Una-Mary Parker is a leading journalist. She
has been social editor for the *Tatler*, and is currently a
partner in Parker and Hobart Associates, a public
relations company. She lives in Knightsbridge,
London.

Una-Mary's two previous novels, *Riches* and *Scandals*, were both international bestsellers, and received
the following glowing tributes:

'Money and passion talk in this novel . . . cleverly
woven and realistically plotted' *Best*

'A racy and accomplished work' *Over 21*

'High society, glitzy lifestyle and exotically wealthy
women . . . compulsive reading' *Hello!*

'Shamefully readable . . . a truly sizzling finish' *Publishing News*

Temptations

Una-Mary Parker

HEADLINE

Published by arrangement with NAL Penguin Inc,
New York, New York, USA

First published in Great Britain in 1989
by HEADLINE BOOK PUBLISHING PLC

First published in paperback in 1989
by HEADLINE BOOK PUBLISHING PLC

10 9 8 7 6 5 4 3 2

ISBN 0 7472 3295 4

Typeset in 10/12½ pt English Times
by Colset Private Ltd, Singapore

Printed and bound in Great Britain by
Collins, Glasgow

HEADLINE BOOK PUBLISHING PLC
Headline House
79 Great Titchfield Street
London W1P 7FN

This is for Baba and Buffy
once more, with feeling.

ACKNOWLEDGEMENTS

I would like to extend my grateful thanks to those who have helped me in the course of my research and who have given me so much encouragement throughout. They include Baba Hobart, Buffy Parker, Mary de Schwarzburg-Gunther, Duncan MacArthur, Doreen Boulding, Nigel Cockburn, Howard Levene, and of course Susan Fletcher, Jackie Cantor and my agent, Susan Zeckendorf.

' " 'Tis one thing to be tempted, Escalus,
Another thing to fall." '

William Shakespeare, 1564–1616
Measure for Measure

Chapter One

The silence of the night was broken by the shrill tones of the telephone, shattering the peaceful darkness and startling Madeleine and Carl into wakefulness.

'What the hell . . .?' Carl reached for the light switch and then looked groggily at his watch. 'Who the fuck's calling us at this hour?'

Madeleine turned over sleepily, her cloud of black hair spreading on the pillows, the white muslin draperies of the four-poster bed festooned like transparent sails in the soft glow of the bedside lamp, cocooning them in a rosy oasis. 'Tell whoever it is to go away,' she murmured.

Carl grabbed the phone. 'Hullo?' His voice sounded terse. There was a pause, and then Madeleine heard him exclaim: 'D'you realise it's three o'clock in the morning? What? Yes, there is a five hour time difference . . . shall I get her to call you tomorrow?' Through half drooping eyelids she saw his muscular legs, tanned from their regular weekends at Oyster Bay, push the sheets away. It was a hot night and his blond hair clung to the back of his neck. Suddenly he glanced at Madeleine, his brown hand cupping the receiver.

'It's your grandfather, calling from England,' he whispered.

1

Madeleine's eyes flew open and she thrust herself into a sitting position, instantly alert.

'You're kidding!' Her heart-shaped face paled against the darkness of her hair and eyes and her expression was deeply shocked. 'He hasn't spoken to us for over twenty years! What does he want?'

'He won't tell me . . . insists on speaking to you . . . I'm sorry, darling, but I think you'll have to talk to him. He sounds in quite a state.'

Gingerly, Madeleine reached for the receiver, bracing herself as she did so. Her autocratic English grandfather had refused to have anything to do with either her or her father since her mother had died. Now, unexpectedly, across thousands of miles of ocean and twenty years of silence, he was reaching out to her from the past as if he desperately needed her.

'Hullo?' she said quietly, though her heart was thumping.

The voice was reedy, imperious and impatient. He'd been kept waiting too long. 'Madeleine? Is that you?'

'Yes, this is Madeleine.'

'George Dalrymple here. Listen, I have to see you as soon as possible. There are things you have a right to know and I don't suppose your damned father has told you everything . . .'

'Just a minute!' Madeleine felt a rush of anger. How dare this elderly man, half forgotten and never mentioned, disrupt them in the middle of the night in this abusive manner! And what did he mean about her father not telling her everything?

Her tone was cold. 'What do you want?'

'I am an old man, Madeleine. I haven't long to live and it's vital I tell you everything before it's too late.' His voice was no less querulous and demanding.

With an effort Madeleine bit back her anger, giving Carl a glance of appeal as she did so. Responding, he reached out for her hand and clasped it tightly.

'Listen,' she said heatedly into the phone, 'neither my father nor I has seen or heard anything from you for over twenty years and now here you are, demanding . . .'

It had been 1965. She'd been three years old and they'd been living in England when her mother, Camilla, had died. To the best of her knowledge Sir George Dalrymple, Camilla's father, had refused to speak to any of them since.

'That wasn't my doing!' the rasping old voice cut in. The conviction in his voice made Madeleine suddenly uneasy. Perhaps it had been her father, Jake, who'd been the one refusing to talk or communicate in any way. It would be consistent with his whole attitude towards his late wife's family. Since Camilla's death, he'd acted as if the Dalrymples didn't exist.

As if Sir George could read her mind, he said, 'Madeleine, you can blame your father for the estrangement. I wanted us to meet but Jake always prevented it. Please fly over here to see me. It is of the greatest importance. I just wish I hadn't left it so long.' Sir George was pleading now and the urgency in his voice alarmed her. She also knew the ring of truth when she heard it, and yet something inside her still resisted the thought of having to face the

3

unknown, from which Jake had so obviously protected her.

Curiosity tempted her to ask: 'What's it about, Grandfather? Why can't you tell me now, or write to me?'

'Impossible! I have to see you. There is too much to tell . . . to explain . . . I shall never rest in my grave unless you know all the facts.' Sir George's voice broke on a quaver.

Alarm threaded its way icily through Madeleine's veins and she shivered. Carl, watching her anxiously, straining to hear what was being said, slid his hand up her arm and stroked her shoulder.

'Are you okay, sweetheart?' he whispered.

Madeleine nodded, her eyes troubled. 'I'll have to go and see him,' she whispered back.

'Are you there, Madeleine? Can you hear me?'

She directed her attention quickly back to the call. 'Yes, I'm here. I can't come immediately because I'm about to hold my first exhibition; I'm an artist, you see. But I'll come as soon as I can.'

'Milton Manor, near Okehampton. In Devon,' Sir George said peremptorily. 'I'll be waiting for you. Come as quickly as you can, please.'

'I will,' promised Madeleine.

'And one more thing . . .' The voice sounded agitated again.

'What is it?'

Sir George spoke swiftly and decisively. 'For God's sake don't tell Jake you're coming to see me, or he'll do everything he can to try and stop you.'

There was a click, the line was silent, and Madeleine

realised he'd hung up. For a moment she sat very still, the receiver resting in her hand like a dead object. Then she replaced it slowly, feeling deeply jarred. It was as if the past, long buried, had been thrust upon her, stirring up half forgotten memories and vague fears that had once filled the mind of a little girl who had called out so often for her mother, and whose cries had gone unanswered. She glanced up to see Carl watching her, his lean face and china blue eyes filled with concern. For comfort, she slid under the crook of his arm, relishing the warmth of his naked body against the sudden coldness of her own.

Her smile was wan. 'How strange to hear from my grandfather like that. What can he have to tell me about my mother . . . do you think there was something sinister about her death?' It was a question she had often asked herself in the past. It might explain why Jake had always refused to discuss his wife and why he had destroyed every photograph of her and every memento. Even Camilla's portrait by the famous Philip de Laszlo, who had painted the society beauties of the day, had vanished from its place above the mantelpiece in their Beekman Place house. Madeleine could vaguely remember that portrait although she'd only been three and a half when they returned to New York from London; it showed a fair-haired woman with pale eyes, wearing a cream lace dress. Most memorable of all were the cascading ropes of pearls that fell from round her neck, almost reaching her lap. Madeleine knew she didn't look at all like her mother; she'd inherited the Shearman black hair and eyes and white skin. Her father's daughter, people called her; a perfect feminine likeness of the powerful Jake Shearman. But that was as far as it went. The likeness was only skin deep.

'That call has disturbed you, hasn't it, Maddy?' Carl whispered tenderly. 'Do you really intend to go and see your grandfather, in England?'

Madeleine turned to look into his face, thankful he was there. But then Carl was always there for her and had been ever since they'd married four years before. She kissed his cheek, near the corner of his mouth. 'I must, darling. Supposing he has something really important to tell me! I'd never forgive myself if he died and I hadn't even made the effort to go and see him. As soon as the exhibition has opened I'll fly over. Is there any chance you could come with me?'

Carl shook his head. 'Not a cat's chance in hell! With the dollar in free fall and interest rates as jumpy as a kangaroo on heat, I'm going to be stuck in the bank for the rest of the year.'

Madeleine sighed, snuggling closer. 'Then I'll only stay for a couple of days. I can't bear to be away from you for longer than that.'

Carl spoke gently. 'Have you thought, Maddy, that your grandfather might be senile and half crazy? You could go all that way and find the whole thing was a wild goose chase! What can he say about your mother that you don't already know, or that Jake won't tell you?'

'That's just the point – Dad has always refused to tell me anything. You know that, Carl. As soon as my mother's name is mentioned he clams up and acts like she never existed. Maybe my grandfather will tell me how she died and what happened.'

'And if it's something unpleasant – and maybe that's why Jake has never talked about it – do you still want to know?'

Madeleine spoke positively, though she looked distressed. 'Yes. I want to know.'

Carl stroked the glossy blackness of her long hair. 'Wouldn't it be better to let sleeping dogs lie?' he asked softly. 'I don't want you getting all upset, honey.'

'I'll be okay.' Madeleine lay back against the lace-edged pillows, recalling what she did know; bare facts, no more than an outline. The story of a glamorous couple who had everything that life could offer until the day disaster struck.

Jake Shearman, at twenty-five, was sure that Camilla Dalrymple was the most beautiful girl he'd ever set eyes on. On vacation from Harvard, where he'd been studying Economics, he and his friends decided to drive from Nice to Monte Carlo one evening, in order to have a flutter in the casino. As the little white ball plink-plinked with monotonous regularity on the spinning roulette wheel under the watchful eyes of the players, and the croupiers called '*Rien ne va plus*', Jake looked up, and through the blue haze of cigar smoke saw her standing there, watching the proceedings with an air of detachment. Her cool English beauty took his breath away. Amidst the more flamboyant and much older French, Italian and Spanish women, she looked ethereal with her simply styled blonde hair and understated ice-blue satin evening dress. Fragile as spring blossom, and delicate as

Dresden china, it struck Jake that she looked as if she'd break easily, as if she'd snap like fine-blown glass or glittering spun-sugar.

'*Faites vos jeux*,' called out the croupier, and like scurrying white rats bony and bejewelled hands pushed and shoved and threw down their different coloured chips, with blind compulsive abandon; greedy faces watched avidly, some a breath away from bankruptcy, others unknowingly hovering on the brink of a fortune. Plink-plink went the little white ball, and a fortune had been acquired or lost. But Jake was no longer interested in the game, so absorbed was he in watching Camilla and noting that she seemed to be on her own. No husband or escort hovered by her side as she glided from table to table, watching the play with absorbed fascination. Then Jake caught his breath; an elderly woman in a blaze of rubies and swathes of sable around her plump shoulders, trotted up and the two women smiled and started talking.

'Have you seen enough?' the older woman asked brightly. She'd been dropping into the casino for years, although she never gambled herself. To her it was a spectacle to show visitors, a little divertissement to while away an hour between dinner and going to bed.

'It's fascinating, Aunt Marion,' Camilla replied. 'And everyone's so smart! There's nothing like this in England.'

'Fifteen years ago, when the Germans occupied France, there was nothing like this here either! But now, as you can see, everyone wears their jewels and

8

puts on their best clothes again. It is good for morale.'

Camilla gazed in wonder as men with fat wallets and women with sharp eyes continued to play as if hypnotised by the whirling wheel.

Jake rose from the table, his few remaining chips in his hand. The moment had come to make his move. Tall, well built and with the black hair and pale skin that characterised all the Shearmans, he presented himself before the older woman with a smile and a slight bow.

She looked up, clasped her hands together and let out an exclamation of joy. 'Jake, my dear boy, what on earth are you doing here?'

Jake kissed her powdery cheek. 'Lady Wantage, how good it is to see you. I'm on vacation, staying with friends in Nice. I thought I'd try my luck tonight . . .' He eyed Camilla pointedly, longing to be formally introduced, smiling his most charming smile.

'Have you two young things met?' Marion Wantage enquired with her usual vague but sweet smile. She turned to the girl. 'This is Jake Shearman, my dear. His late mother and I both came from Boston and we were lifelong friends. This is Camilla Dalrymple, Jake, my goddaughter. She's staying with me at the Hôtel de Paris, as her mother thought she ought to see a bit of France. She thought it would be good for her education,' she added with a roguish smile.

Jake laughed. Camilla's mother could be right. Marion Wantage was an oil millionairess who had married an English baron and had then proceeded to show not only the English, but the international set,

9

what it was to have style. She had permanent suites at the Hôtel de Paris in Monte Carlo, the Beau Rivage Palace in Lausanne and Claridges in London. They were all furnished with her own antiques and paintings, and she had her personal staff ensconced in adjoining suites, so that they were on hand to look after her needs. Widowed now, she still entertained with flair, counting among her close friends Sir Winston Churchill, Somerset Maugham and Jean Cocteau. Any young girl would gain a lifetime's education by spending a few weeks with Lady Wantage, thought Jake.

'So this is your first visit to Monte Carlo,' Jake said conversationally, turning to Camilla. There was something very vulnerable about the way she looked up at him with her misty blue eyes.

When she spoke, her voice was soft. 'Yes, it is.' She looked round the richly gilt baroque room with its shimmering chandeliers and then at the desperate faces that gathered round the gaming tables, watching silently as the atmosphere grew ever more pungent with the smell of expensive cigar smoke. 'But it's a bit decadent, isn't it?'

Jake laughed again. 'That depends on whether you're winning or losing!'

'Shall we go somewhere quiet for a drink?' suggested Lady Wantage.

'I think that's a very good idea,' said Jake, taking Camilla by the elbow.

It was a whirlwind romance. Camilla's parents, Sir George and Lady Dalrymple, invited Jake to stay at Milton Manor, their Devonshire home, and by the time he returned to the States their engagement was announced in *The Times*. They were married in London the following spring, and then Jake whisked his young bride back to New York where he'd bought a beautiful grey stone house on Beekman Place, overlooking the East River.

There were also the weekend home at Oyster Bay on Long Island that Jake's father had left him, and all the trappings belonging to one of New York's oldest and most distinguished families. Jake would one day become President of the Central Manhattan Bank, and meanwhile he enjoyed a senior position without the heavy responsibility that would one day be his. It was an idyllic existence, made all the more perfect by the arrival of their first child, Madeleine. They were fêted by New York society as the 'golden couple' who had everything and it seemed as if nothing could ever happen to cast a cloud over their sunny lives. Then Lady Dalrymple died suddenly from a heart attack, and the shock affected Camilla deeply. She became chronically depressed and Jake was at his wits' end trying to cheer her up. He took her on a trip to Bangkok, suggested she do over their house, loaded her with jewels and furs, but to no avail. It was only when he was posted to the London branch of the bank that she started to brighten up. She also decided that she wanted to remain in Devon with her father, while Jake worked in London.

'But I'll never see you and Madeleine!' he expostulated. 'I want you to be with me.'

Camilla looked stubborn, her beautiful vulnerable mouth set in tight lines. 'Father will need me, now

11

that he's alone. You can come down at weekends.'

They looked at each other, Jake willing to do anything if it was going to make her happy again, Camilla wilfully determined to go her own way.

As time passed Jake did all he could to persuade her to change her mind, saying that if her father needed her, *he* needed her more. It was a battle he never won. Camilla remained down in Devon, and eighteen months later she was dead.

'I've got to find out what happened, Carl.' Madeleine rolled over in the bed so that she lay on her side, facing him. 'Dad's kept me in the dark all these years but tonight, for the first time, I really am determined to get to the truth. If he won't tell me, then I'll fly to England and find out for myself. I . . . well, I feel in a strange way that I owe it to my mother.'

Carl smiled. 'I understand that. Why don't you let me talk to Jake? He might find it easier to discuss things with another man.'

Carl worked alongside Jake at the Central Manhattan Bank, as head of foreign transactions; a position he held through merit and not because he was married to the boss's daughter. From the moment Carl had joined the bank ten years before, fresh from Yale and then Harvard Business School, Jake had been impressed by him. The young man showed brilliance and flair and had a natural aptitude for banking. One day he would make a fitting successor to Jake who had no son of his own.

'I'd rather talk to Daddy myself,' said Madeleine, 'but I'll wait until after my exhibition.' Her first

12

one-woman show was going to be held at the chic Midas Gallery in SoHo in ten days' time, and it was an important career move; something she'd been working towards for years. She snuggled closer, like a kitten seeking warmth. 'I do wish you could come to England with me.'

Carl leaned forward and kissed her gently on the mouth. 'So do I, sweetheart. I shall miss you like hell.'

'Oh, Carl!' She pressed her pale slender body against his strong tanned one and winding her arms around his neck, whispered: 'I'm lost without you.'

Carl kissed her again lingeringly, then leaned back, his eyes twinkling and deep laughter lines fanning out on to his cheeks. He pretended to look solemn. 'You're a naughty girl, sliding up against me like this when you know I've got to get some sleep! What are you trying to do? Make me so tired I'm late for work in the morning, and then have your father sack me?'

Madeleine giggled and pressed herself closer still. Her dark eyes were dancing with fun. 'Now that's a good idea! You get Daddy to sack you and then we'll be free to set off round the world on another honeymoon.' Her pale breasts were crushed against him now and she was kissing his neck just behind the ear where she knew he was particularly sensitive.

Carl let out a groan. 'Maddy,' he pleaded, trying to extricate himself. 'I've got to be at the office in . . .' he glanced at his watch '. . . four hours' time!'

'Four hours,' she whispered, her tongue flicking along the edge of his jaw, her hand reaching down to

13

stroke his thighs. 'In four hours we can do it at least twice!'

'Maddy, will you stop it!'

She continued to kiss him and stroke him, knowing he didn't really want her to stop. Gradually her urgent desire transferred itself to him, so that he too became aroused, his body responding to hers so that they moved in perfect harmony. Lost in sensation, his eyes closed, he let this woman who had been his wife for four years do what she liked with him, as she had done so many times before. They were so deeply attuned to one another that they could convey their desire across a crowded room, and now as they touched and stroked and kissed each other there was no need for words. Madeleine's head was moving from side to side on the pillow now, as she took his hand, so strong and familiar, and placed it between her legs. Carl knew her body as well as he knew his own and he loved to bring her to a peak of excitement.

She moved beneath him now, giving little cries of joy, taking him inside her body and holding him there as if she could never have enough of him, and he thrilled as he heard her cry: 'Give yourself to me, Carl . . . give all of yourself to me.' A moment later, with a mixture of frenzied sweetness and wrenching surrender, they climaxed together with a loving closeness, something they'd done a thousand times before yet found as potent as the first time they'd ever made love.

Patti Ziffren sat at the Georgian desk in the library of her duplex in the Beresford, on Central Park West,

14

looking at the message her butler had taken the previous evening when she and her husband, Sam, had been out at a benefit dinner. She didn't like it. Not at all. Warning bells were ringing in her head and she had a mind to call her brother Jake, to warn him that his ex-father-in-law, Sir George Dalrymple, was trying to contact Madeleine. But what good would that do? Jake would only get into a panic, and God knows he'd suffered enough over Camilla all those years ago, without having the whole thing brought up again. But what, Patti wondered darkly, did Sir George want with Madeleine now?

'Mallaby,' she called to her English butler, who'd been with them for the past fifteen years.

Mallaby came into the room on silent feet and stood at a respectful distance. He was of stocky build with a cherubic face and white hair, and he was slightly in awe, even after all these years, of his employer.

'This message you've left on my bureau, Mallaby,' said Patti without preamble. She knew all the servants were a bit scared of her and she did nothing to dispel their fears. Only Sam, Jake, and of course Madeleine were allowed to see what lay beneath the crusty surface.

'Yes, Madam?'

'When Sir George Dalrymple called from England last night, you didn't, I hope, give him Mrs Delaney's number?'

Mallaby looked shocked and even pained. 'I would never do such a thing, Madam! I merely suggested you might be able to call him back today.'

'Ummmmm.' Patti nodded thoughtfully. 'Thank you. That's all for the moment.'

'Thank you, Madam.'

Tall, angular and in her late sixties, Patti rose from the desk as soon as she was alone again and lit a cigarette. Her shoulders looked hunched in her perfectly cut Ungaro suit and her hands shook slightly. The sunshine streaming in through the long windows passed unnoticed by her. God damn old George Dalrymple! she thought with mounting agitation. He must be kept away from her niece at all costs. But suppose he'd got her number from someone else? It wouldn't be difficult. Madeleine and Carl were a well-known and popular couple. Perhaps he'd already found out they lived on Fifth Avenue . . .

Patti stubbed out her cigarette angrily and immediately lit another, her mind dwelling protectively upon her niece. Madeleine had been a small child when Jake had returned to New York from England, begging Patti to help him bring her up. Patti remembered him saying: 'I've hired an English nanny for her, but it isn't the same as having a mother; I need you, Patti. Someone has to try and take Camilla's place.' And of course, because she cared so much for her brother, Patti had agreed. In a way Madeleine came along like a late godsend, because Patti was unable to have children of her own.

They took to each other at once, the rich socialite with the scratchy manner and the pretty little girl who was everyone's friend. Patti was determined about one thing, though: Madeleine must not be spoilt or allowed to fall into the 'poor little rich girl' trap. She must be encouraged to have lots of friends, learn different sports and be a general all rounder. The first indication that she might become an artist was when Patti found a drawing book full of sketches of their friends; lively bold drawings that were instantly recognisable, often unflattering, but very definitely talented.

'Look at these,' Patti said to Jake one evening, when he was dining with her and Sam. 'The child's brilliant! You must see to it that she has the best art teacher.'

Jake smiled. If Madeleine had hopped around the room on one foot, Patti would have said there was another Anna Pavlova in the family. He flipped through the sketch pad, frowned, and then looked through it a second time.

'They are remarkably clever,' he said in a surprised voice. 'Perhaps you're right. Perhaps she ought to have special tuition.'

'She must go to the Art Students' League when she's old enough, and then you must send her to the Sorbonne in Paris,' said Patti. She picked up the pad and it fell open at a drawing Madeleine had done of her. 'Humph!' she snorted, regarding the thin bony face and piercing eyes her niece had given her. 'If you ask me, Jake, she's too talented for her own good.'

Jake laughed out loud. Madeleine's drawing of her aunt was accurate and deeply observant, even to the frown lines and birdlike way Patti held her head. But it was also faintly cruel. 'Perhaps she'll be a caricaturist,' he joked.

Patti looked him straight in the eye. 'Or a very good judge of character,' she corrected him.

Now, all these years later, Madeleine was a portrait

painter of great talent, admired by those who were not afraid to see themselves as they really were. This exhibition at the Midas Gallery would, Patti hoped, set the seal on Madeleine's success.

She lit another cigarette and, deep in thought, wandered round the library, touching things but not really seeing them, smoking absently, her thoughts miles away. Then she came to a decision. She wouldn't tell Jake what she was doing because it would only worry him. Seating herself at the desk again she reached for the message pad and started dialling Sir George's telephone number in England.

At nine o'clock the next morning, Madeleine left their apartment on Fifth Avenue and Seventy-fifth Street, and took a cab to her studio on Wooster Street in the SoHo area where, when she'd reached twenty-one, her father had bought her a studio at the top of one of the old buildings. Even if she and Carl had been out late she still left the apartment at the same time. Morning was the best time to paint as far as she was concerned, when the light was good and inspiration flowed freely. Today, she wanted to put the finishing touches to the portrait of Dustin Hoffman she was including in her exhibition.

As soon as she entered, the familiar and evocative smell of linseed oil and turpentine assailed her, sharpening her desire to work. The cosy clutter of the studio gave her confidence too; this was her little kingdom, where she could do exactly as she liked and where she could express herself in her painting. Jars filled with brushes, bottles of turpentine, tubes of paint and boxes of charcoal lay scattered on various table tops alongside fragments of sculpture which she collected as a hobby. A jumble of canvases stood propped around, and a sofa, covered with black velvet, dominated the haphazard arrangement of chairs and stools and portable platforms. Above, four skylights in the roof gave a window on to nothing save the clouds that floated overhead in a constant moving show.

Madeleine locked the door for security and then climbed the spiral stairs to the gallery at the far end. Here stood her hi-fi system, flanked by shelves of discs and tapes. A moment later the swelling chords of Rachmaninov's piano concerto in C sharp minor filled the studio and she felt a wave of happiness wash over her that was almost as sensuous as Carl's love-making had been the previous night. Here, in this setting she had created exclusively for her own use, she could reach every part of herself without inhibition, without reserve. She could tap the very source of her talent and ply her skill to her heart's content.

Walking swiftly down the steps again she felt a heady intoxication from just being there. Perching on a high stool, she looked around at all her canvases, savouring the moment. It wasn't always like this. On days when a painting wasn't going well, the sheer frustration amounted to silent raging misery. The likenesses of her sitters mocked her from the walls, saying: Your talent was at its peak the day you painted me – look what a mess you're making today. You can't paint at all, you're a fraud! And the voices in her head would go on and on, as great gulfs of self-doubt enveloped her.

White with anguish, her dark eyes tortured, Madeleine would seize a palette knife and scrape away what she had just painted, obliterating her mistakes before even she could bear witness to them for longer than a moment. And all the time the voice in her head was asking: Can I no longer do today what I could yesterday? Has my talent gone . . . escaped . . . and left me as ham-fisted as a child with his first box of paints? And then she would work feverishly, desperate to recapture the easy flow that came when she felt inspired. She would work until her neck and shoulders felt as if they could no longer support the weight of her head, and her face was tense and drawn. Bit by bit, through sheer determination and concentration on her part, the painting would begin to come right and take on a lifelike quality of its own. And only then would she relax and dare to leave the studio at night – but without a backward glance. The monsters of uncertainty and lost confidence had been slain for today, but a second glance might show them still lurking and she dared not risk that. Once home, Carl would soothe and comfort her with his tenderness and understanding, giving her encouragement, making the failures less painful.

Today it was different. Madeleine's mood was light as the sun shone in bold squares on the studio floor, and the canvases, framed and ready to go to the Midas Gallery, looked brilliantly lifelike. The chords of Rachmaninov's music filled the studio with joy and as she sat there she breathed the air of a summer's day. She could positively taste the sweetness of success, and although she felt a thrill at the thought of her forthcoming exhibition she also felt awe-struck at her own audacity. It had been her father's idea.

'Madeleine,' Jake had said when she and Carl had dined with him one night, 'you have to become better known. How are you going to attract commissions if no one knows you're a portrait painter? You must hold an exhibition, and you've got to get yourself a gimmick.'

After a lot of thought, Madeleine had worked out a gimmick although it went against her artistic nature; but then her father was a businessman and so was Carl, and she knew that if she wanted to become well known she must adopt a more businesslike approach to her art and follow their suggestions.

She reached for her palette and started to mix the colours with a sure and confident eye. Tubes of paint lay before her in a riot of colour: lemon cadmium yellow and dark madder lake; viridian and raw sienna and prussian blue. The very names were like poetry to her ears, suggestive of mysterious and exotic places. What crimson lake of fire was 'dark madder'? What brilliant sky of blue hung over Prussia? And didn't 'raw sienna' conjure up the bloodstained sand of a bullring in Spain?

Lost in a dream world of colours and fantasy, Madeleine worked hard at the background of her painting of Dustin Hoffman, revelling in the fact that she had caught the essence of the actor himself and not the characters he'd played for which he was so famous. Absorbed in her work, she did not notice the time passing and at first was oblivious to the telephone's ring. At last she picked up the receiver and

21

answered. There was a transatlantic click and then she heard a familiar English voice.

'Maddy? Is that you? Are you working? Oh, I'm not disturbing you, am I?' The clear fluting tones, overlaid with bubbling enthusiasm, brought a smile to Madeleine's face.

'Jessica! How good to hear from you. How are you?'

'*Terribly* well, sweetie. I'm ringing about the party you're giving to launch your exhibition.'

'You are coming over for it, aren't you?'

'Wild horses wouldn't keep me away, Maddy!'

'So, what's your problem?' Madeleine asked. She'd known Jessica McCann since they'd both been eight years old and even if they didn't meet very often they were always able to pick up where they'd left off, as if they'd seen each other the previous day. They'd originally met in London, at Lady Eden's school, when Jake had been re-posted to the Lombard Street branch of the Central Manhattan Bank in 1970. He'd brought Madeleine and her Nanny to England with him, and for two years they'd lived in an apartment in the Albany, Piccadilly.

'I'm not going to be able to get to New York until the actual day of your opening. I'll still be in good time, but isn't it maddening?' Jessica was explaining.

'Is the new job working out all right?' Madeleine could just imagine her friend sitting behind her desk in the sales department of the Royal Westminster Hotel, gesticulating as she talked, gold bangles rattling, long red nails slicing through the air.

'It's fabulous!' breathed Jessica fervently. 'It's

22

hard work but I've never enjoyed myself so much in my life. I have so much *responsibility*, Maddy, you've no idea! And this hotel is the last word in glamour; you must tell all your friends to stay here when they come to London. So will it be all right if I land at two in the afternoon, on the fourteenth? It will still give me time to tart myself up before the party begins, won't it?'

'Only about four hours!' replied Madeleine, who'd been wondering when she was going to get a word in edgewise. Conversations with Jessica, as she sparkled and fizzed, were inclined to be a bit one-sided if you weren't careful. 'I'll send a car to meet you at Kennedy. You can stay with us for a few days, can't you?'

'Of course, this is going to be my summer hols! Listen, is there anything you'd like me to bring over? Some little trifle that even the mega-rich Shearmans and Delaneys can't buy in New York?'

Madeleine dissolved into laughter. 'Daddy loves sausages from Harrods,' she replied. 'And – oh!' She paused, struck by a sudden thought.

'Oh, no, Maddy! Please! Not oak-smoked kippers again,' Jessica begged. 'You know the last time I stuffed my hand luggage full of kippers, the *whole* of first-class stank like a fishing trawler! I got some very funny looks.'

'I wasn't going to say kippers,' protested Madeleine, vividly recalling Jessica coming through the arrivals gate from Europe, her nose wrinkled comically, her Gucci hand luggage held at arm's length. 'I was going to ask you to look up my grandfather.'

23

'What d'you mean, in *Who's Who*? Surely you know who he is, Maddy?' Her tone was bantering.

'Of course I know who he is. I want to find out what he's like.' Briefly she related her strange conversation of the night before with Sir George.

Jessica's voice was vibrant with interest. 'My *dear*, how fascinating! What can he want to tell you? Listen, I'm sure I can find out a bit about the family. I know all the gossip columnists very well, and as the Dalrymples would rank as aristocracy they're bound to have your grandfather on their files. Leave it to me.'

'Do be careful,' warned Madeleine, 'I wouldn't want him to think I was checking up on him.'

'Don't worry. I'll make the most discreet inquiries. I say, d'you suppose your mother was involved in some scandal? That would explain why Jake would never tell you anything. I say, how terribly thrilling!' Jessica sounded agog with interest.

On the corner of Wall Street and Broad Street the Central Manhattan Bank rose in a towering block of black glass and steel, reflecting the morning sunshine in dazzling starbursts of light. Carl, getting out of the chauffeur-driven limousine, entered through the bullet-proof glass and steel doors, glad to be off the street where the air was clammy with humidity. The main banking area was modern and impressive, with floors and walls and counters of black and white marble, a steel and lucite escalator gliding smoothly up to the second floor gallery and an artfully arranged jungle of plants that climbed as tall as trees, illuminated by concealed spotlights.

Behind the theatrical façade it was a different matter. Layer upon layer of people, one above the other, filled the glass building from street level to the twenty-eighth floor, the tellers at the bottom of the heap, above them kitchens and staff dining-rooms which opened with breakfast at eight o'clock in the morning and closed in the late afternoon, and above them floor after floor of offices filled with workers sitting at desks under harsh strip lighting, while Fax and Telex machines hummed out their messages from all over the world, telephones rang with maddening persistence, word processors and computers clicked and bleeped, and an atmosphere of high pressure prevailed. With transactions totalling billions of dollars a day, this great throbbing financial animal stood tall amongst its rivals, digesting with relish the quick, the clever and the diligent, while mercilessly spitting out those who could not take the pace.

Carl thrived in the atmosphere. From his office, which led off the gallery on the second floor where all the executive offices were, with the exception of Jake Shearman's penthouse suite, Carl had a good view of the Stock Exchange and the jostling and bustling on the sidewalk below. The knowledge that millions of dollars were changing hands by the minute gave him an almost physical thrill. It was a special fascination he shared with Jake. To them money was a living thing, a plant that would grow and sprout and bear fruit; dividends, equity, loans and interest rates formed a major part of their conversation, and filled their thoughts most of the time. To them money was not a collection of dry figures flashed up on some

25

computer, soulless and dead; it was symbols and signs, meaningful and rewarding, telling a story or painting a picture all of its own.

Carl flipped swiftly through his mail and glanced at the first of the day's authorisations for foreign transactions. Dollars being transferred to Tokyo, Kuwait, Hong Kong and Great Britain. Pounds sterling, yen, deutschmarks and francs coming in from other parts of the world; a fascinating ever exchanging flow of money, giving a picture of trade figures and currency regulations, deficits and profits.

Pressing his intercom, Carl buzzed for his assistant in the adjoining office. 'Averil, can we get started on this lot, please? I'm meeting with Mr Shearman and some clients before lunch, so it's going to be a short morning.'

'Certainly, Mr Delaney.' Averil was the perfect PA. She'd been with Carl for six years and she knew his ways, down to how hot he liked his coffee. Regretfully, Carl remembered she'd be leaving soon because she wanted to move out of New York. Nothing he'd been able to say would make her change her mind. She'd had enough of city life and she wanted out. A moment later she appeared, a pleasant-faced young woman with prematurely grey hair and a gentle smile. She took a seat opposite Carl's desk.

'Right, Mr Delaney. I'm ready,' she said.

An hour later Carl had finished and was striding to the elevator at the other end of the curving gallery that overlooked the bank lobby below. Stepping into its black leather interior, he pressed the penthouse button.

26

Carl and Jake were close. Although devoted to his own father who was an architect in Philadelphia, Carl felt he had much more in common with Jake. He was like the son Jake had never had. To that he owed much of his success, and not, as the gossips insisted, to his marriage to Madeleine. In fact he hadn't met her until he'd been nearly two years with the Central Manhattan Bank and, as he always laughingly reminded Jake, it had been another four years before he'd been allowed near her. 'Well, hell, she was only eighteen and not finished her education,' Jake was apt to protest, although from the beginning he'd secretly hoped Carl would one day become his son-in-law.

Carl had waited, watching Madeleine from afar growing up into a young woman of great beauty and charm, watching her progress as a painter, longing for the time when Jake would give his permission for them to see each other. In the meantime he took out lots of girls but, looking back, it seemed that he was merely treading water, keeping emotionally afloat while he waited for Madeleine. She was everything he'd ever desired in a woman. He felt it was worth waiting until he was nearly thirty to get married.

'Morning, Carl.' Jake greeted him as he entered the President's office. Although his hair was now grey, the years had been kind to Jake, and if anything he was more good-looking than he'd been as a young man. His eyes, almost black like his daughter's, regarded Carl with affection and his manner was one of bonhomie. 'Have a good time last night?'

Carl started, thinking of their love-making when he and Madeleine had luxuriated in each other's bodies

27

with a rapturous knowledge of each other's needs, after they'd taken the call from England. 'Last night?'

'Didn't you have tickets for *Phantom of the Opera*? Weren't you going with Robert and Joan Allord, and then having dinner at Le Cirque?'

'Oh . . . of course.' The events of the night had made him forget. 'Yes, it's a great show! We had a very good time and the Allords sent you their best wishes.'

'Good.' Jake smiled. Then the phone started ringing, and after Jake had taken the call the clients who had come for a meeting were shown into his office and for the next hour Carl became absorbed in discussing the ramifications of a loan to a ship-building company in Scotland. Once or twice he looked at Jake, remembering that Madeleine had told him not to mention the call from Sir George Dalrymple, wondering why Jake always refused to discuss his late wife. As Carl reminded himself, it hadn't happened yesterday but over twenty years ago. Surely the past couldn't be as painful as all that, or wasn't it the pain Jake was trying to avoid?

At last the meeting came to an end and Carl hurried back to his office. He had twenty minutes to catch up on some of his work before he slipped down to the directors' dining-room for lunch. Averil came through from her adjoining office as soon as he settled himself at his desk. She spoke eagerly.

'Personnel have just been on the line, Mr Delaney, to say they think they've found a suitable replacement to take over from me at the end of the month.'

Carl's handsome tanned face showed a flicker of

ruefulness. 'D'you really have to go, Averil?'

She smiled, flattered. 'Yes, I really want to move to New Jersey, Mr Delaney. I've been planning to go for a long time, you know.'

'So what's this new girl like?'

'I don't know her personally, but I've seen her around because she's been working here for over two years in the computer department. You may have seen her, she's got bright red hair. She worked for the Citibank before she joined us and I believe she's very bright.'

Carl sighed, hating changes but knowing now this one was inevitable. 'Interview her for me, will you, Averil? You know what I need – someone as much like yourself as possible.'

Averil flushed, looking pleased. 'Thank you, Mr Delaney. I will.'

She was as good as her word. When Carl returned to the office at two-thirty, having lunched with the chairman of a large aviation company which was starting up in Mexico, she came into his office, closed the door behind her and spoke in a whisper.

'My replacement is in my office right now, Mr Delaney. I've had a long talk with her, and personally I think she'd do the job very well. Her qualifications are good and she seems on the ball.'

Carl asked, 'Is she efficient, d'you think? Quick, with a retentive memory? You know how it drives me crazy if people forget what I've told them.' He knew he was tricky to work for, and demanding too. There'd been a fast turnover of Personal Assistants before Averil.

'I think you'll find she's up to it. Walter Tuffin, the head of the computer department, talks highly of her. She's ambitious, I think,' Averil added, in an even softer whisper, 'and that's a good thing. She'd dead keen to work for you, Mr Delaney.'

'And you're certain she can handle the pressure?'

Averil nodded, positively. 'I wouldn't say so if I didn't believe it.'

Carl sighed wearily. He hated changes in his working routine and the thought of teaching a new girl to do things the way he liked really filled him with dread.

'Okay,' he said at last. 'Show her in. By the way, what's her name?'

'Kimberley Cabot.'

Kimberley, travelling on the subway from Fifty-fifth to Wall Street that morning, hoped against hope that she'd hear if she'd landed the job of Carl Delaney's assistant. As soon as she'd found out that dreary, dowdy Averil Fielden was leaving, she'd gone straight to the head of personnel, George Miller, and persuaded him to recommend her for the post. She'd also made sure her immediate boss, Walter Tuffin, gave her a good reference. It hadn't been difficult. Men always ended up doing what she wanted and George and Walter were no exception.

As if to prove the point to herself, she crossed her long shapely legs with a gentle rasp of nylon stockings as the train hurtled along between stations, and out of the corner of her eye saw three men turn their heads to follow her movements. Kimberley chuckled inwardly. They were all the same, and she was certain Carl

Delaney was just like the rest of them. She'd been watching him covertly for months now, whenever she got the chance – seeing him arrive in the morning, striding purposefully across the lobby, taking the elevator to the penthouse floor, entering the directors' dining-room – a tall athletic figure, far better looking than the average banker, with sexy blue eyes and an engaging smile. She wondered how susceptible he was and came to the conclusion that happily married or not, when it came to the point he'd be just like all the others: easy to seduce.

All she needed now was the opportunity to work for him and then she could start putting her plan into action, the plan she'd begun to formulate in her head long before she'd even heard of Carl Delaney, long before she'd gone to work at the Central Manhattan Bank; a plan that had taken root secretly and furtively when she'd been twelve. Now, seventeen years later, she felt as if every dream and aspiration had led her, sometimes unwittingly and by chance, other times by deliberate and careful planning, to this moment when she could make it all happen for her.

Kimberley had grown up in the Maspeth area of Queens, the youngest of six children born to Ollie Cabot, a truck driver, and his Italian wife, Lucia, who worked in the local delicatessen and believed everything the Pope said. Crammed together in a two family brown and white clapboard house, just like all the others in the area, Kimberley didn't even see a skyscraper for the first twelve years of her life. Warehouses, ugly as aircraft hangars, yards full of trucks, acres of tombstones in the Mount Oliver Cemetery, and rows of small shops like Pat's Liquor Store, Carvel's Icecreams and the 'Lady Finesse' Hairdresser 'for Guys and Gals', made up the scenery as Kimberley looked restlessly around in search of excitement. She attended the Martin Luther King High School, but made few friends. The others seemed content to spend the rest of their lives within the confines of this area, where the most exciting thing that could happen to you would be to go into a jazzed up café called 'Dunkin' Donuts'. Kimberley knew from an early age that she must get away. There had to be life beyond the narrow streets edged with dusty oak and maple trees, and the little Holy Cross Roman Catholic Church her mother dragged her to. There must be somewhere better to live than in the tiny houses that were home to two families and which did not even boast a backyard. Not for her a life of domestic slavery like her mother, with six children and a husband who drank most of his wage packet away.

It was on her twelfth birthday that she begged her eldest brother, Tom, who was twenty, to take her into Manhattan. He had a job as a porter in the Plaza Hotel and his tales of what life was like in the centre of the city had long enthralled her. When they came up from the subway she gasped, looking around her, eyes wide with amazement and little noises of wonder escaping from her open lips. She felt quite dizzy. The towering buildings made her feel she was walking at the bottom of some gigantic ravine and she clutched Tom's hand. The traffic whirled past, a police siren yelped in an adjacent side street, and the crowds jostled on the sidewalk, bumping into them. Kimberley couldn't have been more astonished if she had been dumped on Mars; television was forbidden at home and she'd never been allowed to go to the movies. Everything around her was new and, breathless, she hung on to Tom as he led her through the dusk towards Times Square.

The sight that met her eyes dazzled her and made her heart pound. All around the brilliant blaze of electric bulbs flashed and radiated an incandescent gaudy trail of light on every available rising surface. Glowing advertising signs leapt, glittering, up the side of buildings and around doors and awnings: a scintillating thread of blue and gold and silver, shot with red, lacing the giant buildings together and weaving themselves into intricate patterns. Flickering, swooping, dancing, skimming – the myriads of multi-coloured lights had a life of their own, as they flashed and sparkled in a never ending display. Kimberley had never seen so many lights, hadn't known so much light existed in the world. But there they were, a vivid spectacle of bright spangles illuminating the night, suggesting to Kimberley promised riches and glamour in signs which read 'Marlboro', 'Chevrolet' and 'Sheraton Astor'.

At that moment she knew that when she was grown up she wanted to be rich; to have so much money that she'd never grow old and ugly like her mother; to have so much money that she'd be able to have anything she wanted. Anything on earth. Standing mesmerised, as the traffic screeched and honked around her, she gazed at those advertisements as if hypnotised;

but where others saw rows of dirty electric light bulbs, Kimberley saw chains of diamonds.

From that moment on, she was motivated to one end only: to be rich and successful. Always bright at school, she now threw herself into studying and at sixteen, having gained excellent grades, she left to get a job. Her mother wanted her to continue living at home and take a job in a shop, and for a while Kimberley agreed; but only because the hours allowed her to take a shorthand and typing course at the local community centre. As soon as she'd qualified she was off, living in a small downtown room, but at least it was in Manhattan. Best of all the first job she got was as a clerk with Citibank. She'd learned the ropes fast, had been sent on a computer programming course and given a raise. Four years later she'd joined the prestigious and famous Central Manhattan Bank.

'I'll check if Mr Delaney is ready to see you,' said Averil Fielden.

'Thanks.' Kimberley's heart was pounding as she looked around the office that she hoped would soon be hers. So much depended on the next few minutes. If she got this job she'd really have it made, because Carl Delaney was the key to her future. Thankful she'd decided to wear a smart but demure pale blue linen suit that enhanced her rich auburn hair and creamy skin and that showed off her figure in a subtle and classy way, Kimberley felt a deep sense of excitement. Working hard at school, slogging away at evening classes, sleeping with rich men who bought her expensive clothes and taught her how to behave in public, had given her a certain patina over the years and helped prepare her for this moment. She didn't believe in God, not after the way her Mom had gone on about the sins of the flesh, but she did remember hearing a saying: 'God helps those who help themselves'. Suddenly she smiled, an expression so radiant and confident that when Averil Fielden came back and said Mr Delaney was ready to see her, Kimberley sailed into his office, knowing her moment had finally come.

Jessica grabbed the phone. 'You've delivered the wrong glasses!' she stormed to the supplier on the other end of the line. 'We ordered *fluted* champagne glasses, not tulip-shaped ones! How could you make a mistake like that?' Angrily she doodled on the pad in front of her with her red felt-tip pen. 'I'm not interested in your excuses. We ordered sixty dozen fluted glasses and if they're not here by this afternoon, you can cancel the order – *and* all future orders from us!' Slamming down the phone she looked up at her colleague, Dick Fowler, with whom she shared an office.

'Damned suppliers!' she exploded, her petite frame quivering with indignation. 'They're all the same. When will they ever get anything right? Remember those blankets we ordered from Hobbs? We ordered rose pink and they delivered thirty dozen in a revolting shade of peach!'

Dick nodded sympathetically. 'I think the worst time was when they delivered two hundred chairs for the restaurant, all covered in the wrong fabric.'

Jessica covered her face with her hands in mock

despair, her lazy top-knot of blonde hair threatening to come undone and cascade to her shoulders. 'That,' she said succinctly, 'is what is known as a major cock-up!'

Dick roared with laughter. Jessica, with her exaggerated way of talking and her expressive mobile little face, always amused him. When she'd joined the Royal Westminster Hotel eighteen months before as Assistant Sales Manager, he'd realised there'd never be a dull moment.

Jessica McCann was the eldest daughter of a retired general in the British Army, and her family had hoped she'd make a suitable marriage and settle down by the time she was twenty-two or three; but at twenty-six, she was still pursuing her career with unabated enthusiasm. Tiny, slim, with long blonde hair and round blue eyes that at times made her look doll-like, she had boundless energy and vivacity, and everyone in the hotel adored her.

She could soothe a ruffled guest in seconds, placating them by dealing with whatever problem had upset them. Then she would pacify them further by murmuring there would be no charge for their dinner in the restaurant that night . . . and then, there would be flowers and champagne, and a bowl of fruit or an expensive box of chocolates in their rooms. Her concern if anything went wrong seemed so genuine that most guests, especially the English, ended up apologising for having complained in the first place!

It was a magic formula and that was why she had been transferred from a sister hotel, the Wentworth in Park Lane, where she'd been the Sales and Public

Relations Officer, to the Royal Westminster. She'd also been promoted to Assistant Sales Manager, reporting to Dick Fowler. Their boss, the Director of Sales, was Humphrey Peters, a hard-faced man with ruthless ambition who saw himself as an eventual General Manager. But Jessica and Dick had such a good working relationship that they never allowed Humphrey Peters, with his endless demands, to get under their skin. From time to time bursts of laughter could be heard coming from their office as Jessica did a wicked imitation of a guest or one of the staff, or Dick regaled her with stories of things that had happened before her time.

The Golding Group owned thirty-five hotels worldwide, but the Royal Westminster was their flagship and Jessica had been thrilled at the prospect of working in it. For sheer splendour and elegance it rivalled even their other hotels in Hong Kong, Venice and Washington, all of which were five star hotels, and all of which appeared in listings of the best in the world.

Straddling the west side of Hyde Park Corner, and opposite the lush greenness of Hyde Park, the Royal Westminster was an imposing building, porticoed and pillared and resembling a miniature Buckingham Palace. For tourists, there was the added interest that it had been built in 1775, as the town house of the first Duke of Hastings, and was also opposite the first Duke of Wellington's former home, Apsley House, which was now a museum. Over the years extensions had been added at the rear, where formerly stabling had provided shelter for the Duke's horses and carriages. Invisible from the street, six penthouse suites had also been added, so that the hotel now had two hundred and fifty rooms each decorated and designed by famous designers who specialised in doing up stately homes. But the essential atmosphere of a ducal town house remained. The Golding Group's original investment, which had converted the building from its inglorious temporary use as a hospital into a hotel, had paid dividends. The reported annual turnover was in the region of eighteen million pounds a year.

Jessica's main task at the moment was to get bookings for the principal banqueting rooms; she wanted people to hold their parties at the Royal Westminster and she knew the way to attract them was to sell the idea that it would be like giving a party in a private house. With a large ballroom, a big reception room and several ante-rooms, there was scope to give anything from an exclusive dinner-party for ten, to a ball for five hundred.

Jessica glanced at her page of engagements for the day and let out a yelp. 'God! A Mr and Mrs Cyril Watkins are due any minute. They want to hold their daughter's wedding reception here so I'm going to show them the Armitage Suite.' Re-fixing her hair, she applied some pale lipstick and ran her hands over her neat navy blue suit. 'Then I've got to give luncheon to the managing director of CAC Computers – I'm hoping they'll hold their three-day conference here, next April.'

The telephone rang and she grabbed it, glancing at her watch as she did so. She ought to be down in the lobby now, to meet the Watkins. She hoped this call wouldn't take long.

'Oh, Andrew, hi,' she said, her voice instantly dropping into an easy intimacy. Andrew Seymour had been her steady boyfriend for nearly three years and they shared his flat in Chelsea. He was an estate agent, and both their families took it for granted that in time they would marry.

'We're expected for dinner at eight o'clock,' Andrew was saying, 'and Mother wants us all to wear evening dress.'

'Eight o'clock!' She sounded horrified. 'How can I possibly be changed and at their place by eight o'clock? I've got a wine tasting here this evening and I shan't get away until nearly eight! Why didn't you tell me this morning? Oh, damn, if I'd known I'd have brought a long dress with me, and changed here!'

'Can't you leave early for once?' Andrew sounded cross and slightly disapproving. 'It is my parents' thirtieth wedding anniversary, you know! They've planned this dinner-party for months now.'

'I know.' Jessica tried hard to make her voice sound patient, but it always irritated her when Andrew presumed she could drop everything in order to fit in with his plans. 'And I've bought a decanter for them as a present from us both. It's just that I'm supposed to be hosting this party here, and I've only got a short day dress to change into.'

'Why can't you go home beforehand to change . . . and then you could take a taxi from the hotel straight to Wilton Crescent? We could meet there,' he persisted. She could sense he was getting upset and if that happened the evening would be ruined for both of them.

'I'll work out something, babe,' she said, forcing

herself to sound calm and cheerful. 'In any case, let's meet at your parents' house at eight o'clock. Okay? I must go now because I've got people waiting for me, but I'll see you tonight.'

'Okay.' He sounded grudging.

Jessica dropped the phone back on to its cradle, picked up her clipboard and dashed out of the office and along the corridor to the elevator. If there was one thing she hated it was being late.

She spotted them at once, standing uneasily by the reception desk: Mr and Mrs Cyril Watkins, up for the day from their home near Watford, a middle-aged, working-class couple who had succeeded in making a lot of money from their building company. Switching on her charming professional smile, Jessica stepped forward to meet them, a dainty figure, impeccably dressed, discreetly jewelled, her small intelligent face glowing with vitality. She greeted them as if they were the only people she really wanted to see that day.

'Good morning. How nice of you to come. May I get you some coffee . . . or a glass of champagne?'

They declined, shaking their heads and mumbling something about it not being long since they'd had breakfast.

'Then allow me to take you up to the Banqueting Rooms,' said Jessica smoothly, as if she understood absolutely how they felt. On the first floor, she led them down wide, thickly carpeted corridors, past crystal chandeliers blazing with many lights, silk covered walls hung with eighteenth-century engravings of London, and the occasional gilt console table laden with exotic flowers. The Watkins followed her in awe-struck silence, glancing furtively from time to time at the ornate plaster ceilings and rich hangings. It was all a long way from their semi-detached near Watford.

Jessica flung open double doors at the end of the corridor. 'This is the Armitage Suite,' she announced brightly, leading them into a large baroque style room, decorated and embellished with white plaster garlands, depicting fruit and flowers against a sky blue background. 'Bars are set up at either end for a reception, but of course we have waiters circulating with trays of drinks as well.' Then she walked over to the full-length windows which overlooked Hyde Park.

'When we do a wedding, we usually place the cake here, with pedestal flower displays on either side. It's a good position for everyone to see what is happening, and to have good pictures taken.' Jessica exuded such enthusiasm, and it appeared to be so genuine, that it might have been her own wedding she was planning. Mr and Mrs Watkins were deeply impressed by the magnificence of the room and reassured by the under-standing manner of this helpful young woman. Anxious to do their best for their only daughter, who was marrying a real gentleman, they were determined to make a splash on the great day.

'What d'you think, Mother?' muttered Mr Watkins, who, having made a pile, had so far indulged himself only by buying a BMW.

Mrs Watkins looked at him and pressed her cream cotton-gloved fingertips together. 'It'll do very nicely,' she replied quietly.

'You did say you would be expecting approximately a hundred and fifty guests, didn't you?' Jessica asked, checking the notes on her clipboard.

'That's right,' said Mr Watkins.

'Then this room is perfect for you. Of course if you were expecting more guests, I'd have suggested the ballroom . . .?' She paused, dangling the temptation of something even bigger and grander before their eyes. They hesitated, Mrs Watkins with her head cocked on one side as if she were waiting for her husband to say something. Mr Watkins studied the carpet, wondering who they could ask to fill a bigger room.

'Why don't I show it to you anyway, as you're here?' Jessica suggested, like a hostess wishing to put her best rooms at her guests' disposal. 'It's only down the corridor.' Setting off at a brisk walk, her high-heeled shoes sinking into the deep pile carpet, she led them to a door on the other side of the corridor.

'This room is a copy of the corridor of mirrors in the Palace of Versailles,' she said, as if to prepare them for a shock. When she opened the tall carved doors they stood and gazed in wonder at what seemed like acres of shining polished floor, bounded and held together by endless panels of antique mirrors, mottled and speckled with age, their images reflected a hundred times over. Heavy dull gold draperies festooned the great windows, through which a watery morning sun struggled fitfully.

'I think the other room would do nicely,' commented Mr Watkins hollowly.

Jessica nodded. 'I agree. This room is better at

night, when all the chandeliers are lit. Right, now, would you care to fix up all the details, seeing you're here? It would save your having to come up to London again.' Gently and persuasively she asked what they'd like, whilst skilfully indicating what she thought was suitable.

Thirty minutes later she was back in her office, looking pleased with herself. 'Well, that's all fixed!' she said triumphantly to Dick. 'They've booked the Armitage, plus ten cases of vintage Bollinger, six hundred assorted canapés, eight arrangements of pink and white flowers on pedestals, a three-tiered wedding cake . . . thank God I managed to dissuade them from having a sugar bride and groom on the top! And they want three suites of rooms for the night before. And d'you know something?' Dick looked at her questioningly, amused by her enthusiasm. 'They didn't even blink when I gave them the quote!'

He laughed. 'People never do. Once they've made up their minds to give a big bash, it's all or nothing, regardless of cost. By the way, your lunch appointment is going to be late. Here's the message for you.'

'Great!' Jessica glanced at the scribbled note. 'That will just give me time to dash home to pick up an evening dress for tonight. Andrew and his family have got an attack of delusions of grandeur and I've got to get myself tarted up for this dinner they're giving.'

At that moment the phone on her desk buzzed.

'Hullo? Oh, Peter!' She gave a squeal of delight. Peter Thorn was one of the *Evening Standard*'s leading journalists, and over the years he'd become a good friend, always mentioning the hotel if he could, and sometimes filling her in about celebrity arrivals. 'How are you? When are you coming to lunch with me again?'

His voice was deep and rich, always on the brink of a laugh. 'Is it true Madonna's expected to stay next week . . . for her concert at the Albert Hall?'

'God, I don't know!' she cried aghast. 'We haven't heard anything. Have you checked with Anne Butler in the PR department?'

'She's denying everything, but she always does, and your reservations department says they've no one of that name expected! All very prim and proper they were, and singularly unhelpful. Can you check it out for me, Jessica?'

'Of course I will, but you know I'll have to deny it officially, even if it is true; that's hotel policy. Our guests have to have their privacy protected.'

'I know, I know.' Peter's voice sounded resigned. 'Bloody stupid, isn't it? Her management in Los Angeles have announced she'll be at the Royal Westminster for four nights . . .'

'Typical! They *want* the place swarming with papparazzi and ten thousand fans, because it's good for her image,' Jessica cut in, 'but our other guests are going to hate it! Oh, Christ, I hope it isn't true. Security will go mad, and we don't need that sort of razzmatazz.'

'You will keep me posted, though?'

'Yes, I will, Peter. Listen, I've just remembered something. If I help you over this, will you do a little favour for me?'

'Sure. What is it?'

'Do you know anything about the Dalrymple family? A friend of mine wants to find out about them. They come from Devon.'

'Dalrymple.' Peter paused, deep in thought. 'The name rings a bell, but I can't place it.'

'Sir George Dalrymple. He had a daughter called Camilla, who died over twenty years ago. She was married to an American called Jake Shearman.'

A long piercing whistle came out of the telephone receiver, startling Jessica. 'Yes, I know who you mean,' said Peter drily. 'Why does your friend want to know about them?'

Jessica hesitated, surprised by his reaction. 'Well . . . she . . . she was just interested in the family,' she said lamely.

'Take my advice, tell her to steer clear! There were some very nasty goings-on at the time. I was a cub reporter and I wrote a piece about it, it would be over twenty years ago now. Advise her to have nothing to do with them.' For once he sounded serious, the usual laughter gone from his voice.

'What sort of things?' demanded Jessica. 'Peter, you must tell me. It's too intriguing for words!'

'It's too long a story now. Invite me to that lunch you promised me and I'll give you all the gory details. And you'll keep me posted on the Madonna situation?' It was obvious he wasn't going to be drawn any further.

'Yes, I will. Now, when you are free? Let's fix a date.'

The rest of the day passed in a whirl of meetings and phone calls, including one from an irate customer who insisted she'd been charged for eight cases of champagne instead of six at a reception she'd held recently. It wasn't until five o'clock that Jessica realised she hadn't been home to collect a long dress for the evening.

'Hold the fort for me, will you, Dick?' she begged. 'I'll be as quick as I can, but I *must* go home and change. You don't mind, do you?' she added cajolingly. Dick smiled. Few could resist Jessica's natural and earnest manner, so evocative of a little girl in its candid yet sharp sweetness.

'Run along. I know how hard you have to work to look beautiful!' Dick teased.

'You . . .!' Jessica pretended to look insulted. 'I'll have you know I was paid a compliment on my looks by the General Manager last week.'

Dirk smirked. 'He must have wanted you to do some overtime!'

Jessica arrived at Andrew's parents' house shortly after eight that evening, to find the whole family already drinking champagne and congratulating Mr and Mrs Seymour.

'I'm sorry I couldn't get here before, darling,' Jessica whispered to Andrew, as soon as she had greeted his parents. 'Do I look all right? I had to practically change in the taxi!' With one hand she dug a pin more firmly into her topknot.

Andrew slid his hand round her waist, so tiny he could have encircled it with both hands. 'You look fantastic, Jessie. Here, have a drink. You could probably do with one.'

Jessica rolled her eyes as he handed her a glass of champagne. 'I feel pissed already!' She hissed under her breath. 'You forget, I've come from a wine tasting.'

'But you're not supposed to *drink* at a wine tasting,' he protested, laughing, 'you're supposed to . . .'

'I know! I know!' She waggled her head from side to side. 'You're supposed to swill it round your mouth and then *spit it out into a bucket*! Honestly, Andrew, I could never do that!' Dazzling blue eyes, half joking, half serious, looked up into his, and he felt his heart melt.

Andrew Seymour, twenty-eight and the son of a well-to-do company director, was a keep-fit fanatic and it showed in his physique. Well built and muscular, he towered over the diminutive Jessica, exuding an aura of good health, his dark brown hair shining, his grey eyes clear and untroubled. Three evenings every week at a local fitness club, and games of squash and tennis whenever he could fit them in, were all part of his schedule. He was also ambitious, and since he'd formed Jason and Seymour, Estate Agents, with his best friend, Sandy Jason, he'd flung himself into his work, anxious to be part of the property boom that was sweeping Britain and so far showed no signs of slowing down. And at the centre of his world of working hard and playing hard was Jessica, with whom he shared his life. One of these days he was going to ask her to marry him, although she already knew, of course, that was what would happen. They had an understanding, as his mother told her friends. Neither was in any great hurry to marry, both being wrapped up in their careers, both happy with the way things were.

Tonight, though, Andrew felt sentimental, seeing his mother and father celebrate thirty years together. It seemed such a marvellous recommendation for legalising living together and his eyes grew quite misty as he saw them toasting each other and holding hands.

His voice was gruff. 'We'll be like that . . . after thirty years, won't we, Jess?'

Jessica nodded, her eyes soft and her face gentle. 'Of course we will,' she said, and then because she was Jessica, always ready with a flip remark or a witty barb, she added, 'and won't we be *boring*!'

Andrew tried to hide the way he winced at her words, knowing that she didn't mean to be taken seriously, it was just her way. He forced a laugh. 'We'll be so rich by then, who cares?' he quipped back.

Jessica laughed too. 'Goodee! Talking of rich, I go to stay with Madeleine in four days' time. You hadn't forgotten, had you?'

'No, I hadn't forgotten.'

'I wish you could come too,' she said impulsively. 'I'm going to miss you, sweetheart. Can't you get away? Sandy can manage for a few days without you!'

'There are too many deals to put together at the moment,' he replied, shaking his head. 'We're negotiating on three houses, all million-pound properties, and I must be here to make sure everything goes through all right.'

Jessica nodded, understanding, and rested her

blonde head against the black shoulder of his dinner-jacket. 'That's big business,' she murmured. 'So, shall I give your regards to Broadway?'

Andrew hugged her closer. 'You do that,' he said.

'. . . And let's not stay too late at this party,' she added with a suggestive little look.

Already Andrew felt himself getting aroused. 'You bet we won't,' he whispered back.

Chapter Two

The corner of Spring Street and West Broadway, in SoHo, was jammed with limousines. They drew up at the Midas Gallery, spilling on to the sidewalk the élite of New York society as they arrived in force to see Madeleine Delaney's first one-woman show. Photographers' bulbs flashed. A reporter from *Woman's Wear Daily* jotted down who was wearing whose designs, and columnists noted who was escorting whom, seeing too often the familiar faces of well-known walkers, clinging to the arms of middle-aged bejewelled women. Inside the large white room, a throng already jostled each other in their eagerness to see and be seen, and almost as an afterthought, to look at the portraits of 'Faces of the Famous'. In an atmosphere heavy with perfume mingling with the scent of towering arrangements of white lilac, waiters skimmed around as if they had no feet, carrying trays of champagne and platters of tiny grilled lobster claws.

Madeleine stood near the entrance, her deep amethyst silk dress throwing into relief her cloud of black hair and heart-shaped face as she smilingly greeted everyone and tried to hide her nervousness. Every now and again she glanced over at Carl, seeking reassurance, and he smiled back giving her an almost imperceptible wink. Her father, Jake, was hovering supportively also, helping to introduce the galaxy of guests who included senators and financiers, film stars, and the more élite members of the press. The babble of voices rose in a fever of banal greetings, but then a few people stopped to look up at the spot-lit paintings that covered the walls and gradually the tenor of the party changed. The portraits, brutally raw in their candour, impossible to ignore any longer, struck the assembled company by their electrifying quality.

'She's got real talent!' people murmured, in voices that implied they'd known all along she was going to make it and were gratified to be proved right. This, they observed, was no conventional exhibition of portraits, destined for some drawing-room or board-room. 'Faces of the Famous', depicting men only, was a collection of vibrant studies, swingeingly perceptive, destroying at a stroke the carefully cultivated public images these famous men had taken such pains to present.

'I wonder where she trained?' asked a socialite, who loved 'discovering' people. She opened her glossy catalogue for the first time and skimmed Madeleine's biography. 'Ummm. Educated at Brearley and then she seems to have studied at the Art Students' League before going on to Paris. I see she's won quite a few prizes; she's even had paintings in some major exhibitions. Well, I think she's quite a find. I wonder if she does women.'

Her companion, reading over her shoulder, noted that a leading critic had said Madeleine's portraits contained 'great energy and vibrance'.

'Quite a find!' repeated the woman. 'I must invite her to my next party. Of course, I've known her father for years.'

'I like her style,' commented her companion, 'even if her perception is rather cruel. Look at this one of Nixon!'

They examined the portrait, executed in colours tinged with blue, thickly applied with a palette knife, depicting with brutal clarity the inner doubts and foibles, the fears and quirks, of the man.

'Brilliant, quite brilliant.'

Jake's idea of having a gimmick had worked. No one had ever given an exhibition of portraits of celebrated men, and from the commercial point of view it was a stroke of genius.

Madeleine had aimed for impact and now, as she moved round the crowded room, she knew she had succeeded. People were eyeing her with a new sort of respect; not just as the beautiful daughter of a rich and famous banker who belonged to one of New York's oldest families but as a sparkling and forceful talent in her own right. For a moment she wondered if she deserved this much praise. She had worked hard and studied for years with a single-minded dedication, but what made her paintings special was the strange chemistry that occurred between herself and her subjects that had nothing to do with technique or knowledge. It was as if she could read their thoughts and pick up their secret emotions, as her brush or palette knife, heavy laden with rich burnt umber or indigo blue or carmine, jabbed at the canvas, pinning the underlying characteristics swiftly down as a rare butterfly is pinned to a board. She had the talent; Jake had merely marketed it, with his flair for business.

Her thoughts were interrupted at that moment by the sight of a petite figure with flowing blonde hair, dressed in a swish of black taffeta, hurtling through the packed gallery towards her.

'Jessica!' she cried in delight.

Jessica flung herself enthusiastically at Madeleine. 'Oh, Maddy! This is all so exciting I could die! My dear, I never thought I'd get here! The flight was delayed . . . would you believe it? . . . and when I got to your apartment, you'd already left of course . . . and oh, my God! This is so *thrilling*!'

Jessica spoke breathlessly, her pale English complexion flushed with excitement. Her blue eyes blazed. 'Oh, Maddy, I'm so *proud* of you!'

Laughing, Madeleine hugged her. 'I can't tell you how good it is to see you. I'd never have forgiven you if you hadn't come.'

At that moment Jake Shearman joined them and Jessica flung herself at him too. 'How's my favourite man?' she demanded, looking up into his handsome lined face. He was her ideal older man, and she frequently told him so. 'Why do you never age at all?' she asked. 'I can't tell you how jealous my father is of you.'

Smiling indulgently, he stooped to kiss her on the cheek. 'Welcome back to New York, my dear. I'm so glad you could make it – we were counting on your being here tonight. How was the flight? Did you have a good journey?'

Jessica pulled a comical face. 'If you call seven hours in a plane full of screaming children, plastic food and the worst movie I've ever seen "having a good flight", then I suppose I did. But I'm *dying* for a drink!'

Jake gave a signal and through the chattering throng a waiter appeared.

Jessica sipped her ice cool champagne, then let out a satisfied sigh. 'Oh, bliss! Now, Maddy, I want you to show me everything. I can't wait to see what you've been up to.'

Linking arms, Madeleine began steering her friend through the crowds, pointing out the various paintings. 'What do you think? she whispered.

Jessica eyed her with genuine amazement. 'For God's sake, how did you get all these famous men to sit for you in the first place? I've never seen such a collection of celebrities.'

'That's what everyone wants to know.' Madeleine's dark eyes twinkled with amusement. 'I'll let you into a secret – I relied on their vanity. I wrote each of them a personal letter explaining I was holding a major New York exhibition, entitled "Faces of the Famous", and that it wouldn't be complete without a study of them. I even offered to give them the painting afterwards, if they liked it.'

'And they fell for it?' Jessica, who knew a bit about psychology from working for years in the hotel business, was impressed. Flattery – like remembering someone's name or particular favourite drink – always worked.

Madeleine nodded. 'I did something else too, which

was rather naughty, but it got results.'

'You offered them your body, at the same time!'

They both dissolved into laughter.

'They should be so lucky!' chuckled Madeleine. 'I told, say, Frank Sinatra that Paul Newman had already agreed to be painted; and I told Ed Koch that George Bush had said yes. Jessica, it worked like a charm! In the end ninety percent of them agreed because they thought all the others had accepted. I think they felt they couldn't afford not to be included!'

'You clever girl,' said Jessica approvingly. Then she pranced forward again, diminutive in spite of her spiky heels, exclaiming at every picture as it blazed down from the white walls, glowing under the impact of the spotlights.

'I don't believe it, Maddy! I do not believe what I'm seeing! You've got John McEnroe and Boris Becker – God, isn't he dishy! – Calvin Klein . . . now there's a handsome man for you . . . and isn't that John Fairchild who produces *Woman's Wear Daily*? I thought so! And Bob Hope, Douglas Fairbanks . . . Maddy, who *haven't* you got?'

'Prince Charles,' replied Madeleine instantly. 'I'd give anything to do his portrait.'

Jessica nodded knowingly. 'You can't play tactics with the British Royal Family, but I think I know of a way you might be able to paint him, when you get more established in Europe.'

'You mean you know the password to get through the portals of Buckingham Palace? I bet it's impossible.'

'Not really. You'd have to get a regiment, or a college, or perhaps a city livery company to commission you to do his portrait to hang in their building. Then they approach the private secretary at the Palace requesting the Prince sit for an artist of their choice. Actually, all the Royal Family get painted several times a year for this purpose so you might stand a good chance,' she added thoughtfully.

'Jessica, you're brilliant. And I'd get to go to Buckingham Palace for the sittings?' Madeleine clasped her hands together, thrilled at the thought.

'Or Kensington Palace, depending on which Royal you're painting. You'd also be allowed to go as often as you liked to paint their clothes or robes on a dummy to save them posing for hours and hours,' said Jessica knowledgeably.

Madeleine grabbed her arm, her face intent. 'Jessica, if you could help me fix it up one day, I'd be indebted to you for life!'

Her friend laughed, blue eyes sparkling. 'I'll see what I can do . . . in the meantime, can I have some more champagne? I'm parched!'

'Of course. Oh, I'm so glad you could come over for this party. We go back a long way, don't we?' They had moved to a corner of the gallery, which was less crowded.

'How many years is it?' asked Jessica, savouring her drink. 'We met at school in 1970 so that's . . . oh, Lord, I'm getting old!' she wailed.

'Eighteen years ago.'

Jessica cast her eyes to heaven. 'I remember hating you at first, and thinking you must be spoilt something

57

rotten because your father was so rich and you always wore such expensive clothes.'

'And I remember thinking you were terribly stuck up with your English accent and snobbish ways.'

Their conversation was interrupted by Jake's arrival. His face was the colour of dirty wax, his dark eyes gleaming with anxiety. Beside him Carl was hovering nervously, a deep flush staining his cheeks.

'Madeleine, I must talk to you,' said her father in a strained voice.

She looked up, startled, and then glanced questioningly at Carl. 'What's the matter? What's wrong?'

'I'm sorry, sweetheart.' He shook his head, embarrassed. 'I forgot you hadn't mentioned it to your father . . . it just sort of slipped out.'

Suddenly, she understood. Carl must have told Jake she was planning to visit her grandfather in England.

'I hear you've heard from George Dalrymple,' said Jake sternly.

Jessica gave a sharp intake of breath and was about to say something, but changed her mind.

'Yes, I have,' Madeleine said calmly. 'What's wrong with that? He is my grandfather, after all, and he's asked me to go and visit him. I'd have told you myself, sooner or later, but I've been so busy with this exhibition.'

'You're not to go, Madeleine. I absolutely forbid it,' said Jake. His jaw muscles were twitching and she'd never seen him look so upset. Carl shuffled from one foot to the other, his face still red.

'Let's discuss this later,' whispered Madeleine,

aware now that people around them had stopped talking and were curious to know what was going on. Jessica eased herself out of the group on the pretext of having another look at the paintings, but Carl put his arm round Madeleine's waist.

'She's an adult now, Jake,' he began heatedly. 'If she wants to go and see some ancient relative I don't see why . . .'

'. . . You don't know anything about it.' Jake cut in harshly. 'Promise me you'll have nothing to do with George Dalrymple, Madeleine.'

Madeleine began to feel angry. It was stupid of Carl to have mentioned it to Jake in the first place, without her permission, but at twenty-six she was capable of making her own decisions and she'd already made up her mind, whatever her father said.

'What the hell's the matter?' She spoke so quietly that only Jake and Carl could hear, but her tone was one of suppressed fury. 'Why don't you want me to go? Why have you always refused to talk about anything to do with my mother?'

Jake looked at her for a long moment, and the expression in his eyes was unfathomable. 'I have my reasons,' he said at last. 'Please have nothing to do with your grandfather. If you do, you'll be getting into something you won't be able to handle!'

Carl left early for the bank the next morning, leaving Madeleine and Jessica having breakfast in the Oriental style dining-room of their apartment, which overlooked Central Park. Madeleine had chosen to live on this part of Fifth Avenue, up in the seventies, because of its view; if she didn't get to see the fresh naturalness of trees and grass every day, she felt claustrophobic. Now, through the large window, she watched the landscape in all its summer glory. A variety of greens, so subtle in shade she wondered if it would be possible to capture the tones in oil paints, fluttered and danced in the morning sunshine.

'Look!' she said suddenly, putting down her coffee cup and pointing.

Jessica, who was suffering from a hangover, peered, bleary-eyed. 'What? I don't see anything.'

'On the wall . . . running along the top now . . . see, a beautiful squirrel! They're so tame, you know, they'll eat out of your hand.' Madeleine smiled with delight, watching the squirrel hop on to the branch of a tree and then climb vertically up the trunk. 'Oh, it all looks so beautiful! I might go for a walk later. If it wasn't for Central Park I'd never survive here.'

'Dear God,' murmured Jessica weakly, 'I never expected a city girl like you to go all bucolic on me. It's cold and muddy down there, Maddy, and you'll ruin your smart shoes in fifteen seconds flat! What's brought on this sudden love of the countryside? I'd have thought your scene would have been the Trump Tower atrium more like'.

Madeleine shook her head, laughing. 'It must be old age setting in. Carl and I go to Oyster Bay every moment we can to get away from the city.'

'Well,' rejoined Jessica darkly, 'you'll never find me living in the country. I say, Maddy, have you got any aspirins?'

Madeleine rose. 'Yes, of course. You must be jet-lagged after your flight yesterday.'

'Jetlagged be damned! I've got a good old-fashioned hangover, so there's no need to be so polite.'

A moment later Madeleine returned. She handed Jessica a couple of pills. 'Here you are. Listen, Jessica, I meant to ask you last night, but it was so late when we got back from the exhibition: what were you going to say when my father mentioned my grand-father? You gave a sort of gasp, but then you wandered off?'

'Oh, yes.' Jessica downed the aspirins with a gulp of coffee and leaned back in her chair. 'I talked to a friend of mine, a journalist called Peter Thorn who's on the *Evening Standard*. He seems to know all about your family.'

'Well?' Madeleine looked at her sharply. 'What did he say? Does he know anything about my mother and how she died?'

'I think he probably does. There seems to have been some sort of scandal, a long time ago. He said he covered the case. It was rather peculiar, actually; he said you should steer clear of the family . . .'

Madeleine sat bolt upright, her expression alarmed. 'You didn't tell him about me, did you? I told you to be discreet.'

Jessica cut in indignantly. 'Of course I didn't men-tion you . . . I said a friend of mine wanted to find out about the Dalrymples, that's all. He implied there were some nasty goings-on, about the time your mother died.'

'What did he actually say? What sort of goings-on?' Madeleine felt uneasy, as if a cold hand had clutched her stomach.

'I'm sorry, Maddy, I don't know. Peter and I were supposed to meet for lunch last Friday, but he called off at the last minute because he had to cover a story about Ford being involved in an industrial strike. He'd promised to give me all the "gory details", as he put it. But don't worry, I'll get him to tell me everything when I get back.'

'Jake is trying to keep something from me, isn't he? Oh, I wish he wouldn't treat me as if I were still a child. Whatever he says, I'm going to Devon to see my grandfather.'

Jessica poured herself some more orange juice from a large crystal jug. 'When?'

Madeleine shrugged, her slim shoulders showing through the fine cotton of her robe. 'As soon as possible, I suppose. Now that the exhibition has opened the sooner I go and find out what it's all about, the better. At the moment it's like having a great black cloud hanging over me.'

'Why don't you fly with me, when I return next Monday?' suggested Jessica.

Madeleine's face lit up. 'What a good idea! I'll do that. I hate travelling alone, and I could spend a couple of nights at your hotel, couldn't I?'

'Why not!' Jessica clapped her hands together in delight. 'I'll see if I can get you our Presidential Suite at a special rate!'

'Thanks.'

Jessica sprang to her feet, her hangover forgotten.

'That's settled them. Now, what are we going to do today?'

Madeleine stretched her arms above her head. 'I know what I'm going to do. Take it easy after last night and have a walk in the park. I suppose there are no prizes for guessing what you want to do?' She regarded her friend with knowing affection.

'None at all! You don't think I've flown thousands of miles just to see *you*, do you, my dear?' Jessica bantered. 'I'm off to Bergdorf Goodman, Bloomingdale's, Saks,' she ticked them off on her fingers as she spoke, 'Bonwit Teller, Tiffany's . . . and I *must* pop into Hammacher Schemmer to see what new gadgets they've got.' She gave an excited wriggle at the thought of being let loose with her credit cards.

'Rather you than me,' laughed Madeleine. 'How about meeting for lunch, then? One o'clock at Elaine's?'

'You're on!'

At twenty-past one, Jake Shearman hurried into the Four Seasons, where he was meeting Patti whom he'd summoned that morning to have lunch with him. He found her already seated at his usual table, spikily elegant in a Calvin Klein suit with ropes of pearls wound round her thin neck and the customary cigarette smouldering between her fingers.

She knew why Jake had called her to this meeting, but she wanted to find out how much he knew before she raised the matter herself. She ordered a very dry martini and tapped her elegantly shod foot under the table, irritated at being kept waiting.

At last Jake appeared, flurried and rushed-looking, and slightly out of breath. He kissed her briefly on her rouged cheek.

'I'm sorry I'm late, Patti. I got held up and then the traffic was terrible.'

'You're out of condition,' she remarked disapprovingly. Her voice, gravelly from too many cigarettes, sounded hoarser than ever.

'You're a fine one to talk, with your smoking!' protested Jake. 'Filthy habit! Shall we order or do you want another drink?'

There was complete understanding between brother and sister. They could sound so rude to each other that people, overhearing them, flinched and thought they were fighting. In reality, a staunch affection existed that went back over fifty years, and if anyone tried to come between them they then faced the combined wrath of both Patti and Jake, who were fiercely loyal to each other.

'Of course I want another drink,' said Patti, stubbing out her cigarette and immediately lighting another one. She continued without preamble: 'I hear you had a fight with Madeleine after I'd left the exhibition last night.'

Jake shot her a wary look. 'Who did you hear that from?' If Patti had heard, then most of New York must know.

She shrugged. 'Things get around. So what's it all about?'

'Let's order first.'

'Okay. I'll have the crab mornay and a green side salad; and that second martini you promised me.'

'All right, all right! You sound like an alcoholic.' Jake gave the order to the servile waiter who hovered at his elbow. 'And we'll also have a bottle of the Mondavi Chardonnay, '87, please,' he added.

'Come on, Jake,' Patti said impatiently, 'I want to know why you got me here today.'

Jake sighed deeply. 'Madeleine's been contacted by George Dalrymple and he's asked her to go to visit him in England. I've forbidden her, of course, but I don't think she's going to pay any attention to me.'

Patti looked thoughtful. 'So he got through to her, did he?' she said, almost to herself.

'What d'you mean?' demanded Jake.

'He called me up about ten days ago. I was out, but Mallaby took a message. George wanted to know where he could get hold of Madeleine.'

'And Mallaby told him?'

Patti snorted. 'Don't be such a fool! Of course Mallaby didn't tell him, and neither did I. I called him back to say I wouldn't help but he refused to speak to me, the arrogant old devil! It struck me then that he'd probably got Madeleine's number from someone else, but she hasn't said anything, has she? I gathered from what I heard that it was Carl who told you?'

Jake nodded. 'It was. Apparently he wasn't supposed to, and Maddy and I had a little fracas about it last night. That's when I told her she mustn't have anything to do with her grandfather.'

Patti spoke with deep sarcasm. 'And of course she listened to you! Really, Jake, you can't come the heavy-handed father now. She's twenty-six. That's not the way to stop her going.'

'Then what is? I could tell Carl the whole story, although it's the last thing I want to do, and get *him* to prevent her going to England. But I don't think it would do any good.'

'And you'd be making a big mistake involving Carl. Why should he bear the burden of a secret he must never tell his wife? It would put a terrible strain on their marriage.' Patti dragged deeply on her Marlboro. 'Come to think of it, I wonder if George Dalrymple will tell Madeleine anything about her mother. We may be getting in a panic over nothing. He may just want to see his only grandchild before it's too late!'

'But why now?' demanded Jake, running a hand over the lower half of his face as if checking he'd shaved that morning. 'Why, suddenly, after over twenty years does he get in contact with her now?'

'Look at it this way, Jake. George was pretty ashamed of the whole business himself, at the time. After all, Camilla was his only child. Why should he want to stir it all up again?'

Jake sighed heavily. 'I suppose you're right.' The very thought of Camilla sent a chill through him and he felt bitter that after all these years, during which he'd done his damnedest to protect Madeleine, the memory of what had happened had risen to haunt him again. At the time he'd been driven to the brink of fear and despair by what had happened, and his only consolation had been that his daughter had been too young to understand.

Patti, aware that he was recalling the details of the catastrophe, reached across the table and put her bony and bejewelled hand on his arm. 'Stop thinking about it, Jake,' she commanded angrily, but her eyes were soft with sympathy. 'It won't do any good. George must be very old now, and I think he just wants to see Madeleine. You can't blame him for that.'

Jake remained unconvinced. 'Supposing she makes enquiries in Sherston? It's only a small village; there are bound to be people who remember.'

'So what's the worst that could happen?' Patti puffed furiously on her cigarette. 'If Madeleine finds out anything, she'll just have to learn to live with it, like you have. You can't protect her forever!' Recalling the past, her voice was harsh.

Jake remained silent, brooding.

'You should have married again, of course,' continued his sister.

'You know I couldn't.'

Patti sighed gustily, and her eyes were like dark burning holes in her narrow lived-in face. 'You could have found a way,' she insisted. 'It was wrong of you to let the past deprive you of happiness.'

'I've had a lot of girlfriends,' he protested, but he knew that what Patti said was true. What had happened to Camilla had been tragic and horrifying and it had affected him deeply. But need it have prevented him finding happiness with someone else?

'I suppose you wouldn't talk to Madeleine?' he suggested tentatively. 'Tell her not to go to England?'

'Have you no idea about psychology? Forbidden fruit, and all that? Really, Jake, for a grown man in your position I sometimes think you're exceedingly naive! Now, are you going to finish your wine or not?' she added tartly. 'There's no point in your bringing me to the Four Seasons for lunch if you're going to stare into space all the time, and waste all that good wine.'

Jake's face reluctantly broke into a smile. 'Good old Patti! It always does me good to see you.'

'And so I should think!' she snapped back, but as she looked at her brother her expression was kindly.

Every morning a team of clerks in the Central Manhattan Bank sorted through the mail, dividing and sub-dividing the hundreds of letters before despatching them to the various departments; internal current accounts, deposit accounts, overseas and loan accounts, requests for new cheque books and paying-in books, and letters of general query or acknowledgement, all had to be placed in the relevant baskets to be taken to the various floors of the building. Then there were banker's drafts to be dealt with, and payments authorised by big companies, and several hundred foreign transactions.

By nine o'clock, one of the clerks had deposited on Carl's desk all the documents authorising international money transfers for the day. There was usually a thick stack of these 'yellow forms' as they were referred to, although in fact they were the colour of cantaloup melon. Closely printed, with boxed sections which had to be filled in by the client, stating how much money they wished transferred, they represented the millions of dollars of 'flying capital' as the bank called it, from America to all parts of the world.

Carl was so experienced that a glance told him who

was remitting money, into which overseas bank it was to be paid, and who would be responsible for paying the transfer charges, agents' charges, and the amount being transferred. Accuracy, diligence in checking details, judgment in gauging whether the client had sufficient funds to cover the transfer and complete discretion were required, and Carl was pleased to find that his new assistant, Kimberley Cabot, possessed these qualities. She was quick and sharp and had an instant conceptual understanding of a situation when he explained it to her. As soon as Carl had gone through the authorisations each morning, he called Kimberley into his office and went through each transfer with her. Sometimes the Central Manhattan Bank was used as a clearing house, but mostly transfers were requested by companies who already had current accounts with them. It was her job to feed each form into a special piece of equipment which would record all the details on blue film, so that at any time in the future, if there were any queries, each form could be examined on the microfiche screen.

'I also want you to make sure these companies have sufficient funds in their credit account to allow for the amount they're asking to be transferred,' Carl explained, when Kimberley first started.

'And when I've okayed them, then I bring the forms back to you?' she enquired.

Carl nodded. 'That's correct. Then I pass them on to the President, Mr Shearman, or one of the Vice-Presidents if he's not around, and the money is then transferred by computer to wherever it is supposed to go.'

Kimberley smiled confidently. 'Yes, I know. When I worked in the computer department, I knew the girl responsible for putting these transfers through. Only the President and the Vice-Presidents have the code for foreign transfers, don't they.' She said it more as a matter of fact than as a question.

Carl was impressed. The girl had obviously been keeping her eyes open, learning all she could. People like her went far in the world of banking. 'That's correct,' he affirmed. 'Even I can't put through transfers.'

'Well, it's good it is a secure system,' she remarked placidly.

Carl pulled the stack of forms towards him and started scrutinising each one swiftly and knowledgeably. When he'd checked half a dozen and entered them on the computer on his desk, he handed them to Kimberley, who took them back to her office next door and started the process of recording each form on microfiche. They worked steadily, the rhythm broken by the occasional telephone call, mostly from clients enquiring whether the dollar was likely to rise or fall in the next twenty-four hours.

'I haven't polished my crystal ball lately!' Carl always replied with a laugh, it being forbidden for anyone in banking to give their opinion or prophecy on such matters in case a client held them responsible, at a later date, if they lost money on a foreign transaction. 'Your guess is as good as mine,' he always continued, 'if I knew the answer I'd be a rich man!' It was his standard way of dealing with these queries, and at least the customer felt mollified by the charming way he'd been handled, even if he didn't get the answer he wanted.

Kimberley came back into his office for another batch of forms. 'When I've done these I'll go check on the credit of the ones that bank here.'

'Okay. Thanks.' Carl didn't even look up. All that mattered was that Kimberley seemed to be doing what she was told, and wasn't wasting his time asking stupid questions like some of the girls who'd worked for him in the past. With the exception of Averil, of course, but then she'd been one in a million. Young women like her were rare.

At two o'clock Kimberley came into his office again. 'Can I get you a sandwich or something, Mr Delaney? You really should eat something and it would be no trouble!'

Carl looked up from his desk where the work was still piled high as a result of the noon mail delivery, and saw Kimberley looking at him with concern. Her pale grey eyes looked anxious, and for the first time Carl was struck by her beautiful colouring. Her rich Titian hair framed the pale gold skin of her face, and the green dress she wore enhanced her prettiness.

'I'm okay,' he replied absently.

'I can easily go to the canteen and get you something if you haven't time to go to the directors' dining-room today,' she offered.

The thought of salt beef on rye made Carl's mouth water suddenly. 'Well, are you sure? What about yourself?'

Kimberley smiled and her luminous grey eyes

sparkled. 'I'm fine. I'm on a diet anyway. I'll be back in a few minutes.'

'Thank you.' Carl watched her walk out of the office and noted she had very good legs. Vaguely, as he returned to his work, he wondered if she was going steady.

In a few minutes she was back, clutching his lunch as if she'd brought him an exciting present.

'I bought you an apple as well,' she said, handing him the rosy fruit. 'You know what they say?'

'An apple a day . . .?' he suggested.

Her voice was low and soft. 'An apple for the teacher.' Then she gave a little laugh and hurried back to her own office. With amusement, Carl could have sworn she was blushing.

'I'll only be gone a week, Carl,' Madeleine protested, as she fastened her suitcase. 'Nothing much can happen in a week.'

'I wish you weren't going at all.' Carl's tone was grim. 'Your father had another go at me yesterday. He made it sound positively dangerous . . . your going to see your grandfather. I wish to God I could get away and go with you.'

Madeleine came over to where he sat on the side of the bed and put her arms around his neck. 'I wish you could too, more than anything, but what can go wrong? Dad's making this whole thing sound like I was going behind the Iron Curtain or something! I'm only going to spend a couple of nights with my grandfather; I'll be with Jessica for the first day and the last couple of days in London, so there is not much risk of my coming to any harm! I'll phone you if there's a problem, darling.'

Carl held her close. 'Why can't your father come clean with me, and tell me what's wrong?'

Madeleine replied slowly and thoughtfully. 'I have a feeling that Dad's never got over my mother's death, and as he hasn't spoken to my grandfather for twenty years, maybe he blames him? Until I find out how my mother died we can't begin to unravel the mystery, but it's become obvious that Dad and Grandfather hate each other and that my mother is the bone of contention between them.' She pulled away from him and looked urgently into his face. 'I've got to go, Carl. Once and for all, I've got to find out why the subject of my mother is taboo, and this is my only chance.'

Carl kissed her tenderly. 'I know, sweetheart. I do understand. What worries me is that this Sir George Dalrymple sounds like a nut case; suppose he tries to keep you at Milton Manor?'

'You mean . . . like a prisoner?' Madeleine threw back her head and laughed. 'Don't be ridiculous, sweetheart! This is the twentieth century. Milton Manor may have been built in the times of Queen Elizabeth I, but that's all. You're letting your imagination run away with you, and you're supposed to be the hard-headed businessman; I'm the artistic one that's supposed to have a head full of fantasies, you know!'

Carl joined in her laughter, and the tension between them broke. But he still added: 'You promise to phone me if anything is wrong?'

'I promise,' she replied gaily, but as she boarded the jumbo jet that evening with Jessica, at JFK, she couldn't prevent a wave of nervous apprehension from sweeping over her. After all, her father was not given to hysteria, and yet his attitude to her visit to England bordered on panic.

Chapter Three

The fiery dawn, blazing the sky with vivid streaks of red and orange, streamed through the port windows of the jumbo jet like a celestial furnace, startling Madeleine from a deep sleep. She glanced at her watch. Six-thirty. In an hour and a half they'd be landing at Heathrow. Peering out of the window she could see the Irish Sea below, dazzling and sparkling like a lake of fire, then the plane tilted towards the east, the fire was suddenly extinguished and the waters were dark and mysterious again. Within moments the wild tumultuous sunrise had faded to a misty gold and the passengers were beginning to stir. Madeleine stretched her legs and looked at Jessica who was sitting, curled up under a blanket, beside her. An air hostess came bustling down the aisle, looking amazingly fresh, and the compartment was filled with the pungent aroma of coffee.

'Hi,' said Jessica, opening her eyes and blinking. 'What time is it?'

'Half-past six. You slept well,' replied Madeleine.

'It was the second dry martini before takeoff that did it. God, I look a mess!' Jessica regarded herself in her compact mirror. 'I can't wait to get home and have a bath. Anyway, I'm thankful I don't have to go to work today. We can laze around and Andrew can take us out to dinner tonight.'

'Yes. I'm glad I don't have to go down to Devon until tomorrow. I wish Carl had been able to come, though,' Madeleine added wistfully. 'I always miss him when I have to go away to do a commission or something.'

'That's the worst part of being a working woman. In the hotel business there are times when I don't get to see Andrew for twenty-four hours, and there's nothing I can do about it. You at least have some choice about when you're going to paint someone; I have to jump to, when I'm told! The trouble is, Andrew doesn't always understand the demands the hotel makes on me. It worries me sometimes,' she added, with a touch of anxiety in her voice.

'But you'll get married to him one day, won't you?' asked Madeleine. To her marriage was the most wonderful thing in the world. She couldn't bear to think of life without Carl and she longed for her friend to experience the same happiness.

Jessica replied positively. 'I'm sure we will, but not just yet. I've got a long way to go in my career before I settle down. There are a lot of things I want to achieve first.'

'Such as?' To Madeleine, Jessica had got about as far as a woman could get in the male-dominated hotel business.

'There's so much that is still a great challenge, that's what attracts me to the business. Of course what I'd *really* like is to have my own hotel. Nothing enormous, you know, but very elegant and exclusive with only fifty or sixty rooms and a superb dining-room with a chef from Paris. And I'd like to do all the little things that you can never do in a big corporation.' Jessica was fully awake now, her voice eager as she spoke.

Madeleine looked at her questioningly. 'What sort of things?'

'Oh, personalised writing-paper for each guest, a valet on hand night and day to look after their clothes, a fully stocked fridge in each room – and I mean fully stocked. Containers of fresh sliced lemons every day, bowls of olives as well as nuts, a variety of Twinings best tea to go with a kettle and fresh milk and nice crockery . . . Oh, Maddy, if I had my own hotel, I'd make staying there the most memorable thing that had ever happened to anybody!' Her voice trailed away, aching with yearning. Then she sat bolt upright and turned to Madeleine. 'In every bathroom I'd supply terry towelling robes, and not just shampoos and bath oil but moisturisers, toothpaste, nail polish remover, hair spray – all beautifully packaged in the hotel colours. Most important of all, each guest would be able to control the temperature of their own room. There is nothing worse than being stuck in a too hot or too cold place and not being able to do anything about it.'

Madeleine looked impressed. 'You've certainly given it a lot of thought, but wouldn't the work be horrendous? I mean, in a hotel you never stop, you don't even close at the weekends like a big store. Surely it would be a killer?'

Jessica's voice was vehement. 'Absolutely not. When you come to think of it, Maddy, the parallel to running a big hotel is running a big house! You've got all the same elements – cleaning, laundry, marketing, cooking, dealing with staff, and lots and lots of guests! I love it,' she added unnecessarily.

'I can see you do!' Madeleine smiled at her friend's enthusiasm.

'I don't suppose it'll ever happen but it's a lovely dream.' Jessica sighed then suddenly leaned forward, peering across Madeleine to study the landscape just visible below. 'Look, we're over England. That's Cornwall and Devon, just down there.'

Madeleine looked down on the patchwork of tiny fields, visible through the drifting clouds of morning mist.

'We'll be landing soon,' Jessica commented brightly. 'Just time for another cup of coffee.' Madeleine's heart suddenly lurched as she looked at the countryside below. By tomorrow, she would be down there among those lush green fields where her grandfather lived. And by tomorrow she'd know whatever it was he wanted to tell her!

The train roared into Okehampton station, and with a squeal of grinding brakes, screeched to a standstill. Stepping down on to the small country platform, Madeleine paused to look round and get her bearings. She had called Sir George from her suite at the Royal Westminster the previous evening and the butler had informed her that Jenkins, the gardener, would meet her at the station. Dust and grass pollen hung heavy in the afternoon air, and as she walked towards the exit sign she could feel the heat of the tarred platform through the fine leather of her shoes. There wasn't a sign of anyone and she was just wondering whether there was a taxi service in this remote part of the world when she spotted an elderly man wearing a tweed jacket and cap, standing beside an ancient Riley in the deserted carpark.

'Excuse me, are you Jenkins?' she asked, going over to him.

He nodded, and without saying a word took her case and put it in the boot of the car. Madeleine climbed into the back, acutely aware of his unfriendly attitude. His manner seemed almost hostile, and as he turned out of the station yard she caught a glimpse of his profile. His mouth was closed in a grim line.

Once outside Okehampton, the roads became narrow winding lanes, edged by hedgerows eight feet high, almost blotting out the sky at times as they drove through what felt like a green tunnel entwined by a profusion of wild flowers.

'I'd no idea it was so pretty here,' Madeleine exclaimed spontaneously as she caught flashing glimpses of wild myrtle, golden oxslips and hawthorn through the car windows.

Jenkins did not respond. Gripping the steering wheel fiercely as if unused to driving, he stared solidly ahead, his back stiff and forbidding.

'Have you always lived here?' she asked in an effort to make conversation.

His voice was flat. 'I was born 'ere.'

Madeleine leaned forward with interest. 'Really? And have you worked for a long time for Sir George?'

'Goin' on forty years.'

It was on the tip of Madeleine's tongue to ask if he remembered her mother but something stopped her, an instinctive feeling that told her she was treading on forbidden ground. The back of his thick red neck, and the hunch of his shoulders expressed more enmity than if he had snubbed her. She angled herself to adjust her hair in the windscreen mirror, and met his eyes, watching her intently. Embarrassed, she drew back and looked out of the window. There had been something disturbing about his furtive stare.

At last the car slowed down, and taking a left turn Jenkins turned into a driveway banked by hydrangeas, their pink and blue flowering heads drooping in the strong afternoon sunshine. At the end of the drive stood Milton Manor.

Built of shimmering grey limestone in the middle of the sixteenth century, the façade was surmounted by Dutch style gables, highly decorated with scrolls scalloped out in curving lines. Madeleine climbed out of the car and stood looking up at what had been her mother's home. The house itself was E-shaped, the centre porch embellished above the door with the Dalrymple coat-of-arms carved in stone. High mullioned and transomed windows, their hundreds of tiny glass panes winking like jewels in the sun, gave the place a friendly and inviting look, and for a moment she laughed at herself for having been so apprehensive. Milton Manor was nothing more than a beautiful, typically English country house, surrounded by elms and oaks, the garden brimming with summer flowers, the atmosphere redolent of peace.

At that moment an elderly butler opened the heavy brass studded front door and took her case from Jenkins.

'Good afternoon, Madam. Please come in. Sir George is waiting to see you in the library.'

Madeleine followed him into the large hall, cool and dark by contrast, aware that it was furnished with heavy carved tables and chairs with walls lined with old family portraits. Hunter, as she later came to realise he was called, led her down a corridor, tapped briefly at a door at the far end and ushered her into the library.

The first thing that hit her was the intolerable heat of the room. As if she'd opened a furnace door a great blast engulfed her, sucking out her breath and parching her skin. Then she noticed that a blazing log fire filled the grate, and in spite of the warm afternoon all the windows were tightly shut and the curtains half drawn. Fighting a feeling of suffocation, she walked forward and saw an old man hunched in a chair before the fireplace.

'Hello, Grandfather,' she said softly, taking his blue veined hand and looking into his face.

Sir George was small and wizened, his pale skin stretched tightly over his angular skull, a few wisps of silver hair fringing his ears. His shrunken neck disappeared into a collar several sizes too big for him, and for a moment Madeleine was reminded of a dead goat she'd seen in the desert when she'd been a child, parched dry by the sun. Only his eyes were alive; they were pale blue and glittered with a feverish intensity as if an explosion was about to take place in his head. It was as if he were bursting with something he could no longer keep to himself.

'I came to see you as quickly as I could,' she said, drawing up a chair.

'So you're Camilla's child?' The voice was a rasping whisper.

'Yes, I'm Madeleine. I believe I was a baby when you last saw me.' She spoke gently, as if to a child, so as not to excite him more. His blue eyes searched her face anxiously.

'You were three.'

'Was I? I'm afraid I don't remember.'

George Dalrymple turned his head to look at the fire, and the reflection of the flames made his eyes look like blazing sockets in his face. Madeleine shifted uncomfortably. There was something terrible and fearful in those eyes, as if he had looked into the pit of hell and could not forget what he'd seen. The heat was stifling now, closing in around her, making her sweat. Her hair stuck uncomfortably to the back of her neck. Suddenly he spoke, his voice stronger but his sentences disjointed.

'There are things you should have been told . . . things that have been kept from you. I told your father it was wrong . . .'

A sense of unreality swept over Madeleine, almost making her dizzy for a moment. The grating voice of her grandfather, the cloying hothouse atmosphere of the room, the mystery that surrounded Camilla . . . was it only a few days ago that she'd been the centre of a sophisticated New York crowd, living a normal life? She felt as if she'd been swept back in time, to another age and another existence. For a split second she almost felt as if she *was* her mother.

'What have you got to tell me, Grandfather?'

He turned sharply to look at her again, taking in her

pale chiselled features, her large dark eyes and the cloud of black hair that framed her face.

'You don't look like Camilla,' he rasped accusingly. 'You take after your father.'

'I know! All we Shearmans have dark colouring. What was my mother like?'

George Dalrymple rubbed one of his bony knees as if it hurt; a nervous restless gesture, a sign of inner pain. Only his eyes continued to work, seeing things Madeleine couldn't fathom, lost in memories of long ago.

'She was beautiful.' There was so much pain in his voice that Madeleine almost winced. 'She had blonde hair . . . down to her waist, blue eyes, a lovely nature . . . she was a good girl.'

'You must have loved her very much.'

It was as if she hadn't spoken. 'My only child,' he continued. 'I can remember the day she was born.'

Madeleine felt a great rush of pity for this old man, and her eyes brimmed. His loss had been her loss also, the only difference being that she would never know how much she had lost, whilst he could gauge it day by day in terms of loneliness and grief.

Impulsively she laid her hand on his thin arm. 'I wish we had met before now,' she said. 'I don't know why my father didn't want us to be friends.'

'I do!' he cut in, harshly. 'He never understood. Camilla meant no harm. She was led astray.'

Madeleine's mind worked quickly, his words conjuring up a series of pictures she'd never thought of before.

'You mean she had a lover?' she asked. 'Did she

run away with him?' That would explain Jake's refusal to talk about her.

'No! No, nothing like that!' said Sir George vehemently. Then he lapsed into silence once more while Madeleine sat there, sweltering in the incandescent heat that glowed from the fireplace, wondering if she dare ask more questions.

At that moment Hunter came silently into the room and, bending, spoke to Madeleine in a half whisper.

'Sir George always takes his nap at this hour, Madam. May I show you to your room?'

Madeleine followed him up the red-carpeted oak staircase, and into a large cool chintzy room where summer fragrances floated in through the open windows. A maid had already unpacked for her.

'I hope you have everything you need,' said Hunter. 'Dinner is served at seven-thirty, Madam. If there is anything you require, the bell is over there.' He indicated a press button by the side of the Adam fireplace.

'I'd like some iced water,' said Madeleine immediately.

As soon as the water had been brought to her room by a young maid, Madeleine stripped off and ran a bath in the adjoining old-fashioned bathroom. Half an hour later, cool and refreshed and wrapped in a big towelling sheet, she went and leaned out of the mullioned window overlooking the garden. A haze of soft colours, interspersed with wide bands of lush grass, lay spread like a woven tapestry from the terrace of the house to the encircling shelter of tall oak, elm, and beech trees. Roses bloomed in profusion, mingled with phlox, love-in-the-mist and dark blue lobelia. She could see Jenkins, in his shirt-sleeves now, kneeling by a border of pinks, tying the stems to strong sticks. Once again she felt lulled by the tranquillity of the place. What was it her father had said? 'You'll be getting into something you can't handle.' What was there to handle? she asked herself. A broken old man, still grieving for the loss of his daughter? A family fight that had nothing to do with her?

After a while, she went and lay on the comfortable bed, still feeling the effects of her night flight from New York. Within a few minutes she was fast asleep.

A small square table, laid for supper with crisp white napery and silver, had been placed in the middle of the library. Hunter, and the young maid Madeleine had seen earlier, hovered ready to serve.

Like a stiff old crab uncoiling itself shakily from a sand dune, Sir George creaked jerkily to his feet and tottered over to the table. Madeleine slipped into the seat opposite him, suddenly aware that she was ravenous. She'd only had coffee for breakfast, and lunch had been a sandwich on the train. Hunter placed the first course in front of them: lobster laced with lemon mayonnaise on a bed of delicate lettuce leaves. He filled their glasses with a fine Ladoucette au Chateau du Nozet, which she noticed was a 1983 vintage. Sir George hardly ate anything. While Madeleine tucked in hungrily, he picked at his food with a fork and sipped a little wine, his hand so shaky he could barely hold the glass. From time to time she smiled encouragingly, but he did not seem even to notice her presence.

They had just begun the next course, tender pink lamb with succulent vegetables, when Sir George suddenly looked up at her, his blue eyes a ferment of passion.

'It was wrong of your father to try and protect you!' he burst out querulously.

Madeleine blinked, startled by the suddenness of his attack.

'I suppose he had his reasons,' she said, abashed.

'Reasons?' The rasping voice rose. 'Let me tell you . . .' He broke off as Hunter filled his glass with red wine. For a moment a bewildered look moved fleetingly across his face as he looked up at the butler, and then he shrank back like a tortoise retreating into its shell. 'No matter,' he mumbled. 'I'll tell you later.'

At last dinner was over, the table cleared away and the servants withdrawn, leaving a tray of coffee and brandy on a side table. Sir George hobbled back to his chair by the fire, which had been stoked up again with a fresh supply of logs, and Madeleine took a chair near him hoping at last the time had come when he would tell her everything.

'You were saying my father shouldn't have been so protective towards me – what did you mean by that, Grandfather?'

'He should have told you everything.' The old man was rubbing his knee again, back and forth, back and forth, his blue veined hand moving jerkily. 'I know he didn't or you'd have come before. You don't know anything about my beautiful Camilla . . .' The words were like a lament, heavy with sorrow.

'Tell me. I want to know,' she urged.

'She was led astray. It wasn't her fault. None of it was her fault. She didn't mean to harm anyone.' The short sentences came rattling out, sharp and grating and with mounting agitation. 'Jake wasn't fair . . . he blamed her . . . but she needed help.'

In spite of the stifling heat in the room, something in his tone made Madeleine's flesh tingle, as if she'd been brushed by a draught of cold air. 'What sort of help?'

'She was led astray,' he repeated. His breath was rapid now, his hands shaking as if from ague and his eyes were pools of agony. He seemed to be reaching some sort of crisis.

'I'm sure she meant no harm,' said Madeleine, soothingly. She felt scared now, not of what he might be about to tell her, but of his obvious distress. 'If you'd rather talk about it tomorrow . . .' she began.

'No! You don't understand. Time is running out and there will be no one, once I'm gone . . .' She noticed he was having difficulty in getting his words out now and a dull red flush stained his cheeks.

'Your mother was involved in something terrible, but it wasn't her fault. You must realise that, even though it nearly led to your death!'

Madeleine recoiled, her heart missing a beat. 'Don't you mean *her* death?'

He looked at her sharply for a second and then he said: 'I knew you hadn't been told. No, *your* death! And when I'm gone there'll be no one to . . .' His voice faltered, and his eyes glared into hers with a look of desperation. From his throat came a long drawn out gurgling rattle.

Madeleine sprang from her chair, appalled. 'Grandfather!'

Sir George made another attempt to speak, opening his mouth wide, his eyes beseeching. Then suddenly he shrank and withered before her, as if retreating from life. A moment later he collapsed.

Jessica awoke to find Andrew nuzzling her, his hands sliding up inside her nightdress, his tongue flicking round the edges of her ear. For a moment she lay still, pretending to be asleep, frantically trying to remember which day of the week it was. If it was Sunday . . . then her eyes flew open and she gave a little gasp. It was Wednesday, the day the management of the Royal Westminster were holding a Derby Day reception and luncheon for three hundred of their most valued clients.

'God, I've got to get up!' she exclaimed, wriggling out of Andrew's arms and jumping out of the bed.

'Wait a minute!' He made a grab for her wrist but she eluded him, running to the windows and pulling back the curtains. Their flat overlooked the centre gardens of Paulton's Square, in Chelsea, and at the top end she could see the red buses going up and down the King's Road. 'Thank God it's a fine day, not that it matters as we'll be indoors, but it does make it jollier!' Now she could be assured that the ladies would be wearing pretty summery dresses and perhaps extravagant hats.

'Surely you needn't go yet? It's only seven o'clock.' Andrew had awakened with a rigid erection and was annoyed at having his advances spurned.

'Darling, I *must!*' said Jessica, slipping off her pale blue silk nightdress and hurling it on to the bed. 'There's a hell of a lot to do before everyone arrives at noon. This is one of the biggest days in our calendar. Now, what shall I wear?' She stood poised, naked, winding up her blonde hair into a loose topknot as she surveyed the contents of her wardrobe.

Andrew lay back, marvelling at the perfection of her pale petite body; her breasts were rounded like small ripe melons, her flat stomach was taut and firm, her smooth long limbs and tiny feet reminded him of illustrations in children's books of fairies and sprites. And then he was assailed by her smell, exciting and warm, emanating from her discarded nightdress. Suddenly he was angry. This wasn't the first time she had skipped away, like a naughty child, just when he felt overflowing with love and desire for her. Most mornings she was out of bed and dressed before he'd even come to his senses; most evenings she was too tired when she got back from work to do anything but eat a little supper and then fall asleep.

'This is bloody ridiculous!' he stormed, clambering out of bed. 'What sort of a relationship is this?'

Jessica turned to look at him, noticing the painful bulge in his pyjama trousers. Her face was contrite.

'I'm sorry, sweetheart! It's just that today is *terribly* important. Couldn't we wait until tonight?'

'No, we bloody well couldn't!' Seizing her, he lifted her up and flung her back on to the bed.

'Andrew!' she cried, annoyed. 'I don't want . . .'

He silenced her with a kiss, holding her so close to him she could hardly breathe. She could feel the heat of his body, strong and urgent, thrusting against her and as strongly as she had resisted him a few minutes before, so now did she find herself ignited with a passion to match his.

'No . . .' she protested with a little moan. 'No, please stop it! Please, Andrew. You know I can't resist it when you do that . . . oh, God!' She gave a little sob. 'It's not fair!' His hand was stroking her where she was most sensitive, his face buried in her neck. With velvety fingers and silky voice he continued to arouse her.

'You've no idea how much I love you,' he whispered.

Jessica found herself sinking into a whirlpool of desire and as hard as she tried to fight against it, because today of all days she couldn't be late, so her resistance crumbled like a sandcastle against a rising tide. She gave a final whimper, but then as she felt his penis thrusting hotly inside her she clung to him, crying his name, matching her rhythm to his, unable to control herself any longer. Her ears were filled with his urgent cries and her body was flooded with his juices as she reached a shuddering peak herself. Then they collapsed in each other's arms, spent and gasping for air. For several minutes they lay like that, their limbs entwined, their breath mingling and their eyes closed. Then Jessica opened hers and saw that the hands of the bedside clock were at eight o'clock.

'Christ!' she exclaimed, wriggling out of Andrew's arms. 'Have you seen the time? Now I'm going to be seriously late!' She slid off the bed and rushed into the bathroom, the passion of a moment before turned into silent anger. Andrew has taken advantage of me, she thought, and it isn't fair. He knows I can't resist him when it comes to sex. He knows . . .

She caught sight of her reflection in the mirror. Her chin was red from the stubble of his chin. Damn! Now she'd have to wear a thicker makeup to disguise the tell-tale marks. Fuming, she dabbed her face with cold water while she ran a bath. Why the hell did he have to tempt her like that when he knew she couldn't be late for work? Knowing she was being unreasonable yet unable to help herself, she climbed into the bath with a groan of exasperation.

At that moment he came into the bathroom and stood looking down at her.

'That was a damned stupid thing to do!' she exploded, when she looked up and saw him. 'Now I'm going to be at least half an hour late, and Dick will be going crazy trying to cope without me.'

Andrew looked distressed. 'I'm sorry, Jess darling. I wanted you so much. I love you so much.'

Jessica retorted swiftly, 'There are lots of times when I want you, but if you're busy or too tired . . .' her voice trailed off. 'It was taking advantage of me!' she added as if she'd only just thought of it.

Andrew's eyes opened in amazement and for a moment he looked as if he was going to laugh. 'Since when have you been the sort of shrinking Victorian violet that *anyone* could take advantage of?' he asked carefully.

Jessica threw him a cross look. 'Oh, you know what I mean. I wish you'd understand that my job is important. You deliberately set out to . . .'

'You didn't need much persuading, did you?' he

protested, suddenly angry again. 'Come on, Jess, you like it as much as I do. Don't give me this line that I forced you to have sex against your will!'

Suddenly her eyes brimmed. 'I know,' she said, her voice catching, 'but you don't seem to understand how important the hotel is to me. They've put me in charge of all the arrangements for today and it's terribly important.'

Andrew knelt down beside the bath, his athletic body curving naturally into graceful and very masculine lines. Gently he stroked her hair.

'I love you,' he said simply. 'I love you and I need you. I want us to get married one day so that we can spend the rest of our lives together. Of course it upsets me when you put your work before us, I sometimes wonder if you still love me at all!'

'Of course I love you,' she replied, dabbing her eyes with a face flannel. 'But you must understand I'm under a lot of pressure at the hotel. I'll be home early tonight – we could have waited until then.'

Andrew rose abruptly. 'I don't think we should have to make appointments to make love; it's supposed to be a spontaneous thing, like it was when we first met.' Angrily, he turned away and walked out of the bathroom and back to their bedroom. A few minutes later, wrapped in a bath sheet, Jessica followed him.

'I'll get back as early as I can this evening,' she said in a conciliatory tone as she struggled into her clothes as quickly as she could. She was going to have to do her makeup in the taxi.

'Well, I don't know when I'll be back,' Andrew replied sulkily, 'so don't hurry on my account.'

Jessica made a little grimace behind his back. Andrew was going into one of his martyred moods; she'd have to work like hell when she got home tonight to jolly him out of it and reassure him she still loved him.

When she arrived at her office Dick Fowler was already hard at work.

'I'm sorry I'm late,' she apologised. 'What's happening?'

Dick handed her a sheaf of notes. 'Masses of calls for you. Here are all the messages. Basically, seven people have called to say they can't attend the luncheon, for various and boring reasons; someone wants to bring his secretary . . . I said I didn't think there was room which is a bit of a lie now that seven people have dropped out, but I'll leave it to your discretion. Oh, and yes, the florist has been delayed; their van has broken down.'

'Wonderful, just what I need to hear!' rejoined Jessica sarcastically. 'At least all the table centres will have been arranged overnight, so they'll only have to put them out when they get here.' She scanned her messages, then reached for the master seating plan. A layout of their banqueting rooms, printed on a large sheet of paper, lay before it. On to this the banqueting manager had drawn circles, each one numbered, to represent the tables. The larger circles were for twelve people, the smaller ones for ten. During the previous week Jessica had written each guest's name beside the table, and she'd also compiled an alphabetical list linking the names with the number of the table they were sitting at. Now, with people dropping out, she'd have to do some rearranging.

'Number six will have only eight guests now, and number thirty-two, nine,' she muttered aloud, making notes. 'Oh, hell, three of those who have dropped out were on table number twelve. I wonder if I can fill the gaps with some of the press!' Juggling the names around, she was interrupted by the phone. 'People really are the limit!' she cried when she replaced the receiver. 'That was the managing director of Gates Chemicals – you know, they always hold their conference here – saying he and his wife can come after all!'

Half an hour later, she rushed with the amended list to the typist in the adjoining office. 'Make these alterations on the table plan we're pinning on the easel,' she said, 'and have you finished typing out the sticky labels the guests are going to be given to wear?'

'Yes,' said the secretary, who was already swamped with work.

Then Jessica ran along to the Banqueting Manager's office. He would have to inform the porters and waiters, so that they laid up the tables for the right number.

'Alterations, as usual!' she cried, handing him her notes. 'At least it's not as bad as when we have a charity ball and some stupid titled chairman keeps on altering the numbers right up until it starts!'

Then she hurried to the scene of the action, the ballroom and the Armitage Suite. This year, the hotel had decided to bring all the fun and attractions of the Derby Day race-meeting into the banqueting rooms. There were stalls laden with buttonholes, red carnations for the men, pink roses for the ladies; green- and white-striped awning and white trellis screens sectioned off a champagne bar and Pimms enclosure; tick-tack men were taking 'bets' in aid of a well-known charity, and there was a tent serving strawberries and cream which had been decorated with scarlet and white tulle looped with red velvet ribbons. By the entrance, 'racing' cards and mock enclosure badges were to be handed out as the guests arrived, and at the far end a small bandstand had been erected on which the band of the Grenadier Guards would play appropriate music.

Jessica walked round checking every detail, noting the waiters were putting out large jugs of freshly squeezed orange juice to go with the champagne for anyone who wanted Buck's Fizz. Then she had a word with the technicians, who were arranging enormous television screens in the four corners of the ballroom, so people could watch the racing, live, from Epsom. Finally, she checked the thirty tables, set with their best Limoges china and crystal glasses. The Chief Steward, who had polished all the silver until it shone, was checking that everything was in order. The pure white damask tablecloths and napkins, which had been washed and pressed in the hotel's laundry, were virginally smooth. Jessica had also arranged for a designer she knew to do a centrepiece for each table, using various people's racing colours, executed in silk ribbons. The effect was both smart and colourful, and when the bowls of pure white flowers arrived it would look better still. Pleased with the effect, she was turning to leave the ballroom when she saw the President of the Golding Group, Robert Scholtz, who had flown in from California that morning to preside over the function. He entered with the General Manager hovering by his side.

Robert Scholtz, a florid man in his fifties, was revered and feared by everyone in the Group, and as he approached Jessica felt her colour rise and her heart start to bound.

'Good morning, Jessica,' he beamed, shaking her hand. The fact that he even remembered her name both impressed her and made her more nervous. He was head of over thirty-five major hotels, worldwide; why should he remember who she was? Before she could do more than murmur 'Good morning', he continued: 'I hear you've done a great job getting today organised!'

'Thank you, Mr Scholtz,' she replied, a trifle breathlessly. 'I think we're in for a big success. All our most important clients are coming and we're expecting a lot of good press people.'

'Let me see a copy of the guest list.' He was still being charming, but she was not taken in by his apparent niceness. Robert Scholtz had the reputation of being a cold ruthless operator who would not tolerate inefficiency or sloppiness.

Thankful that she had her file tucked under her arm, she whisked out the typed list. 'This copy is for you,' she said smoothly.

A flicker of pleased surprise registered on his red veined face and his small eyes looked at Jessica penetratingly. 'Well, thank you.' Without another word he strode off in the direction of the kitchens, obviously intent on carrying out a snap inspection there. The last thing Jessica heard him say was: 'Now, about today's menu . . .'

Thankfully she slipped down to the main lobby, to make sure the brass edged notice-board stated where the lunch was going to be held. With any luck she'd acquitted herself well in the eyes of the almighty President, but the day was not yet over.

Andrew Seymour found it hard to concentrate on his work that day. As a partner in a thriving estate agency, he had to be on the ball, showing people round the more upmarket London houses they specialised in selling, negotiating prices in an ever rising market. Sometimes the asking price bore no relation to the actual value of the property, and yet there was always someone ready to pay these exorbitant amounts, and to Andrew's constant surprise the buyers were not necessarily rich Arabs or Asians but English people who fitted into the nouveaux riche bracket.

He'd already shown five lots of people round various properties that morning, and now he'd have to wait and see whether they'd make an offer or not. All his persuasive charm and basic knowledge of psychology were stretched daily; he had to decide first, when clients approached him saying they were interested in a house, whether they were genuine or not. A lot of people 'house hunted' as a hobby, because they had nothing better to do. Others were sincere but did not have the finance and did not qualify for a mortgage or bank loan. There were others still whose intentions were genuine, but when it came to the point they could not quite make up their minds. Andrew, in the six years since he'd formed Jason and Seymour, had rarely been wrong about a client.

Today, though, he suddenly felt fed up with the whole business. He was tired of dashing from property to property, extolling the delights of marble fireplaces, mosaic jacuzzis and custom-built kitchens. He was bored with calling small backyards with a few tubs 'private gardens', and converted garages 'bijou residences'. Most of all, he hated the sham of describing 'magnificent views' from windows that actually overlooked a couple of dusty trees and a patch of scrubby lawn.

Sighing deeply, he asked one of the secretaries to say he was out next time the phone rang. The reason, he knew, for his feeling so disgruntled was Jessica. She was the most bewitching, maddening, enchanting and thoroughly irritating woman he'd ever known, and he loved her more than anything in the world.

'What's your problem?' his partner, Sandy Jason, asked him as they paused for a mid-morning cup of coffee in their Knightsbridge office. 'You look as if you'd won the pools but forgotten to post your coupon.'

Andrew gave a wry smile. 'I think I'd like to live in the country,' he announced, as if the thought surprised even him.

'You'd have to commute,' said Sandy, who was younger than Andrew, and liked the city life. 'Getting up at dawn to be here in time; going home in the dark for six months of the year! Not my idea of fun, and wouldn't Jessica hate it?'

Andrew didn't answer. Of course Jessica would hate it. It would mean she'd have to give up her twelve-hour day working at the hotel, and settle down to a normal life. He didn't need Sandy to tell him that it wasn't Jessica's idea of happiness.

'God dammit!' he exploded, pounding the desk so that his coffee spilt. 'All I want to do is marry her, have two or three kids and live in a nice house in the country.'

'Awfully bourgeois, don't you think?' Sandy cocked a quizzical eyebrow at him. 'What about your social life? Wouldn't you miss going to restaurants and the theatre and the cinema? You actually think Jessica's going to swap those high-heels for green wellies?' He chuckled loudly. 'Not a hope in hell, old chap.'

Andrew replied hollowly. 'I know. I'm not even sure I can persuade her to get married at the moment. Oh, God, I hate all this women's lib stuff, every woman thinking she can have her cake and eat it. My mother didn't put a career before my father, she was the perfect wife. Why the hell do all these girls want to be so bloody emancipated?'

Sandy rocked back in his chair, dissolving with laughter.

'You are in the dumps, aren't you? What's the little lady done to bring all this on? Don't forget the reason you were first attracted to Jessica was because she was a go-ahead career girl! There's no good trying to change that now.'

Andrew grinned sheepishly. 'You're right, of course.'

'Come on, old chap. Let's go to the pub and have a drink. Drown your sorrows. Give her a bunch of flowers or something. If she's being tricky that'll soon bring her round.'

Andrew glanced across at his partner. 'You obviously don't know Jessica very well,' he commented drily.

The last of the guests had drifted away in a cloud of euphoria, brought on by a lavish luncheon, flowing drink, and an ambience of luxurious splendour. Jessica, her feet hurting in the neat high-heeled shoes she always wore, sank into a chair at one of the now empty tables, and surveyed the mess. Dirty glasses, lipstick smeared table-napkins, discarded race cards and wilting flowers covered the surface of all the tables in the ballroom, but at least the occasion had been a brilliant success, and she didn't have to help clear it all away. An army of minions, still busy washing up behind closed doors, would see to that. A waiter offered her a glass of champagne.

'Thank you, that would be lovely,' she said. It would be her first drink of the day. Rule number one for hotel staff – never drink on the job. The Banqueting Manager joined her, and so did Dick Fowler and Anne Butler, the Director of Public Relations.

'You look tired,' said Anne, 'but it seems to have gone very well.' Her tone was grudging. She'd always been jealous of Jessica, with her natural flair for organising.

'Good for business, too,' said Dick. 'At least fifteen people told me they plan to hold their functions here again, next year.'

'And you'll write to them this afternoon, confirming the dates, won't you?' joked the Banqueting Manager.

'Thank God everyone came,' remarked Jessica, who had slipped off her shoes under the table. 'I had a word with the organiser of the annual Flower Ball and she told me The Prince and Princess of Wales have accepted to come to the next one. Isn't that good?'

Anne Butler's eyes gleamed. 'Give me the details when you get back to your office, will you? We can get masses of publicity for the hotel if *they're* coming.'

At that moment, as they all sat round relaxing and chatting about the success of the day, Robert Scholtz put his head round the ballroom door, accompanied by the hotel's General Manager.

'Oh, Christ!' muttered Jessica under her breath, trying to get her feet back into her shoes.

'Ah, Jessica, there you are!' said the President, striding over to them. 'Can I have a word with you?'

'Yes . . . of course.' Clumsily, she got to her feet. Robert Scholtz led her to a corner of the ballroom, away from the others.

Jessica tried not to sound anxious. 'Was everything all right?'

'Splendid. Splendid,' he replied, nodding. 'Why don't we sit down.'

They sat at one of the tables; it had just been cleared by a waiter and looked bare and derelict. Jessica eyed him nervously, wondering why he wanted to talk to her.

Robert Scholtz didn't waste words. 'You've been happy working here, haven't you?'

Jessica's face flamed. Oh, God, he's going to sack

101

me, was her first thought. He thinks I'm hopeless and he's going to tell me to go! Why else would he want to speak to her alone? It was obvious he was sparing her from embarrassment in front of all her colleagues.

'I love working here,' she stammered.

'Good. Good.' He always repeated himself. 'And you're committed to working for this company?'

Jessica looked at him wonderingly. 'Absolutely,' she replied firmly.

'Right. Right.' He stuck out his thick lower lip and his eyes were piercing. 'We were wondering if you'd be able to take on the job of Director of Sales? Humphrey Peters is being posted to the Temple Hotel in Hong Kong and has to leave here sooner than expected. The situation will become vacant in three weeks' time. Are you prepared to take it on?'

Jessica sat mesmerised, as if she couldn't believe what she was hearing. She heard herself blurt out loyally: 'But what about Dick Fowler? He's been here much longer than me!'

'We think you're more suited to the job. Today you have proved it.'

'There's nothing I'd love more,' Jessica admitted fervently. Director of Sales was the top rung of the ladder as far as she was concerned, the one post she'd been striving towards from the beginning. It would offer her immense challenges and scope for her talents, and it would put her in a position of great power.

She looked up at Robert Scholtz who was still watching her intently. 'Thank you for offering me the post,' she said, more formally. 'If you really feel I can do it, I'd be delighted to accept.'

'We can go into the details later, but there is just one other thing . . . I don't know how you're placed but . . .' he paused, his voice speculative. It was as if he were trying to decide something.

Jessica raised her eyebrows questioningly. 'Yes?'

Robert came straight to the point. 'You would have to live in the hotel, as you'd be on call day and night. You're not married, are you? That would be no problem, would it?'

Chapter Four

With maddening regularity, the grandfather clock in the hall ticked on, the small noise seeming loud in the silence that pervaded the rest of the old house. Madeleine, sitting uneasily on one of the hard carved chairs near the front door, waited with growing impatience. The doctor had been in the library with Sir George for what seemed like an interminably long time now and her anxiety was growing with every irritating tick-tock.

Around her in gloomy opulence the polished Jacobean furniture cast heavy shadows, lit only by a brass lamp that hung from the low ceiling. Restlessly, Madeleine got up and opened one of the dark panelled doors that led off the hall. Darkness and a musty smell assailed her as she reached for the light switch; a dining-room with more heavy furniture met her gaze. Although spotlessly clean, it had the unlived in atmosphere of a museum. She almost expected to see little signs indicating the period of the oak table and chairs.

Madeleine turned away, shutting the door behind her, and then she crossed the hall to see what lay behind the other door. Again solid blackness lay before her, but when she found the switch she was surprised to see a warm pink glow bathing the room in a flush of light, turning it into an inviting rosy bower in an otherwise severe house. Decorated in muted shades of pink and blue and cream, with brocaded walls, delicate French furniture and a richly woven Aubusson tapestry carpet, it was essentially a very feminine room which she guessed must have been her grandmother's drawing-room.

Fascinated by the wash of soft tints spread at her feet, she bent down to look closer at the giant cabbage roses, embroidered from palest pink to deep carmine. Against a sky blue background the design twirled and curved into creamy stems, mingled with leaves in a variety of soft greens, and tucked among the beige scrolls and ribbons that bound the roses loosely together were little gentian violets, worked in purple silk. So absorbed was she in following the pattern, that it wasn't until she was in the middle of the room that she paused and straightened up. Then she gasped, stunned, her eyes moving with growing horror around the room. Every surface, from the gilt console tables to the concert grand piano, from the magnificent marble mantelshelf to the little occasional table, were covered by framed photographs of a beautiful young woman with fair hair and mocking eyes.

Madeleine blinked as a creeping coldness swept over her. She knew the face and yet she didn't know it. There was something strangely familiar about it, and yet it was unknown and alien. And the eyes, hundreds of them, watched her wherever she moved, ringing some far distant chord in her childhood memories.

Suddenly gripped with fear, she began to feel dizzy. The over-furnished, prettily cluttered room, airless and cold, was alive with Camilla's face, for that was whom Madeleine knew it to be. Paralysed, she stood there on the variegated embroidered roses unable to escape the silent stare of this woman who had been her mother, and a silent scream of panic filled her throat. The roses began to swirl round her feet. Camilla, in a hundred different poses and settings, seemed to be advancing on her, closing in, suffocating her, challenging her with those mocking eyes . . .

'Your mother was involved in something terrible . . .' The words filled her mind. So real was the sensation of danger at this moment; so malevolent did all those faces seem as they clustered, floating, pressing in on her, mocking images swirling around her head, that she fled, stumbling wildly, her hand clasped over her mouth to stop herself from screaming.

She found herself back in the hall, her heart pounding so that she felt almost sick. What had it been? She felt as if she'd experienced a tangible human assault, and had been filled with such real terror that all she could think of was escape. 'Oh, Carl, I wish you were here,' she whispered under her breath. 'I don't understand what's going on and I'm scared!'

'Are you all right, Madam?'

Startled, she looked up to see Hunter watching her anxiously.

'I'm fine,' she replied, suddenly feeling foolish. 'I was just looking around. Er . . . none of these rooms seems to be used much!'

'Sir George often sits in the drawing-room when the weather's warm,' he replied, indicating the room she'd just come out of, 'but the dining-room is never used these days. Can I get you a drink, Madam, while you're waiting for the doctor?'

'Some coffee, please,' she replied.

Dr Thurlow came out of the library a few minutes later, looking grave.

Madeleine looked at him questioningly, her heart sinking as if she already knew what he was going to say.

'Why don't you sit down? You look pale,' Dr Thurlow told her. He seated himself in one of the carved chairs near her and spoke gently, the wrinkles round his tired eyes making him look strained.

'I'm afraid he's had a stroke. He's unconscious and I've used the telephone in the library to call an ambulance. The sooner we get him to hospital the better, but until tests have been carried out it's impossible to know the extent of the brain damage,' he explained.

Madeleine steeled herself to ask the obvious question. 'Will he recover?'

He gave her a sympathetic smile. 'It's too soon to say, and of course one has to remember he's over eighty. But everything will be done for him. I understand you only arrived today, Mrs . . . er . . .?'

'Delaney. Yes, my grandfather asked me to come and visit him. I live in New York.'

Dr Thurlow nodded. 'Yes, I see. Well, I don't know Sir George very well. I've been in this practice for just over a year and I've attended him only once, for mild angina.'

Madeleine watched as Sir George was stretchered into an ambulance. The doctor suggested she wait at the house as there was nothing she could do for the time being. 'We'll keep in touch,' he promised.

'You think he'll regain consciousness?' she asked anxiously.

'We can only hope.'

A minute later the white ambulance, its blue light flashing, slid away and Madeleine went slowly up to her room. Sleep was impossible. The events of the past few hours, following on her flight from the States, had left her both emotionally and physically exhausted. She climbed into bed and turned out the light, but the pictures in her mind kept flashing vividly before her, disturbing her deeply. Most of all she felt bewildered by her experience in the drawing-room below. It was almost as if she'd been physically threatened by something . . . but what? A room full of old photographs was nothing to be afraid of. Perhaps jetlag, combined with the shock of her grandfather's collapse, had caused her imagination to play tricks? As an artist, of course, she was perhaps more aware of people's faces, and especially their eyes, and maybe being confronted with dozens of photographs of her mother had been more traumatic than she'd realised?

Switching on the light again she reached for her book and started reading. Now was not the time to let her imagination run away with her.

The next morning, the doctor drove over to Milton Manor himself to break the news to Madeleine.

'I'm afraid your grandfather died in the early hours of the morning,' he said gently. 'They did everything they could, but he had suffered a massive stroke.'

Madeleine felt a deep pang of regret, although she'd half expected the news to be bad. The old man had looked so frail the previous evening, except for the glittering feverishness in his eyes. And hadn't he begged her to visit him because 'time is running out'. It seemed he might have guessed himself that the end was near, and that was why he'd been so desperately anxious to see her.

'Thank you for what you did,' she said.

'I'm sorry I couldn't do more.'

When he left, Madeleine went to the kitchens to tell the servants Sir George had died. Hunter and the household staff took the news gravely, but Jenkins wept, slow tears trickling down his withered cheeks.

'I'd like you all to know that although my grandfather has died, I will see that you are all taken care of. I'd like you to stay on here until further notice, and as soon as I can I'll let you all know what's happening,' Madeleine said, to reassure them. Maybe Sir George had left everything to her, and maybe he hadn't; whatever the outcome she didn't want the servants to worry about their next pay cheque.

'Thank you, Madam,' said Hunter, acting as spokesman. 'That's very kind of you. Will you be staying on yourself?'

'Certainly until after the funeral,' Madeleine replied.

Carl was in Jake's office when Madeleine's call came through later that day.

'Hi, sweetheart,' Carl greeted her. 'How's it going?'

110

'Grandfather died early this morning,' he heard her say.

'Christ! Wasn't that a bit unexpected? What happened?'

Jake looked up sharply from his desk. 'What's going on?'

Carl explained briefly.

'. . . so it's all been a bit traumatic,' Madeleine was saying.

'Is she all right?' Jake demanded. 'Here, let me speak to her.' He seized the phone from Carl. 'Madeleine? What's happening? Are you okay?'

'I'm fine, Daddy. Just a bit sad that Grandfather died before I could get to know him, and before he could tell me anything. You're going to have to tell me why . . .'

'You're coming home right away, I hope?' Jake interrupted.

'How can I?' said Madeleine. 'There's the funeral, and there will be other things to see to. Listen, you've got to tell me what's been going on. Grandfather said my mother was involved in something terrible . . . something that nearly led to my death! He was starting to tell me all about it when . . .'

'He was senile, Madeleine. He imagined things, that's why I didn't want you to visit him,' Jake cut in quickly.

'He wasn't senile!' protested Madeleine. 'I'm certain of that. He said there was something I must be told, because once he was dead . . . there'd be no one! You must know what he meant? He said you should have told me years ago. Come on, for goodness sake, I'm not a child.'

'Madeleine, your grandfather's mind went when your mother died.'

'Then why did you tell me I'd be getting into something I couldn't handle, if I came to see him?' she challenged.

'For that very reason! I wanted to protect you from the demented wanderings of an old man,' he retorted.

'Daddy . . .' Jake could hear the doubt in her voice. 'Daddy, if it's the last thing I do, I'm going to find out about my mother. Can I speak to Carl again, please?'

Jake handed back the phone, feeling immensely relieved. With old George Dalrymple dead the chances of Madeleine finding out what had happened were fairly remote. Of course there were always the village people, but he doubted they'd talk. They, too, had lived in fear at the time and would wish the past forgotten.

Carl stayed late at the office that evening as he had a stack of work to get through, and besides he didn't much like the idea of going back to an empty apartment. Madeleine had said she was going to be away longer than expected, and the prospect of being on his own for the next week or so did not appeal. What had he done with himself when he'd been a bachelor? Already he'd forgotten. There had been girls, of course, lots of girls, and they'd gone to the movies and out to dinner, he supposed; sometimes there'd be a party at a friend's place and sometimes a group of them would sit up all night, drinking and talking. But mostly he'd ended up in bed with the girl he was dating.

Looking back, he found it hard to reconcile the carefree young man he'd been with the responsible banker he was today, and just for a fleeting moment he wondered what it would be like to recapture the hedonistic pursuit of pleasure that once he'd taken for granted.

Kimberley was working in her office next door and idly he wondered what she did with her evenings. An attractive girl like that must surely have a busy private life, he thought. Immersed in work, he forgot about her again until he heard her come into the room.

'Are you off now?' Carl asked conversationally.

Kimberley was cradling a small plate in her hands which she brought towards him, like a child offering a gift.

'I wondered if you'd like a piece of my birthday cake?' she said. A slice of chocolate gâteau filled most of the plate, which she set before him on the desk. 'The girls in my old department gave it to me at lunch-time,' she added. A smear of creamy filling had stuck to her finger, and carefully, like a cat, she licked it clean.

'Is it your birthday today?' Carl felt very remiss. He should have known; he should have got her a small but suitable present and a card. Jake always gave his secretaries presents on their birthdays and at Christmas.

Kimberley giggled. 'Yes, but who wants to advertise they're a year older!'

Carl eyed the cake, wondering how he was going to avoid all that cholesterol without hurting her feelings. 'Going anywhere nice tonight?'

'No. Just home,' she said lightly.

'Ah, a family party. How nice.' Carl rose, thinking

that if she was leaving now he could tip the chocolate cake down the can and she'd be none the wiser.

'I live alone,' Kimberley said simply. 'I thought I'd watch TV and then have an early night.'

'On your birthday?' Carl stood looking at her, amazed.

'I had planned to go out with some friends, but one of them got ill so the plan was scrubbed.' Kimberley smiled at him, not a trace of self-pity on her face.

Carl felt embarrassed. Not only had he not realised it was her birthday, he hadn't got her a present, and now she'd told him she was going to be on her own.

'Say, let me at least get you a drink?' he said quickly.

'No, really. It doesn't matter,' she protested, still smiling.

Carl had a brilliant idea. He went to the built-in fridge in the corner of his office, where he always kept a selection of both hard and soft drinks for important clients, and took out a bottle of Moët & Chandon. It was ice-cold.

'I hope you like champagne,' he asked, but it wasn't really a question, more a statement. Suddenly he was rather glad of an excuse to have a drink and a chat with someone. It would help ease his own loneliness, and also pass the time. He poured the wine into two tulip-shaped glasses and handed her one.

'A very happy birthday,' he said, raising his glass, 'and may you have many more of them.'

Was it his imagination or did Kimberley seem less servile, less the willing little assistant at that moment, and more a self-confident woman? She'd dropped into the chair in which his clients usually sat, long legs crossed, head thrown back in a gesture of expectancy, grey eyes regarding him with languid interest.

'Thank you,' Kimberley said. 'This is very nice of you.'

'It's the least I can do,' Carl replied, suddenly noticing her cleavage was like a valley, a cleft between two snowdrifts. He dragged his eyes away and went back to sitting behind his desk. 'I hope you're happy here in the bank,' he said, 'we like everyone to be happy.' It was all he could think of to say, and even to his ears it sounded trite and banal.

'Sure, I love my job.' Kimberley nodded confidently. 'I always wanted to work in a bank, ever since I was a little girl.'

Carl asked her about her family and noticed that she was not very forthcoming. Conversation was stilted and awkward, and Carl refilled their glasses. He and Kimberley had so little in common except for their work that bridging the gap between them conversationally was proving more difficult than he'd anticipated. Maybe it had been a mistake to offer her a drink after official working hours. Now that dusk had fallen there was something unusually cosy and intimate about his office, in a now almost silent building with only the night security people patrolling the corridors. Down below on Wall Street, the evening rush was over, and the sidewalks were silent and deserted under a lavender sky. For a moment he felt as if he and Kimberley were the only people left alive.

'Here, have some more to drink,' Carl said, topping up their glasses and breaking the awkward silence between them. He didn't usually drink much but tonight he felt like it. After all, there was no Madeleine to go home to and no engagements to keep. He was a free agent, and the wine was lifting his spirits so that he was feeling quite elated. He decided to open a second bottle.

'Your wife is away in Europe, isn't she?' Kimberley asked, shifting her position in the chair so that her tight skirt rose higher, exposing her thighs.

Carl looked at her legs, and to his surprise felt himself getting aroused.

'That's right, and I heard today she's going to be away for at least another week or so,' he said, hearing through a faint roaring in his ears the regret in his voice.

'That must leave you at rather a loose end,' Kimberley remarked, looking at him with unnerving directness. 'What are you going to do with yourself while she's away?'

Carl knew instantly what she meant and, suddenly embarrassed, he averted his gaze. 'I don't know.' He laughed awkwardly and took another gulp of his drink. It was a long time since a girl had propositioned him and, half flattered, half shocked, he rose and went to look out of the window. It would never do to get involved with someone in the bank, and besides there was Madeleine, he thought. He'd always been faithful to her and they had a great sex life together.

He felt a hand in the small of his back and, turning sharply, saw Kimberley standing by his shoulder.

'Where would be the harm? Who would ever know?' she whispered, and he could smell the scent from her hair, heady and exciting as she moved closer.

'No, Kimberley,' he heard himself say, but a voice in his head asked – who *would* know? What *would* be the harm? The champagne had really got to him now and he felt as if he could do anything; break all the rules and not get caught, have himself a ball and escape the consequences! He could do as he liked and he needn't be answerable to anyone.

'No, Kimberley,' his voice sounded almost pleading; but she was pressing herself against him now, like a cat, insinuating herself against his side. Why am I arguing? he asked himself. Why the hell am I saying no? My mind is saying no, but my body is saying yes . . . I can't resist you, Kimberley. Yes, I want you . . . Yes, I need someone tonight.

Carl's mouth sought hers, and found her lips softer than he'd expected. She kissed him back with a gentle sweetness, a trust that was almost childlike, and he put his arms around her and held her close. As he closed his eyes, his mouth on hers, the complacent thought passed through his head that here was a girl who would be no trouble; here was a girl whom he could trust to be discreet.

Kimberley eased herself out of his arms, her eyes never leaving his face, and slowly started to undress. Carl went quickly to the door of his office, looked out into the corridor to make sure no one was about, then locked both his office door and the one that led to Kimberley's. When he turned back, Kimberley had gone into his adjoining private washroom.

'Come and join me?' she called out, and he heard her switching on the shower. Struggling out of his clothes, his wild elation mounting, he entered the little washroom which was in semi-darkness. Kimberley stood underneath the warm spray of water, her red hair loosened so that it fell damp and clinging to her white shoulders. In her hands, she held a bar of soap which she was twisting round and round between her palms until they were creamy with suds. Then she reached out for Carl, drawing him into the circle of water with her, smoothing the slippery lather over his chest and down to his hips, while he stood spellbound, mesmerised by the magic she was weaving. Steam rose all around them, misty and soft in the dim light, and all Carl could think of was that he wanted this moment, so full of exciting anticipation, to last forever.

'Do you like that?' she whispered so softly he could hardly hear.

'Kimberley . . .' He buried his face in her streaming red hair, sucking the white skin of her neck, sliding his hands round her buttocks where the flesh was yieldingly soft. Her hands had slipped down to his groin now, manipulative and coaxing, gentle and unhurried.

'I need you. God, I need you badly,' he groaned. 'Take me inside you?'

'Soon,' she promised, then she slipped out of his arms and slid round the back of him, pressing herself close, stroking him with soapy hands from behind and in front.

Carl raised his face into the jet of warm water and felt as if he was being borne down swirling rapids, half drowning, his mind lost in the sensuality of the moment, his body throbbing with the most piercing pleasure he had ever known. He was being carried on a journey of flooding turbulence, of hot whirlpools and rivers bursting their banks. Great waves surged him onwards and upwards uncontrollably, on a tide whose currents swept away all else but the ecstasy of the moment, and turning, he lifted her off her feet and thrust himself inside her. Impaled, Kimberley clung to him, her head thrown back so that her red hair flowed in the water like a trail of blood, her white throat working on the brink of a cry. Savagely, with the desperation of animals tearing each other to pieces in a prehistoric act of lust, they possessed each other, while the steam rose about them and the warm jet of the shower played a dance on their naked bodies.

Sir George's funeral took place at the nearby village church of St Olaf's. Madeleine, accompanied by Mr Marks, of Spindle, Coutts and Marks, her grandfather's solicitors, drove the short distance through the narrow winding streets of Sherston and arrived just as the coffin was being lifted out of the hearse. Gathered outside the entrance to the church were groups of village people, mostly women with shopping baskets and toddlers in their arms. They stood in respectful silence as the oak casket was borne aloft, a wreath of white flowers from Madeleine resting on the lid, and the bell in the church tower tolled its solemn song. As soon as Jenkins drew up at the gates and Madeleine stepped from the car, she was aware that the local interest had shifted sharply from the coffin to her. Dozens of people turned to stare, their mouths expressionless but their eyes flickering with furtive interest. Was it her imagination or did the figures seem to huddle closer as she approached? Madeleine had the unpleasant sensation of being more than a local curiosity. When she looked into some of the faces, acknowledging their presence with the hint of a polite smile, eyes were instantly averted; feet shuffled; there was a perceptible drawing back amongst the front ranks, like animals sensing fear. She turned to look at Mr Marks to gauge his reaction, but he seemed not to have noticed anything amiss and returned her look with a friendly smile.

The Vicar greeted her in the porch, shaking her hand and leading her up the aisle to a pew in the front, where Mr Marks joined her. The servants from Milton Manor sat behind; Hunter ramrod stiff and dignified, Jenkins strangely clean-looking in a shiny dark suit. The organ was thundering richly, reverberating through the twelfth-century church, and she recognised the strains of Bach. Musty, dark and damp-smelling, the only light in the church came in through narrow medieval windows, while two ineffectual candles spluttered on the altar.

Madeleine picked up her prayer book and was once again aware that she was being closely observed. Turning slightly to see if any of the villagers had come into the church, she noticed an elderly woman, beautifully dressed and with a sweet, lined face, looking in her direction. Beside her sat a dark-haired man in his early thirties; he too was looking at her.

Then the older woman smiled, a charming smile that lit up her face, so that laughter lines became deeper, fanning on to her cheeks. The young man's smile was more diffident, but he inclined his head in a friendly fashion as if he, too, knew who she was. Madeleine nodded back, not having any idea who they were.

The service was short followed by the interment in the churchyard. Madeleine noticed the plot had been dug beside her grandmother's grave: 'Emily, beloved wife of George Dalrymple and mother of Camilla. 1900–1946'. Then she looked around, wondering if her mother had been buried here too.

It wasn't until they were out of the churchyard, watched again by the villagers who had maintained their vigil, that the older woman approached Madeleine, her hand outstretched and a compassionate expression on her face.

'My dear, you won't remember me,' she said. 'My name's Alice Stewart . . . this is my son, Philip. The last time I saw you, you were only two or three but I'd have recognised you anywhere. You had large dark eyes and that wonderful dark hair even then.'

'How do you do? You must have been a friend of grandfather's,' replied Madeleine, smiling back. She had liked the look of this woman from the moment she'd set eyes on her in the church, and her son looked pleasant enough, too.

'I've known George for over fifty years. He was a wonderful person, always so kind. So kind.' For a second she gazed into the distance dreamily, as if remembering past pleasures. Then she looked at Madeleine again, her bright blue eyes soft and affectionate.

'And of course Camilla was my best friend,' she said.

Madeleine's eyes widened. 'You knew my mother?'

'Of course I knew your dear mother, we used to play together as children. Oh, we had such fun! We were debutantes the same year, and we went to all the parties together. Ah, those were happy days.'

'I'd love us to meet sometime,' said Madeleine impulsively. 'I'm over here for a bit longer. Could I call you? Maybe you and your son could come over for lunch?'

'We'd love that, wouldn't we, Philip?' Alice Stewart turned to her son who had been listening to his mother's reminiscences with amusement.

'Sounds great,' he agreed, catching Madeleine's eye.

'Then that's fixed. I'll call you tonight. I'm sorry I can't ask you back to the Manor now, but I've got to talk to grandfather's solicitor.' She indicated Mr Marks, who was waiting by the car for her.

'Of course you have, my dear,' said Alice, patting her arm, 'and we shall look forward to hearing from you. I can't tell you what a pleasure it is to see you again after all these years. Camilla's little girl! George must have been very proud of you.' With a wave of her white-gloved hand Alice Stewart walked gracefully away. Philip gave Madeleine a broad grin.

'See you soon, then,' he said.

Back at the Manor, Hunter had set the table in the library as usual, and stood ready to dispense drinks. Mr Marks asked for a small sherry and Madeleine had vodka and tonic. Drained by the morning's events, she wanted to get everything settled, so that she could decide what to do with the old manor house if, as she strongly suspected, her grandfather had left it to her.

'Let's take our drinks into the garden,' Madeleine suggested. 'It's such a lovely day.'

'That would be very nice,' replied Mr Marks. He was a prim-looking man in his forties, with receding sandy coloured hair and pale blue eyes that frequently blinked. When he looked at Madeleine, he blinked even more. Her beauty, emphasised by her simple black dress and the blackness of her hair, riveted him. He had never seen anyone quite like her. Clutching his briefcase, he followed her out on to the terrace and to a wooden bench under a spreading cedar tree.

'I have Sir George's Will with me,' he said eagerly. 'Shall we get the business out of the way now, before lunch?'

Madeleine smiled at him and nodded, aware of the effect she was having on him. His sandy eyelashes flickered madly, like moths beating their wings against a window, as he withdrew the document from his case.

'It is really quite straightforward, Mrs Delaney. Sir George made this Will in 1965, and apart from a bequest of five thousand pounds to a Wilfred Arthur Jenkins . . .'

'He's the gardener,' Madeleine interrupted.

'. . . apart from that,' Mr Marks continued, 'he has left Milton Manor, all its contents, lands, effects, livestock, stocks and shares, etc, to his only child, Camilla Mary Shearman, née Dalrymple, of 1027, Beekman Place, New York City.'

Madeleine started, hearing her mother's name spoken as if she were still alive. Not noticing her surprise,

Mr Marks continued: "In the event of Camilla Mary Shearman pre-deceasing me, her daughter, Madeleine Elizabeth Shearman, on attaining the age of twenty-one, shall inherit my estate in entirety." '

'That's me,' Madeleine said unnecessarily. 'My mother died when I was a child.'

Mr Marks raised his eyebrows, and then took a swift sip of his sherry. The funeral, the presence of this beautiful young woman, and the heat of the sun as they sat in the garden, were too much for him; he felt quite unsteady and rather emotional.

'Then you are the sole heir, Mrs Delaney,' he quavered. 'I hadn't realised your mother had died, but then I've only been with the firm for the past eight years and I don't think we've had any dealings with Sir George in that time. He obviously didn't think it necessary to make a new Will when your mother passed on, as he'd already made provision for you.'

'Yes, I see,' said Madeleine thoughtfully. What Mr Marks said was perfectly reasonable, but she still thought it strange.

'Will you be living here?' he asked.

'I don't think so. My husband and I live in New York, where he works with my father. I'm a painter, so it doesn't matter where I live, but Carl won't get transferred to England for several years yet so I think I'll sell the house.'

A tinge of disappointment cast its shadow over Mr Marks' face. 'Well, if I can be of any help, let me know. I can put you in touch with several estate agents, but of course you do realise that nothing can be done until after probate has been agreed?'

Madeleine looked bewildered. 'Probate?' she asked.

'That is the assessed value of the property,' Mr Marks continued, 'and when probate has been fixed there will be Capital Transfer Tax on the value of the estate to pay. It could be as long as a year before you will be able to put Milton Manor on the market.'

'As long as that?' Madeleine had no experience of these things and had imagined she could have everything settled and done within weeks. 'Do I keep the house open and running until then?' she asked.

'It will be easier to sell when the time comes, if you do. Empty houses do not have the same appeal to buyers,' Mr Marks explained. 'Of course, before anything can be done, it will be necessary to obtain a copy of your late mother's Death Certificate in order to prove your claim.'

'Can you do that for me?' Madeleine asked, suddenly experiencing a feeling of helplessness. All her life she'd had things done for her and she'd never had to think about business, because all her interests and all her energy went into her art. Jake had looked after her and arranged everything for her, ever since she could remember, and in the last few years Carl had taken over. She knew what a bank statement looked like but she didn't think she'd ever even seen a tax form in her life.

As if sensing that she felt out of her depth Mr Marks leaned forward, his face alight with eager helpfulness. 'If there's anything I can do, at any time,' he murmured in a rapt voice, 'please feel free to call on me, Mrs Delaney.'

'I will,' Madeleine replied, smiling with relief. 'In the meantime, is it all right if I tell Jenkins about his inheritance?'

'Yes, of course. Quite all right,' said Mr Marks.

When he left an hour later, Madeleine wandered back into the garden in search of Jenkins. The afternoon had become golden and languid, the air so still and the silence so heavy that the persistent humming of the bees, hovering dizzily above the lavender bushes, was the only sound to be heard. Sweetly pungent, the scent of new mown grass drifted towards Madeleine as she paused, standing to look around her at the immaculately kept flower-beds and hedges. It seems a pity to sell this beautiful old place, she thought, and yet she knew she didn't want to stay here.

Jenkins was kneeling by the herbaceous border, pulling out weeds. He'd changed out of his shiny suit and was wearing his usual brown cord trousers and an open-necked shirt.

'Jenkins,' Madeleine said gently, knowing he must be feeling the death of her grandfather almost more than any of them, 'I thought you'd like to know Sir George has left you five thousand pounds in his Will.'

Jenkins paused in his weeding for a moment, staring at the rich brown soil, his face flushed.

'Thank you, Mam,' he said at last.

Madeleine stood watching him for a few more minutes, wondering how she could bring the conversation round to her mother. 'You've been working here a long time, haven't you, Jenkins?' she said, suddenly feeling nervous.

'I have that,' Jenkins replied slowly.

'I expect you've seen changes in your time, haven't you?' A breeze came ruffling through the trees as she spoke, and she raised her hands to her head, trying to control the dark curls that fluttered round her face.

'No, Mam. Nothing much changes in these 'ere parts.' His thick workman's hands tugged at an obstinate dandelion root.

'But you must remember my mother?' Madeleine said reasonably. 'After all, if you've worked here for forty years . . . you see, I don't remember her at all, so it's nice to meet someone who must have known her.' She tried to sound casual, as if it didn't matter all that much to her, but her heart was pounding in her rib-cage, as she felt herself drawing nearer to the truth.

'I remember her,' Jenkins grunted grudgingly.

'What was she like? Tell me about her.'

Jenkins' voice was flat in its finality. 'There's nothing to tell.'

Madeleine felt taken aback by his surliness. 'But Sir George wanted me to know about her, that's why he asked me to fly over from America!' she exclaimed. 'What happened to her, Jenkins? You were here then – you must know!' A hint of desperation had crept into her voice.

The old gardener rose to his feet, rubbing the earth from his thick fingers for several moments. Only then did he look at Madeleine, his eyes veiled, his mouth stern. 'Some things are better left alone,' he said, and with that he turned abruptly away, walking in the direction of the kitchen garden.

His dismissal of her was absolute; the broad chunky outline of his receding figure so forbidding she froze, unable to run after him. At that moment it hit her that the mystery of Camilla went far deeper than she'd realised. It went beyond Jake and his refusal to discuss her; it went beyond an ordinary family feud. Something had happened that Sir George had wanted her to know, and whatever it was Madeleine was convinced that Jenkins was somehow involved.

Chapter Five

Jessica came rushing down the front steps of the Royal Westminster shortly after seven, gesticulated wildly at a passing cab, and jumping in gave the driver her address in Chelsea. Her mind was in a turmoil. To have been offered the job of Director of Sales by Robert Scholtz was so fantastic, so unbelievable, that she felt quite breathless. But, oh! She put a hand to her mouth and closed her eyes for a moment. What on earth was she going to say to Andrew? How could she possibly breeze home and say to him, 'Oh, by the way, I'm moving out as my new job will require me to live in the hotel!'

Jessica groaned inwardly, imagining his reaction. On the other hand she couldn't turn down this opportunity either. It was a chance in a million, and besides, if she did it would give all those chauvinistic directors of the Golding Group a perfect opportunity to cite her as a typical example of a girl who could have had a brilliant career, but didn't because she put her private life first!

'Blast and damn!' Jessica muttered under her breath, as the taxi rattled down Sloane Street. Why was life so unfair? she asked herself. Men didn't have to choose between their work and the person they loved – so why should she?

As soon as she let herself into the flat she could hear television blaring in the living-room. Andrew was watching a panel game, nursing a whisky and soda, the evening newspaper on his knee.

'Sorry I'm late,' she said gaily, trying to smother her feelings of guilt. Flinging off her spiky heels, she flopped on to the sofa beside him.

'D'you want a drink?' he mumbled, never taking his eyes off the screen.

'Not for the moment,' Jessica replied. 'What would you like for dinner?' As she said the words she knew the role of housewife, on its own, would never be enough for her. She needed the stimulation of working in an exciting job; she loved the tensions of living in the fast lane, with every day bringing new adrenalin-charging challenges. The thought removed all lingering doubts from her mind; she *had* to accept the post Robert Scholtz had offered her.

Andrew wrenched his eyes away from the TV. 'What's all this domesticity bit? I thought you'd be tired after your big "do" at the hotel, so I've booked a table at L'Escargot.'

'Oh, Andrew!' Jessica felt deeply touched, because it was so unlike him. Usually she cooked something from the deep-freeze, or he went out and bought a Chinese takeaway. 'What a lovely surprise! I adore L'Escargot.' She slipped her arm round his neck and kissed him on the cheek. 'We'll be able to celebrate . . .' she began, and then stopped. Her innate sense of timing told her that this was not the right moment to tell him her news. '. . . to celebrate the fact I've got the whole weekend off,' she ended instead.

Andrew took her small slim hand and squeezed it. 'I'm sorry about this morning,' he said gruffly.

Jessica responded swiftly. 'It was my fault too. I was really uptight. So much depended on today going well.'

Andrew didn't ask how her day had gone. Instead he launched into a lengthy description of how he'd shown a two-million pound house in Regent's Park to an Arab, who'd declared it was too small for all his wives and children.

'We did get an offer for the broom cupboard, though,' he added.

Jessica's eyes widened. 'What d'you mean, the broom cupboard? Not a real broom cupboard?'

'A real broom cupboard,' Andrew insisted. 'You know Haversham House, that block of flats near Harrods? The owners have converted what used to be the caretaker's room on the second floor landing, where he stored his cleaning materials and vacuum cleaner, into what is referred to as a "London pied-à-terre".'

'You have to be joking!' Jessica started laughing, not taking him seriously.

'I kid you not. It has a shower, an electric kettle and a sofa-bed, and we sold it for what it would cost to buy a two-bedroom cottage in Essex!'

'Andrew!' Jessica looked quite shocked. 'That's dreadful!'

'So are prices, in the most fashionable parts of town, but who am I to complain? If I'm going to be able to buy a country mansion one day, and keep you in the luxury to which you've become accustomed,

I've got to make a killing while I can. Surprisingly, there's always some bugger stupid enough to pay!'

Jessica looked away quickly, then reached down to pick up her discarded shoes. 'I'll go and change before we go out,' she said quietly, slipping from the room.

Alone in their bedroom, which she'd decorated with green and pink Laura Ashley fabric three years ago, her guilt deepened. It was as if she were betraying Andrew by planning a whole new life for herself that did not include him. Worse than that, she hadn't even the courage to tell him now. Ever since the moment Robert Scholtz had spread at her feet a future so glittering, so fantastic as to be almost unbelievable, she knew what she had to do. It wasn't a question of choice really. The only choice left to her was when to tell Andrew.

L'Escargot, in the heart of Soho, was crowded as usual when they arrived, and while they waited for their table they sat in the bar area, drinking an aperitif. Andrew was still talking about the houses he and Sandy Jason had on their books, and how the property boom was going on and on in a seemingly endless upward spiral. A medium size London house now cost as much as a mansion with extensive grounds in the country.

'It's the best investment in the world,' he declared stoutly. 'Stocks and shares are dicey, even gold and silver has its ups and downs, but bricks and mortar go on forever!'

'Yes, Andrew,' Jessica said patiently, her eyes flickering round the dimly lit bar and into the restaurant beyond. 'Someone should clear that table of dirty glasses,' she said fretfully. 'I hate it when tables aren't cleared immediately. Don't you think we should ask for the menu? We could be deciding what we want and giving our order while we wait. Someone should have brought us one.'

Andrew regarded her with a smile that masked his irritation.

'Sweetheart, can't you be off duty for just a little while? How this restaurant's run is no concern of yours, as long as we get a decent dinner.'

Jessica looked abashed, not realising she was still acting as if she was in charge of everything.

'I'm sorry, Andrew. It's habit really. I'm so aware of everything, in a restaurant or a hotel; it's second nature to have my eyes everywhere, checking that the staff are doing everything properly!'

'Well, I'm sure the manager here is perfectly capable of running the show without your help.' He spoke flippantly, and even jokily, but Jessica got the point. She was out with him and she ought to be relaxing and putting him first.

'You're right and it's a very bad habit!' she scolded herself disarmingly. 'I must remember: *I am here to relax and enjoy myself!*' She made it sound like a slogan.

Andrew regarded her fondly. 'At these prices, sweetheart, you certainly are. Never mind, Jess, once we're living in the country you'll soon get out of the habit. You know, I was thinking . . .' And he went on to describe the type of house he had in mind for them, stressing the necessity of a large garden 'for the children to play in'.

Jessica said nothing, her eyes fixed on the piece of lemon floating in her gin and tonic, unable to look him in the eye and tell him she'd be moving into the Royal Westminster within the next three weeks, and that there she'd be living for the foreseeable future.

Feeling like a traitor, she let him ramble on while she sipped her drink and began to wish she'd never been offered the damn job in the first place. She ought to tell him, but how could she ruin his evening when he was being so sweet and generous, thinking he was giving her a glorious time? He'd never understand, now or at any time, that she needed to fulfil her ambitions, to feed the starving desire to be an achiever that consumed her day and night.

'What will *you* do, if we live in the country?' Jessica asked at last, because this was a part of his Grand Scheme that he never seemed to consider.

Andrew grinned. 'I shall be the Lord of the Manor! A gentleman farmer! The local squire!' he joked.

When she'd stopped laughing, she said: 'I suppose you could still be an estate agent, dealing in country properties instead of London ones.'

'That's what I had in mind, while you work for the Goose and Gander Inn, instead of the Golden Group Inc!' he quipped.

Jessica tried very hard to look amused but she felt jarred by his mockery. It underlined his basic feelings; he would continue to pursue his career while she settled for any job, even if it was second best. Never before had she realised how much her future in the hotel meant to her. If she didn't realise her full potential there she'd never forgive herself.

Dinner was rather strained as she tried to steer the conversation back to generalities, and for once there were yawning black pits of silence between them; but when they got back to Paulton's Square Andrew took her to bed and made love to her gently and sweetly, as if to obliterate his rough and demanding treatment of her that morning. It was almost as if, in an unspoken way, he understood the complexities of her nature, although she knew he didn't. Andrew didn't understand her at all. He was like all men, convinced that his occupation was much more important than that of any woman's; convinced also that the old-fashioned values his mother had modelled herself on were the right ones. She ached with tiredness and longed to curl up and go to sleep, but Andrew was being so loving that she hadn't the heart to tell him how she felt. And I do love him, she told herself as she submitted to his embrace, but I will love him less if I cannot follow my own destiny. And that was the reality of it.

The next morning she awoke cold and stiff, the duvet having slipped over to Andrew's side of the bed, as a pale grey dawn filtered through the small Laura Ashley print. Outside, a dawn chorus of London birds shrilled away, almost rivalling their country cousins with their lusty singing. Getting silently out of bed, Jessica knew she had to get to the Royal Westminster and submerge herself in its atmosphere before Andrew awoke and her resolve of last night vanished. She knew she couldn't face him with the truth yet, and yet she couldn't bear to lie to him for much longer either.

Having dressed in a navy blue dress and high-heeled shoes, she put on a minimum of make-up, brushed her hair, and leaving it hanging loose crept out of the flat without disturbing him. Breakfast would have to wait until she got to the hotel and then, for once, she'd spoil herself and order the full menu from the chef: grapefruit, eggs and bacon, croissants, toast and marmalade, gallons of coffee – the lot. It wasn't every day she could indulge herself like this and she decided it was her reward for getting in to work two hours before everyone else; but in her heart she knew it was 'comfort eating' because she was worried.

When she arrived the whole place seemed to be slumbering, bedroom curtains drawn and lights dimmed, but behind the scenes she knew the day's activities had already begun. Many of the staff of three hundred would have already arrived; the chambermaids would be collecting the linen and towels from the laundry rooms, which were steamy warm and sweet with the smell of starch; the goods entrance round the back would already be bustling with activity as the produce for the day, ordered from the chef's market list, was delivered. There'd be fish from the north Atlantic, its flesh firm and the eyes checked to make sure it was fresh. If the eyes were sunken it would be sent back with anything else that was less than perfect. Then there'd be lychees from China and cherries from California; onoki mushrooms from Japan and ripe avocados from Spain. Like a cornucopia of the world's finest products, the kitchens would begin to fill up with all the most exotic fruit and vegetables obtainable. Truffles came from the king of truffles in France, Monsieur Pebe, and chocolates from the house of Godiva. Baby sweetcorn from Thailand and miniature bananas from Jamaica were unpacked for spot checks on weight and quality; the finest beef from Ayrshire in Scotland and the most succulent lamb from New Zealand were placed in the walk-in fridges. Oysters and escargots, venison and guinea-fowl, sun-ripened apricots and tiny wild strawberries arrived in profusion, so that the air grew sharp with the tang of mingled smells.

Cleaners, waiters, florists and maintenance people would be arriving and slowly the hotel would be waking up to another long day. Soon, guests would be having their breakfast trays taken to their rooms, complete with a posy of flowers in a little Limoges vase, and the daily newspapers. Reception would be busy checking arrivals in and departing guests out, and as the morning progressed the tables in the restaurant would be laid for luncheon, the bars would be restocked, and down in the cellar the Sommelier would be checking his stock of 250,000 bottles of various red wines and his 80,000 bottles of assorted white wines, fewer in number because hotels don't have to invest, long term, in white wine as they do in red.

As Jessica made her way up to her office, she felt a sudden and enormous pride in the whole place. It epitomised true excellence with elegance and its reputation of being London's top hotel was not unjustified. From its marble lobby to its penthouse swimming-pool, it was as smooth-running as silk, and that was because everyone pulled together, she thought, with one object in mind: to make the clients welcome and keep them happy.

By ten o'clock she felt as if she'd done a day's work, so advantageous had her early morning start been. When the phone rang she was well into her stride.

'Sales Department,' she said crisply.

'Is that you, Jessica?' asked a hesitant voice.

'Maddy! How good to hear from you. How are you?'

'Great! You sounded so fierce I wasn't sure it was you.'

Jessica laughed. 'Sorry, I was expecting a business call. So what's happening? Are you coming up to London?'

'I'm flying back to the States early next week, because there's nothing I can do here until probate has been agreed, and that could take months and I'm desperate to go home.'

'Missing your dearly beloved?' teased Jessica. 'I don't know. You old married couples, you're worse than the people who come here for a dirty weekend!'

'I shall ignore that remark, Miss McCann,' Madeleine declared, pretending to sound offended. 'I was going to invite you and Andrew down for my last weekend here, because I'd love to see you, but now I'm not sure if you deserve it!'

'Maddy! You beast! We'd *adore* to come!'

How much easier, thought Jessica, as she replaced the receiver a few minutes later, to tell Andrew about her new job whilst they were staying with Madeleine.

'I'm going to make a list of the things I'd eventually like shipped to the States,' Madeleine told Hunter.

'Do you think you could get out all the silver for me to see?'

'With pleasure, Madam,' he said. He was enjoying there being a young mistress around the place, although it was only for a few more days, and he and the rest of the staff felt enormous gratitude to her for saying she'd keep them on at Milton Manor, even if it was a year before the house could be sold. 'Shall I set it out in the pantry, Madam? There is quite a lot of it, stored in the strong-room in the cellar.'

'That would be fine.' Madeleine smiled at the butler, hoping the new tenants, whoever they were, would want to keep him on. Hunter had been so helpful to her since she'd arrived, getting hold of the solicitor for her, contacting the undertakers and arranging many of the details of Sir George's funeral, and she felt very grateful. Jenkins she was not so sure about. After her encounter with him in the garden two days previously, he'd seemed to be avoiding her, leaving cut flowers for the house on the kitchen table and then scuttling back into the garden before she could say anything to him. Madeleine decided not to press him further about Camilla. It was, after all, Jake's job to tell her what had happened, and she intended to see that he did as soon as she got back to New York.

Meanwhile, armed with a notepad and pencil she started to take stock of the contents of Milton Manor, deciding what she'd sell with the house and what she'd take home. A lot of the furniture would have to remain; it was far too heavy and large to fit into their apartment and would not blend with the light modern decor. But some of the smaller pieces would go well in the weekend house at Oyster Bay. The paintings were a different matter. She would definitely keep them. Many dated back to the sixteenth century and were portraits of her Dalrymple ancestors; stiff stylised paintings, so unlike her own work, but immensely valuable and of great historical interest. Listing them carefully, she authenticated a Gainsborough, two Lelys, a Joshua Reynolds, and a priceless sketch by Inigo Jones. Her grandfather's art collection, she reckoned, must be worth in excess of eight million dollars. Persian rugs, some fine pieces of Dresden china and a beautiful brass candelabra were added to the list. That left only one room in the house to examine: the drawing-room. Madeleine had managed to avoid going into the room of a thousand eyes since the night of her grandfather's collapse, and she still shuddered whenever she thought about it. The incident had shaken her so badly that she'd dreamed about her mother's face every night since then, seeing again those mocking eyes closing in on her.

'Hunter,' said Madeleine, keeping her voice light and nonchalant, 'could you open up the drawing-room for me?'

'Yes, Madam. Will you be using it when you have guests this weekend?' he asked, hopefully.

Madeleine seized the chance to act as if it were just another room in the house and of no special importance to her. 'That's right. Open all the curtains and shutters and give the place a good airing. And put some flowers in there, too. I'll have a look at the furniture and paintings tomorrow.'

'Very well, Madam.' Hunter withdrew, a look of

delight on his face, as if he couldn't wait for the weekend.

That evening, after Madeleine had eaten a light supper in the library, she decided to have a look at the books which filled the shelves from floor to ceiling, in ranks of gold tooled leather bindings. There must have been four thousand of them, she reckoned, as she pulled the mahogany library steps into position and climbed up to look at the upper shelves. Her hand smoothed the spines of the works of Sir Walter Scott, Charles Dickens and Jane Austen, all first editions. On the shelf below, were books on history and further along a collection of illustrated books about wild animals. As Madeleine continued her exploration, noting down books that would be of special interest to Carl, she found a treasure trove of literature. Never in her life had she seen so many valuable books in one collection, or so many fascinating ones. She reached out and lifted from the shelves a copy of Milton's poems. He was her favourite poet and she decided to take this volume back to the States with her, in spite of Mr Marks saying nothing must be removed from the house until it had been valued for probate. Who's going to miss one little book? thought Madeleine, tucking it under her arm.

She was just about to rearrange the remaining books on the shelves so a gap wouldn't be obvious, when she spotted a black volume, old and dog-eared, tucked away at the back. Withdrawing it and blowing away the dust that clung thickly to it, she saw it had no title on the spine or on the front cover either. Flipping it open and realising it was handwritten, sometimes in

141

ink, sometimes in pencil, she climbed down the steps and went and sat on the sofa. A cloud of dust arose, making her sneeze as she clapped the covers together to get rid of the cobwebs. It was obvious it had been hidden at the back of the shelf for years.

Opening the first page, she saw the handwriting was large and rounded and difficult to read; but it seemed to be some sort of journal, although there were no dates anywhere, nothing to indicate what day or month or even year it had been written. An entry caught her eye:

'Tonight we met in the barn where the crossroads used to be: the King of Darkness, Power of Power, was in our midst.'

Feeling suddenly uneasy, Madeleine skimmed through a few more pages, only able to make out certain words: 'pagan rite – spirit of hell-fire – allegiance to Satan –' and then a horrifying passage, written in red ink: '. . . covered in oil and smeared with the blood of a hare, the spirit entered my body . . .'

Madeleine involuntarily threw the book away from her, hurling it towards the fireplace where it landed with a thud by the brass fender. Whoever had penned that journal had been involved in witchcraft and black magic, something she greatly feared. When she'd been at school a lot of her friends had become fascinated by the occult, and had frightened each other to death with tales of sticking pins in waxen images in order to harm an intended victim, or being able to cast spells over people by obtaining a lock of their hair, or even a photograph. When their teacher found them playing with an ouija-board one day and

142

learned about their morbid interest in malfeasance, he hadn't been so much angry as full of warning. Madeleine had never forgotten him saying that to play around with the spirit world was highly dangerous: 'If you dial a telephone number and get it wrong, you can always hang up,' he explained, 'but if you should make contact with an evil or mischievous spirit, there's no hanging up. You're stuck with it.'

Madeleine shivered as she looked at the evil little book lying on the hearth. She didn't even want to touch it again, so strong was her superstition, and she wondered if her grandfather had realised it was up there, tucked behind the volume of Milton's poems. And what was she going to do with it now? she asked herself. She couldn't leave it there, flung down so violently that it had landed open and face down. Hunter would wonder what on earth she'd been doing. Then she rose to her feet, telling herself she was being stupid. How could a book hurt her? She didn't plan to read it, or be influenced by its contents, and if it was as old as she thought it could be of local historical interest. Bending down, she picked up the volume and placed it on a side table.

The next day was Friday, and having breakfasted in her room Madeleine went down to the kitchen, to go through the weekend menus with the cook. Jessica and Andrew would be arriving in time for a late supper and she wanted to give them something light. Hunter had just finished laying out the silver in the pantry.

'Good heavens, I'd no idea there was so much!' Madeleine exclaimed, looking at the collection of glittering pieces that covered the large pantry table and were also laid out on a side dresser.

'A lot of it is Georgian, Madam,' Hunter explained, 'and there are also some very fine Queen Anne salt cellars. Of course this tray is only Victorian, but it is very pretty, isn't it?' He picked up a large silver tea-tray, edged and handled with intertwined ivy leaves, the Dalrymple family crest engraved in the centre.

'Very pretty,' she agreed. 'How did my grandfather come to have so much, though? There's enough here for a dinner party at the White House!'

Hunter smiled. 'I believe Sir George entertained a great deal in the old days, when Lady Dalrymple was alive. I should say, Madam, that most of this silver has been in the family for several generations. These candelabra are particularly beautiful, I think.' He indicated four matching candlesticks, each two feet high, embellished with cherubs and garlands of leaves and grapes, the five candle branches shaped like the stems of a vine.

'They're exquisite. My God, my husband will be thrilled when he sees all these things – he loves silver.' Madeleine continued to examine the treasure trove. There were butter dishes, shaped like scallop shells, ornate tea and coffee pots, minute cream jugs and sugar bowls lined with sapphire blue glass. A collection of entrée dishes complete with lids blazed as a ray of sunlight coming through the window caught their polished surfaces. Then, like a conjuror demonstrating his favourite trick, Hunter unrolled a length of green baize, displaying dozens of shining forks and spoons.

'It's too amazing for words!' said Madeleine. 'I've never seen so much silver in one place in all my life. You'd better put it away for safe-keeping, Hunter. I'm not sure if it's insured.'

'I'll lock it up again, Madam. The drawing-room is ready, by the way, if you wish to use it now?'

'Thank you, Hunter.' Madeleine went into the corridor that led to the hall, and was passing the open library door when she saw a movement, no more than a flickering shadow by the fireplace. The french windows were wide open and, conscious of security after seeing all that silver, she hurried into the room to see who it was. She glanced round quickly but the room was empty, the only movement the gentle swell of the curtains as a sudden gust of wind whipped across the lawn and through the open windows. Nothing seemed to have been disturbed, and yet she was sure someone had been in the room. Shrugging, she closed the windows and then made her way to the drawing-room.

Hunter had obviously been hard at work for the curtains and wooden shutters had been opened, letting in the fresh morning air, and there was a smell of lavender furniture polish and full blown roses. Madeleine walked to the centre, breathing steadily, waiting for some reaction, testing the atmosphere as a bather tests the temperature of the water. Her gaze shifted from the swirling roses in the tapestry carpet, up to the brocade-covered chairs and sofas, and then higher still to the black grand piano that stood in the corner. Fixing her eyes on the array of framed pictures that cluttered its surface, she looked unflinchingly into the face of Camilla, challenging the mocking eyes and the beautiful face to scare her. It was almost an anti-climax when she felt nothing. All that stood before her in a silver frame was one of many black and white photographs of a woman's face, looking over her shoulder into the lens, the features clear-cut and delicate, the eyes direct, the mouth half smiling.

Relief swept over Madeleine, coupled with a feeling of foolishness. This whole business was causing her to let her imagination run away with her and she'd been getting fanciful. Laughing a little at herself, she wandered round looking at the other photographs, picking up little objets d'art that lay scattered about, taking stock of the room as a whole. It was a very pretty room, in fact, and there was nothing sinister about it at all. It must have been the shock of her grandfather's collapse that first evening, coupled with jetlag and general apprehension, that had led her to feel the place was filled with evil, she thought. On the other hand, there were too many pictures of her mother for anyone's taste; the room was totally swamped by them. Deciding to put most of them away in the drawer of a Queen Anne chest that stood against one wall, she stacked them up in twos and threes, being careful not to damage the frames. Gradually the room began to look larger and seem more airy, the mirror above the mantelshelf reflecting the pastel blues and pinks and gilts that harmonised so perfectly with the colours of the carpet.

There were only a few more pictures left to put away. Madeleine went over to the table by the window. Reaching out for the largest, which was gilt-framed, she picked it up. A second later she let out a yelp as if she'd been stung, and the photograph went crashing to the floor, the glass exploding in a shower of brittle shards that stuck to the carpet like tiny quivering arrows. Camilla's face stared up at her and for a moment Madeleine thought she was going to faint.

Hunter came hurrying into the room. 'Madam, are you all right? I heard a crash . . . oh, dear, I hope you haven't cut yourself!'

Automatically, Madeleine looked at her hands, although she knew she wasn't hurt. Then she turned away from the window, realisation making her head spin and her throat dry up. 'No, no I haven't cut myself . . . could you clear away this mess, please?' she stammered, then she rushed out of the room, her trembling legs hardly able to carry her.

For how could she tell Hunter that the scrawled inscription on the photograph – 'To Father, with love from Camilla' – was written in the same hand as the writing in the journal she'd found the previous evening!

Jessica and Andrew arrived late that evening, having taken a taxi from Okehampton Station because Jessica wasn't sure which train they were catching.

Madeleine went to the door to greet them, her black hair tied off her face by a ribbon, her casual white slacks standing out in the velvety purple twilight that was rapidly enshrouding the silent countryside.

'Am I glad to see you both,' Madeleine exclaimed with feeling, as they entered the house.

'Finding the countryside boring, sweetie?' enquired Jessica.

'Boring, no. Nerve-racking, yes,' replied Madeleine. 'Anyway, come and have a drink, and we'll talk later.'

'This is a lovely place you've inherited,' Andrew remarked, as they settled themselves in the library where Hunter had arranged a cold buffet supper, with freshly caught lobster and salad. 'Do you really want to sell it?'

Madeleine nodded. 'I most certainly do. Nothing would induce me to live here now.'

Jessica, who looked slightly drawn and pale, gave Madeleine a quizzical glance. 'Have you found out how your mother died? Was it here, in this house?'

'I don't know, but I do know what she was up to before she died,' Madeleine replied grimly.

Andrew raised his eyebrows, and looked at her enquiringly. Jessica leaned forward, anxious not to miss a word. 'Why, what was she up to?' she asked.

'Black magic.'

'*What*? Oh, for God's sake, Maddy . . .!' exclaimed Jessica.

'I mean it,' said Madeleine seriously. Then she told them what had happened, including what her grandfather had said before he died. 'When I realised today it was my mother who'd kept a journal about her experiences . . . well, I can tell you, I freaked out! Ever since that time at school . . . my God, Jessica, I can understand now why my father didn't want me to know anything when I was a child.'

'And you really think she got involved in witchcraft and that sort of thing?' Jessica asked, her blue eyes as round as saucers. 'I thought all that sort of thing went

148

out in the Middle Ages! You *can't* have got it right!'

'I promise you I have. I just knew something was wrong that first evening. I remember Grandfather saying she'd been led astray, and that Jake didn't understand . . .'

'I don't suppose he would,' said Andrew drily. 'Don't tell me you two girls honestly believe in this sort of thing?'

'I certainly do,' Jessica said emphatically.

'So do I,' agreed Madeleine. 'I know from the articles and books we read at school that the power of evil is one of the strongest forces there is.'

Andrew leaned his head back in the armchair, his legs stretched out in front of him, and his laughter filled the room.

'I don't believe it!' he chortled. 'Intelligent young women like you; educated career girls . . . Oh God, you have to be joking! You can't believe in all that twaddle?'

Jessica and Madeleine smiled at him in a condescending manner.

'Witches' covens are springing up all over the States,' said Madeleine. 'It's no laughing matter.'

'Black magic is rife in this country too,' Jessica added. 'But to think your mother was involved . . .!'

'Okay,' Andrew said reasonably. 'Let's have a look at this journal?'

'That's the strange thing, it's vanished,' Madeleine said.

'*Vanished!*' exclaimed Jessica.

Andrew smirked and said nothing. Madeleine looked at him, wishing he'd take the situation seriously.

'I left it on the table, over there, last night. This

149

morning, when I passed the door, I was sure there was someone in here, but when I came into the room it was empty. Later on in the day when I came to look for it, out of a sort of morbid fascination, it had gone. I'm sure whoever was in here this morning took it.' Madeleine indicated the table on which she'd left the journal.

Jessica gazed over at the table, which stood in a side window, as if she expected to find an answer. 'So it could have been seen by someone passing the window, from the garden?' she suggested.

'Ah, a budding Agatha Christie,' teased Andrew.

'Oh, do shut up,' said Jessica. 'I'm only trying to find a rational explanation. Have you any idea who could have taken it, Maddy?'

'I think it was Jenkins. He's been the gardener here for the past forty years, and I'm convinced he knows the whole story. And I can tell you something else, he sure as hell doesn't want me to find out anything. He completely clammed up when I tried to ask him about my mother.'

'This is absolutely *fascinating*!' Jessica crowed, all tiredness gone. 'You've *got* to find out what it's all about.'

Later, after supper and several glasses of wine, Madeleine took them into the drawing-room where Jessica begged to be allowed to look at some of the photographs of Camilla. While Andrew scoffed gently, Jessica pored over the framed prints, but Madeleine looked away, busying herself by taking another look at the little silver snuff boxes and trinkets that lay scattered about. All she wanted now was

150

to get home to Carl and a life of normality.

'Let's go up to bed,' Madeleine said at last.

'Suits me,' said Andrew with a grin. Then he turned to Jessica and gave her a playful smack on the bottom. 'Are you going to walk up the stairs . . . or fly up on your broomstick?'

The rain started to fall at dawn, obliterating the countryside as it lay bleakly under grey, low-lying clouds. Jessica was awakened by heavy splattering on the bedroom windows, and as she lay listening to it she planned what she'd say to Andrew. The thought made her stomach contract nervously because she knew he was going to be absolutely furious. If only I'd told him earlier in the week and got it over, she fretted, glancing over at him as he lay slumbering. It never failed to surprise her how young he looked when he slept; almost boyish, his face smooth and relaxed, his mouth tilting up naturally at the corners. He's going to be hurt, she reflected.

For a fleeting moment Jessica contemplated turning down Robert Scholtz's offer, seeing herself and Andrew continuing as they were, enjoying their comfortable lives in their smart London flat; each going to work in the morning, and then coming home at night, sure of each other's affections, confident in their future together. The picture was rosy and contented, and also safe. That's the trouble, she thought, easing herself into a sitting position in the bed. It's *too* contented, *too* safe.

As the rain continued to hiss on the terrace below the window and the gentle sough of the trees grew stronger, Jessica knew it wasn't enough; not while she had the chance to soar to the peak of her career, to enjoy the power and the satisfaction the future held out to her. In ten years' time, maybe. She'd only be thirty-six then and there would still be plenty of time for getting married and settling down with a family. But not yet. Not now.

Jessica lay down again, her mind finally made up. She couldn't put off telling Andrew any longer.

By ten o'clock the rain had turned into a blinding deluge, drumming on the window sills of the manor, turning the lawns into a squelching carpet and running in muddy streams down the pathways.

They sat in the library, Madeleine and Jessica chatting while Andrew slouched in an armchair reading the *Daily Telegraph*. From time to time he looked up and glanced out of the windows as if hoping the storm would magically cease.

'Not much chance of going for a walk in this weather,' he commented bleakly.

Jessica glanced up quickly, breaking off in the middle of saying something to Madeleine. Something in the disconsolate tone of his voice made her heart quicken, reminding her again of what she had to do.

'Oh, Andrew!' she said, as if she'd just remembered something. 'I've been meaning to tell you – Robert Scholtz, you know, the President of the Golding Group – was over from the States a few days ago and, well, he's offered me the job of Director of Sales.' She pressed her hands together to stop them shaking. 'It's the most wonderful opportunity – of course it means much more money, too – and it's a *terrific* feather in my cap! It's one of the top positions in the hotel!' She was aware she was gabbling, her words running one into the other.

Andrew put down his newspaper, a pleased expression on his face.

'Well done, Jessie,' he said quietly.

'Congratulations! Why didn't you tell us before?' Madeleine enthused. 'I know you hoped you'd get to be made Director of Sales one of these days, but isn't this much sooner than you expected?'

'Yes, it's because the person who is doing it now is being transferred to another of our hotels in Hong Kong. It's not official yet, I think there'll be an announcement in a week; in the meantime no one at the Royal Westminster knows. It's going to be a bit of a shock for Dick Fowler, whom I work with, but that's life, isn't it?' Jessica gesticulated, her gold bangles chinking as she talked. She was sitting very upright now, her tight jeans emphasising the slim vibrance of her body, her feet in the inevitable high-heeled shoes tucked beneath her.

Andrew regarded her with lazy approval. 'And so when does this new job start, darling?'

Jessica looked across at him, her little face suddenly tight, her eyes defiant. 'In about three weeks, I think. There is just one snag that's not going to thrill you . . .' She gave a forced laugh, brittle and tense. 'They want me to live in. It's part of the hotel policy . . . all senior management have to be on site twenty-four hours a day.'

There was a stunned silence. Madeleine was the first to break it. 'Live in? You mean live in the hotel?'

'That's right. I'll be given a room, probably on the top floor. It won't be a suite or anything grand like that, but it doesn't matter because I'll only be using it to sleep in,' Jessica replied. Now she'd actually told Andrew she felt her courage and conviction returning.

'Thanks very much for consulting me before you accepted!' Andrew said angrily.

Jessica flushed. 'Well, how could I refuse a chance like this!' she said defiantly. 'Come on, Andrew, it's not the end of the world. I will have time off, and some weekends, too. It doesn't change anything between us.'

'Oh, you don't think so?' he said bitingly. 'Well, I think it changes everything.' And without another word he rose, flung down the newspaper and strode out of the room. A moment later they heard the front door slam.

'He can't have gone out in all this rain . . . can he?' Jessica rushed to the library window, and looked out. 'It's still *pouring*! Oh, what a fool! He'll catch his death of cold!'

'You can hardly blame him, Jessica,' Madeleine said reasonably. 'It must have been an awful shock for him. Didn't you think he'd be upset? God, Carl would kill me if I announced I planned to sleep at my studio in future, because I wanted to get on with my painting.'

'That's different, you're married!' Jessica wailed, throwing herself back on to the sofa. 'I knew Andrew would hate it. I've been dreading telling him, but Maddy, it's *my* life! I ask you, how could I possibly turn down an opportunity like this?' She brushed her eyes angrily with the back of her hand, her voice breaking on the edge of a sob. 'It's not going to alter our relationship.'

Madeleine regarded her with quiet amazement. 'Of course it is, Jessie dear. When will you see Andrew? Occasional evenings, sometimes at weekends? After three years of living with you it's pretty hard on him suddenly to find you're actually moving out.'

'From Chelsea to Hyde Park Corner is hardly the other side of the world, for God's sake!' Jessica's voice rose to a querulous squeak. 'I thought you'd understand, Maddy! That's why I waited until this weekend to tell Andrew, because I was sure you'd back me up.'

Madeleine shook her head. 'Sorry, Jessica. I'm with Andrew on this one.'

For the rest of the weekend the atmosphere was strained. The rain continued to fall in a slanting curtain, and the house seemed filled with a chilling dampness that seeped through the skin to the bones. Forced to stay indoors most of the time, they read, watched televison and conversed in a stilted fashion. Jessica began to pray for Sunday evening when they were due to return to London, as Andrew's cold fury was getting her down. Never one to harbour grudges herself, she sparkled and fizzled again within minutes of having a fight, and couldn't understand why he didn't also. At last Andrew suggested they should catch an earlier train.

'What a pity, but with the weather being so miserable I think you're right,' Madeleine said, understandingly.

'I'd come back to London with you now if I could, but I've got a final meeting with Mr Marks, the solicitor, tomorrow morning, before I fly home on Tuesday.'

As they got into the taxi waiting to take them to the station, Jessica turned and flung her arms round Madeleine.

'It's going to be ages before I see you again!' she cried. 'Wish me luck in my new job, Maddy.'

'Of course I wish you luck,' Madeleine replied warmly. 'It's your life, honey, and I really hope everything works out for you.'

'Thanks.' Jessica fought back emotional tears.

Madeleine kissed Andrew on the cheek. 'Goodbye, Andrew, and thanks for doing a valuation on the house. When I get around to selling it, maybe you could handle the sale for me?'

'Of course I will, Maddy dear.' Andrew looked at her fondly. 'Take care of yourself, and don't let this business of your mother get you down. After all, it's all in the past.'

'I know.'

'And give my best regards to Carl.'

'Yes, give Carl my love and a big kiss from me,' Jessica chimed in, sticking her head out of the taxi window.

'I will. Goodbye.' Madeleine watched as the taxi drove off, its tyres sending out sprays of muddy droplets. Then she went back into the house to start packing.

At nine o'clock the next morning Mr Marks arrived, a drab beige raincoat a couple of sizes too big for him protecting his dark suit from the steady drizzle that had now replaced the heavy rain. His blinking eyes reminded Madeleine of a mole's, coming out of the darkness and confused by the light. She led him into the library and offered him coffee. He appeared to be slightly agitated.

'There is a slight hitch in the proceedings,' he said as he sipped. 'It is causing a delay in proving your claim on the estate, and I shall have to get some details from you.'

'What sort of details? What do you need to know, Mr Marks?'

'Well, the problem is, Mrs Delaney,' he paused to stare into her face, his eyes blinking rapidly, 'so far we have been unable to find any trace of your mother's death certificate.'

Chapter Six

Carl left the Central Manhattan Bank shortly after six,
telling his chauffeur he wouldn't be needing him. Then
he hailed a cab to take him to Kimberley's apartment,
La Première, on Fifty-fifth and Broadway, a towering
block opposite a popular diner that did a good impression of being a forties restaurant. That morning she'd
suggested he spend the night with her and, spellbound,
knocked out by her sexuality, he agreed, telling her to
go early so they wouldn't be seen leaving the bank
together. Already, he thought with amazement, I'm
slipping into the games some married men play. He was
appalled at how easy it was.

When he arrived, Kimberley had already changed
into loose silk pyjamas, her feet bare, her red hair
cascading round her shoulders like burnished copper.
She'd lit the apricot-shaded lamps in her luxuriously
furnished living-room, throwing into relief the dark
brown suede sofas and chairs and cream fur rugs, all
presents – as the apartment itself had been – from
previous lovers. As Carl stepped into the room he felt
as if he'd walked into a box of delicious chocolates:
rich, dark and tempting. Kimberley padded over to the
drinks tray, her legs visible through the green silk, her
bare arms creamy and smooth.

Carl had been fantasising about this moment all day.

When Kimberley handed him his drink, he put it on a side table and took her in his arms. This was what he'd come here for, his senses told him; to lose himself in the warm body of this voluptuous woman with the white skin and the Titian hair. Without saying a word, he pushed her down on to the fur rug, pinning her beneath him, tearing away the clinging silk of her pyjamas. Kimberley curled herself round him, welcoming him with little moans. Demented and losing control, Carl ripped away the last of the silk, revealing her perfect body and flawless skin. Without bothering to remove his own clothing, he took her savagely, his face scarlet and his breathing heavy; he was desperate to possess this woman who had so suddenly bewitched him. His passion reached flash point too soon, maddening him. There was something elusive about this girl that he was unable to capture. She was giving nothing of herself away. At last, with a final surge, Carl poured his life into her, desperate to have her and hold her and make her his; but as he raised his eyes to look into Kimberley's, all he saw was an expression of smiling detachment. Carl buried his face in her neck, unable to bear what he saw.

'You're hot,' she said, brightly. 'Would you like a drink?'

He shut his eyes tighter, ready to weep in this moment of acute anti-climax. He had started out wanting a purely sexual thrill, a bit on the side, a diversion from his loneliness with Madeleine away, but somehow in the past few hours he had hoped for something more from Kimberley. Now he realised, she had nothing more to give. It was obvious, looking round the apartment, that she could not have afforded to furnish it so lavishly from her earnings; she didn't get enough from the bank even to pay the rent. Painfully aware that he was one of many, he accepted her offer of a drink and felt ashamed of his own naivety.

While Carl lay fast asleep, his mouth slightly open and his breathing deep and regular, Kimberley slid out from between the brown satin sheets and crept, naked, to her kitchenette. It was four o'clock in the morning and the humidity of the city, still noisy and active at this hour, made her feel hot and sticky. Going to the ice-box she got out a tin of 7-up and jerked back the metal tag. A loud hiss penetrated the heavy silence of her apartment and she paused, listening, but Carl did not stir. Kimberley's mouth curved in a smile. Let him sleep . . . while he could. Soon he'd be too worried even to want to go to bed!

Perching on a kitchen stool, her bare feet swinging clear of the cork floor, she leaned forward until she could rest her elbow on the windowsill. From here she could look south, down Broadway, and watch the constant ebb and flow of traffic and the dazzle of lights that now, from the twenty-fourth floor, looked like tiny pinpricks. She remembered another night, a long time ago, when a little girl had stood in Times Square, and all around her the lights had sparkled and shone in gold and silver, red and green and shimmering blue. They'd spun a promise of excitement and untold wealth that was soon going to be fulfilled. Not long to go now, she assured herself, and then all her dreams would become a reality. She'd have everything she'd ever wanted; the jewels and furs, the exquisite clothes, a lovely house and cars . . . Soon it would all be hers, thanks to Hank Pugsley; and thanks also to Carl Delaney, although he didn't know it yet.

Twelve months before, whilst sitting in a singles bar one night, Kimberley had met Hank Pugsley. Not met, exactly, although that's what she'd tell her friends, but been picked up by Hank. He was middle-aged, married and exceedingly rich. He was also very fat and unattractive, with lank greasy hair and small eyes, but that didn't bother Kimberley. He might be good for a dress and even a fur, so she wasted no time in inviting him back to her apartment, and in doing so, ditching another man she'd agreed to meet that night. Men like Hank were 'fillers in', as she described them to herself; someone who would fill in the time until her lucky break came along. Meanwhile, they allowed her to live in a nice apartment and dress smartly.

Kimberley discovered that Hank owned a company called Brandt's Motors. They sold spare parts for cars and trucks and operated from New Jersey. Hank ran a small office in downtown Manhattan, but the reason for that, he explained leeringly, was because it gave him an excuse to stay in town some nights instead of going back to his wife. It was a story Kimberley had heard a thousand times before and she shrugged, bored. Men were all the same, from her father onwards, and they sickened her.

'I've got a big outfit, you know,' Hank declared, disappointed by her lack of interest in him, 'and I make a stack of dough!'

'Oh, yeah?' She studied her long nails, painted a frosted pink, and wondered when he'd go.

Anxious to impress, and puffed up with his own importance, he helped himself to some more of her brandy and started bragging.

It was the greatest mistake he was ever to make in his life!

'D'you know how I get away without having to pay much tax?' he demanded proudly.

Kimberley looked up, instantly interested. He might, she thought, have something useful to say. 'No? How d'you do that?'

Hank leaned back on her brown satin pillows, his sweating shoulders staining the fabric almost black, his cigar filling the air with its pungent stench.

As Hank explained Kimberley became more and more attentive, making mental notes of everything he told her, memorising details with a mind that was like a trap.

'It is my money, after all,' he concluded smugly. 'I'm not robbing my customers and I reckon I should be able to keep as much of my own money as I want. After all, I've earned it. Why should I let the fucking IRS get it all!'

'How clever,' Kimberley said slowly, and she meant it. She rolled over on to her stomach so that she was facing him, her large breasts swinging pendulously. 'Have a little more brandy, honey,' she said affectionately.

Flattered, and pleased by his own cleverness, Hank told her more, his small beady eyes gleaming with cunning.

What held Kimberley's particular interest was that the millions of dollars he was transferring to a numbered account in Switzerland initially went through the Central Manhattan Bank, where his company had an account. Probing gently, careful not to appear too interested because he thought she was a budding model and models didn't usually bother with high finance, Kimberley finally got out of him everything she wanted to know.

Over the next few months, she was able, surreptitiously, to check out what he'd told her. Sure enough every couple of weeks large amounts were transferred from Brandt's Motors to Zurich. Kimberley started to formulate a plan; and that was where Carl came in.

Madeleine walked with Mr Marks to the front door and stood talking to him on the steps of Milton Manor.

'I'll get the details from my father,' she told him. 'You say if we had the exact date and place it would help trace my mother's death certificate?'

'Exactly so.' Mr Marks still looked slightly agitated. It was a reflection on the good name of Spindle, Coutts and Marks that they were unable to do a simple thing like trace a death certificate, and in the circumstances, highly embarrassing.

'I'm just so sorry that it will delay things even more . . .' he continued, his voice drifting away as if he didn't know how to finish the sentence.

Madeleine shrugged. 'It can't be helped. I'll get the information to you as soon as possible. In the meantime, thank you for all you're doing.'

'Oh, not at all! Please don't mention it.' He darted her a grateful look under his quivering eyelashes, and got into his car. 'We'll be in touch then, Mrs Delaney?'

'We will,' Madeleine promised him with a smile.

It wasn't until later in the morning that she realised she would probably be able to get her questions answered sooner than she'd realised. Alice Stewart and her son, Philip, were driving over for luncheon today. Alice would be sure to remember when and where Camilla had died.

They arrived at one o'clock, with Philip at the wheel of his Aston Martin. Alice Stewart, unperturbed by the speed at which her son drove, emerged from the vehicle unruffled, an elegant figure in a silvery grey dress, her white hair curly and fluffy round her face.

'My dear, it's sweet of you to invite us over,' she said, holding out her hands in greeting as Madeleine came forward to welcome them. Alice glanced up at the Dutch style gables and scroll carved stonework of the old manor, and smiled.

'My goodness, it's a long time since I've been here! George used to entertain a great deal, but when he became a widower, he found it more difficult.'

Madeleine led them into the drawing-room for drinks before luncheon. Alice, she noticed, had turned small talk into an art form, and charmingly and captivatingly she kept the conversation going with her reminiscences of bygone days when Milton Manor had been the setting for many a lavish party.

'I can even remember Camilla's coming-out ball here. There was a pink and white marquee in the garden, and your grandmother had arrangements of big white michaelmas daisies everywhere,' she recalled. 'It looked so pretty.'

Hunter announced lunch and they all went through to the stately dining-room, which now sparkled with use and smelled of sweet scented stock from the garden.

'You must have missed my mother when she married Daddy and went to live in the States,' observed Madeleine, as Hunter placed plates of fresh asparagus in front of everyone before filling their glasses with wine.

'Yes, indeed!' Alice nodded vigorously, her pearl drop earrings shimmering as she moved her head. 'But then of course I got married myself, and went to live in London until my husband inherited our place from his father.'

Madeleine leaned forward eagerly. 'Were you living here when my parents returned to England in 1964 . . . when I was two?'

'No, we were still in town then, but we often came down for weekends, and sometimes I'd bring Philip over to play with you.'

He looked at Madeleine and smiled. She smiled back politely, but it wasn't Philip she was interested in at this moment. She spoke with sudden urgency: 'And were you here when my mother died?'

Madeleine wondered what she'd done wrong. Alice

had almost recoiled and was now ashen-faced, her pale lipstick taking on a mauvish tone.

'What did you say, my dear?'

Madeleine spoke carefully, never taking her eyes off the older woman's face; it was as if a mask had been pulled down over the features, blanking out all colour and expression. 'I asked if you were here, in Devon, when my mother died?' she repeated clearly.

'Oh, yes . . . I mean, no . . .' Alice was looking at her strangely. 'It's . . . it's such a long time ago, I can hardly remember,' she added lamely. Madeleine glanced at Philip who was watching his mother with a puzzled look on his face. Alice fiddled with the long ropes of pearls that hung round her neck . . . like the pearls, Madeleine thought suddenly, that she remembered round her mother's neck in the portrait by de Laszlo.

'But did she die here, or up in London?' persisted Madeleine. 'The solicitor told me this morning they can't trace her death certificate. If I knew exactly where and when she'd died, it would be a great help.'

Alice's manner had changed. From being a talkative outgoing woman full of vitality and friendliness, she'd suddenly become withdrawn, almost furtive-looking. 'You must ask your father about all that.' In spite of the quaver in her voice she spoke with finality. Then, with astonishing panache and social dexterity, she plunged straight into a dissertation on the treatment of mildew in roses. Philip, obviously relieved that what looked like a sticky moment had passed, offered his contributions and the conversation turned to gardening.

Madeleine, leaning back in her chair, felt both disappointment and growing disquiet. Whatever had happened to her mother, Alice Stewart wasn't going to talk about it either.

Carl had been in a meeting with Jake all afternoon. Now, as he returned to his office, he found Kimberley waiting for him, her translucent grey eyes clear like cold marble, but her mouth tilted into its accustomed smile.

'Have you a moment?' she asked, standing opposite him as he sat at his desk sorting out papers.

Carl looked up warily. The last two nights had been a great mistake, he'd decided. No harm had been done, but nevertheless he'd been extremely foolish to fall into the cliché of the boss and the secretary having an affair; now he planned to extricate himself gently and pleasantly, as if he were sure their fleeting relationship had meant no more to her than to him.

'Sure, but I'm a bit busy, as you can see . . .' he began in a friendly fashion, but something in her expression cut him short.

'This is important, Carl.' Kimberley no longer called him Mr Delaney when they were alone. She sat down on the chair opposite him, looking businesslike, her hair swept back into a neat chignon, her black and white suit with padded shoulders an indication that she was now into power dressing.

'What is it?' Carl asked.

'I have a friend called Hank Pugsley. He owns a company called Brandt's Motors of New Jersey, and he banks here, with us.'

Carl's mouth tightened. If Kimberley was going to have the damn cheek to ask him to arrange a loan for one of her lovers, she had another thought coming to her. 'So?' he snapped.

Undaunted, Kimberley went on to explain Hank's method of tax dodging. 'It's quite neat, really,' she explained. 'Some time ago he started a phoney company in Switzerland, called Michaux Internationale. Every two weeks Hank is sent a fake invoice from Zurich, sometimes amounting to hundreds of thousands of dollars, for machine tools and various spare parts. He then sends the money to Zurich, but of course it goes into his numbered account, as Michaux doesn't exist.'

'I'm not with you, Kimberley,' Carl said, frowning. 'Why are you telling me all this?'

'Because I've thought of a way of stopping him.'

Carl was taken aback. 'By reporting him to the IRS, d'you mean?' He thought for a moment. 'That could be a problem, especially from the bank's point of view. We would be using privileged information and that would constitute a breach of trust.' He looked at her. 'Apart from which, why do you want to spill the beans on a friend of yours?'

Kimberley smiled, amused. 'I have a much more interesting proposition than that to put to you.'

'What are you talking about?' Carl's stomach contracted uneasily and a prickle of fear shivered down his spine. 'You don't intend to blackmail him?'

'You're head of foreign transactions, right?' Kimberley continued, as if she hadn't heard him. Carl nodded, mute with apprehension. Kimberley continued: 'Whenever you receive one of Hank's instruction forms authorising money to be transferred from his business account at the Central Manhattan Bank to Switzerland, to pay Michaux Internationale's invoices, you have to pass it to Jake Shearman after you have done the initial paperwork. I know you've been receiving them, because I've been watching.' She paused, to let the words sink in. 'Jake Shearman and two of the Vice-Presidents are the only people who have the code for transferring large amounts of money by computer to foreign countries. I trained in computers and I'm a computer programmer, so I do know what I'm talking about,' she added, her voice an urgent whisper now.

Carl was watching her as if hypnotised; her cold clear eyes held a hint of fanaticism, binding him to her, immobilising him so that he sat still, almost mesmerised, his brain reeling at the implications of what she was saying.

'You have access to Jake's office. I want you to borrow that computer tape which has the key to the foreign transactions code, and let me have it for an hour. In that time I can make a copy and you can put the original back in Jake's office.'

'I still don't understand, Kimberley,' Carl said heavily, but a voice inside his head said, You understand only too well. He had to play for time while he decided how to handle this situation. He felt caught on the hop; unprepared. Kimberley was in control of the position at the moment and she knew it. She'd deliberately chosen a moment, during working hours in the Bank, when she knew he wouldn't be able to

170

make a scene. She leaned towards him now, her eyes fixed on his face. Carl felt himself recoil as she spoke.

'This is my plan, Carl,' she said. 'Every time you get instructions from Hank Pugsley to transfer money to his Swiss account, you give it straight to me. I will put it through the computer, using my copy of the tape with the coded key, only instead of transferring it to Hank's account I will be transferring it to a numbered account at a bank in Zurich which I opened six months ago.'

Carl closed his eyes, shock and fear turning him ice-cold, making his heart pound. He knew what she was going to say before she said it. He'd made love to her in the shower . . . in her apartment . . .

'Don't think of refusing, Carl. I doubt if your wife and your father-in-law would appreciate receiving a copy of the tape recording I made of you screwing me in my apartment last night.'

The silence in his office was palpable, locking them together in a fearful conspiracy. Her words thundered in his head, holding him in a vice of torment. He'd let himself be manoeuvred, by the oldest trick in the world, into a situation where he was ripe for blackmail, and unless he could think of a way out of this mess he would only fall deeper and deeper into Kimberley's clutches.

'Let's make a deal,' he heard her say. 'We'll split the money because neither one of us could pull this off singlehanded. That's fair, don't you think?'

Carl sprang to his feet, anger and panic engulfing him. 'You're off your trolley!' he whispered furiously.

'No, I'm not. There's no way we're going to get

caught. Hank isn't going to find out the money isn't reaching his account because he never gets sent bank statements from Switzerland; he told me himself it would be too dangerous in case they fell into the wrong hands. Even if he were to, what can he do about it? He's acting illegally himself, pretending to pay for tools that don't exist in order to defraud the IRS. He wouldn't dare squeal! Believe me, Carl, we can cream off several million dollars and no one will know.'

'If you think I'm going to go along with this crazy scheme . . .' he muttered, running his hands through his hair. What scared him most of all was that he knew Kimberley's plan could be made to work. He *was* in a position where it would be easy to 'borrow' the computer tape for a short while from Jake's office, providing he did it in the late afternoon when Jake and the two Vice-Presidents had left the bank; and Kimberley knew what she was doing so she would have no problem in making a copy. After that, all he had to do was pass over Hank Pugsley's instruction forms to Kimberley instead of Jake for processing, and as she'd said, Hank was unlikely to do anything but stop sending the money if he did find out what was happening.

Carl looked at Kimberley, realising she'd worked everything out, down to the last detail, and in a moment of self-loathing he wondered how he'd ever thought her attractive. Fool! Fool! How could he have let himself get caught like this? For a moment he contemplated telling her to go to hell; he even contemplated rushing up to Jake's office to tell him what had happened, but he knew if he did he'd be finished. Madeleine might forgive him an indiscretion, although she'd be deeply hurt, but her father would not. Jake lived by a rigid moral code, especially where the bank was concerned. Sleeping with a member of the staff and thereby putting oneself in a vulnerable position, would in Jake's opinion show a severe lack of judgment; and a sense of judgment in banking, as in politics, was essential.

'You really haven't got any option, have you?' Kimberley was saying. 'You've got to be part of my plan or your whole future lies in ruins. You can kiss goodbye the prospect of being the next President of the Central Manhattan Bank if you don't go along with it.'

What she said hit Carl like a physical blow. He would lose everything he'd worked for if Jake were to find out, and if her scheme was to go disastrously wrong he'd lose everything anyway. Carl went to his washroom, shuddering as his eyes caught the shower, remembering her standing there naked. Splashing cold water on his face, his mind spinning down into a bottomless void that was filled with horror and anger, he cursed himself for being such a fool as to have succumbed to mindless lust for a pretty girl.

Carl awoke at five o'clock, his head throbbing and his limbs rigid with tension. For two nights now he'd only slept fitfully, spending most of the time on his back gazing up at the ceiling, while his mind reeled in a frenzy of worry as the slow hours ticked away. How could he ever have got himself into this situation? The question chased itself round and round in his brain until he thought he'd go mad. He cursed himself for his moment of weakness, and thanked God that Madeleine was not there to witness his torment. And yet he longed for her too. None of this would have happened, he thought unhappily, if she hadn't gone away. In the four years of their marriage he hadn't so much as looked at anyone else, although they'd often been apart for days at a time if she was away on a painting commission. Yet this time, during that one crazy irresponsible moment, he'd wrecked everything.

The guilt he felt overshadowed even the events of yesterday afternoon, when Kimberley had demanded he get the computer tape from Jake's office. Feeling sick with fear he'd knocked on the door and, finding it empty, walked in and gone straight to the safe where the tape was kept. He knew how to open it in seconds. When he'd married Madeleine and become 'family', Jake had made him privy to a lot of highly confidential material and that included the combination to his private office safe.

Holding his breath, he turned the knob twice clockwise until it rested at 6. Then he turned it once anticlockwise, stopping at 9, and clockwise once again until the tiny arrow got to 5. A final turn and the door opened. Carl's mind raced as he reached for the tape, at the same time extracting some other papers, as a cover, in case he was caught. Then he closed the safe and hurried from the room. Kimberley was waiting for him in his office. Without a word she took the tape from him.

Drenched with sweat, Carl sank down on to the

chair behind his desk and watched her go back to her own office. He tried to work but found himself shuffling papers about, as the longest hour of his life began. Whenever the phone rang he jumped with fright; when anyone knocked on his door wishing to see him, he felt himself grow tense with fear. He could imagine Kimberley copying the tape in the computer department, spinning some lie no doubt to explain what she was doing to anyone who asked. For a moment he was almost grateful that she was so adept at lying and so skilful at deceiving. Anyone with fewer wits about them would surely get caught.

At last she returned, a satisfied smirk on her painted lips. Carl grabbed the tape from her, collected the papers he'd also taken from Jake's safe, and within five minutes had returned the lot. No one had seen him, as far as he knew, going into Jake's office either time, but the strain of the afternoon had left him with a blinding headache.

Slowly now, as if his mental agony had transferred itself to his body, he eased himself out of the four-poster bed and padded into the adjoining bathroom, which Madeleine had designed in soft shades of pink marble. Relaxing in a tub of very hot water, which he felt would help him unwind more than a shower, he planned to get to the office before Kimberley. It was imperative he did something to put an end to her scheme before everything got out of hand. Supposing he offered her money? Persuaded her to leave the country? But how much money would it take?

Carl shook his head in silent anguish. She'd want millions, because that was what she'd said she could get from robbing Hank. Where the fuck was he going to get millions to give her? He didn't have that sort of money, and he couldn't go to Jake or Madeleine because of course they'd want to know why he needed it. Supposing he borrowed it from someone else . . .? But that was no use; he'd have to provide collateral, and that would involve Madeleine and her father again. In a gesture of furious despair, Carl picked up a flask of perfume that stood on a ledge by the bath and flung it at the opposite wall. In a shattering of glass, a pungent trail of Claude Montana scent drifted towards him, bringing Madeleine's presence into the room as strongly as if she'd been standing there.

'Oh, Jesus,' he groaned, stepping out of the bath carefully so as not to cut his feet. Picking up the broken shards, he wrapped them carefully in tissue and dropped them in the waste bin. Madeleine would be home very soon now and he wondered how he was going to face her.

An hour later Carl strode into his office.

'What the hell . . .?'

Kimberley, standing by his desk, turned to look at him coolly. 'Hank should be putting through a transfer to Zurich any time now. I was going through your morning mail to see if there was any sign of it.'

'How dare you touch my things?' Carl stormed. 'What the fuck d'you think you're doing?' He found his hands were trembling and he'd broken out in a sweat.

Kimberley looked at him insolently. 'Keep calm, it hasn't arrived yet in any case. But I'll keep a look out for it, so don't think you can go slipping it to Jake Shearman behind my back.'

'Goddamn you!' Carl stared at her with revulsion, hating himself even more than he hated her. What had he ever seen in her? 'I'd like to kill you!' he breathed in her face.

'Or fuck me?' she scoffed, crudely.

'Enough people have done that already,' he snapped, turning to leave the office. He walked along the corridor, blinded with rage, bile rising sourly in his throat. When he came to the first-floor gallery he paused to look down on the main banking area below. Clerks were arriving for work; nice, simple men and women, bent on doing a good job, content to receive their pay packets at the end of the week and go back to their families every evening. For a long moment Carl envied them their uncomplicated lives, and then he wondered at the turn of fate that had sent him a secretary in the shape of Kimberley Cabot. Down among the stretches of black and white marble and chrome and lucite, ordinary decent people were going about their work, while in his office a she-devil had taken possession. Carl suddenly wished with all his heart that he could turn the clock back to a couple of weeks ago.

Madeleine hurried out of the arrivals terminal at JFK and into the waiting car. It was over two weeks since she'd seen Carl, and now that she was nearly home the longing for him intensified, making her wonder how she'd managed without him for so long. She glanced at her watch. Provided the traffic into New York

177

wasn't too bad, she might just catch him before he left for the bank.

Settling herself in the back of the large limousine, she tried to plan her day, but her thoughts kept straying back to her husband. They'd talked constantly on the phone, of course, almost every day, but it wasn't the same. She closed her eyes, imagining his arms round her, his mouth demanding, his body pressing against her. Aroused, she opened her eyes again, wondering if she could persuade him to stay home with her for a while. Surely it wouldn't matter if he was late for work just this once?

When the familiar outline of Manhattan appeared on the horizon, her heart gave a little twist of excitement. Only another twenty minutes and they'd be on Fifth Avenue, drawing up outside No. 944.

The moment she entered the apartment she knew Carl had already left. There was an emptiness and silence about the apartment that suddenly chilled her and sent a great wave of childish disappointment sweeping over her. She'd been convinced she'd make it in time . . . and couldn't he have hung on a little longer before leaving for the bank? She'd even hoped for a moment that he might be at JFK to meet her. Tears welled in her eyes, but then she wiped her cheeks angrily. God, how old was she? Four? Six? How ridiculous to get upset because Carl wasn't there.

At that moment Teresa appeared to take charge of her luggage. Madeleine greeted her and said she'd like some coffee.

'Right away, Mam,' said Teresa. 'Did you have a good trip?'

'Yes, thank you. Has everything been okay here?'

'Yes, Mam.' The maid didn't seem to want to linger, and picking up one of the suitcases, added: 'I'll get your coffee and then I'll do the unpacking.'

'Thanks.' Madeleine blew her nose and went into the living-room to phone Carl. At least she could talk to him, even if she couldn't see him until this evening.

The bright morning sun streamed in through two large windows, dazzling and highlighting the all white room, where the Thai silk festooned curtains resembled thick whipped cream and the carpet was like a drift of soft snow. White was piled on white, in thick cotton and silk upholstery, in pleated muslin lampshades and bleached ash furniture. The only spots of colour in the room were provided by two portraits, one of Carl and one of Jake, which she'd painted some years before. The one of Carl, looking impossibly blond and handsome, hung above the white marble fireplace, and the one of Jake was on the opposite wall above a writing-table. Madeleine glanced at them as she entered the room, wondering with a fresh eye brought about by absence if they weren't too strong for such a delicate-looking room. Especially the portrait of Jake. She'd forgotten how totally dominating it was, depicting her father sitting at his desk in the bank, his face composed in serious lines.

She went over, idly, to have a closer look and was suddenly struck by something she'd never noticed before. His eyes had the same mocking watchfulness that she'd seen in the eyes of Camilla's photographs.

The chilling look was not as pronounced in the photographs, but it was definitely there; a wariness, a guardedness – and a knowledge! But a knowledge of what? A shared experience? A secret known only to them? Madeleine put her hand to her face in a gesture of bewilderment, wondering if it was only she who could sense these things. Maybe this gift of reading a person's soul was what made her the painter she was. Maybe her artist's eye was seeing something that others didn't see. With a little shudder she turned away. The portrait was much too strong for this room, she decided. Maybe she would give it to her father as a present.

That evening Carl was home early, wiping out her disappointment by arriving with an armful of pink roses. She hurried across the hall to greet him, her arms outstretched.

'Hi, Maddy. Welcome home.' He kissed her tenderly.

'It's so good to be back, you've no idea.' Madeleine ran her hand through the thickness of his hair at the nape of his neck. 'I'll never stay away so long again.'

'You couldn't help it, sweetheart. Is everything all right . . . do you have to go back again?'

'At some point I'll have to supervise the sale of the house but it won't be for ages yet.' Madeleine took his arm and they walked slowly into the living-room, where she'd already put a bottle of champagne in a silver ice-bucket. 'I've missed you so much, Carl. You've no idea. I wish to God you'd been with me.'

'So do I!'

Madeleine looked at him sharply, wondering if anything was wrong. She'd had such a strange fortnight, overcast by death and doubt and mystery, that maybe she was letting her imagination run away with her; but he'd spoken with unusual vehemence.

'Well, thank you, honey. I didn't know you missed me *that* much!' she joked coquettishly.

Carl flushed, and grabbing her again kissed her, long and hard. 'I'll show you how much I missed you,' he said lightly as he released her.

'I was hoping you'd say that,' she replied with a wicked grin. 'That's why I've given Teresa the night off.'

'Scheming woman.' He pretended to spank her bottom, but he put up no resistance as Madeleine drew him towards the bedroom. Suddenly she stopped, and turning towards him put her arms round him again. Pressing her cheek to his, she whispered: 'Oh, I love you, Carl, and I need you so much.'

'I need you too,' he whispered back as he held her close, and he was glad she couldn't see his face, or the deeply troubled look in his eyes.

'Can we meet for lunch, Daddy?' Madeleine asked Jake when she phoned him the next morning.

He seemed to hesitate for a moment and she knew he was trying to delay their inevitable confrontation. But after a moment he said:

'Yes, of course, my dear. I can't manage today but how about tomorrow?'

'That would be fine.'

'La Caravelle at one?'

'Perfect. I'll see you then. 'Bye, Daddy.'

When Madeleine entered the restaurant the next day, in a simple white suit with gold jewellery, there was a flutter of interest. Heads turned, elbows nudged and voices dropped to whispers.

'That's Madeleine Delaney . . . did you see her exhibition?'

'Wasn't it brilliant?'

'I wonder who it is she's meeting?'

'Ah . . . here comes Jake Shearman!'

They made a handsome couple, father and daughter, as they were seated at one of La Caravelle's best tables, reserved for VIPs only. Both tall and slim, Madeleine's black hair framed her exquisite face in a riot of fluffy curls, while Jake's grey hair and tanned lean face gave him a distinguished air.

'It's good to see you again,' he remarked, smiling, when he'd given their order. 'How was England?'

Madeleine looked at him askance. 'England was fine; pity I can't say the same thing about my grandfather!'

'That remark's in rather poor taste, isn't it?' Jake remarked mildly. 'I'm sorry you had to suffer the shock of George dying, just after you'd arrived.'

'But you're not sorry he's dead,' Madeleine observed.

Jake raised his eyebrows, and looked at his daughter in surprise. 'What a strange thing to say! George was an old man and he'd been slightly crazy for years. I would have thought his death, to use a cliché, was a merciful release. I warned you not to go to see him, Madeleine. I knew it would be no picnic.'

She levelled her gaze at her father, her voice steady. 'Daddy, there's no point in your trying to hide anything from me. I found out a lot of things when I was staying at Milton Manor, but I need you to fill in a few details. I want to know what happened to my mother.'

Jake gave a false laugh, and threw his arms wide in a gesture of bravado. 'Why are you so obsessed with the past?' he demanded. 'It's over and done with, and now that George is dead that's the end of the chapter. The end of the Dalrymples.'

'It's not, Daddy. You forget *I'm* half a Dalrymple, and Grandfather has left me a wealth of family heirlooms. Just because my mother's dead we can't pretend the family never existed!'

Jake didn't answer.

'My mother got involved in black magic, didn't she?' challenged Madeleine.

'Where did you hear that nonsense?' Jake had paled, but he did not falter. 'From George, no doubt! Surely you don't believe . . .'

'I found her journal in the library, hidden behind some other books. It described a black mass . . . and other things.' Madeleine broke off, shuddering. 'Jenkins was involved, too, wasn't he? He stole the journal the day after I'd found it, and when I asked him about my mother, earlier, he'd refused to say anything. He was obviously trying to cover up the truth.'

'Jenkins?' repeated Jake, shaken. 'Good God, is he still around? I thought he'd have been dead years ago. Now listen to me, Madeleine . . .' He leaned across the table in a confidential manner, his voice lowered. 'There *was* some talk of a witches' coven or some such stupid thing, going on in the village of Sherston years and years ago, but your mother was certainly not involved. I believe she was a bit intrigued; she may have jotted down notes of what she'd heard, but that was all. As for Jenkins, he was just the gardener. I don't know what sort of trash George has been filling your head with, but as I've told you he was senile. He probably didn't know what he was saying!'

At that moment the waiter interrupted them, to serve the poached salmon they'd ordered and to refill their wine glasses. Jake looked around the restaurant waving gaily to a few friends he saw at the other tables, obviously anxious to change the conversation.

'There's Oliver Strong,' he remarked. 'Did I tell you, Madeleine, that he's going to run for Congress?'

'I'm not interested in Oliver Strong,' she said mutinously. 'I don't care if he's going to be President! Grandfather said that at one point my life was endangered by what my mother was doing . . . now, for God's sake, Daddy, I have to know what happened! It's important to me.'

'Keep your voice down. People are looking at us,' Jake said tensely. 'I don't want to hear any more of this rubbish.'

'Well, there's one thing you're going to have to tell me,' said Madeleine. 'I need to know exactly when and where she died, because right now there's no trace of her death certificate!'

Jake hurried round to his sister's Beresford apartment

as soon as he'd said goodbye to Madeleine and seen her into the waiting car. Patti, who was about to leave for a bridge party, greeted Jake with her customary acidity.

'Really, this is most inconvenient! Couldn't you have called me up first?' Her voice was more gravelly than usual and a haze of blue cigarette smoke surrounded her like an aura.

'I'm sorry, Patti, but I had to talk to you urgently.'

'Oh, well, you'd better sit down then,' she said, waving him to a chair in her large cluttered living-room. 'What's the matter?'

Briefly, Jake repeated his conversation with Madeleine.

'Oh . . . my God!' Patti sank on to one of her pale pink sofas, more angular-looking than ever in a sharp navy blue Chanel suit and a plethora of gold chains. 'What are you going to do?'

'I don't know,' he said, wretchedly. 'Why the hell didn't George make a new Will after . . . Patti, I wish to God you'd stop smoking!' Irritably he waved his hand, trying to disperse the smoke.

'Do stop being so neurotic, Jake.' Nevertheless she stubbed out her cigarette in a large marble ashtray. 'I think you're going to have to tell Madeleine everything,' she said reflectively. 'You can't hide the truth from her now.'

'I can't, Patti, I can't. She's found out enough as it is. Christ, how I wish George had just gone and died quietly without involving Madeleine in the first place, then she need never have known anything at all.'

Patti eyed him sympathetically, although she still

spoke harshly. 'Pull yourself together, for goodness' sake. Why don't you call up this solicitor – what did you say his name was, Marks? – and tell him in confidence what happened. He'll understand why you don't want Madeleine to find out the truth, and then let him sort out the legal side of George's Will. No one's going to dispute that Madeleine is the rightful heir to her grandfather's property!'

'I suppose I could.' Jake sounded doubtful.

'Of course you can, stop being so negative.' Patti's restless hands reached for her gold and jewelled cigarette case. 'You've gone this far to protect Madeleine, why can't you go further?' She lit her cigarette and dragged on it with obvious pleasure.

Jake looked at her, his face still anxious. 'Jenkins is the danger,' he said quietly. 'Thank God he apparently clammed up when Madeleine questioned him about Camilla. But can he be trusted not to talk in the future? Madeleine says she's going back to Milton Manor to sort out the contents, when she sells the house.'

Patti puffed thoughtfully. 'Couldn't you silence him with a nice fat cheque?'

Jake looked startled. 'That's not quite my style, Patti. I don't think I've ever paid out hush money in my life.'

'There are times,' she said severely, 'when you should forget you're a banker and try to act like a normal man. If the thought of paying off Jenkins makes you feel squeamish, *I'll* damn well do it. Now I must go, or I'm going to be late for my bridge party.'

186

'I'll think about your suggestions,' said Jake, as they left her apartment together.

'I know you'll do the best for Madeleine,' Patti's eyes twinkled for a moment, 'and next time, Jake, call me up before you come rushing round for advice!'

Chapter Seven

'Have you heard the latest?' Dick Fowler barged in to Jessica's large new office, which bore the sign 'Director of Sales' on the door. He was doubled up with laughter.

'What's happened?' Jessica looked up from her desk, glad that they were still friends. Her promotion over Dick could have caused a rift between them, but he had been the first to congratulate her when the news had been announced, and seemed genuinely glad for her.

'Room Service have just phoned through to say that a client in Room 102 has ordered four breakfasts!' chortled Dick.

Jessica looked perplexed. 'What, for him and his wife?'

'Wife be blowed! He's a single booking. The waiter who's on duty for that floor is on his way down to report to you.'

Jessica's expression was a mixture of amusement and exasperation. 'Security haven't noticed any hookers patrolling the corridors again, have they?'

Six months before, in spite of the stately grandeur of the Royal Westminster, they had been forced to have a purge on prostitutes who slipped into the hotel late in the evening and then cruised up and down the corridors, tapping on bedroom doors where a form ordering only one breakfast hung from the door knob.

During one night Security had rounded up eighteen of these ladies of the night, and from then on hotel policy had changed. Single women entering the hotel were now politely approached by a member of staff, inquiring if they needed assistance. Genuine women guests liked the courtesy; hookers took the hint and left, and the word soon got round that their presence was not welcome. There hadn't been any trouble for months now, thought Jessica, hoping it wasn't all going to start again. That sort of thing gave any hotel a bad name.

There was a tap on her office door. A young Italian waiter, smartly dressed in black trousers and a spotless white top with a mandarin collar, entered at Jessica's request and came and stood respectfully before her desk.

'I hear 102 has got company?'

'Yes, Miss.'

Jessica tried to hide her amusement at the young man's obvious embarrassment. 'Yes?' she said encouragingly. 'Who's in his room with him?'

There was a long pause as the waiter swallowed with difficulty. 'Three young ladies,' he said at last. 'All in the bed.'

Jessica started, visibly surprised. '*Three*?' she exclaimed. '*Three*?' She turned to Dick Fowler, whose self-restraint had given way and who was leaning back in his chair, roaring with laughter.

'This isn't funny,' said Jessica, trying to sound

severe. 'We'd better get Mr Powell to deal with this.'

'He's on sick leave . . . remember? And Mr Wolfson's at a two-day hotel conference in Paris.' Kenneth Wolfson was the General Manager, and Denis Powell his assistant.

Jessica swore silently and looked back to the waiter. 'Thank you for letting us know. That will be all.'

'Thank you, Miss.' He scuttled out of the office as if relieved.

Dick looked speculatively at Jessica. 'That leaves you . . . or would you like me to handle it?'

Jessica responded immediately in her usual gutsy fashion. 'Oh, I'll deal with him. If he thinks he can use this hotel like a bordello he's got another thought coming! Anyway, I can't wait to see what this Casanova of the corridors is like.'

For a moment it crossed her mind that Andrew would really enjoy hearing all about it tonight, but then with a pang she remembered there was no more Andrew in her life. When they'd returned from staying with Madeleine in Devon he'd issued her with an ultimatum.

'It's me or the hotel, Jessie,' he'd said, and from the sadness in his voice she knew that he'd already realised what her choice would be. She had wept copiously, arguing for hours that she could manage both, but Andrew had been adamant. The hotel was going to consume her, twenty-four hours a day, and they'd hardly ever see each other – just for odd nights here and there and the occasional weekend.

'You must see it can't work.' Andrew's voice had been quiet and reasonable.

'But I love you!' Jessica had wailed. It was no use. She knew she couldn't turn down this chance, and Andrew knew their relationship could not continue while she insisted on working at this level. On the day she'd moved out of their Chelsea flat, taking just her clothes with her to the hotel, while her parents stored the rest of her possessions in their house, she'd wept as if her heart would break. That the pain she was going through was self-inflicted did nothing to alleviate her sorrow. After three years of living with Andrew, it was over. She had never felt more torn between wanting to stay and wanting to go. For a long moment she was bitter at the price she was having to pay to further her career, and just hoped to God that in the long run it would be worth it.

Jessica looked up at Dick, then she jumped to her feet and straightened her slim shoulders. 'Okay, I'm ready to do battle with this over-sexed stud. What's his name?'

Jessica leaned across the reception desk to speak quietly to the clerk. 'Can you tell me which gentleman is Mr Stratford Stevenson, when he comes down from his room?'

'Certainly, Miss McCann.' The uniformed clerk glanced round the lobby. 'Here he is now, coming out of the elevator.'

Jessica spun round and a look of incredulity spread across her face. 'What . . . *him*? Are you sure?' she croaked.

'Absolutely certain. He booked into Room 102 two days ago.'

'Right!' Jessica strode across the lobby, her high heels clicking on the white marble flooring.

'Mr Stevenson? Good morning, I'm Jessica McCann, Director of Sales. May I have a word with you, please?' With distaste she shook Stratford Stevenson's hand and led him to the seating area, where low sofas and brass-edged coffee tables stood clustered under an oasis-like arrangement of tall plants.

Jessica sat down facing him, thinking that never in her life had she seen such an unattractive man. Short and greasy-looking, with dark strands of hair plastered over his bald head, his ferret-like eyes slithered to and fro as they ranged over her body from her head to her feet.

'What can I do for you?' he asked throatily, his thick lips barely moving.

Wondering how much he had to pay to get a girl, let alone three, Jessica tried to hide her revulsion.

'I understand you have three . . . er . . . guests staying in your room,' she said.

'So what?' Mr Stevenson shrugged and looked at her boldly. 'They're my guests and I can have whom I like in my room.'

'Certainly you can,' she informed him pleasantly, 'but by law all persons staying overnight must register. We must have a record of all guests in case of fire or any other unforeseen happening. Apart from which –' here she drew a deep breath, determined to remain in control of the situation – 'our policy at the Royal Westminster is to charge for all guests who stay here.'

'I'll pay for whatever they have to eat or drink!'

'I'm afraid you'll do more than that, Mr Stevenson. The accounts department will be adding the overnight charge for your three guests to your bill,' Jessica said firmly.

Mr Stevenson made a sickly attempt at smiling. 'Oh, come on, be reasonable. My little friends aren't doing anyone any harm,' he protested.

'I'm sorry, but it's hotel policy.'

He leaned forward and looked at her insolently. 'That's like charging me corkage for screwing!'

Jessica rose, dignified in spite of her diminutive height. 'If you choose to put it that way, Mr Stevenson, that is *exactly* what we are doing. Thank you for your time. Goodbye.' Then she turned away, leaving him gaping after her.

'And *so*,' Jessica said, as she regaled Dick back in her office, 'shall we charge him corkage at beer rates or champagne rates?'

For the rest of the morning, Jessica was busy putting the finishing touches to the 'Glorious Twelfth' special dinner she was organising for August 12th. The first batch of grouse to be shot that morning would be flown down from Scotland and served in the hotel's Fantaisie Restaurant, where she had planned a Scottish theme for the evening. Salmon, caught in the River Dee near the Queen's Scottish residence, Balmoral, was on the menu, and Jessica had got the chef to order haggis from Edinburgh. The tables were going to be covered with tartan table-cloths, and in the centre of the room there would be a magnificent free-standing decorative arrangement of stuffed grouse strutting on a bed of heather, thistles and bracken, which she'd hired from a local taxidermist.

'The restaurant is fully booked for the evening,' the restaurant manager had informed her the previous day.

'Thank God for that,' Jessica replied. 'I sent out six hundred expensively printed notices to everyone I could think of. It's a relief to hear they've responded!'

Satisfied that she'd done everything she could to ensure that the event, which was in three days' time, would go well, she glanced at her watch and gasped when she saw it was already twelve-thirty. In fifteen minutes she was meeting her friend from the *Evening Standard* in the cocktail bar. Taking the elevator up to the sixth floor, she ran along to Room 217 and, opening the door, flung herself across the room, whipped a packet of tights out of the chest of drawers and started to change. Room 217 was now home to her, a neat impersonal space furnished with a bed, an armchair and some plain furniture suitable for staff. Adjoining it was a tiny bathroom in which, she told her friends, it was not only impossible to swing a cat – there wasn't room to swing a mouse either. Jessica spent as little time in here as possible. Sleeping alone depressed her and she wasn't used to it yet. There'd been many mornings when she reached out for Andrew as she awoke, only to find her hand hitting the bedside table. At least, she thought, looking round as she slipped into a pink linen dress, I don't have to make my own bed or do my laundry.

A few minutes later, her filofax and hotel bleeper in her hand, she rushed into the bar just ahead of Peter Thorn.

'Peter!' she greeted him rapturously, kissing him on both cheeks. 'It's been *far* too long since we last met. Come and sit down and we'll have a jolly strong drink before lunch.' Jessica ordered champagne cocktails, asked for menus so they could take their time deciding what to order, and carried on a voluble conversation with Peter at the same time.

'So, how's the new job?' he asked, when he could get a word in edgewise. 'You're quite the business executive these days, aren't you?'

Jessica laughed, her eyes glowing. This was what she liked; meeting people, entertaining, being in luxurious surroundings, organising special sales events, having the power to make things happen.

'It's *divine*!' she said fervently. 'I've got so many ideas for attracting people to come here. D'you want to know what my latest plan is?'

'I doubt if I shall be able to stop you telling me.'

Undaunted by his teasing, she continued: 'I'm going to introduce a special Christmas scheme, for couples who don't have children. They'll be given a stocking full of little presents with their champagne breakfast in bed. We'll have a traditional lunch in the restaurant, and I'll have jugglers and fire-eaters and other entertainers. We'll put a giant tree in the lobby and show a really good film in the ballroom, and at night there'll be carol singers followed by dinner and dancing!'

'And the next day guests take out a bank loan to

pay for it all, I suppose,' grinned Peter. 'Sounds a fun weekend to take a girlfriend on . . . I'm not so sure about a wife!'

'Peter, you're *wicked*! Oh . . . that reminds me.' Jessica collected her thoughts quickly, so she could give Peter an edited version of her weekend at Milton Manor, without involving Madeleine. 'You were going to tell me about the Dalrymple family. I heard a rumour when I was down in Devon the other month, that one of them was involved in black magic. Is it true?'

Peter looked at her askance. 'Is the Pope a Roman Catholic? You bet it's true! I told you I had to cover the story – about twenty years ago, mind you. Jesus, it was awful!' Then he leaned towards Jessica and quietly, so as not to be overheard in the crowded bar, told her what had happened.

'Oh . . . my God!' breathed Jessica when he had finished. Her face had gone pale, and she looked horrified. 'Is that really true?'

Peter nodded. 'Witchcraft still exists all over the country, you know, even in this day and age. But that was a particularly nasty episode. It gave me the creeps, I can tell you. I read that old Sir George Dalrymple had died recently. Of course he claimed at the time that he'd no idea what was going on, but I'm not so sure.'

Jessica glanced at her menu, so she wouldn't have to meet his eyes. What he had told her was so appalling she felt quite shaken. And one thing was certain . . . there was no way she could ever repeat it to Madeleine.

* * *

Carl froze as he looked at the form on his desk. Kimberley had already gone through his papers before he'd arrived and she'd placed this one right on top. With a feeling of sickening dread he picked it up, scanning the authorisation for three hundred and sixty thousand dollars to be paid by Brandt's Motors Inc of New Jersey, to Michaux Internationale, Zurich. Hank Pugsley's signature was scrawled along the bottom of the form, to which was pinned an invoice supposedly charging for machine tools imported from Switzerland.

At that moment Kimberley came briskly into Carl's office. Her face showed not a trace of emotion. She nodded when she saw he was examining Hank's form.

'I'll go back to my apartment at lunch-time and pick up the copy of the coded tape I made,' she said in a whisper. 'I'll put the transfer through the computer at about five o'clock when everyone's gone. If anyone should see me, I'll say I'm checking up on a client's current account to see if he's got sufficient funds to cover a foreign transfer.'

'You've got it all worked out, haven't you?' Carl said hollowly, knowing that nothing was going to change her mind now. She was quite determined to embezzle Hank's money, and although he knew her scheme was as foolproof as any scheme could be, the element of risk made him feel quite ill.

'Of course I've got it all worked out!' she snapped. 'This is not a job for amateurs.'

Carl went through the morning's mail, giving her instructions on the dozens of other transfers that were going through. At last he leaned back in his swivel chair, his shoulders aching with tension, his head throbbing. Kimberley sat opposite him with her notepad on her knee, watching him closely all the time. If he so much as reached for the phone her eyes darted to his face, trying to gauge what he might be about to do. In an atmosphere heavy with distrust and dislike he tried to concentrate on his work, but it became more and more difficult as the morning wore on. What astounded him more than anything was that he had been fool enough to have been taken in by her seductive little girl manner at the beginning. Looking at her now, cool and calculating, with her hair drawn back into a neat chignon, it seemed impossible that this was the same girl who had drawn him to her in the shower and set him afire with her sexuality, transporting him into a fever of desire. It rankled to know he'd been one of many and that he'd allowed himself to be used and manipulated by her. Anger and wounded pride, mingled with fear, vied bitterly in his mind.

Painfully, he nerved himself to ask her one more question while steeling himself to hearing the answer.

'Do you still see Hank Pugsley?' he blurted out awkwardly.

Kimberley's full mouth curved into a smile.

'Jealous, are you?'

Carl flushed deeply and she looked more amused than ever. Her translucent eyes sparkled with malice.

'Why should I be jealous? You mean nothing to me,' retorted Carl.

'That's not what you told me when we were in bed!' Kimberley rejoined swiftly. 'But to answer your question . . . I stopped seeing Hank after he'd told me about his scam. He thought I was a model and at that point I didn't want him to know I worked in this bank, of all places.'

The phone buzzed on Carl's desk, making him jump. He pressed the key to line one. 'Hello?'

'Jake here. Can you come to my office, Carl?'

Guilt flushed through him in a tidal wave. 'Sure, Jake. I'll be along right away.' Then he caught Kimberley's eye.

'I don't know why you're looking like that, Carl. We haven't done anything yet!' she said mockingly.

'I know.' He sighed heavily, feeling as terrible as if they'd already committed the felony. Jake had put his trust in him from the beginning, guiding him through the intricacies of high finance, investments, backing loans, and banking practices, encouraging him every step of the way, grooming him eventually to take over; and here he was, about to betray the man who had been like a father to him. Then there was Madeleine! Carl closed his eyes for a moment. To think about her was more than he could bear.

Jake wanted only to discuss the financing of a new aircraft factory in Ireland. The Central Manhattan Bank had agreed to lend sixty million dollars for the project, but as Carl sat listening to his father-in-law, he felt as if his and Kimberley's sordid involvement was written clearly all over his face. Shifting uneasily in his seat, hardly able to concentrate, he oozed guilt from every pore.

'Are you all right?' Jake asked at length.

Carl started. 'I'm fine. Just a bit of a headache, nothing really.'

Jake's lined face creased into a kind smile as he looked at Carl benevolently. 'Why don't you and Madeleine go down to Oyster Bay this weekend? You could do with a break, and you haven't had much of a chance to be with her recently.'

'Yes, I'd like that. I'll talk to her about it tonight.' The thought of a couple of days by the ocean, staying in the rambling holiday house with its garden leading on to the beach, might help to take his mind off the mess he was in, for a short time anyway.

'That's settled then,' said Jake. 'Now, about this scheme . . .'

Carl looked up swiftly, his heart pounding again. 'What?'

'The scheme to launch this aircraft factory,' Jake explained patiently. 'You'll have to arrange the transfer of dollars to Dublin, and I want you to be at the directors' meeting next week. They're flying over on Tuesday to discuss the final details with us. Is that all right by you?'

'Oh . . . oh, sure,' said Carl hurriedly.

'Right. Now don't forget to mention the weekend to Madeleine. You look tired and you could do with a break.' Jake placed a hand on Carl's shoulder as they walked to the door of his large office.

'I'm fine, but thanks anyway,' Carl replied.

When he got back to his own office, he still felt shaken.

Kimberley sat at her desk watching until the hands of the brass wall clock in her office reached five o'clock.

That was when the clerks went home, and the computer room would be deserted. It was now ten to five. She slipped her hand into her purse and extracted the tape. It fitted snugly into the large patch pocket of her suit. With it she put a pack of cigarettes, so if anyone noticed a bulge she could make a joke about smoking too much. Then, with closed eyes, she ran through the program she'd have to feed into the computer, to get access to her account in Zurich. Her account number she knew by heart: 23007 4810 66792, followed by the code word, HURRY. Provided she wasn't disturbed it was going to be a cinch.

'Working late?'

'That's right.' Kimberley, entering the computer room, acknowledged Liz who was one of her former colleagues. Liz was still at her desk, fiddling with a computer print-out. 'They're a bunch of slave drivers around here, aren't they?' Kimberley added jokily. The tape felt as heavy as a brick in her pocket and twice as large. She shuffled the handful of papers she was carrying. 'Can't stop to talk. Mr Delaney wants something checked out right away.'

'Anything I can do to help?' Liz asked. She was a heavily-built girl, with a florid face and strong body odour. Kimberley had always disliked her.

'Don't worry,' she said breezily, 'it won't take long, and it's rather nice to be back in here again.' She went over to an empty desk and pretended to be checking her papers in order to play for time.

'I'm not in a hurry,' Liz persisted. 'What do you want to check?'

'No, it's all right, really.' Her hair was sticking to the back of her neck now, and her hands trembled. 'Go, Liz, for Christ's sake, go,' her mind implored, as the fat girl sat there in a broadly striped dress that resembled awning fabric, a bland smile on her face.

'What's it like working for Mr Delaney?' she asked, settling down for a gossip.

'Look, honestly, he's waiting for me upstairs, and I must get on with this,' Kimberley said desperately, yet anxious not to appear rude and possibly arouse Liz's suspicion. 'Let's meet for lunch one day soon, and then we can have a good talk.'

'Well, if you're sure . . .' Liz sounded mollified, though still reluctant to leave. Slowly and laboriously, she gathered her things together in her chubby hands, watching Kimberley all the time.

'Sure I'm sure!' Security would be coming round at any time now and it was vital she switch over the tapes, enter the transfer and put the original tape back before the computers were switched off for the night.

Liz started walking slowly towards the door, and then she stopped and turned back to Kimberley. 'Did you hear that Julie's boyfriend had left her? D'you know, he just packed his bags and went . . . didn't even leave her a note! Did you ever hear anything as dreadful as that?'

Sweat was pouring down Kimberley's back now and she felt as if she could scream. This goddamn fat ugly boring girl seemed determined to stick around and she felt like hitting her. Time was running out. And the transfer had to be put through today.

'Don't tell me now . . . save it for when we have

lunch together,' she said, forcing a smile. 'I've got to concentrate on this or Mr Delaney will be furious at my taking so long.'

'Okay.' Slowly Liz lumbered away and Kimberley waited, listening, until she was sure the girl had really gone. Then, with her heart in her mouth, she seated herself swiftly at the main computer and removed the tape containing the program for clients' current accounts. In its place she put the tape from her pocket. The green screen flickered off and on again, and then sprang to life in a flurry of numbers and figures. Her copy tape was working perfectly! Gasping with excitement, her heart pumping violently, Kimberley knew at that moment that her scheme, planned and plotted for so long, was really going to work.

Concentrating intently, her fingers tapped smoothly and knowledgeably on the keyboard. ACCESS GRANTED spelt itself out on the screen . . . and she took a deep breath, forcing herself to keep calm. With Hank's authorisation on top of her pile of papers, she began to enter the details. First she had to feed in the number of his account at the Central Manhattan Bank. 0037246 Z18. The screen responded without a hitch. Then she tapped out the amount to be withdrawn from Hank's account. Again the result flickered up with perfect accuracy. 'This is fantastic,' she thought exultantly. It was going better than she could have dreamed in her wildest dreams. The next thing she had to do was transfer the money to her own Swiss account, instead of his. She entered the code for the Zurich Banque Internationale, and the irony that it meant tapping out HURRY was not lost on her. Her fingers flew over the keys, every nerve straining in her body, listening in case anyone was coming. Her heart was hammering so hard she could barely breathe now: HURRY . . . and then a wave of pure physical pleasure when the screen flashed up the details of her own Swiss bank account. Not long now . . .

She leaned forward, the unearthly green glow of the screen reflecting on her pale skin and grey translucent eyes. For a moment she looked as if she was at the bottom of the sea, the clear green waters holding her still in a breathless moment; but the illusion was broken as she shifted her position, frowned, and then tapped out the number of her account. 23007 4810 66792. There was a pause and then she entered the amount. Another pause, a flicker, and then the words CREDIT RECEIVED flashed up.

Kimberley hardly remembered what happened in the next few minutes; all she knew was that the precious tape was back in her pocket, she'd replaced the original one in the computer, and she was hurrying up to her office, not stopping until she was safely behind her desk again. There she leaned back in her seat to regain her breath and composure, wishing her heart would stop thudding. Not that it mattered. She was now three hundred and sixty thousand dollars richer.

Chapter Eight

Madeleine laid down her hog's-hair brush and stood back, head tilted to one side, lips pursed. The portrait was shaping up nicely: Dwight Lasmo, President of Phoenix Oil and an Opec minister, looked back at her from the canvas with a stern resolve that matched the figure's in the carved chair opposite. At the last sitting she had outlined his features in a wash of burnt umber mixed with turpentine and linseed oil, and in just that one session she had captured the essence of the man. Now, as she mixed the right paints to form the basis for flesh tones, she felt the strange but familiar chemistry between herself and her subject stirring within her again. It was as if she was in tune with what was going through his mind, intuitively picking up his thoughts and feelings.

The finished portrait was going to surprise quite a few people, she thought, as she started to work on his eyes. No one would guess, meeting him casually, that the cold ruthless exterior hid a man consumed by self-doubt and a sense of inferiority. She spotted a vulnerability in his expression when he didn't think anyone was looking at him, and she guessed he found keeping up a protective public image a great strain. Nevertheless, she would paint him as she found him, even if it did mean exposing something he'd rather keep hidden, because her artist's integrity did not allow her to lie on canvas.

'Would you like to listen to some music?' she suggested. He was beginning to flag, and his eyes were growing blank from boredom. Music would give him something to concentrate on.

'I'd like that very much, but won't it distract you?' Dwight asked.

Madeleine shook her head, laughing. She put down her palette and brushes and went up to the hi-fi in the gallery, a slim vibrant figure in a tightly belted white boiler suit, a white bandeau holding her hair off her face. 'I don't even hear it when I'm painting,' she admitted honestly. 'Which do you prefer? Pop? Classical? Opera? Ballet? I've got most things here.'

Dwight ran the tip of his tongue tentatively across his bottom lip and spoke with sudden diffidence. 'Have you any of Frank Sinatra's records . . . or Andy Williams'?'

Madeleine suppressed a smile. 'Of course! No record collection would be complete without them,' she said gaily. She might have guessed he'd choose an oldie and a goodie like Sinatra or Williams; a safe familiar choice that would remind him of when he was a young man.

With the strains of a well-known love song filling the studio, she went back to work and was soon in her own world again, unaware of everything except the face before her. And then a thought slanted its way into her brain, making her pause, wondering, for a moment. She'd suddenly remembered that first night at Milton Manor, when she'd come across all the photographs of her mother and had experienced a profound inner knowledge of what Camilla had been like. It was the same when she painted a portrait. She would look at a person, and intuitively know what their inner self was like; insecure as now, in Dwight Lasmo, or corrupt, or avaricious, or lecherous, or even just plain stupid. It was all there, in their eyes; it was like looking into their soul and seeing their very being.

She might only glimpse it for a fraction of a second, but once observed it stayed in her mind and was transmitted, through her hand, on to the canvas. Madeleine paused for a moment, brush poised, brow furrowed. No matter how hard she tried to dismiss her memory of that first night, it was an undeniable fact that she had seen an expression of evil in her mother's eyes. Or could it have been fear? Madeleine felt confused now, her powers of recall blunted by the passing of time. Perhaps her imagination was playing tricks . . . had played tricks with her that night? Perhaps Camilla had been frightened of something, all those years ago, and that fear had transmitted itself to Madeleine through the photographs? Was it terror and not evil that had manifested itself to her? The thought took hold, gripping her mind in a paralysis that made her put down her brush, unable to continue painting.

'Do you mind if we stop now?' she asked Dwight Lasmo in a small voice. It was nearly time anyway; she'd been painting for almost two hours.

He looked relieved. 'I don't mind at all. It's more tiring than I thought, being painted, isn't it?'

Madeleine nodded distractedly. 'Yes . . . yes, it is tiring,' she agreed. She started cleaning her brushes in a jar of white spirit. The sharp smell filled the studio, as much a part of her life as the Claude Montana perfume she always wore. Dwight Lasmo took his pocket diary out and riffled through the pages.

'I have another sitting next Thursday, at noon – is that right?' he asked.

'That's right.' She smiled briefly. 'I'll look forward to seeing you then.'

He approached the easel. 'May I have a look?'

'Of course.' She stepped aside so he could see better. 'It's coming on very well.'

Dwight stood before the canvas, his face filled with awe. 'That's amazing . . . that's exactly how I feel!' He turned to her with a look of wonder, tinged with suspicion. 'How do you know what I'm feeling . . . what I'm like inside?'

Madeleine shrugged. 'I don't know, but I suppose it's what enables me to paint portraits.'

Dwight studied the canvas again. 'It's quite uncanny. I've never even seen a photograph of myself that made me feel it was really me, but this is exactly how I see myself.'

Madeleine smiled. 'Good. I'm glad you like it. It will be even better when it's finished. We'll do a lot more next Thursday. Now, if you'll excuse me . . .?'

'Of course.' He gave the painting a final pleased look. When he had gone, she tried to do some more work, but her day had been ruined. A thought, so sudden and unexpected, so horrifying she dared not even name it, had now taken hold and she knew she would not be able to rest until she found out if she was right. She must seek out the truth now, no matter how terrible the revelation. It stood to reason, she told herself, wondering why it had never occurred to her before, that if no death certificate could be found for her mother, then there could be only one possible explanation.

Patti Ziffren felt deeply exhausted. Last night she and Sam had attended the Labour Day Fantasy Ball, in aid of Cancer Research, and this morning she regretted going. Once she'd enjoyed dressing up and attending parties every night, but now, she decided, she was too old for that sort of thing. Sam still enjoyed social-ising, but then it was different for him. He settled himself in a corner with his brandy and cigars, sur-rounded by all his old cronies, talking business until the early hours. That, to Sam, was like being drip-fed the essence of life itself. Patti had to keep up with all the other women and that could be hard work; being the best dressed and bejewelled; being the wittiest and best informed; being the most brilliant because that was the standard she'd set for herself when she'd been Patricia Shearman, the young and beautiful daughter of Henry Shearman who owned the Central Manhat-tan Bank.

That was a very long time ago, she reminded herself now, as she applied her lipstick. Her father was dead, the bank was now a public company. At least Jake was its President and being his sister still had a certain cachet.

Patti sat at her dressing-table, looking at the

reflection of a pale, drawn-looking woman with severely arranged dyed blonde hair, and she didn't like what she saw. How had she arrived at this moment in her life? she wondered wearily. Where had all the fun gone? She was tired of the whole eternal social round: the shopping for clothes each season, the regular trips to fashionable resorts, the ladies' lunches and the bridge afternoons. And she was bored with seeing the same faces and eating the same caterer's food and looking at the same florist's arrangements everywhere she went.

Absentmindedly, she reached for the blue enamelled cigarette box, wondering how she could avoid going out to dinner tonight. She watched herself in the glass as she lit the cigarette, the skin round her lips puckering into a concertina of tiny folds. Her eyes looked hollow, and with a tiny stab of panic she was suddenly aware of her own mortality. That cough . . . it wasn't any better. She smoked too much, she knew that, but it brought her an immeasurable amount of comfort. In fact she couldn't contemplate a life without cigarettes; from the first one in the morning to the last one at night, she enjoyed every puff. She didn't care what people said, smoking was her one pleasure in life and she wasn't going to give it up.

Slipping her slender black-stockinged feet into smart black high-heeled pumps, she went to the dining-room, and found Sam already seated at the breakfast table, reading the *New York Herald Tribune*.

Patti helped herself to coffee, strong and black, and with it took a couple of aspirins. A fresh cigarette

212

smouldered in an ashtray beside her cup.

Sam glanced over at her. 'Hung over?'

Patti looked at him. 'I didn't drink that much,' she snapped with some asperity. 'I just have a headache. I think I'll cancel lunch today.'

Sam nodded noncommitally. He was a short rotund man, with a cheerful round face and thick white hair. Nothing ever seemed to irritate him and he was renowned for his joviality, a quality that sometimes drove Patti crazy.

'I'm off to Hartford to look at some interesting real estate that's become available, but I'll be back this evening,' he said, folding the newspaper. 'Have we anything on tonight?'

Patti seemed to shudder. 'Dinner – but I think I'll cancel. I'm beat.'

'Why?' Sam inquired blandly. 'We weren't late last night.'

Patti took a deep drag of her cigarette. 'I don't care whether we were late or not, I'm beat,' she repeated. Then she started coughing, a deep rattling cough that sounded as if her lungs were being torn apart.

'Nasty cough!' Sam observed, rising to leave the table. 'You shouldn't smoke so much, Patti.'

'You . . . you can talk!' Patti spluttered, her eyes watering with exertion. 'I never see you without a great fat cigar . . .' The rest of her words were lost as she coughed and wheezed.

'But I never inhale. Never.'

'Well, bully for you!'

By noon she felt better, and was helping herself to a martini when she heard the doorbell to her apartment

213

ring. A minute later she heard Madeleine's voice in the hall. Patti went to greet her.

'Just like your father – always arriving unexpectedly!' she remarked tartly. 'Now you're here, you'd better stay for lunch I suppose.'

'Hello, Aunt Patti.' Unabashed, Madeleine kissed her pale cheek. 'You're looking very smart. Are you sure I haven't come at a bad moment? Are you going out?'

'I wouldn't have invited you to stay to lunch if I'd been going out.' Patti's voice switched to huskily welcoming as she asked: 'What would you like to drink?'

Madeleine glanced over at the drinks cabinet. 'I'd love some Perrier.'

'Huh! Designer water, what next? Well, come and sit down and tell me what you've been doing – and how is that divine husband of yours?' Patti lit a cigarette, and perched on the edge of an upright chair as if she was about to jump up again. 'You're getting too thin,' she observed sternly.

'Can we talk?' Madeleine blurted out as soon as the butler had left the room.

'I didn't suppose you'd come here to discuss the stockmarket. What's the matter, Madeleine?'

Her niece hesitated, as if she didn't know where to start. Then she said: 'I suppose Daddy's told you all about my trip to England?'

Patti nodded. 'I gather your grandfather died as soon as you arrived. Rather bad timing, I must say.'

For once, Madeleine didn't smile at her aunt's abrasive manner. 'The thing is, Aunt Patti, a problem's arisen over Grandfather's Will. The solicitor can't trace my mother's death certificate, and I find that very strange. And Daddy won't give me any of the details, like when or even where she died.'

Patti's mind worked quickly, wondering what she was going to say. She'd plead ignorance, of course; say she was in New York when it all happened and that she wasn't sure of the details. But that wasn't going to make the problem go away; nor would it satisfy Madeleine.

'Surely,' Patti said reasonably, 'if someone's been dead for more than seven years, it doesn't matter whether the certificate can be found or not.'

'I don't know,' Madeleine replied, spreading her hands in a helpless gesture. Then she looked at her aunt, her eyes wide with anxiety and bright with unshed tears. 'Why am I being kept in the dark, Aunt Patti? I had a terrible thought this morning when I was in the studio, and you must tell me if I'm right. I really can't take the strain of not knowing any longer.'

Patti stiffened. Surely Madeleine couldn't have hit upon the truth? No, that was impossible. From what Jake had said, she had only the vaguest idea of what had happened, certainly not enough for her to have drawn any conclusions.

'You must remember I was here, in New York, living my own life at the time,' Patti said with asperity. 'I don't know that I can help you.' She stubbed out her half smoked cigarette and automatically lit another.

'If there is no death certificate,' said Madeleine

slowly, 'and my mother's death is shrouded in such obvious mystery, then I can only conclude that . . . well . . .' she floundered, hardly able to put into words what she was thinking, '. . . perhaps her death was never reported?' she concluded.

Patti watched her closely, observing the emotional struggle that Madeleine was trying to control.

'Never reported?' Patti repeated. 'What do you mean?'

'I mean . . . was her death kept a secret . . . has my father refused to talk about it because she was murdered? Is that it, Aunt Patti? Was my mother murdered? Did my father kill her?'

The telephone buzzed on Jessica's desk. It was Kenneth Wolfson, the General Manager of the Royal Westminster.

'I'm calling all department heads for an emergency meeting this morning, Jessica,' he informed her. 'Be in my office at nine-thirty.'

'I'll be there,' she promised, wondering what had happened. Every morning there was a brief meeting in the Manager's office to discuss any points arising out of the day's programme, such as a banquet with a member of the Royal Family attending in which case extra security would have to be laid on, or the arrival of a VIP who might need extra looking after, or something as mundane as a broken boiler that needed fixing; but that usually took place at ten o'clock. Heads of departments only met once a week, to report on the bigger issues, and that meeting had been yesterday.

Jessica shrugged and, rising from her desk, went

into Dick's office next door.

'D'you know what's up? Why are we being summonsed by the great white chief?' she asked.

Dick grimaced. 'I've heard a nasty rumour, so it's probably to do with that.'

'What sort of rumour?'

'I've heard the unions are threatening to bring out all the hotel staff on strike unless we meet their new overtime pay demands within twenty-four hours. This time tomorrow we may be making the beds and serving in the bar . . . even cooking in the kitchens! Don't you just long to see Kenneth Wolfson and Denis Powell down on their hands and knees, scrubbing the floors!' he laughed.

Jessica looked dumbfounded. 'You've got to be joking!'

'I wish I was. It's true, Jessica. I popped in to the kitchens earlier this morning, and everyone's downed tools. They're busy painting placards with slogans painted on them like: "We're not slave labour" and "Management is exploiting us".'

Jessica looked startled. 'My God, they're not going to lobby for public sympathy, are they? That would be very bad publicity for the hotel.'

'As far as I could tell, from the mutterings, they plan to parade around the front hall and in the street outside the entrance,' Dick replied.

Jessica clasped her head, appalled. 'Oh, Dick, this is serious! No wonder Kenneth Wolfson has summonsed us all. D'you really think we're in for a serious strike?'

'I hope not, but it's a tricky position.'

217

'If only we were a smaller hotel, then we could sack the lot of them and employ non-union workers.'

Dick agreed. 'They don't seem to understand in this business that there's no such thing as work-to-rule. If there's a job to be done you stay and do it until it's finished.'

'As if I didn't know! But management can't give in over this, Dick. If they do, every hotel in the Group, from Bahrein to Turkey, will be under threat of a strike from their staff, demanding higher overtime pay.'

'I know, I know,' replied Dick, shaking his head.

At nine-thirty all the management personnel were squeezed into Kenneth Wolfson's office. The atmosphere was tense. Jessica, seated next to the Banqueting Manager, Mike Lyle, raised her eyebrows questioningly.

'Any news?' she whispered, as Kenneth Wolfson shuffled the papers on his desk, cleared his throat and prepared to talk to them all.

'No,' murmured Mike, 'except that there's to be a meeting with the union spokesman at noon.'

'Maybe something will be resolved then,' said Jessica hopefully.

Mike replied drily. 'I very much doubt it. They mean business this time.'

Kenneth Wolfson was brief and to the point. 'We have a serious problem on our hands, with a staff walk-out threatened at noon tomorrow unless we meet their overtime demands. The staff are on a go-slow today, and we need you all to do everything you can to keep this place running smoothly.'

218

There were nods and grunts of agreement from everyone.

Kenneth continued: 'Should we not be able to come to a satisfactory settlement with the unions, then you must all be prepared to help keep the place running as best you can. There will be a rota of those of you who will be put on to bedmaking and cleaning the rooms, those of you who will look after the front office and guests' luggage, and then of course there will be the kitchens and bars to be manned. We have a day in which to make these contingency plans, should the strike go ahead, and I would like each of you to return to your office now, so that you can plan for your individual departments.'

Amid a scraping of chairs and muted mutterings, the management rose, their faces grim. Every one of them had the interests of the hotel at heart, or they would not today be in the position they occupied. To keep everything running smoothly, from fresh flowers in the vases to fresh sheets on the beds, was of paramount importance to them all. The golden rule of running a hotel was that no matter what, the guests' comfort must come first.

Jessica rushed straight down to the reception desk in the lobby to see if any VIPs were due to arrive within the next twenty-four hours. She might have to get them into another hotel if the Royal Westminster couldn't look after them properly. Anne Butler, from the public relations office, went with her. It was going to be her job to keep the story of the strike out of the newspapers and she was deeply angered by this disruption.

'What d'you want?' she asked Jessica, almost crossly, as they arrived at the reception desk together.

'I want to see if we've got any VIPs arriving,' Jessica replied. 'They won't exactly relish finding this is a do-it-yourself establishment!'

Anne didn't smile. She looked at Jessica as if she were a skittish schoolgirl. Contemptuously she said, 'Why bother asking reception? I have the list of celebrities due to check in. Tomorrow it's the President of CBS television arriving for a couple of days, and the day after there's some actor from California.'

At that moment, Denis Powell, the Assistant Manager, came hurrying up to them. 'Ah, there you are, Jessica,' he said, smiling in spite of the situation. Denis had been with the Golding Group for twenty-five years, much of which he'd spent working in their hotels in the Middle East. He'd been at the Royal Westminster for eight years now and was renowned for his charm, whether he was talking to one of the maids, a maintenance worker, or a celebrated guest.

'Good morning, Mr Powell. Is there anything I can do for you?' Jessica asked, while Anne just stood there, saying nothing but looking harassed.

'There is something I'd like you to do for me, Jessica,' he said warmly. She was a favourite of his, and they shared a great sense of comradeship. 'We've got Bernard Scheller arriving on Thursday for a ten-day visit.'

Anne cut in with a hint of I-told-you-so in her voice. 'That's the actor I was telling you about.'

Denis Powell turned and looked at Anne with sad eyes as if he pitied her effort at seeming in the know.

'He's not an actor,' he said, 'he's the famous composer and conductor. He's over here from the States to give a concert at the Royal Albert Hall.'

Anne flushed angrily and shrugged, but Jessica's face lit up as she exclaimed: 'Oh, how fantastic! I've got all his records! I'll see if I can get him into the Dorchester or Grosvenor House, in the event of the worst happening.'

Denis Powell looked at her approvingly. 'Great!' he said, nodding. 'Make contingency plans for him because he's a very important client. He will only ever stay in five star hotels, so we don't want him upset in any way. He's a rather demanding guest, Jessica, and I want you to keep an eye on him the entire time he is here. He entertains a lot, mostly in his suite, so make sure he has everything he wants.'

'I will,' she promised. 'It will be a pleasure . . . I've admired his work practically all my life!'

Denis smiled. 'I wouldn't tell him that,' he joked, 'it'll remind him of his age!'

'And don't ask him if he's in the Top Twenty because he doesn't write that sort of music!' rejoined Anne, with a bitchy laugh. It annoyed her that although she was the Public Relations Officer, it was Jessica who got the nice jobs, like looking after the more important of the hotel's guests.

'I'll see he has everything he needs,' said Jessica, ignoring Anne, 'and I'll check all the details now.' She sped over to the reception computer and tapped out the name on the keyboard: Bernard Scheller. There was a pause of a couple of seconds, and then the screen read: 'Arriving Heathrow, 7.45am on

Thursday 7th September. Hotel's Rolls-Royce to meet him and bring him straight to hotel. Expected time of arrival: 8.30am.' Then there were some details giving his American Express card number and home address, which was in Sardinia.

Jessica felt excited, hoping the strike would be averted so he could stay. She'd met many so-called VIPs in her time, but rarely one as talented and famous as this.

The silence in the room was almost palpable. Madeleine was sure Patti could hear the thundering of her heart.

'Is that what happened?' she asked, her voice heavy with dread. Now that she was about to find out the truth, she suddenly wished she'd taken her father's advice and pushed the whole thing to the back of her mind. What good was the truth going to be to her now, anyway? It wouldn't bring her mother back. It wouldn't change the fact that her childhood had been lonely, despite Aunt Patti's devotion. It wouldn't bring her peace of mind; in fact it would only serve to underline the sense of loss she'd always felt. Worse, the truth might reveal something about her father that she'd rather not have known.

Patti Ziffren reacted with a shower of cigarette ash and billowing smoke. A racking cough tore into her lungs.

'Good God, child!' she spluttered. 'Of course your mother wasn't murdered! What on earth gave you that idea?' She was deeply shocked. This was all Jake's fault. If he'd handled the situation better

Madeleine's imagination would never have run away with her like this, allowing her to conjure up terrible visions.

'How could you think your mother had been murdered?' she demanded, when the worst of her coughing fit had subsided. 'I've never heard of such a ridiculous thing in all my life . . . And to suggest it might have been Jake! Really, Madeleine, you're getting carried away by this whole thing. Your stupid old grandfather has filled your head with nonsense – why, Jake wouldn't hurt a fly, and you know it!'

'I was wrong to think that Daddy might have had anything to do with it,' Madeleine admitted, 'but something sinister did happen, I'm quite certain about that. Something so terrible that Dad won't even talk about it. It's driving me crazy . . . wondering . . . not knowing . . . and now not being able even to find a death certificate.'

Patti, anxious to reassure Madeleine yet unable to tell her everything, sounded harsh. 'Oh, for goodness sake, pull yourself together. You're getting obsessed.'

'I'm sorry,' said Madeleine contritely. 'I never used to think about my mother all the time, but recently, since my trip to England . . .' Her voice faltered and Patti felt a deep wave of compassion for her. Madeleine had been too protected all her life and now she was being exposed, in the worst possible way, to a situation she did not understand, with half truths getting mixed up with sheer fantasy and only a little knowledge. What the girl needed, she thought to herself, were some hard facts, but they could only come from Jake.

'Listen to me,' she scolded, as if her niece were a little girl again, 'I'm sure your trip to England was upsetting but there's no need to make a major drama out of it. Whether Camilla's death certificate can be found or not is immaterial. You have inherited your grandfather's estate and in due course I gather you're going to sell it. That's it. End of story.'

Madeleine remained silent, toying with her glass of water, her long black eyelashes casting a fringed shadow on her pale cheeks.

'I know exactly what's the matter with you,' Patti suddenly said sharply. Madeleine looked up.

Her aunt was sitting very upright, lighting another cigarette. 'This whole business,' she began, 'has suddenly made you realise you haven't *got* a mother! As a child you never asked about her, you know. You were perfectly happy with your father and all your toys, and the time you spent with me. You accepted the situation which, for some reason, you are refusing to accept now. It may be sad, but it's something you've got to come to terms with, sooner or later. All this hoo-haa with your grandfather has merely made you realise what you've missed.'

Madeleine nodded slowly, recognising the wisdom and truth of her words.

Patti looked at her directly. 'Now let me tell you something. You don't have a monopoly on being motherless, so you must stop feeling sorry for yourself. You have a father who loves you very much, a fantastic husband, and for what it's worth, you've got me.' Her eyes were tender now, belying the abrasiveness of her words.

Madeleine's eyes swam with unshed tears. 'Oh, I do realise, and I am grateful, and I'm especially grateful to you for all you did when I was small.' She gave a deep sigh. 'Perhaps Daddy was right when he said I shouldn't have gone to England; I do feel more confused and disturbed than before, and of course my curiosity really has been aroused.'

Patti snorted. 'Well, you know what they say? "Curiosity killed the cat!" Now, do me a favour and put away that wretched glass of water and have something decent to drink! Lunch will be ready in a few minutes, so you can pour me another martini. Then I want you to advise me on my bedroom. I'm going to have it redecorated. I hear Chinese yellow is the "in" thing this year . . . but do you think it will go with my complexion?' Artfully she diverted Madeleine and was pleased to see a little colour returning to her cheeks. Later in the day she would get hold of Jake and tell him that things couldn't continue as they were. Madeleine was going to have to be told something, even if it wasn't the whole truth.

The atmosphere in the hotel was strained and Jessica could feel trouble in the air like a storm about to burst. In the lobby and kitchens, the go-slow was snarling up the normal smooth-running efficiency, and upstairs beds remained unmade so far and Room Service was taking an hour to produce a pot of coffee. As she hurried back to her office she saw a group of porters and house electricians clustered in the corridor, deep in discussion. A few of them glared balefully at her as she passed. She tried to ignore them but it was difficult.

Of all the hotel staff these were the ones with whom she sympathised. They worked all hours – often having to dismantle and clear the ballroom at three o'clock in the morning, only to re-set it with tables and chairs for a breakfast conference or exhibition. Heavy sofas and grand pianos and stages had to be trundled around, spotlights had to be re-angled and microphones set up and tested. Sometimes these men worked for forty-eight hours at a stretch, with only a three- or four-hour break while a function was actually in progress; not long enough to go home but too long to be hanging around without a comfortable place to sit.

Jessica crossed her fingers, thinking of Kenneth Wolfson at this moment in talks with the union spokesman. By this time tomorrow an agreement would either have been reached, or they'd all be working flat out, no matter how menial the task, ensuring that the Royal Westminster kept running. It would be a major calamity and cost the hotel thousands of dollars; it would also be bad for its image, and Anne, in the public relations department, was going to have her job cut out in dealing with the press. But nothing, Jessica knew, would force them to close, even for a few days. The three hundred and eighty members of staff might go on strike, but the management were going to have to keep the show on the road, somehow.

Two hours later Dick put his head round her door, a jubilant grin spread across his face.

'I've just heard – it's all over! The strike's off.'

Jessica jumped to her feet, arms waving, bangles rattling. 'That's terrific! What happened?'

'The management has offered an increase of twelve percent on overtime pay, and the union are satisfied,' said Dick.

'Thank God for that. Now I get to meet Bernard Scheller – we were going to have to send him to another hotel if the worst had happened!'

'Bernard who?'

'Bernard Scheller! Oh, Dick, you must have heard of him?' Jessica looked scandalised. 'Didn't you see *Beneath the Shadow* or *Ring of Light*? He composed the theme music for them, and masses of other films as well.'

Dick shrugged. 'Never heard of him, but I'm not a great one for music, myself. So, what's he doing staying here?'

Jessica gave a little wriggle of excitement. 'He's flying in from Boston, and while he's in London he's giving a concert at the Albert Hall. Mr Wolfson has asked me to look after him and see that he has everything he wants.'

'Oh, yes?' Dick grinned, his tone full of innuendo.

'Don't be silly! He's at least a hundred and three,' she giggled. 'He's been composing and conducting for *years*.'

'Well, I'd wear two pairs of tights when you meet him if I were you. I've heard all about these composer chaps.'

'Dick, you're disgusting!' shrieked Jessica. She grabbed a sheet of paper from her desk and, screwing it into a ball, threw it at him. Dick, laughing loudly, ducked and shadow boxed. Relief at hearing the strike had been averted made them feel quite childishly light-hearted, and they were still playing about when the door opened and Anne came into Jessica's office, her lips tight with disapproval.

'I came to tell you the strike's officially off,' she said in a schoolmistressy way.

Jessica and Dick tried to smother their laughter.

'W . . . we know,' spluttered Jessica.

Anne drew herself up and spoke pettishly. 'Then some of us can get on with our work, can't we?'

'Oh, yes, that's right,' agreed Dick, pretending to be contrite. 'Now I don't have to be chief washer-upper in the kitchens, I'd better get back to the boring things of life!'

'And *she* . . .' muttered Jessica under her breath as she watched Anne depart ' . . . is a calamity looking for a disaster!'

'But the big white chief must think a lot of her,' observed Dick. 'I heard she'd been given a rise . . . and a dress allowance.'

Jessica smiled sweetly at him. 'Really? I wonder what she spends it on?'

Two days later, Jessica was down in the lobby by twenty past eight to meet Bernard Scheller. Dressed in a chic little dark blue suit with navy tights and high-heeled navy shoes, she'd done her makeup with extra special care that morning, and for once her topknot was smoothly and securely fixed. Taking a seat among the oasis of tall plants, from where she could watch the entrance, she longed for a cup of strong coffee. Room service didn't apply where living-in staff were concerned and she usually had coffee and croissants at her desk, but today that would have to wait. Tapping her foot nervously, she kept her eyes on the revolving glass doors, so that as soon as the car appeared she could alert reception to the great composer's arrival.

At this hour the lobby was still and empty; the white marble floor gleaming like an ice-rink, the towering arrangement of fresh flowers on the centre table the only touch of colour amid the elegant grey decor. It would be a different scene within an hour. Stacks of luggage would be coming and going, as guests departed or checked out, the air would be filled with foreign accents, all the phones at reception would be ringing and there would be a general hurrying to and fro.

At that moment the smooth lines of a Silver Cloud Rolls-Royce glided up to the main entrance and a chauffeur in grey uniform jumped out to open the passenger door.

It was Jessica's first glimpse of Bernard Scheller. As he got out of the car and hurried through the revolving glass doors, she had an impression of a tall man, immensely broad-shouldered, exuding charisma and a sense of power that made her falter momentarily before she went forward to greet him. He looked younger than in his photographs, with a lean hawk-like face and a mane of hair greying at the temples. What struck her most were his eyes. Slightly hooded, they were the most incredible shade of dusky dark blue, like a twilit sky.

Stepping forward, she extended her hand. 'Good morning, Mr Scheller. I'm Jessica McCann, Director of Sales. Welcome to the Royal Westminster.' It was

229

her usual greeting, an automatic patter that came to her without thinking, but this morning she wasn't even aware she was speaking. Bernard Scheller's eyes seemed to be catching hold of her senses, paralysing her, as she stood looking up at him.

'Good morning,' he replied courteously, without smiling.

Porters were rushing out to the car to unload his luggage and the receptionist was poised, alert, an ingratiating smile on his face.

'What can I get you to drink, Mr Scheller, while we check you in?' Jessica asked, as she led him over to the desk. 'Coffee, tea, perhaps a Bucks Fizz?' She was aware of him handing over his American passport and being given a registration form to fill in.

'I'll have herb tea, please.'

Jessica signalled to a hovering waiter, seated Mr Scheller at a nearby table so he could write in more comfort, and discreetly and without fuss arranged for the porter to take his luggage up to the Roxborough Suite where she had already ordered champagne, a bowl of exotic fruit and a large box of liqueur chocolates to be placed, with the compliments of Kenneth Wolfson. Bernard Scheller was to be given the VIP treatment for the duration of his stay, and she was determined nothing would go wrong.

Madeleine and Carl arrived at 'Highwinds', Oyster Bay, Long Island, late on Friday evening. The white weatherboard house, with its verandah and wooden steps down to the beach, had belonged to the Shearman family for many years, and it was here that

230

Madeleine had spent weekends and holidays when she was a child. A resident housekeeper kept the place in order, with the help of a gardener, so that at any time either Jake, or Carl and Madeleine, could announce their impending arrival and everything would be in readiness for them.

Madeleine went out on to the verandah as soon as they arrived. Long Island Sound lay quiet and peaceful, the waters hardly seeming to move, the last light of day descending gently on Locust Valley and Bayville. It was her favourite view; always the same, always there. Carl came out to join her, his hands in the pockets of his cream linen trousers, his attitude one of forced casualness.

'Can I get you a drink or anything, honey?' he asked.

Madeleine turned to smile at him. She'd been looking forward to this weekend ever since he'd suggested it, and she was determined not to mention her mother, or Milton Manor, or any of the things that had been preying on her mind lately. Carl seemed to have worries of his own and looked deeply strained. She made up her mind that these precious two days together, on their own, were going to be perfect.

'A nightcap might be nice,' she replied softly, 'before we go to bed.'

Carl looked out to sea, nodded silently, then went back into the house to fix their drinks. When he came back, Madeleine drew him down on to a swing sofa, and slipped her hand into his.

'This is the life, isn't it?' she murmured with a contented smile.

'Ummm. We should come here more often,' Carl replied, gazing out to sea.

They sat in companionable silence until he rose slowly and stretched. 'I think I'll go for a short walk,' he said, and she thought he sounded awkward, as if he felt guilty at not inviting her to join him.

'Okay, sweetheart,' she replied mildly. 'I'll have a long lazy bath . . . and then we can go to bed when you come back, can't we?' Madeleine reached out to catch his hand and press it to her cheek.

'Sure, honey.'

'Will you be able to see? It's almost dark . . . don't go falling into the sea!'

Carl gave a little laugh. 'No chance of that. I won't be long.'

Madeleine watched him go, longing for him filling her heart. If anything were to happen to him! She dismissed the fanciful thought, banishing it because she could not bear even to contemplate a life without Carl and his love. He filled her life in every way; even the success of her painting was due to his reassurance and support. She thanked God, with every fibre of her being, that she never had to worry about him cheating on her. In a day and age when philandering husbands were looked upon as the norm, she counted herself as one of the luckiest women in the world because Carl had always been faithful to her.

A cold shimmering dusk hung like a grey veil over Oyster Bay as Carl walked slowly by the water's edge. He'd taken off his shoes and the sand oozed spongily between his bare toes. The breeze ruffled his hair. He'd had to get away from Madeleine for a little while, the feverish torment of his mind making it difficult for him to act naturally with her. One word hung in the air before him: regret. It ate into his mind, night and day, driving him crazy. Regret . . . regret . . . He kicked savagely at a stone, hurting his toe, almost rejoicing because it was another type of pain. How could he have let himself be seduced by Kimberley? It was unthinkable. Unbelievable. He licked his lips and tasted the salty air on his mouth; salty as the tears he could not shed. In one wild unguarded moment, he'd ruined his life.

The thought was so shattering he paused and turned to look to the horizon with unseeing eyes. Even if Madeleine never found out, even if he and Kimberley got away with embezzling Hank Pugsley's money, he'd ruined his life because he'd let himself down. That was as bad as betraying Madeleine, Jake and the bank. He'd done something that could produce only self-loathing, and for the rest of his life he would be treading a knife's edge until . . . until when? Until Kimberley had stolen enough money? Until Hank or the Central Manhattan Bank found out?

As he stood there, the waves spending themselves in lacy frills about his ankles, and the darkness closing in around him, he almost wished he could step forward into the sea and keep walking, the waters getting deeper . . . He could feel the waves closing over his head, pressing down on him, filling his lungs, while a heavy blackness bore him away into oblivion.

With a strangled cry of anguish, Carl turned and started walking back to 'Highwinds'.

* * *

Madeleine was sitting up in bed, reading, when he got back.

'Had a nice walk?'

'Great!' He tried to keep his voice light and steady. 'You should have come too, lazybones.'

Madeleine laughed. 'Lazybones yourself. I bet you I'll beat you at tennis tomorrow.'

'You're on.'

'Carl . . .' She reached out to him, her eyes tender and her mouth soft. A moment later he was in her arms, and they were holding each other close. 'You smell wonderful,' she murmured, pressing her face against his, 'like the seashore.' She trailed her fingers through his hair, closing her eyes, so all her other senses were aware of him.

'My love . . .' The words were wrenched from his throat, as he started to take off her nightdress. 'My darling love.' At last she lay naked on the coverlet, her smooth curves catching the light, her breasts twin pinnacles and her hair a cloud of blackness on the pillow. Carl thought he had never seen anything more beautiful.

Madeleine clung to him, responding and wondering why there was such heartbreaking intensity in his movements and pain in his face. For once he was rising to an early climax, as if unable to control himself, and there was desperation in his manner, too. Madeleine decided not to try and ride the same wave of passion as Carl. Although deep, her arousal did not match his, and so tonight she decided that she would give of herself only for his pleasure. Sometimes it happened like that and she didn't mind, for the mental satisfaction she derived from making him happy was at times almost as joyous as reaching her own physical release.

Holding him in her arms, blending and shaping her body to his frantic one, she felt as old as womanhood itself; as old as the earth or the sea that lapped on the shore, and as old as the moon that cast a silvery glow on the sands. She felt like a mother, comforting her troubled child, holding him safe within the circle of her love. But then Carl climaxed with such violence that he bucked and reared his head as he plunged deeper into her hot wetness, crying out her name. Madeleine knew suddenly, instinctively, that something was dreadfully wrong.

Chapter Nine

'Is there anything else you want, Mr Scheller?' Jessica asked, sitting perched on a chair in his suite, a notepad on her knee. 'I've made all the arrangements for your press conference in the Armitage Suite tomorrow morning at nine-thirty, and I've ordered a car to take you to your rehearsals after that.'

Bernard Scheller had been staying at the Royal Westminster for three days and as Kenneth Wolfson had warned her, he was a demanding guest.

'I told you I'd invited some friends over for drinks this evening, didn't I?' he asked, in his faintly mid-European accent.

'Sixteen guests at seven o'clock, for champagne, up here in your suite,' Jessica replied immediately without having to consult her notes. 'And you would like the chef to make some phyllo pastry parcels filled with a hot chilli mixture, and also some grilled baby lobster claws and a large dish of crudités.'

Bernard nodded, his expression, as always, serious. He was a man with a permanently guarded manner, a barrier to protect himself from the adulation of the general public, who flocked round him in sycophantic adoration and would have bled him dry if he'd allowed them to. Only after three days was he becoming relaxed with Jessica, whose manner was so utterly professional.

'We'd better have some whisky as well,' he observed. 'Not everyone likes champagne.'

'Right.' Jessica made a note on her pad. Bernard intrigued her, although nothing was going to induce her to reveal her curiosity. All she knew about him was that he was Austrian by birth, and that he'd studied at the Curtis Institute in America before going on to become a world famous composer and conductor with the Boston Symphony Orchestra. That much she had gleaned by reading a short biography of his life on the back of a record sleeve. It had gone on to say he was a first rate pianist as well, and had made many television appearances and recordings with the New York Philharmonic and Symphony Orchestras as well as the Vienna Philharmonic Orchestra.

Bernard passed a weary hand over his hooded eyes, and let out a great sigh. 'God, I'm tired. This touring is too much.'

'Where will you be going this year?' asked Jessica, a hint of sympathy in her voice.

Bernard shrugged. 'Milan, Tokyo, Moscow, Sydney . . . God knows. I shall be flying to a dozen capitals within the next few months.'

'That must be very unsettling.'

He raised his thick dark brows. 'Unsettling, but I'm afraid very necessary. When I am in Boston in two weeks' time I have a big engagement and it will be an important concert. The President and his wife are flying in for it and the evening is going to be relayed live on television. And so it goes on . . .' he added, spreading his hands expressively. 'Month after month I tour around the world. It is important to my career.'

'And where is your home? Where do you go between tours?' asked Jessica, fascinated.

Bernard's expression changed, grew softer and more relaxed. 'I have a house in Sardinia. Ah, there I find peace and quiet. That is where I do my composing. It is so wonderful, after months and months of travelling and living out of suitcases, always being on show . . . to live in a swim suit and feel the freedom of my own house! To be near to nature is necessary for my creative powers. I go to Sardinia to re-charge my batteries and cleanse myself from the pollution of city life.'

Jessica nodded, impressed. Beneath the superficial glitter that surrounded him, Bernard was obviously a very sincere person, and she liked the unaffected way in which he spoke. Here was somebody, she told herself, who had not let success and fame go to his head.

'Can I ask you one more thing?' she heard Bernard say as she prepared to go back to her office. Jessica's heart sank. It was all very well being helpful and seeing that, as a VIP in the hotel, he was being looked after. But she had a mountain of work on her desk, and there was no doubt about it – Bernard Scheller was time-consuming!

'Yes, of course,' she said brightly. 'What can I do for you?'

His reply took her completely by surprise. 'I'd like you to have dinner with me, after my guests have gone tonight?'

Jessica looked at him and found herself impaled on a pair of twilight blue eyes that were looking intently at her.

She flushed. 'That's very kind, but I'm on duty,' she said, suddenly embarrassed, while her mind reeled, wondering why he should want to have dinner with her.

Bernard shrugged. 'So what? Presumably you've got to eat, so why can't you eat with me downstairs in La Fantaisie?'

'Well . . . yes,' she floundered.

A glimmer of amusement showed in his eyes. 'Then that is settled, and I hope you'll join my other friends for drinks up here first?'

'Thank you.' A sudden thought occurred to her. 'How many shall I book the table for?'

His look was penetrating, and for the first time since she'd met him the corners of his mouth quirked up at the corners in a rather attractive fashion. 'For two,' he said smoothly. 'Just you and me.'

For some unaccountable reason, her heart started hammering in her chest.

She dressed with care that evening, up in the little hotel room that was 'home' to her now. When she entered Bernard's suite, he greeted her with an appreciative expression before introducing her to his friends. Jessica glanced round at the assembled company, and knew that Anne Butler would have killed to be present tonight. There was a famous television presenter, a bestselling author, a well-known Hollywood film producer and a man-eating actress in a fake snakeskin dress that plunged to her navel. Standing by the bar, a celebrated journalist and the chairman of a large newspaper group were demolishing a plate of canapés, proving her point that the richer people were, the greedier they became. In her time at the Royal Westminster, she'd seen whole buffets, piled high with food, stripped bare in minutes by a group of millionaires who acted as if they hadn't eaten for months.

More people were arriving and Bernard was introducing her as 'My friend, Jessica McCann', which she found very gratifying. He could so easily have referred to her as the hotel's Sales Director. The women guests were kissing Bernard on both cheeks and the men were giving him bear hugs and slapping him on the back. It made Jessica realise what a popular man he was. Sipping champagne she mingled happily, aware that the other guests were wondering where she fitted into Bernard's life. She could see the speculation in their eyes, hear their curiosity as they asked how long she'd known the great man.

'You're English, aren't you?' asked a German industrialist's wife. She made it sound like an accusation.

Jessica opened her blue doll-like eyes very wide as she smiled back innocently. 'No, I'm not,' she replied.

'No?' The woman's drop emerald earrings wagged aggressively. 'Then what are you?' she added rudely.

'I'm Scottish,' Jessica smiled sweetly. 'The McCanns come from Ayrshire.' She turned to face a scruffy-looking young man in black leather, a straggle of greasy hair hanging to his shoulders. Jessica thought with amusement of what must have passed through the head of the commissionaire

241

downstairs when he saw this apparition coming through the revolving doors.

'Good evening,' she said, hoping to make him feel at home. 'My name's Jessica McCann. What's yours?'

'Ignacio Herrera,' he replied shyly.

'Of course!' Jessica felt herself blushing. He was the most famous flute player in the world, even more famous than Bernard Scheller. 'What brings you to London?' she asked, feeling weak. I mean, she thought to herself, there are VIPs and VIPs and this is all too rich a mixture, even for me. I prefer to be behind a desk doing the administration, not having to meet all these living legends.

'I'm playing in Bernard's concert at the Albert Hall,' Ignacio replied. 'Are you coming?'

'Of course she's coming to the concert!' Bernard butted in, as he joined them, flinging an arm round Ignacio's shoulders. 'You are coming, aren't you? I have a ticket for you,' he added, looking questioningly at Jessica.

'If I can get time off, I'd love to,' she replied, thrilled.

'Then it is settled!' Bernard moved on, his charismatic personality filling the room as he talked to friends like a king to his courtiers.

At last the party was over, and everyone had departed in merry groups, leaving Jessica and Bernard on their own in a suddenly silent suite. It was at that moment that she realised he was really a deeply lonely man. She could sense it in the lines of his serious face and in the droop of his broad shoulders; like a lot of famous people, she realised intuitively, he had a thousand acquaintances but few real friends, and it was obvious he couldn't bear to be on his own. He was pottering disconsolately around the room now, straightening things that had already been straightened by the waiters, fiddling with the empty glass in his hand.

'Our table will be ready – would you like to go down to the restaurant now?' Jessica suggested with a sudden warmth born of secret sympathy for this great man who was basically so alone.

'Yes. Yes, that would be good,' he replied, glancing over at her.

In the muted lighting and hushed atmosphere of La Fantaisie, they were shown to a table in an alcove, intimately tucked away from the mêlée of other diners, discreetly placed so they could see but not be seen. He took control of the menu and wine list, and Jessica let him. It was rather nice for once not to have to be in charge.

'That was a good party,' Jessica remarked, in an effort to make small talk. 'I think everyone enjoyed themselves.'

'I hope so.' Bernard seemed steeped in gloom. 'Too many of them are sycophantic, though. Forgive my language, but they are what we call Star-Fuckers.'

Jessica nodded, understanding him. 'But you must have a lot of real friends,' she observed.

'From the early days . . . yes, but when you get to my age and you are never in one place for long, it gets harder to make new friends. I see my real friends from time to time, but we are all working hard – you know

243

how it is.' His hooded eyes gazed sadly at the other diners, mostly couples. 'Sometimes one has the feeling,' he added, 'that everyone has someone, except oneself.'

Jessica's heart went out to this great but lonely man, who gave so much pleasure to others but who seemed so deeply isolated within himself. As if he could read her thoughts, he spoke again.

'It's the loneliness that I don't like,' she heard him say. 'I have no wife now, you know. My marriage ended in divorce, and I find it very difficult having no one to share my life with.'

It flashed through Jessica's mind that she'd heard that line before and that it was a very old one, but on this occasion she couldn't help but be touched by his words. Suddenly he smiled, the twilight blue eyes lighting up unexpectedly.

'Corny, eh?' he mocked in a self-deprecating tone. 'I know. The corniest story in the world but it just happens to be true. My existence is so nomadic it's impossible to form permanent relationships, but like all men I need someone by my side; someone to love.' He grew serious again. He glanced at her left hand. 'You're not married, I see!'

Jessica tried to give a light laugh, but it didn't quite come off. 'Not in this job, I'm not! No husband would stand for the hours or the fact I now have to live in the hotel.' For a moment a shadow crossed her face as she thought of Andrew. He certainly hadn't been prepared to stand for it.

Bernard sighed deeply. 'You must be lonely too, sometimes?'

Jessica shrugged, realising she was getting into deep waters.

'I don't have the time,' she lied. 'The days go so fast.'

An uneasy silence fell between them as the waiter served their first course of Consommé Fedora. Bernard was the first to speak again.

'Do you think we could console each other a little? Ever since I met you I've been fascinated by you . . .'

Jessica broke off his proposal by sitting very upright and shooting him a sharp look. 'Certainly not!' Her expression was deeply offended.

'Please don't get me wrong,' Bernard protested, looking distressed. 'I didn't mean, can I whisk you up to my suite after dinner and take you to bed! What sort of a man do you think I am?'

Jessica was beginning to wonder. So far the script for the evening was following the lines of a cheap romantic novel. 'Powerful, rich celebrity whisks hotel sales director off her feet and tries to carry her off to far lands.'

'I don't know what sort of a man you are, Mr Scheller, and I don't propose to find out,' she said evenly. 'I'm here to do my job of seeing you are properly looked after in the hotel. Nothing more.'

'Oh, Jessica, I understand. I've expressed myself badly.' He ran a hand across his forehead in a gesture of distress. You sure have, she thought crisply.

'Of course I fancy you,' he continued. 'I wouldn't be a normal man if I didn't, but there is something more.' His hooded eyes held hers for a moment. 'I think I'm falling in love with you,' he said slowly.

'Well, that's not very sensible. You'll be gone in a week and you'll never see me again.' Her voice rose, half joking, half serious, as she tried to control the sudden trembling of her limbs.

'I know.' He looked down at his plate. 'But do me one favour, please. Just one thing. You will come to my concert, won't you? I'll give you a ticket and you must come to the party afterwards. Please?'

Jessica spoke evenly. 'I'd like that very much. Thank you.'

'Good.' Bernard raised his wine glass and toasted her. 'Here's to your coming to my concert.'

'Here's to your concert,' she said pointedly.

The letter arrived by the morning post, propped up against the silver coffee-pot on the breakfast tray Teresa carried into Madeleine and Carl's bedroom. Carl was already in the shower, but Madeleine, relaxed after their weekend at Oyster Bay, still lay in bed, in no hurry to get up. The weekend seemed to have done Carl good, she thought as she reached lazily for the letter. The tension of the first night, when he'd made love to her so frenziedly, seemed to have passed by the next morning, and as they swam and played tennis and listened to music in the evenings, watching the changing moods of the sea from the verandah, he'd seemed to unwind. And there was something else: he'd never been so loving and devoted. It reminded her of the days when they'd just married, only this was better. There seemed to be a greater depth to Carl's feelings as he talked to her, and his love-making had been ardent, as if he couldn't do enough to show her how much he loved her. It was the difference, she thought, between the passion of new love, which always holds an element of selfishness, and the selfless giving of a love that is deeply consolidated, full of understanding and a special knowing. Madeleine smiled contentedly to herself, still basking in the after-glow of their weekend together. With Carl's love to support her, she knew she could handle whatever the future might hold.

Madeleine looked at the letter more closely, realising it was from Mr Marks, the solicitor from Okehampton. Pouring herself some coffee, she shrugged. The weekend had taught her that the most important thing was her marriage, and if that was all right, the mystery surrounding her mother was of little importance by comparison. Ripping open the envelope, she took out the typed letter.

It was, of course, couched in legal jargon, a lot of which she didn't understand. For example Mr Marks had written: 'The said Mrs Madeleine Elizabeth Delaney, née Shearman, must prove her mother's death, as her claim to the inheritance is *per stirpes*.' What the hell did that mean?

'Carl,' Madeleine called out, and at that moment he came back into the bedroom, his wet blond hair the colour of tawny sand, a blue towelling robe round his shoulders.

'Carl, what does *per stirpes* mean? It sounds like a dreadful disease!'

He raised his eyebrows and then caught sight of the letter in her hand.

'It means progenitor of family . . . an ancestor.'

'Ah!' Madeleine glanced back at the letter. 'The solicitor says I've got to apply for a court order of presumption of death, "see Nc Probate Rule 60 (1)" – oh, for goodness sake, why can't he write in layman's language – and that "an order for leave to swear to the death will be made by a registrar of the Principal Registry, under section one of the Supreme Court Act of 1981." Carl, I don't understand a word of this! What am I supposed to do?'

'Let me see.' Carl sat down on the edge of the bed, and skimmed through the letter. 'Nothing for the moment, darling. Mr Marks says he will keep you informed, so it looks as if he can make the claim on your behalf.'

Madeleine sank back against the pillows, relieved. 'Thank God for that. The last thing I want to do is have to go back to England. I suppose I can't sell Milton Manor meanwhile?'

'I'm afraid not.'

'What a nuisance. Andrew – you know, Jessica's ex-boyfriend – called me on Friday to say he thought he had a buyer.'

Carl rose and started dressing. As she watched him, Madeleine could see he was getting tense again. Tight-lipped and silent, he was selecting a tie from the closet, choosing a pair of cuff-links from the little alligator jewel case she'd given him, and deciding which shoes to wear.

'Have you got a very busy day ahead of you?' she asked gently. She'd have to talk to Jake soon, if pressure of work was having this effect on Carl. Although he seemed in a hurry to get to the bank she could also

248

detect a hint of dread in his attitude, and that was uncharacteristic of him. Usually he was brimming with enthusiasm about his work. Suddenly the weekend seemed a long time ago.

'No busier than usual,' he said, almost coldly.

A few minutes later he was gone, his breakfast almost untouched, the strain showing in his eyes as he bent to peck Madeleine on the cheek.

Folding up Mr Marks' letter and putting it back in its envelope, Madeleine decided to drop into the bank at lunch-time and show it to Jake. If only she could get him to talk, just give her a few details like the date of her mother's death, or whether it took place in Devon or in London, she might be able to stop what was obviously going to be a long drawn-out case. She also made up her mind to tell him that Carl was working too hard.

At ten o'clock she had a meeting with her frame maker, the man who could enhance or ruin the look of one of her portraits by producing something too heavy or too light, the wrong shade or the wrong texture. The importance of having exactly the right frame was paramount. Madeleine and Leo Parramon would spend hours with sections of planed or carved wood, plaster casts, different shades of paint from soft grey to dull gilt, and often fabric to stretch tightly over the wood. Sometimes, of course, she would pick up antique frames in Christies or Sotheby's, rich ornate gilt affairs with scrolls and twirls and baroque swags, suitable for an old-fashioned formal study. Madeleine herself preferred to get Leo to make more modern frames. His most revolutionary were made of lucite, designed so cleverly that they glittered like clear water with shards of brilliant light filtering through them.

'What shall we do with Dwight Lasmo?' she asked, laughing, as she and Leo sat on one of the sofas in her studio and looked at the finished portrait of the oil baron. Leo sat with a large pad on his knee, making little sketches, his eyes narrowed and his head on one side.

'You've used a lot of dark, rich tones,' he noted. 'Browns, greens, blacks – what sort of room is he going to hang it in?'

'The boardroom of Phoenix Oil. It's a dark panelled room, with ceiling lights and dreary furnishings. Gilt would look hideous. How about ebony?'

Leo, bearded and arty-looking, raised his brows, impressed. 'Ebony's not a bad idea,' he agreed. 'With maybe a narrow fillet of bronze?'

'I like it!' Madeleine exclaimed.

'Okay. Now what else needs framing?' He turned to several more finished canvases propped around the studio.

They worked together for a couple of hours, designing between them a variety of frames for all her most recent works.

'I suppose you want most of these by yesterday?' Leo asked, as he rose at last to go.

Madeleine laughed. 'What's wrong with the day before? Seriously, Leo, the only one that's urgent is Dwight Lasmo's. I've promised him he can have it in a couple of weeks.'

Leo groaned. 'A couple of weeks, she says! No,

there's no hurry, Leo! A couple of weeks will do just fine!' He leaned forward and kissed her on the cheeks. 'You're a slave-driver, Madeleine. Okay, a couple of weeks it will be. I'll get all the others to you as soon as I can.'

'Got all the dimensions?' she called after him as he hurried off down the street.

'What do you take me for? A fool?' he bantered back.

Madeleine grinned after him. Leo was a great guy and a good friend. Whatever happened, she knew he'd deliver on time. Then she glanced at her watch. If she was going to catch Jake before he went out to lunch, she'd better hurry over to Wall Street right away.

The meeting to discuss the sixty million dollar loan to the new aircraft factory in Ireland was drawing to an end at last. Jake, seated at the head of the table in the boardroom of the Central Manhattan Bank, smiled at the directors, squared up the papers before him and spoke.

'Then we're agreed to lend them the money, on the terms we've discussed?' Jake asked.

They had spent over an hour going over all the figures, and Carl, his head aching, longed to get back to his office. Another authorisation from Hank Pugsley had arrived that morning, asking for three hundred and twenty-one thousand dollars to be transferred from Brandt's Motors, to Michaux Internationale in Switzerland, and he knew Kimberley was aware of the fact. At five o'clock she'd be going down to the computer room again, to divert the money to her own Swiss account, and he felt as if his head was going to split with anxiety.

Carl heard the other directors agreeing to Jake's proposal, and the decision to lend the money was finalised.

Business over, everyone rose, gathered up their papers and left the boardroom. Carl was just turning to go himself when Jake called out to him.

'Carl, can you spare me a moment? I'd like to have a word with you.'

'Sure.' He turned to look at his father-in-law, his heart skipping a beat. 'What can I do for you?'

'I've got to lunch now with the president of Citi-Telecom, but I'd like to discuss the transfer of money to that car plant in Italy. I'm not happy with the arrangements at the moment. Shall we say three o'clock in my office?'

A wash of relief swept over Carl. God, he thought, if I don't get a grip on myself I'm going to be flipping every time any little thing comes up.

'Fine, Jake,' he replied, trying to keep his voice steady. 'I'll be with you at three.'

As Carl turned to leave, he caught Jake's eye and gave a forced smile. Was Jake watching him strangely? He couldn't be sure, but the feeling of uneasiness remained as he returned to his own office.

Kimberley came up the steel and lucite escalator from the main lobby, where she'd been dealing with a query, and found Carl had just returned from the board meeting. Together they entered his office. She immediately shut the communicating door to her office, so they could not be overheard.

'Everything all right?' Kimberley asked immediately.

'So far,' Carl replied tensely.

'Right. I'll go back to my apartment in my lunch break and bring back the copy of the computer tape so I can put the transaction through, as usual, when everyone's gone home.'

Carl groaned. 'Can't you give it a miss this time?'

'Oh, for Christ's sake!' Kimberley's voice was low and impatient. 'You only have to counter-sign Hank's transfer and put it through the normal channels. I had to take the risk of making a copy of the computer tape; you only had to sneak it out of Jake's office for an hour! And I have to go down to the computer room, switch the tapes over and put through the transactions, while you sit up here on your arse, twiddling your fucking fingers!' she added coarsely. 'I can't see what you've got to panic about!'

Carl dropped heavily into the chair behind his desk, his face a grey mask of anxiety. 'Hank Pugsley's going to find out, sooner or later, I'm sure. The man would be a fool if he didn't notice hundreds of thousands of dollars were missing from his account.'

'How often do we have to go through this, Carl? I've told you Hank doesn't get sent bank statements from Switzerland. He's never going to know his money's missing until he goes over there to get it. By that time, I will have got as much as I want. We've nothing to fear from Hank.' Kimberley perched on the edge of his desk in a familiar fashion, her long black nylon clad legs crossed. 'Anyway,' she continued, 'you know as well as I do that Hank can't do anything about it, even when he does find out. He's not going to want to go to prison for tax evasion! There's no way he'll squeal.'

Carl looked at her with loathing and fear. He'd done everything he could think of to put an end to her scheming, including telling her to keep all the money she'd stolen, if only she'd stop now; but it was no use. Yet he had to have one more try.

'You've got over a million dollars from Hank's account already. Isn't that enough? Do *you* want to go to prison, when we could stop right now and no one would be any the wiser?' Carl demanded. 'Why push your luck?'

Kimberley looked at him for a moment, her grey eyes cold and reptilian, her red hair afire from the sunlight that streamed in through the windows. Then she laughed in his face, a laugh that sent a shudder through him.

'Quit now?' she mocked. 'You're out to lunch! This is the neatest little scam ever thought up and if you'll only quit panicking we'll end up with millions.'

Carl closed his eyes as the inevitable stared him in the face. Kimberley had no intention of quitting and she was going to drag him along with her.

'Christ, I wish I'd never set eyes on you,' he burst out hoarsely.

'You should have thought of that before you fucked me!' she shot back venomously. 'You couldn't get enough of me in the beginning, could you? You were begging for it . . . in the shower . . .

back at my apartment. You were quite happy to get involved with me then and have your fun! But of course it's different now, isn't it? You're having to pay the price for your little fling and so you want out. Well, no chance, Buster, we're in this together, and we're going to go on until I say so.' Kimberley raised her head defiantly, her eyes never leaving his face.

Carl jumped to his feet, enraged. 'I'd let you damn well broadcast that tape of us in bed, if it wasn't for my wife,' he stormed. 'There's only one reason why I'm doing this: to protect her. I care for her more than anything else in the world – more than my job, more than what Jake will do to me if he finds out, more than *anything*. That's the only goddamn reason I'm letting myself be blackmailed. Otherwise I'd go straight to the police.'

'Too late for that now,' Kimberley retorted sardonically. 'You're as implicated as I am, so we'd go down together. I knew you'd never go to the police, not even at the beginning. You're too interested in protecting yourself, so don't give me that trash about your wife.'

Carl spun on her, his fists clenched, his eyes bulging with rage. 'Get out of my office!' he cried harshly.

Kimberley shrugged. 'I'm going anyway. Have you forgotten we've got another of Hank's transfers to put through? I'm going back to my apartment now to pick up the tape.' She strode purposefully to the door that led to her office, where she collected her handbag. Then she went down the elevator to the lobby. Once in Wall Street, she hailed a passing cab and gave the driver her address.

A minute later Carl left his office too; if he didn't

get out of the building for a short while, something in his head was going to explode. Quietly, he shut the door behind him.

His office remained still and empty for a few minutes longer, the atmosphere still charged with tension, the sun laying a warm band of light across Carl's desk. The phone rang several times, but then cut off as there was no one to answer it. Dust motes in the still air hovered uncertainly. Then the door leading to Carl's washroom opened slowly and silently, and, half fainting and holding on to the wall for support, Madeleine emerged.

When Jessica arrived at the Royal Albert Hall, the vast domed building was already swarming with people, blocking the traffic with their cars, pushing their way into the many entrances round the circumference of the building, and standing in groups waiting for friends. Large posters on the front hoardings announced, 'Bernard Scheller in concert, conducting the Royal Philharmonic Orchestra!' and across them, stickers announcing SOLD OUT.

Jessica, in a pale yellow evening dress, her golden hair loose down her back, joined the crowds, swept along by the atmosphere of excitement. This was Bernard Scheller's second London concert in ten years and over five thousand people of all ages were cramming into the Hall to hear his music. In the vestibule, she joined a long line to buy a programme, listening to the snatches of conversation around her, suddenly feeling very proud that she actually knew him.

He had given her a front seat in one of the Grand Tier boxes. As she took her place, the view was breathtaking. She was surprised, although she'd been to the Albert Hall before, by the richness of its gilt baroque ornamentation and red plush drapes. Built on the lines of a Roman amphitheatre, thousands of people sat on rows of gilt chairs in the well of the hall, and in row upon row of raked seats which stretched up to the first tier of boxes. Three more tiers, like velvet-lined jewel cases, rose to the roof where those who could not afford expensive seats stood or walked around the circular gallery.

Tonight the place was packed, and there was a buzz of expectancy as people chatted in undertones or read their programmes. The orchestra were taking their seats now, under banks of brilliant lights that made their instruments shine brassily, and soon the air was filled with strange muted notes as they tuned up. A frisson of excitement ran, tingling, down Jessica's spine. She consulted her programme. The first item was the score Bernard had written for the award-winning film, *Silver Apples of the Moon*.

The audience seemed to be settling now as Jessica looked around, and the musicians seemed poised, ready to begin. At that moment a dazzling white spotlight pierced the semi-darkness, and Bernard Scheller strode forward from the wings. A tremendous roar of welcome erupted from the gallery to the pit so that the very building seemed to shudder.

Jessica's breath caught in her throat as Bernard surveyed the vast audience that stretched from his feet upwards to the gods, and then he bowed, his stage presence holding everyone's total attention. The power he exuded was like the sun bursting forth over a dark landscape, and his personality seemed to fill the hall as he held five thousand people in his thrall simply by standing there. And this is the man, she thought wryly, who confessed to being lonely.

The music started. Mesmerised, Jessica sat back and let it carry her on a journey of such exquisite pleasure that she forgot where she was. It transported her to forests, lushly carpeted by a mist of bluebells; to a meadow where wild poppies quivered in a summer's breeze; to a shoreline where jagged rocks glistened as waves came pounding in from some distant ocean; to a sunset that dipped away and faded with intolerable sadness, marking the end of a day, a year, a lifetime. The throbbing music soared with such unbearable sweetness that Jessica found herself aching, hurting, thrilling with indescribable emotions.

When Bernard Scheller laid down his baton, the tears were coursing down Jessica's cheeks.

The giant dome of the Albert Hall seemed to lift, the walls expand, the little lights in their silk shades shiver, as thunderous applause rocked the building. Jessica dabbed her eyes in embarrassment. The ovation lasted several minutes. Bernard acknowledged the acclaim, still immaculate in his white tie and tails. It seemed as if the audience would never stop clapping, but at last he picked up his baton and a hush descended as everyone settled down to listen again.

Jessica remained transfixed, marvelling at Bernard as he controlled this huge orchestra, bending it to his will, coaxing it, commanding it, ruling it with a power that was absolute. With strong hands beating a tempo and dark blue eyes flashing to and fro, he brought the music to life and took the audience with him in an unforgettable journey of sound.

When the concert finally ended in a tumultuous surge of applause, Jessica sat back, exhausted and drained. The music had moved her so deeply that as she made her way to the large reception room where the party was to be held, she felt as if she moved in a dream, languid with emotion, transported to another world.

The room was already full of people and she recognised several of them from the drinks party in Bernard's suite. The great man had not yet appeared, timing his entrance to the exact moment when he knew it would have the greatest impact. Jessica found herself, a glass of champagne in her hand, talking to an elderly couple who seemed to know him well; but all the time her eyes were straining to watch for his arrival, to see him face to face again, and marvel at his sheer genius.

At last he stood in the doorway, as perfectly dressed and groomed as if he were just setting off for his first engagement of the evening. His twilight blue eyes surveyed the crowded room with satisfaction. Instantly he was surrounded by a mob of well-wishers, kissing him, patting his shoulders, fawning over him in a wave of adulation. Jessica, holding back, watched as he slowly made a circuit of the room, edging foot by foot, as people gathered close, hanging on to his arm, eager for a word. He got to Jessica, gave her a brief smile and then was swept past her by a rush of new arrivals. A moment later he had gone, with only the top of his head visible as he was almost jostled to the far end of the room.

Jessica was filled with an unexpected feeling of deflation as she found herself standing alone in his wake, looking after him. It was as if she'd gained something marvellous from the night, but somehow lost it too as she watched his figure recede.

Madeleine's first instinct, almost animalistic in its desire to run away and hide, was to get to her studio as quickly as possible. Hurrying down to the lobby from Carl's office, hoping against hope she wouldn't bump into him or her father, she rushed into the street and managed to give the driver of the cab she hailed the address in Wooster Street, SoHo.

Shock stunned her senses. She couldn't even cry. Unawareness, borne of numbness, took hold of her and before she knew it they were outside her studio and the driver was hollering: 'That's three dollars-fifty.'

Dazed, she handed him a five dollar bill. 'Keep the change,' she mumbled, as she got out and fumbled for her keys.

All her brain could do was repeat over and over the things she'd heard Carl and Kimberley say. Surely this was a nightmare; surely she'd wake up in a moment, safe in bed encircled by Carl's arms, to find this whole thing was a bad dream! But what they had said to each other kept stabbing at her mind, indelibly committing itself to her memory.

Carl and Kimberley? It's impossible . . . it can't be true . . . As she sank, trembling, on to the studio sofa, every part of her cried out in rejection. And they were embezzling money from one of the Bank's clients! What was she going to do, say to Carl? The horror of what she had discovered sent her mind spinning and tumbling in fragmented directions, as she tried to grapple with a situation that an hour previously would have seemed utterly impossible. Carl and Kimberley? Madeleine rejected the thought violently, swerving away from it with revulsion. There must be a mistake . . . she couldn't have heard aright. Carl loved her, she knew it. He was honest, too; he'd never in a million years commit a felony . . . and yet with her own ears she had heard him discuss the money they were embezzling!

Then she recalled something else, something Carl had said: 'There's only one reason I'm doing this: to protect her'. Kimberley is blackmailing Carl, thought Madeleine. She's forcing him to steal, because if he doesn't . . . And then the tears sprang to her eyes and she rocked herself to and fro, hugging a cushion. Carl *did* love her. He was doing this only to protect his wife. Madeleine forced herself to concentrate on this because it was what mattered most. To protect her from finding out he'd been to bed with Kimberley, he'd allowed himself to be blackmailed. And then she remembered Carl saying, 'I care for her more than anything else in the world'. That was what she had to believe; that was what she had to hang on to if she was going to avoid falling apart.

Nevertheless, she was wracked with uncontrollable

sobbing for a love betrayed and a trust broken. She cried for a long time and then, dabbing her eyes, wished with all her heart she'd never gone to the bank today. When she'd arrived Jake's secretary had told her he was in a meeting, and so she'd gone along to see Carl, only to find his office empty. Thinking she'd freshen up in his washroom while she waited for him to come back, she suddenly heard angry voices: Carl's and Kimberley's.

Why hadn't she made her presence known then? Because, as she caught what they were saying, she'd become paralysed and gripped by a terrible fascination to hear more, and it was at that moment that she realised Carl was in very real danger. If this Hank Pugsley – she marvelled at herself for remembering the name – were to find out he was being robbed blind, the scandal involving the bank would rock New York and Carl would get a long prison sentence. Jake would be disgraced as well. The implications were too terrible to contemplate, thought Madeleine as she blew her nose and tried to pull herself together. Perhaps it was a blessing in disguise that she *had* gone to the bank after all.

Grief at Carl's unfaithfulness was swamped beneath anger towards the girl who could bring about his downfall, who had tempted him and led him into this mess. Revenge filled her heart now. She loved Carl and she would do anything to save their marriage.

Positive action was what was needed now, she told herself, as she rose from the sofa and went to make some coffee. Carl had got himself into this terrible mess and she didn't want to probe the whys and wherefores – she just wanted to get him out of it so that things could get back to normal, the way they'd been before. But paramount in her mind was another thought: Jake must never find out what had been going on, or he'd never trust Carl again.

Chapter Ten

'Jessica, have you checked this proof?' The Assistant General Manager stood over her desk, flapping a sheet of white paper before her.

Jessica glanced up nervously. Proofreading wasn't exactly her forte, but she'd pored over the wording of an invitation the hotel was sending out to ask people to a promotional breakfast party, and was sure it was all right.

'Yes, why? Is something wrong?' she asked.

'Thursday isn't spelt "Thirsday"!' Denis Powell said crossly.

Jessica clapped her hand to her cheek. 'Oh! My God, is that what it says? I think they employ complete idiots at that printing firm. Sorry, I'll change it.' She grabbed the proof from him and made the alteration with a red pen.

'You're sure everything else is okay? The new menus and wine lists?' Denis queried, his voice heavy with doubt.

Jessica flushed. This was the third mistake she'd made in two days and her self-confidence was shaken. Usually she was so careful about checking proofs; she'd never forgotten the disaster that had happened when she'd worked at the Wentworth Hotel, and the press office had passed a proof giving the wrong date.

Two hundred and fifty people had turned up a day early for a dinner-dance!

'Of course I've checked everything else,' she said brightly, 'but I'll go over it one more time, just to make sure.'

'Please do.'

When Denis left her office, she tried to concentrate on the latest sales figures before her, but the numerals jumped around the page and after a few minutes her concentration slid away and she found herself thinking of Bernard Scheller again. Ever since the night of the concert, that unforgettable figure standing on the podium, filling the Albert hall with the sound of his music, had been in her thoughts. Jessica hadn't seen him since that night, and now that the concert was over she doubted if she'd have to do anything more for him except to see him off when he left in two days' time. The thought filled her with unaccountable depression. Bernard had made a deep impression on her and, confused, she tried to analyse her feelings. One thing was certain, she'd never felt like this about Andrew. Theirs had been a gradual love, built initially on mutual tastes and a foundation of friendship. They had grown into love during the months before they started living together, so that it had seemed a natural thing to do. This obsession of hers with Bernard was something else. She felt as if he'd cast a spell over her.

This is crazy! she told herself, throwing her pen down on the desk with characteristic impatience. I don't even know Bernard. I don't know anything about him, except that his music thrills me to the core.

Somehow Jessica managed to get through her work that day without making any more mistakes. At six o'clock she was due to welcome another arriving VIP, a famous and aging film star called Lynette Herbert, who was in London to promote her biography. Just as Jessica was greeting her, she saw Bernard come out of the elevator and go into the bar. He was alone.

'Can I get you a glass of champagne while you check in, Miss Herbert?' Jessica asked, trying to keep an eye on the entrance to the bar and look after the guest at the same time.

'I never drink. That's why I've kept my looks,' Lynette Herbert replied, with an expansive smile.

Jessica smothered the amazement she felt at this elderly woman thinking she was still beautiful. She'd had so many face-lifts that her skin was stretched into a parchment mask, and her heavily mascaraed eyelashes made her eyes look like aspic-covered orbs in a nest of spiders. Laboriously, Lynette Herbert started filling in the registration form, her passport held tightly so that no one would see her date of birth.

Jessica tapped her foot, trying to curb her impatience, watching the bar entrance all the while. Bernard might come out at any minute and she was longing to see him again. She glanced at her watch. He'd only been in there about five minutes; if she got this bag of bones and silicone up to her suite quickly, Bernard might still be drinking when she got back.

'Let me take you up to your suite, Miss Herbert,' Jessica said pleasantly, when the last of the formalities had been completed at the reception desk.

Lynette Herbert wasn't to be hurried. When they

got to her first-floor suite she insisted on Jessica showing her how to work the remote control on the TV, how to dial for room service, and how to unlock the fridge. 'And remember to tell them,' Miss Herbert commanded in a reedy voice, 'that I only like Melbix toast for my breakfast.'

'I'm sure that can be arranged. Now, if you'll excuse me . . .' Jessica was practically hopping from one foot to the other in her urgent desire to get away. Bernard might have left the bar by now; he might even have left the hotel to go out to dinner.

'Can someone press my suit?' The aged voice was plaintive. 'I'm appearing on breakfast television tomorrow morning, and I must have my suit pressed.'

Swiftly, Jessica rushed to the bedside table and, picking up the receiver, dialled 9. 'Please send the ladies' maid to Room 101,' she said as soon as she got through, then hurried to the door, intent on escape. 'There'll be someone along in a moment to see to your suit, Miss Herbert, and if you want anything else just dial 5. Now if you'll excuse me, I have to get to a meeting.' Without waiting for a reply Jessica slipped out of the suite and ran down the corridor to the elevator.

Bernard Scheller was standing in the middle of the lobby, looking out through the revolving doors as if he were waiting for someone. Jessica gulped, and started walking across the lobby, trying to look casual.

'Oh, good evening!' she put on a surprised voice as soon as she got level with him. It suggested he was the last person on earth she expected to see at that moment. The dark blue eyes turned to look into hers and she could have sworn Bernard Scheller looked relieved.

'Hello, Jessica. I saw you here a few minutes ago, but you were with someone. I was looking for you.'

'Oh!' There was a whole gamut of emotions in the way Jessica said it. Then she added in a professional way: 'Is there anything I can get for you?'

'Maybe there is.' He regarded her seriously, his mouth unsmiling.

'Yes?'

'I'd like you to have a drink with me.' Bernard spoke slowly.

Jessica answered simply. 'Thank you. I'd like that.' Inside her something had begun to tremble.

'Let's go up to my suite, it's too noisy in the bar,' he said firmly.

'All right.' Well, why not? Jessica asked herself defensively. It's unlikely he wants to give me dictation or ask me to put a call through to Timbuktu, but what the hell! In her present restless mood, she felt a sudden need for adventure. Patting her pocket to make sure she had her bleeper with her in case she was needed urgently, she followed Bernard into the elevator.

The view from his suite was spectacular, and gave Jessica something inconsequential to chatter about. A few people on horseback were cantering along Rotten Row as the early evening sun filtered through the lush greenery of Hyde Park; mothers were gathering up their children to take them home, and a couple of boys were walking their dogs.

'What will you have to drink?' Bernard asked, cutting across Jessica's banalities about its being a nice evening.

'Vodka and tonic, please.'

Silence fell like a smothering blanket as he poured the drinks. Jessica shifted position nervously on the large white sofa.

Suddenly Bernard swung round and looked at her. 'I asked you to have a drink with me because I want to talk to you, Jessica.'

'Oh!' Again she packed a lot into the monosyllable.

'Is that all you can say . . . "Oh",' he mocked gently, and then he smiled, a smile of such rare warmth that his face lit up with an inner radiance.

'Well,' Jessica stumbled, confused, 'what do you want to talk to me about?'

'I wanted to tell you why I haven't seen you for the last couple of days.'

'I expect you've been busy!'

'No, Jessica, I have not been busy. I've been thinking. I've been trying to work out in my mind what I should do about you.'

Her hand began to shake at his directness. She was also amused. In this feminist age no Englishman would have dared to make such a remark. She regarded him silently with round blue eyes.

'Jessica . . .' Bernard reached for her hand and held it tightly in both of his. 'I know this sounds crazy because we've only known each other for such a short time, but I'm in love with you.' His voice was richly tender. 'I told you I was lonely, but that isn't my reason for wanting you now. Please believe me. I love

270

you, and I think you love me, although you may not yet realise it.'

'I – I do . . .' she stammered. 'Yes, I think I do.'

He stood, feet apart, a powerful bull of a man looking down at her with penetrating eyes. Then he leaned forward, took both her hands, and pulled her gently to her feet. A moment later they were in each other's arms, drawn together as if by a magnet. Jessica seemed to hear the clash of cymbals and the roar of drums in her ears. Bernard *was* his music; all the passion and the pathos, the exultation and the bitter sweetness, were what made up this incredible man. As he kissed her deeply, her senses swam and she felt almost faint.

'Bernard . . .' She gasped, looking up at him, the top of her head barely reaching his shoulder. She suddenly felt scared. Could she bear this much emotion? Dizzily, she leaned against him, trying to catch her breath, knowing that she had never felt like this before.

Bernard looked down at her with moist eyes and slowly started to undress her, stroking her breasts and hips and thighs as he did so with hands that were both strong and gentle. As if he were handling a precious instrument, he caressed her body, tuning it finely, preparing her for the moment when he would take her and possess her and make her his. Surrendering to the domination of Bernard's mouth and hands, Jessica found herself filled with physical rapture, as he had filled her soul with music on the night of the concert. When the pressure had built up in her so that she could bear it no longer she cried out for him, wanting

271

him with a desire that was consuming her senses.

Bernard entered her with a quick hot thrust, lifting her to greater heights of ecstasy than ever as he plunged wildly . . . until, like a searing, crashing crescendo, Jessica cried out as orgasm after orgasm convulsed her and sent her mind spinning off into space.

It was a week since Madeleine had overheard the conversation between Carl and Kimberley in his office, and it had been the most agonising week of her life. Carl still had no idea she knew anything. With a superhuman effort, explaining away her distracted manner by saying she'd caught a form of flu that was going around, Madeleine struggled through each day, spending most of her time at the studio. At night, she went to bed early, complaining of headaches and tiredness, and so far Carl believed her.

How long she could keep this up she had no idea. All she knew, in a kind of blind terrified way, was that she didn't want Carl to find out she'd discovered what was going on; not until she'd decided what to do, and how to do it.

A plan was taking shape in Madeleine's head and, amazed by her own lust for revenge on Kimberley, she lay awake in bed at night long after Carl had fallen asleep, plotting just when she'd make the first move. It would have to be soon because the longer Kimberley had to embezzle funds, the greater the risk to Carl . . . and of Jake finding out!

Hour after hour it all went round in Madeleine's mind as she tossed and turned, her mind in a fever, her heart breaking. What really hurt, of course, was the fact that Carl had gone to bed with Kimberley Cabot. Madeleine knew that was why she was taking an almost diabolical relish in planning to bring about the girl's downfall. Whilst Madeleine cared about the reputation of the Central Manhattan Bank for her father's sake, she didn't give a damn about the money that was being embezzled, nor about Hank Pugsley. All she cared about was wreaking revenge on the woman who had seduced her husband, and in whose hands he could be ruined.

Oh God, Carl, how could you? her mind screamed in the dark. How could you have betrayed me, even for a moment, even if it meant nothing to you . . . And then the tears would flow, hot and salty, into her pillow and she would stuff the quilt into her mouth to deaden the sounds of her sobbing.

Saturday dawned wet and humid, one of those days when clothes cling clammily to the skin and the atmosphere is stifling. Madeleine arrived at her studio early; Carl had gone to play golf with friends and wouldn't be back until the early evening. The day stretched before her like a thousand other Saturdays, only this one was going to be different.

At two o'clock she entered the lobby of La Première, on the corner of Fifty-fifth Street and Broadway. It hadn't been difficult to find out where Kimberley Cabot lived, and Madeleine's 'wrong number' call from a street telephone a few minutes before had confirmed that she was in. A security man sat behind a desk, heavy set and watchful. He was talking to a couple and Madeleine slipped quickly to the elevators before he had time to question her. To her relief, the elevator doors opened as she reached them and two women, chattering loudly, got out. A moment later the doors slid shut and she was alone in the claustrophobic container that rose through the building, as swiftly and silently as a snake, hissing when it drew to a standstill on the twenty-fifth floor.

Apartment 279 was on the right of the landing, and as Madeleine stepped forward trying to quieten the thumping of her heart, Kimberley's door seemed to her like a black and forbidding face. She pressed the bell, and waited. A muffled movement on the other side of the door made her aware that Kimberley was peering through the spyhole. Madeleine looked steadily into the little glass lens, aware that she was eyeball to eyeball with her most deadly adversary.

'I'd like to talk to you, Kimberley,' she said, in as calm and level a voice as she could muster. 'It really would be to your advantage if we met, and I know you're there because you answered the phone to me a few minutes ago.'

The silence that followed was stunned and hollow. After a few moments Madeleine heard the rattling of security chains and bolts. Then the door opened very slowly, and there stood Kimberley. Today there was no makeup on her face or fancy clothes to give her a look of cheap allure. Instead there was a freshly scrubbed young woman in faded jeans and a T-shirt, with her riot of fiery curls held back with a scarf.

'What d'you want?'

Madeleine fancied she sounded more fearful than

insolent. 'Do you mind if I come in? I think it's time we had a talk.'

Reluctantly, Kimberley opened the door wider and stepped aside. Her grey eyes were alert now, sharp and shining. With a sideways jerk of her head she indicated that Madeleine should enter.

By daylight, the living-room which Carl had thought resembled the inside of a box of chocolates looked more like a tip for the used wrappers. Newspapers, magazines, clothes, overflowing ashtrays and dirty cups and glasses were strewn around. Down one side an untidy assortment of books was stuffed on to a couple of shelves.

Fastidiously, Madeleine picked her way across the room to the sliding glass screens that led on to the balcony. Pushing one further open she stepped out, as if to seek fresh air. The implied insult was not lost on Kimberley.

'What do you want?' she asked harshly.

Nonchalantly, taking her time, Madeleine picked at the flaking paint on the railings without looking at her. At last she said: 'I overheard you and my husband talking when I was at the bank the other day. I know exactly what you're up to.'

Kimberley's head jerked up and her face flamed. 'What the fuck . . .!'

Willing herself to look calm, Madeleine continued: 'I was in the washroom adjoining my husband's office while you were both discussing the embezzlement you are carrying out at the bank. I must say, you didn't leave out a detail!' Her voice was dry and grating.

In the silence that followed the only sound was the

roar of the traffic hundreds of feet below. Madeleine's face was as pale as the other's was scarlet. Then Kimberley swore obscenely, and her hands started working nervously. Unmoved, Madeleine continued: 'I heard all about the money you are stealing from Hank Pugsley's account . . .'

Kimberley's eyes nearly popped out of her head. 'You *know* him?' She stared disbelievingly at Madeleine, who shrugged, letting the girl think what she liked.

Smoothly, Madeleine continued: 'I also heard how you blackmailed Carl into taking a coded tape for the computer from my father's office so that you could make a copy of it. And I heard how you go down to the computer room late in the afternoon, when everyone's gone, to put through the false transaction! Actually, I don't think there's much I don't know.'

Madeleine watched as Kimberley, just inside the room, slid down on to one of the brown suede sofas, noticing how marble white she'd turned. She knew she had the upper hand now. No matter how much pain this girl had caused her Madeleine could, if she wished, have her begging for mercy.

'I suppose you know it's only a matter of time before you're caught? It's a terribly dangerous game you're playing.'

An expression of wild defiance crossed Kimberley's face. 'It wasn't dangerous until you came poking your fucking nose in,' she cried angrily. 'Now I suppose you're going to go running to your fucking daddy!'

Madeleine's dark eyebrows rose a fraction as she stood looking coolly down at the girl. 'That's why I'm here, Kimberley, to tell you I've no intention of saying anything to my father. I think if he were to find out, it would kill him.' She looked away, momentarily unable to bear looking at this woman, imagining Carl in bed with her . . . kissing her . . . taking her into his arms and making love to her . . . Below, to the south, Broadway lay like a glittering ribbon, winding its way through the rigidly square blocks of New York, and for a moment the scene blurred as she fought for control of herself. When she spoke again her voice was steady.

'I'm here because I want to protect my father, and by protecting him I shall inadvertently be sparing you and my husband.'

'Does Carl know you've come to see me?'

'Carl has no idea I've found out what's happening.'

Kimberley sounded unbelieving. 'How come?'

'He left his office shortly after you did that day. He'd no idea I was in the washroom.'

'So now what? D'you plan to blackmail *us*?' Kimberley gave a short harsh laugh and Madeleine had to dig her nails into the palms of her hands to prevent herself from hitting the girl. Something about Kimberley as she sat on the sofa, with her legs sprawled wide and her breasts swelling out of her low-cut T-shirt, filled Madeleine with revulsion. The girl reminded her of a vixen in a permanent state of heat.

'Could we have some coffee?' she asked ignoring Kimberley's question. 'I could use some, and I expect you could too.'

Kimberley looked at her, startled. 'Fuck the coffee! Why the hell are you here?'

Madeleine turned away from the balcony railings and re-entered the living-room of the apartment. 'It's so much easier to talk over a drink,' she responded smoothly.

Uncertainly, and looking deeply disgruntled, Kimberley rose and went into the small kitchen across her central hallway. Noisily she poured water into a percolator. A few moments later Madeleine followed, her hands in the pockets of her suit, a relaxed smile on her face. She spoke casually, as if she'd dropped in to see a friend. 'Nice place you've got here. Have you had it long?'

Kimberley shot her a venomous look. 'Over a year.'

'Ummm. I've always liked this part of town.' Madeleine glanced around the neat kitchen, which was obviously used more for assembling deli food and drink than cooking. Rows of expensive crystal glasses, from champagne flutes to tumblers, were arranged along two high shelves, under which hung man-size coffee cups. At one end of the counter a wine rack was fully stacked with clarets and burgundies and several bottles of Dom Perignon. Beside it were jars of cashew nuts. When Kimberley opened the fridge to get some milk, Madeleine noticed it contained nothing but cocktail snacks and trays of ice-cubes. A hooker's kitchen, she thought, with everything a hooker needs for entertaining. But Kimberley was no ordinary hooker. She was a highly intelligent young woman; ingenious, manipulative and cunning. Also highly dangerous!

'Oh, you've got a microwave oven!' Madeleine suddenly exclaimed. 'Are they any good? My housekeeper's always urging me to get one, but I wasn't sure how useful it would be.'

Kimberley swung round on her in a sudden burst of fury, her voice an explosive screech, her eyes blazing. 'What the fuck are you playing at? You barge in here, uninvited, tell me you know what's going on – and then you start waffling on about fucking cookers as if this was a tea party! What the hell's your game?'

Madeleine looked at her with a smile, maddening in its serenity.

'Well?' Kimberley yelled.

Madeleine's fingers smoothed the folds of one of Kimberley's tea-towels, which had 'The Big Apple' printed all over it in scarlet lettering.

'I believe in conducting myself in a civilised manner at all times,' she said with a touch of hauteur. 'There's no point in getting rattled, Kimberley. If you've any sense you'll keep on the right side of me. I know enough to put you away for a long time.'

'Your precious husband's in this as deep as I am!' retaliated Kimberley sharply. Then she fell silent, glowering at the percolator, recognising the truth.

Madeleine continued to admire the kitchen fittings as if nothing had happened, watching Kimberley all the time out of the corner of her eye. She fiddled with a bottle opener, the handle shaped like a banana, and she examined a cookie jar with a picture of a naked dancing girl on the lid. The coffee had another minute to go before it was ready, so Madeleine wandered back into the living-room, as if bored. When Kimberley brought the two steaming cups through she found Madeleine sitting on the brown suede sofa, powdering her nose from a gilt compact, her initials set in diamonds on the lid so that they glinted in the light.

'Right,' Madeleine said, as if she'd suddenly made up her mind to get down to business, 'as I told you, my main concern is to make sure my father never finds out what is going on, but I also want to prevent Carl from getting caught for his part in this business.'

Kimberley continued to maintain her sullen silence while she scrutinised Madeleine's face, as if looking for clues.

'To enable me to protect the two people I care about most, I must ask you *not* to tell Carl I've come to see you today.' Kimberley opened her mouth to protest but Madeleine raised her hand to silence her. 'It's vital Carl doesn't know I'm aware of what's going on, because if he did he'd blow the whole works and you'd be for the high jump.'

'Crap!' Kimberley cried.

'I do know Carl better than you,' Madeleine said coldly. 'At the moment he's going along with you in order to protect me; no other reason. His feelings about Jake are secondary. If you want to stay around, this meeting between us never happened, okay?'

Her dark eyes flashed and her tone was commanding. Madeleine was suddenly amazed by her own strength. Where had this sudden rush of self-confidence come from? A week ago she'd have been a quivering mass, begging Kimberley to leave Carl alone; now she felt strong enough to face anything, and with a flash of insight she knew it was because she still loved her husband. She would do anything for him, even face this tough little cookie who hadn't a scruple in her body.

Kimberley reached for a pack of menthol cigarettes and, lighting one, dragged on it deeply. 'Okay. I don't give a damn whether Carl knows we've met or not! What I want to know is, what's your angle? If it concerns him, he'll have to know. As we're lovers, it will be difficult keeping anything from him.'

Madeleine felt a slow burn of anger building inside her, but with a supreme effort she quelled it, knowing she must remain calm at all costs or she'd play right into this girl's hands. 'As you're *not* sleeping with my husband,' she said succinctly, 'my only concern is what is going on at the bank.'

'Ah-h-h!' Kimberley dragged out the word sardonically. 'If it isn't blackmail . . . it's a cut you're after!' She was silent for a moment, inhaling her cigarette thoughtfully, then she pounced venomously. 'How d'you know Carl isn't planning to go away with me, when all this is over and we've got enough money? Huh?' She leaned towards Madeleine aggressively. 'That's the plan, you know. He's crazy for me, but as you and your father hold the purse strings this is the only way we can get enough money together.' She gave a coarse, harsh laugh again. 'Don't imagine he's sticking around because he loves *you*! He told me he only married you for your money.'

Madeleine rose with dignity and stood looking down at Kimberley. 'There seems little point in continuing this conversation,' she said icily. 'I was going to offer you a large sum of money if you'd stop putting through these fraudulent transfers, but it seems you have a totally unrealistic fantasy in your head which you'd rather pursue. A pity,' she added reflectively, 'because when I arrived I'd intended giving you a large cheque, and the opportunity to leave the bank without anyone finding out what had been going on.'

She could see the inner conflict tearing Kimberley apart as she wondered if she hadn't blown an easy way out. Madeleine didn't give her the opportunity to say anything, though. Curtly she continued: 'It's too late now, of course. As far as I'm concerned, you can go on embezzling funds until you're caught.'

Kimberley sprang to her feet, chagrin, fury, and regret written all over her face. 'You . . .!' she began explosively.

Madeleine turned at the door to make her parting shot. 'Remember. Don't tell Carl I've been here today. If you do, I'll go straight to my father and tell him everything. Every single thing,' she added clearly.

The door slammed behind Madeleine, and Kimberley sank on to the sofa, her legs suddenly weak, her brain reeling with shock. At that moment she could have killed Carl for being so fucking stupid. Fancy not knowing his wife was in the washroom while they talked! Rage and fear swept through her, paralysing her thoughts and making coherent reasoning impossible. She lit a cigarette with trembling hands, trying to remember everything Madeleine had said, but it didn't add up. The fucking crazy bitch had talked in riddles – and why had she come to visit in the first place? To offer hush money? To beg Kimberley to leave Carl alone? It hardly mattered, Kimberley thought. Madeleine, powerful with knowledge, was in a position to blow them all sky high. She wouldn't, of course, because she wanted to protect Carl . . . but what about that crap about protecting Jake Shearman? Jake needed about as much protection as a shark from a minnow!

Today had been a game of cat and mouse, but where was it leading?

Slowly and distractedly, Kimberley started cleaning up her apartment, remembering she had someone coming to see her that evening. She piled clothes into the closet, and stuffed empty coke tins, old newspapers and the contents of overflowing ashtrays into the trash can. But all the time her mind was spinning in spirals of panic, wondering whether, in spite of Madeleine's warning, she ought to tell Carl what had happened.

At last, as if in need of comfort, like a child counting the money in its piggy bank, she slid her hand behind the padded bedhead and, groping, felt for the large envelope. Unlike Hank Pugsley she'd asked the bank in Zurich to send her monthly statements because she needed the reassurance of knowing her account was steadily increasing. It made all those dollars that flashed across the computer screen as she keyed in the transfers seem real. In a way, the knowledge that she had so much money stashed away made *her* seem more real too. A woman of wealth. A somebody, after a lifetime of being a nobody.

Kimberley unfolded the latest bank statement, and

felt an almost physical pleasure as she read the balance at the bottom of the right-hand column: one million, seven hundred and eighty-two thousand dollars. She let out a sigh of rapture. Soon it would be two million dollars . . . and then three . . . providing that goddamn wife of Carl's didn't screw everything up for her.

For a moment Kimberley contemplated getting out of New York now, right this minute. She could pack a small case. She had her passport and enough cash on her for a one way ticket to Zurich. She could be there by tomorrow and no one the wiser. Carl certainly wouldn't go looking for her, that was for sure. The idea took hold and grew; better to get out with under two million dollars, she reflected, than wait to be caught with three. She even got as far as opening her closet to decide which clothes she'd take with her.

But then she remembered something, something so tempting she couldn't resist closing the doors firmly again and abandoning her escape plan . . . for the moment, anyway.

Hank Pugsley was due to put through another transfer within the next week to ten days. It could be for as much as three hundred thousand dollars. Kimberley decided to wait. If Madeleine hadn't done anything so far, and she must have known for nearly two weeks, then she was unlikely to do anything immediately. Kimberley decided to take a chance. She'd wait for just one more transfer before getting the hell out of New York.

Madeleine walked briskly up Broadway to Central

Park. In spite of the winos and vagrants who raved and ranted by the park's perimeter, she decided to walk back to her apartment on Fifth Avenue. In her present frame of mind, the sense of danger, the risk of being mugged, attacked, or even assaulted, was what she needed to cleanse her from the feeling of sleaziness she'd experienced in Kimberley's apartment. She glared angrily at a drunken bag lady who looked as if she was going to cause trouble, and quickened her pace.

She felt contaminated, and more emotionally disturbed by her meeting with Kimberley than if she'd been physically attacked. The last hour had drained her, and yet it was beginning to sink in that she'd actually scored. Kimberley had been left bewildered and confused, there was no doubt about that in Madeleine's mind. The girl hadn't known what was happening and Madeleine's mission had been totally successful. Yet, the memory of Kimberley made her flesh crawl. How could Carl have . . .? She closed her eyes and tried to shut off the visions that came to haunt her all the time now. She must concentrate on the positive aspects of the task she'd set herself, and now that she'd completed phase one of her plan she must go ahead with phase two. It wasn't going to be such a walk-over either. Phase two was going to be dangerous and tricky.

For a second Madeleine's heart sank, wondering if she had the strength to carry on, but then she thought of Carl. If I didn't love him so much, she thought, this whole nightmare would be impossible. And if I wasn't sure he loved me too, in spite of everything, I wouldn't be able to carry on.

She could see her apartment block through the trees

now and with a rush of thankfulness she broke into a steady jog, oblivious of the passers-by who wondered at the elegant young woman in a grey linen suit and high-heeled black shoes, trotting briskly along.

Home was a haven. Madeleine wanted a hot shower to rid herself of the last essence of Kimberley, so that when Carl got back from his golf she'd be as calm and composed as possible.

'There's an urgent message for you, Madam,' said Teresa, when Madeleine let herself into the apartment. 'I've written it down on the pad by the phone.'

'Thank you.' With her heart skipping a beat, Madeleine's eyes flew to the notebook she always kept on the hall table by the phone. Could Kimberley have discovered . . .? She snatched it up, frightened for a moment, then let out a long sigh of relief. It was from Jessica. Please call her urgently at the Royal Westminster. She had something amazing to tell Madeleine.

Smiling now, grateful for any distraction, Madeleine went into the living-room and started dialling Jessica's number. Typical Jess, she thought, as she waited to be put through to the sales office, dramatising the most trivial situation. She'd probably been given a rise, or was having her office re-decorated.

Five minutes later Madeleine sat dumbfounded, hardly able to believe what her friend had told her.

Chapter Eleven

'We really would be very sorry to see you go, Jessica,' Kenneth Wolfson was saying in a stunned voice. 'Are you sure you've given this enough thought?'

Jessica sat in the General Manager's office, feeling slightly stunned herself. The past week had been the most extraordinary of her life and she hardly knew or recognised herself by her actions. Swiftly and with barely a backward glance she was doing a complete turn about, throwing to the winds all her previous adamantly held views on work versus a private life. Where was the old Jessica, who had given up Andrew and the prospect of a secure marriage and future because her job prospects at the Royal Westminster were more important?

After Bernard had made love to her the previous week – was it only a week ago? it seemed like years to her now – he'd asked her to stay with him forever. Just like that! Jessica-I-love-you-and-I-want-to-spend-the-rest-of-my-life-with-you! And to her amazement, Jessica had heard herself agreeing in a whole-hearted rush of emotion that left her dizzy. Never in her life had she felt such heady ecstasy as when she was with Bernard. Her new feelings were obliterating everything that had mattered to her previously. There was no past, no present either; the future was all she could see now, stretching to infinity like a glorious avenue. And that future was totally filled by Bernard.

'Of course I'll stay with you, darling,' she'd whispered, as a cold blue dawn stole over the rooftops of London. 'I'll stay with you forever.' What was she saying? She didn't care. All she knew was that she'd found a paradise within the circle of Bernard's arms, a heaven she couldn't resist. Then Bernard had hugged and kissed her with a wild abandon that had thrilled every cell in her body, and together they had lain close, planning the future.

It was only during the following day as she rushed about the hotel giving lunch to a restaurant writer, setting up meetings to discuss forthcoming events, greeting VIPs in the lobby and sending out invitations for a reception, that the full impact of what she was planning hit her forcibly. Bernard's last words, as she slipped out of his suite before breakfast, suddenly rang in her ears with appalling clarity.

'First we will be going to Boston, my darling, then on to Washington and New York, and after that Milan, Paris, Tokyo and Sydney. Then, when the tour's over, we'll spend the next four months in my house in Sardinia, where I do my composing.'

It all sounded fantastic, but tottering along the corridor to get to her own room, the realisation dawned on her that by going with Bernard, she'd be leaving her job in the hotel. The thought took her breath away – but then so did Bernard! Feeling overcome by this turn of events which was making her feel as if she were being whisked along on a runaway big dipper, she was overcome by conflicting emotions. She'd broken off with Andrew so that she could give her all to the Royal Westminster, yet here she was, about to chuck in the chance of a lifetime in the hotel business, for a man she'd only known a few days. It was crazy! She needed to have her head examined! But . . . sitting at her desk, she also knew that the most wonderful, glorious and fantastic thing had happened to her. She'd fallen in love with a man in a million, and he was in love with her. All her life, in everything she'd done, she'd let her head rule her heart; she'd made sensible decisions and afterwards been grateful that she had. This time, the temptation to let her heart rule her head, and lead it where it would, was so strong she had no desire to fight it. Why not give way to these glorious emotions? Just for once?

All morning Jessica's mood swung between wanting to go away with Bernard, and wanting to stay and follow her career. There seemed no reality in the prospect of going to Kenneth Wolfson to hand in her resignation, but there was no reality in the thought of her dream-like future with Bernard either.

How can I be doing this? she asked herself distractedly, her lazy topknot of blonde hair coming loose as she shook her head, her small fists clenched on her desk. I'm about to give up everything I've spent six years working for. It's lunacy! Oh, but what delicious lunacy. Her mind and body still reeled from Bernard's love-making the previous night; four times she'd surrendered to his ardent passion, letting him take her again and again as if he couldn't have enough of her. Virile enough for a man half his age, skilled as only a man of experience can be, Bernard had awakened her to delights she didn't know existed. Where, Jessica demanded, as she picked up her pen, am I ever going to find a man like that again? She'd be a fool to turn her back on such a rampant consuming love that was burning her up even as she sat at her desk. At lunch-time she came to a decision. She'd go and see Kenneth Wolfson and tell him she was leaving.

'Of course I've thought about it, Mr Wolfson,' Jessica said, sitting as taut as a Jack-in-the-box before somebody lifts the lid. 'I know it's very sudden . . . and I'm very sorry to inconvenience you like this.'

'Frankly, Jessica, I think you've had a brain-storm,' he said. He spoke kindly, and in a fatherly fashion, but there was concern in his eyes. 'You've only known Mr Scheller for a short time . . . a week! . . . and you don't know anything about him. Don't you think you're being unwise in giving up your career, when you've got such a brilliant future, for what I can only describe as a wild infatuation?'

'It's *not* an infatuation!' Jessica said indignantly. 'Don't you believe in love at first sight? That's what's happened for both of us, and I'm not a starry eyed eighteen-year-old, you know, Mr Wolfson. I do know what I'm doing and although it may seem a bit quick off the mark to others, if feels *right* for us!' Her gilt bangles chinked as she gesticulated, anxious to get her point across.

Kenneth Wolfson remained silent, looking at her with a worried expression.

'I realise I must work out my notice, of course,' Jessica continued hurriedly. 'I wouldn't want to let you down by just walking out this minute but I am determined to live with Bernard. You've been so good to me but –' she spread her hands in a gesture of helplessness – 'what else can I do?' Her piquant little face looked genuinely puzzled.

'If we weren't so frantically busy here,' said Wolfson, shaking his head, 'I'd suggest you had three months' leave of absence so you could get this – this thing – out of your system, but I'm afraid it's impossible right now. And I'm afraid there can be no question of our keeping your post open, should you change your mind.'

'I won't,' Jessica said firmly. 'I've always adored my job, but this is something else.'

He spoke drily. 'It certainly seems to be! Very well, Jessica, with great reluctance I'll accept your resignation and I'll have a word with Denis. Maybe we can find a replacement immediately, which would mean you could leave quite soon.'

'Really?' Jessica's blue eyes blazed with delight.

Wolfson, in spite of his misgivings, smiled indulgently at her. She looked like a little girl who'd been promised a treat.

'I can't promise, Jessica, but I'll see what I can do.'

'Thank you, Mr Wolfson. I'd be terribly grateful. You've been so understanding.' She sprang to her feet, looking vibrantly alive and brimming with enthusiasm.

It was in the evening, while she was changing to dine with Bernard, that Madeleine returned her call.

'You're what?' gasped Madeleine, when Jessica told her the news.

'It's true!' chortled Jessica. 'I'm *madly* in love! Oh, Maddy, I'm absolutely *dying* for you to meet Bernard. He's the most fantastic man that's ever lived! And . . . guess what? . . . we're going to the States! Well, he leaves tomorrow, and I'm following as soon as they've found a replacement for me here. We can see lots of each other!'

'It'll be lovely, your being in the States,' Madeleine was saying in a shocked voice, 'but, Jessie, isn't this all awfully sudden?'

'Don't *you* start!' exclaimed Jessica. 'I've had it all from our General Manager. Do I know what I'm doing? What do I know about Bernard? Oh, Mr Wolfson gave me the whole works, telling me it was all infatuation. What does he know?' Her voice rose plaintively.

'Yes, but you've always been an obsessive person, Jessie.'

'What d'you mean, obsessive?' Jessica sounded quite offended.

Madeleine laughed. 'I mean, whatever you do, you go for it hell-for-leather! One hundred percent! There are no half measures with you, are there? You threw yourself into the hotel business as if life didn't exist outside the Royal Westminster, and now you're doing the same thing over this new boyfriend. Are you going to give up work altogether?'

'Well, I'll have to, won't I?' Jessica was deeply disappointed that Madeleine did not share her euphoria. 'I'm going to be living in hotels, not running them, all over the world for eight months of the year. All my time will be taken up looking after Bernard!'

'Ummm.' There was silence on the line.

'I thought you'd be excited for me,' Jessica wailed. 'You've no *idea* how much in love I am!'

'I'm sorry, Jessie. Of course I'm pleased, if you're happy. I'm in shock still, I suppose. Somehow, I'd imagined you always in the hotel business. You've seemed so dedicated to it.'

'Well, that was *then*. This is *now*!' Jessica replied, relying on her own form of logic.

'Have you told Andrew what's happened?' she heard Madeleine say.

'I haven't talked to Andrew for weeks. Anyway, it's got nothing to do with him now. Remember, it was Andrew who really broke off our relationship, because he couldn't stand my working so hard. I wanted us to carry on as usual, but he wouldn't have it!'

She heard Madeleine sigh deeply.

'Maddy . . .' her voice caught fractionally. 'I am going to be all right, you know. Don't sound so upset. I want you to be happy for me!'

'I'm not upset, honey, just a bit worried for you. I couldn't bear it if you ended up having regrets.'

'I *promise* you I'm doing the right thing, everything's going to be fine,' Jessica pleaded. It meant a great deal to her to feel she had her best friend's blessing, especially as she still had to face her parents and break the news to them. They'd been very upset when she and Andrew had split.

'Jessie, I wish you all the happiness and luck in the world,' Madeleine said warmly, 'and I can't wait for you to come over.'

Jessica beamed instantly. 'I'll let you know as soon as I do. Anyway, how are things with you? Painting any more famous faces?'

'I'm fine . . . and busy.'

'And that *divine* man you're married to . . . how is he? Still making a fortune?'

'Carl's fine.'

Jessica's ever mobile and expressive face changed from a grin to a faint frown. Madeleine sounded . . . well, sort of strange. Could the shock of hearing about Bernard have affected her that much, or was she upset about something else?

'Are you all right, Maddy?' she demanded.

Madeleine's voice came across the line stronger now, as if she were making an effort. 'Yes, everything's great, and I'm longing to see you again.'

'You're sure you're okay?'

'Of course!' Madeleine protested stoutly.

'Right then. I'll be in touch.'

'Good luck, Jessie.'

Jessica replaced the receiver, her brow still puckered. She could have sworn Madeleine was keeping something back.

Jessica spent the night with Bernard again, and it reaffirmed in her mind that, no matter what anyone said, she was doing the right thing. They hardly slept at all, passing the dark hours in deep and wonderful conversation, planning their lives together, in between making love. Bernard was flying off in the morning so every moment was precious, because she wasn't sure when she'd see him again.

'I'm going to write a symphony, when we get to Sardinia,' Bernard whispered, as the song of the dawn chorus from the birds in Hyde Park filtered through the open window, 'and I'm going to dedicate it to you.'

Jessica felt lost for words. It was the most beautiful thought she'd ever heard, and emotionally she reached out and clutched his hand.

'My little angel, my little love,' Bernard murmured, his twilight eyes looking deeply into hers, thrilling her so much she felt the mounting pressure of sexual arousal again.

'I can't live without you,' she moaned, running her hands over his broad shoulders. 'Oh, God, I hope I can get to America soon.'

'I'll be waiting,' he promised, slipping his hand between her legs, touching the seat of her excitement, stroking her with strong yet gentle fingers as the tension built up inside her. Then she slipped her legs around his hips drawing him closer, her eyes glazed, her mouth partly open.

'I shall *die* if you don't come inside me,' she cried out, clinging to him. 'Oh, Jesus . . . Bernard, oh, oh, Jesus . . .' She rocked her head from side to side on the pillow, half crazed with desire, straining to feel his strength filling her, pushing up hard inside her . . . hard . . . hard . . . The world turned upside down amid an explosion of blazing stars and the heavens

295

were torn apart, as she let out a scream, rocked to her depths by a searing climax.

Later that day, as she tried to keep awake at her desk, Jessica received a call from Kenneth Wolfson. Her position as Director of Sales had been filled. She was free to leave the hotel within a week.

It was Monday, two days after Madeleine's visit to Kimberley's apartment. Carl left for work as usual and Kimberley, on the lookout for another transfer from Hank, was already in his office when he arrived.

She glanced over at him as he entered. 'So how was your weekend?' she asked with a touch of insolence.

Studiously, Carl avoided looking at her as he took his seat behind the desk. 'Fine, thank you,' he replied with icy politeness.

'Really?' Kimberley drew out the word, her voice flat with doubt, her pellucid grey eyes looking searchingly into his.

'Yes.' Carl glanced up at her, genuinely surprised.

'Well, aren't some people lucky!' she rejoined, shrugging. Then she turned away and went next door to her own office. Carl frowned at her retreating figure, wondering what she was implying. Had something happened? He glanced through the stack of transfers to be dealt with on his desk and noted with relief there was nothing from Hank Pugsley, but had she seen him over the weekend perhaps? Could Hank have discovered what was going on?

Carl's heart started to thump heavily and unpleasantly and his hands felt clammy. Torn between the desire to question her and find out if there was any-thing wrong, and the fear that if he did he wouldn't like what he heard, he remained at his desk trying to work, avoiding contact with her as much as possible. But even her presence in the adjoining office felt threatening. Like an unseen menace, breathing poison into the atmosphere, Kimberley went about her work, while Carl was forced to breathe the same air, and listen to her voice on the phone and her typewriter as it clacked; and all the time there was the redolence of deep fear between them. They were united in executing a serious crime and now they could not even communicate with each other, so great was the antipathy between them. If they were partners in crime they were also the bitterest of enemies.

At twelve-thirty, Carl heard a light tap on his office door. A moment later Madeleine entered, her arms full of shopping and her manner cheerful. Seeing he was on the phone, she mouthed: 'Hi, Carl!' before dropping her parcels on to a chair.

He put his hand over the mouthpiece. 'I'm talking to Tokyo. I'll be with you as soon as I can,' he whispered.

'That's okay,' she whispered back, smiling. Through the open doorway into the adjoining office, she could see Kimberley working at her desk. At that moment the PA looked up, as if conscious of being watched, and the two women's eyes met and locked. Madeleine held the stare coldly, and after a moment Kimberley's eyes flickered away and her gaze dropped back to her work.

Carl hadn't noticed any interchange between the

two women, and Madeleine thought how tired and haggard he looked as he sat hunched over the phone, quoting figures to some businessman in Japan. Madeleine had come to his office today hoping to find it empty. Carl lunched with someone almost every day and she was sure Kimberley took her lunch break to go shopping. Now she would have to rethink how she was going to carry out phase two of her plan. She needed just a few minutes alone in Kimberley's office . . . she was sure the answer to getting the girl finally out of their lives lay there. Carl was still on the telephone. Madeleine wandered around, looking at the pictures on his walls as if they were a source of profound interest. Then, out of the corner of her eye, she saw a bank clerk enter Kimberley's office and say something to her. She strained to listen.

'Can you go to his office right away? He wants to give you the details of the dollar transfer to Kuwait, for the Voltex Construction Company,' the clerk was saying.

Kimberley swore loudly. 'That'll take hours! I wanted to go to lunch now!'

'Sorry. Mr Watts said it was urgent.'

'Oh, hell!'

Madeleine tensed, straining to hear what was happening. If Kimberley were to leave her office now, while Carl was still on the phone . . . God, she'd have to act fast! There was a terrible element of risk but she might just have time.

Carl was gesturing to her to sit down. 'I'm going to be some time yet,' he whispered, putting his hand over the mouthpiece.

'Don't worry about it,' Madeleine replied softly. The longer the better, she thought. Strolling nonchalantly towards the door that led to Kimberley's office, she was just in time to see her backview flouncing out with obvious irritation, banging the outer door after her.

Madeleine didn't waste any time. With a backward glance to make sure Carl was still engrossed in the papers before him, from which he was quoting, she slipped through the open door and made straight for Kimberley's desk. She knew exactly what she was looking for, because she'd seen it in Kimberley's apartment; a black leather filofax, very like her own. She hadn't been able to examine it then, but now as her eyes swept feverishly over the clutter on the desk, she knew that it was vital she should find it. With every nerve straining to listen for either Carl coming off the phone or Kimberley returning for some reason, she looked around without disturbing anything. Files, papers, ledgers and transfer slips lay stacked up on every surface. She saw a memo signed 'Kimberley Cabot', lying on the desk. Swiftly she folded it in half and stuffed it into her pocket. It wasn't what she was looking for, but a copy of Kimberley's signature would certainly be useful.

She continued her search. The office was a mess and there were even some files heaped up on the floor down one side of the desk. Then she saw it! The black diary-file, together with Kimberley's purse, on the floor by her swivel chair behind the desk. Madeleine grabbed it and undid the press-stud clasp, her heart pounding and her hands shaking. Was there time now? Should she slip it under her jacket and go to Carl's washroom, where she could examine it without fear of being disturbed? But then she'd have to put it back where she found it, and if Carl had finished his call – No, she decided. It was now or never.

Because her own Filofax was identical, Madeleine knew the layout by heart; where the ordinary diary section was, and the address book section, the parts devoted to 'Accounts', 'Projects', 'Finances', 'Daily Planner'; there was also an index for classified listings like the telephone number of the TV repair company, or the electrician or the carpet cleaning company, and this was followed by an index headed 'Restaurants'. Madeleine knew what she did if she wanted to jot down something confidential. The question was, did Kimberley's mind work in the same way? Carl always teased Madeleine about this, saying no man's mind could ever be as inventive – and illogical – as a female's. Who but a woman, he joked, would put the number of her bank Cashpoint card under 'S' for shopping? He'd fallen about with laughter the day he'd discovered that.

Automatically, Madeleine flipped open the address section of Kimberley's Filofax at 'S' . . . maybe for Switzerland? Her pulse quickened. SPRITZA COOL BAR. STANTON'S GARAGE. BUNNY STEINBERG. JOSH STANTON. Nothing. Then she turned to 'C', for cash, perhaps? CAR HIRE. CHANTERELLE COUTURE. NANCY CLAVELL. Madeleine's eyes skimmed the entries. Nothing. She continued her search, a frantic feeling of the minutes ticking away filling her with desperation. 'M' for money; nothing. 'D' for dollars; nothing.

Sweat was breaking out all over her body now and her hands were sticky. Please God, let it be here, she implored under her breath. Give me a break, God, before anyone comes into the room and discovers me rifling through the diary of Carl's assistant. How would that look? What the hell would she say? At that moment she was struck by a brainwave. Oh, why hadn't she thought of that before! 'O' for overseas, or off-shore! That must be it! When she looked at the 'O' listings her heart nearly stopped. Orthodontist insurance number indeed! Grabbing a scrap of paper she jotted down the row of numbers: 23007 4810 66792. Then she closed the Filofax and replaced it carefully beside Kimberley's purse again. Checking that she'd left everything as she found it, she was already standing in the doorway of Carl's office as he came off the telephone. She tried to look cool, but beads of perspiration were plastering the black curls to her forehead and her clothes were sticking to her.

'I don't think your air conditioning's working properly,' she observed. 'It's terribly hot in here.'

'Is it, sweetheart?' Carl replied vaguely. He was busy making notes.

'I think I'll freshen up. How about some lunch, if you've got time?' Madeleine braced herself to enter the washroom, forcing herself to control her emotions, for the last time she'd been in here her world had fallen apart.

'Sure. I'd like that,' said Carl, looking up and smiling at her. 'Are you all right, Maddy? You look very flushed.'

'I'm fine,' she replied with forced gaiety, 'I'm hot

because this place is like an oven!'

They lunched at a nearby fish restaurant, with Madeleine keeping up a flow of light chatter so that Carl would not suspect how worried she was about him. She longed to reach across the table and tell him that soon, with any luck, it would all be over; but caution prevented her. The nightmare was far from over yet and it was vital he did not suspect the part she was playing in bringing about Kimberley's downfall. If he knew, if he had even an inkling of what she was up to, he'd get edgier than ever and then Kimberley would notice, and the whole thing could blow up in their faces.

It wasn't until Carl suddenly made a remark during lunch, that Madeleine realised she'd been absorbed in this terrible business to the exclusion of everything else.

'Have you heard any more from that fellow, Marks?' he asked.

'Who?' For a split second she stared at him blankly. The names that had been running round in her mind lately were Kimberley Cabot, Hank Pugsley, Brandt's Motors and Michaux Internationale. 'Marks?'

'How many Mr Marks' do you know?' Carl teased. 'You couldn't think of anything except the mystery surrounding your mother's death and your grandfather's Will, and now you don't even remember who I'm talking about!'

'Sorry, darling,' Madeleine flushed. 'I've been so involved with my painting, and you know how everything else goes out of my head when I've got a lot of commissions,' she lied.

302

'Even so, Maddy!' He looked incredulous. 'What's happening over your mother's death certificate? Has Mr Marks applied for a court order of presumption of her death?'

Madeleine shook her head. 'I don't know. I'll call him up tomorrow and find out what's happening.' She didn't want to talk about it right now. There was nothing she could do for the time being anyway, and the solicitor had said he would keep her informed and let her know when her claim had been granted in the British courts. Far more important was what she had to do next: find out where Hank Pugsley hung out and go and see him.

'You're so *kind*!' sobbed Jessica. 'Thank you all so much.' She wiped away the tears as Kenneth Wolfson, Denis Powell, Dick Fowler, Mike Lyle, Adolph, the Restaurant Manager, and even Anne Butler, toasted her with champagne as she clutched the going-away present they'd all clubbed together to buy her. It was a beautiful dark red leather jewel case, the inner compartments lined with cream suede.

'It's beautiful!' gasped Jessica. 'I just hope Bernard gives me some jewellery to put in it.'

Everyone laughed at her comical expression.

'Well,' said Denis Powell, patting her shoulder, 'you know what will happen the next time you come to this hotel, don't you?'

Jessica looked mystified.

Denis explained. 'There'll be someone in the lobby to greet you with a drink, while you check in, and Mr Bernard Scheller and Miss Jessica McCann will head our list of visiting VIPs and you'll be given the full treatment.'

Jessica looked appalled. 'Oh, *no*! I don't want to be treated any differently, and knowing me I'll probably forget anyway and start rushing around checking all the other bookings and seeing how many events we've got in banqueting!'

'Oh, I'm sure you'll take to the life of a lady of leisure without any trouble,' Anne Butler interjected, a hint of spite in her eyes.

'Don't worry – I will!' retorted Jessica spiritedly.

'So where are you going to be actually based?' Dick asked. He knew he was going to miss Jessica like hell; even in a crisis she was good for a laugh.

'In Sardinia, I suppose, where Bernard has a house, but it's lucky I like hotel life because I'm going to be moving from one to another for eight months of the year.'

Anne's eyes narrowed. 'You poor thing. How unsettling for you!' Her insincerity was not lost on Jessica, who smiled sweetly and replied: 'A nomadic existence, my dear. Goodness knows how I'll survive!'

'Jolly exciting, though,' interjected Dick, missing the point.

'Fascinating,' said Kenneth. 'I know the Far East very well, working for the Golding Group out there, but I'd love to travel around Europe.'

Anne had one more barb to hurl at Jessica. 'So when are you actually getting married?'

'Married?' echoed Jessica, pretending to look shocked. 'Goodness, what a bourgeois idea! I don't know if we'll *ever* get married, but then, I never did think a bit of paper made any difference to a relationship.'

Anne's lips tightened in anger and her eyes looked flat and sullen.

'Well, we're certainly going to miss you,' Denis said hastily. 'The old Royal Westminster isn't going to be the same without you.'

'Don't say that, or you'll make me cry again,' Jessica implored. 'If Bernard wasn't a man in a million, you wouldn't be getting rid of me so easily.'

At last the drinks party came to an end and Jessica was kissing everybody goodbye – even Anne – and then hurrying up to her room to finish packing. In an hour's time she was leaving the hotel and going down to Guildford, to spend her last night in England with her parents. Early tomorrow morning her father would be driving her to Heathrow airport, where she'd catch the flight to Boston; and Bernard would be waiting for her.

An hour later a porter came up to collect her luggage. Having taken one last look at the small room that, for a short time, had been home to her, she followed him down in the elevator.

As soon as she stepped into the lobby an enormous sense of loss enveloped her, making her throat dry and her eyes sting. This lobby was to her the heart of the hotel, and she remembered the first time she'd entered it, feeling terrified because she'd just been transferred from the Wentworth, and this new job at the Royal Westminster was so important to her. It had seemed so vast and strange, with its stretches of white marble flooring, the long reception desk, the elegant oasis of furniture and plants, and the sweeping staircase that led up to the first floor. She remembered all the thousands of times she'd crossed this lobby on her way to the bar or the restaurant, or to meet a guest; and those Christmases when the centre table of flowers was replaced with a giant tree shimmering with little lights. She remembered the glamorous occasions when they'd had a grand ball or dinner, like the time the Prime Minister had attended a Conservative Party banquet, and they'd placed vases of blue flowers everywhere. And then there were the thousands of people she'd met, right on this spot, many of whom had become her friends.

The tears slid down her cheeks as she realised a chapter had closed in her life. Never again would she know the changing moods of this public place which had become as familiar to her as her old home; still with expectancy through a thousand dawns, clamouring with people and voices and shifting luggage at high noon, quiet as a mausoleum at dead of night. She would never belong in this spot again, or be any part of its day to day activity. Already she felt she'd left it all behind, and that she was a mere shadow standing here now blending in with arriving guests and departing tourists, no longer belonging. Unnoticed and invisible. Only her memories lingering now.

Jessica moved swiftly to the glass revolving doors and into a waiting cab, as if she could not bear to hang around any longer. Her career in the hotel business was over forever.

*   *   *

The telephone rang just as Madeleine was getting out of the bath.

'It's for you, Mrs Delaney,' said Teresa, tapping on the door. 'It's a Mr Andrew Seymour, calling from England.'

'Tell him I'll be right there.' Madeleine grabbed a towelling sheet and, wrapping it round her sarong-style, hurried to the phone by her bedside. She had a strong feeling she knew what he was calling about.

'Hi, Andrew. How are you?'

He sounded agitated. 'Maddy, d'you know what's going on? I rang Jessica at the Royal Westminster, because I wanted to know what she'd like me to do with a box of tapes she left in my flat, and they told me she'd left! Left to get married!' The hurt and shock in his voice was painful to hear.

'Oh, I'm so sorry,' said Madeleine sympathetically, 'it all seems to have happened so quickly . . . and I don't know if she's actually getting married,' she added, hoping that might soften the blow.

'I don't believe this is happening,' he said slowly. Then there was a silence on the line as if he were bracing himself to ask the next question. His voice croaked. 'Who is he?'

'Bernard Scheller,' Madeleine replied quietly.

'Bernard Scheller? Isn't he . . .?'

'That's right. The composer.'

'Jesus! He's old enough to be her father! What the hell's going on?'

'Andrew, that's all I know. I was as surprised as you are when I heard. It seems he was a guest in the hotel –'

'Where can I get hold of her?' he cut in.

'I don't know.'

'Oh, come on, Maddy!' She could sense his fury mixed with anguish. 'You're her best friend, you must know. And I'll find out sooner or later, so you might as well tell me now.'

'I'm not being evasive, Andrew. I honestly don't know where she is at the moment, except that she was due to join Bernard in Boston before going on to Washington and New York. I'm expecting her to get in touch with me. Shall I get her to contact you?'

Andrew groaned heavily. 'I don't suppose she'll want to. Christ, I wish she'd let me know what she was doing before going off like that. What I don't understand is, why has she given up work? That hotel meant everything to her. Hell, she even turned *me* down because of it! Then this bastard comes along . . . Couldn't anyone stop her? She must be out of her mind! It'll never last!'

'Andrew,' Madeleine said gently, 'I do know how you're feeling, but Jessica is a grown woman. She has to be left to make her own decisions.'

'Oh, I know, but it's all my fault, really. I should never have forced her to choose between me and the hotel. God, what a fool I was! But even when she did, I sort of hoped she'd get tired of it in time, and we'd get together again.'

'I know. I'd rather hoped the same, for both your sakes,' said Madeleine understandingly.

'Oh, well . . .' He sounded dispirited, his voice hollow. 'Tell her I called, will you, Maddy?'

Madeleine's heart ached for him. Andrew had

308

taken a gamble and lost, and for a moment she felt quite angry with Jessica for being so unpredictable and flighty. But that was Jessica all over; part maddening, part lovable, as dazzling as quicksilver but with a heart of gold. Jessica probably thought Andrew no longer wanted her and that was why she hadn't told him about Bernard. Certainly she would never have set out to hurt him intentionally.

'I'll tell her to call you the minute I hear from her,' she assured him. The last thing she wanted was to get involved, or start acting as a go-between, but at least she could pass on Andrew's message. After that it was up to Jessica.

Andrew replaced the receiver slowly and gazed out of his office window, ignoring the fact that there were two people waiting to talk to him on the other telephone lines. They could wait; he had to collect himself before he could talk to anyone. The shock of hearing what Jessica had done was a bitter blow, doubly painful because he blamed himself.

'Are you all right, old chap?' Sandy inquired from his desk opposite.

'I'm okay.' Grimly Andrew took the first waiting call, dealt with a minor query, then took the second.

An uneducated woman's voice came on the line. 'I saw your board outside an 'ouse on the corner of Eaton Square,' she said. 'I'd like to look over it.'

Andrew winced at the flat vowels and the dropped aitches. She was obviously a working-class woman and he felt he ought to warn her about the price. It would certainly be beyond the range of anyone but a rich American or an Arab.

'Certainly, Madam,' he replied politely. 'I know the one you mean. It is a freehold property though, and the price is three million pounds.'

'I wants to see it,' said the woman doggedly.

'Very well, Mrs . . . er . . .?'

'Latimer,' she said, almost crossly. Her tone seemed to say, Stop messing me about.

'Mrs Latimer. Would this afternoon, at three o'clock, be convenient?' Andrew cast his eyes to heaven as he spoke . . . this was going to be a complete waste of his time, but they didn't call themselves 'an agency who takes a personal interest in their clients' wishes' for nothing.

'Yes.' Mrs Latimer hung up abruptly.

'I bet she just wants to see what the inside looks like,' Sandy remarked when Andrew told him. The house in question had been featured in the *Evening Standard* a few days before and had aroused much interest, having a swimming-pool in the lower ground floor, and a garden with trees and a little stream full of goldfish on the roof. It was a coup for the Jason and Seymour Partnership that they had been appointed sole agents by the owners, who lived in Spain, and whom Andrew suspected made their money by drug pushing.

'D'you want me to show the house for you?' Sandy asked Andrew. 'You look beat.'

Andrew shook his head. 'I'll live. If I can just get Jessica out of my mind I'll be fine. Goddamn it!' He pushed himself away from the desk on his swivel chair with a violent movement. 'What have I done, Sandy?'

he groaned. 'How could I have been such a bloody fool! Jessica and I were made for each other . . . and I let her slip through my fingers. Oh, God, what a mess.'

Sandy, who had overheard Andrew's conversation with Madeleine and who had gathered what had happened, looked cynical.

'If she's as flighty as she sounds, could be you're better off without her,' he remarked.

Andrew flushed with anger. 'She's not flighty at all! How could she have held down a job, like she did, if she was flighty? It's obvious she's been seduced by this old man who must have some hold over her.'

'Humph!' Sandy snorted. 'If you believe that, you'll believe anything! Forget her, Andrew. That's my advice. There are plenty more fish in the sea.'

Andrew paced up and down their smart pale blue carpeted office, so filled with bitter regret and anger that he could hardly speak.

'It's nearly three o'clock,' Sandy reminded him.

'What? Oh, hell.' Picking up his car keys he strode out of the office without saying another word.

When he arrived at the large, imposing, porticoed house in Eaton Square, he double-parked his car, risking a fine, and went to wait on the doorstep for Mrs Latimer. The wind raced gustily along the pavements, sending the first of the autumn leaves spinning into whirlpools of dust, while overhead an uneasy sky pressed down on the city. Jessica, why didn't you talk to me before you rushed off like that? Jessica, did our years together mean so little to you? Lost in his anguished thoughts, Andrew did not at first notice a

311

large grey Rolls-Royce, driven by a uniformed chauffeur, glide up the street and stop. A minute later the chauffeur was holding open the passenger door for a buxom woman in her thirties, who alighted and tottered forth on thick legs and high stiletto heels.

'Are you the agent?' she demanded, looking at Andrew.

He recovered himself in time to smile politely and acknowledge that he was.

'I'm Mrs Latimer,' she announced unnecessarily. 'I wanna see round the 'ouse.'

'Of course.' Andrew had changed his mind about Mrs Latimer's ability to afford three million pounds for a London house. Plump, with a mane of dyed blonde hair, a too short blue skirt and a tawny-coloured fox jacket, her coarse heavily made up face bore the hostile expression of a woman who knows she is not socially acceptable, although she has enough money to be so. And Mrs Latimer had enough money; that was for sure. Her diamond solitaire earrings and ring, with a stone as big as a lump of sugar, assured Andrew that here was a possible buyer. How she came upon her money he didn't want to know, he was merely there to make the sale. He proceeded to show her around the house.

For someone who had probably started life humbly, Mrs Latimer showed typical superciliousness when it came to the finer points of carved cornices, Adam fireplaces and parquet floors. But then he remembered the three percent he and Sandy would be making out of the deal and he gave Mrs Latimer a sickly smile. After all, business was business.

At last they finished the tour of ten bedrooms with bathrooms en suite, four reception rooms, large kitchen and utility rooms, and all the mod. cons. of this des. res., not forgetting the swimming-pool, sauna, jacuzzi and roof garden, complete with fish, and fowl in the shape of two London sparrows.

Mrs Latimer stood in the spacious marble hall, her hand on her hip, her expression that of someone who has entered a bar and is waiting to be served.

'I suppose it'll do,' she remarked grudgingly. ' 'ave to be painted over, like. Colours are dull, but it'll do. I'll 'ave it.'

Andrew was still reeling with shock when he got back to the office. 'It's sold . . . to the most *ghastly* woman, but at least it's sold!' he told Sandy. 'God knows what she's going to do with it! Probably decorate the drawing-room in leopard skin patterned fabric and the bedroom in purple satin, but who cares?' The sale had cheered him up. 'Not a bad afternoon's work,' he added modestly.

'There's a message for you on your pad,' said Sandy. Something in the forced casualness of his voice made Andrew look at him anxiously.

'Jessica called,' Sandy said breezily. 'She left her number, so you can call her back.'

Madeleine poured a couple of drops of linseed oil on to the blob of white paint on her palette, and worked it in with the tip of her brush. When she was satisfied with the consistency, she leaned forward and very carefully, with a feather-light touch, added the highlights to her portrait of Pearl Ermintrude, one of New

York's leading socialites. This was the part she liked best. Adding those little dots and streaks of white that brought the face to life and gave it added depths. Especially the eyes. It was amazing what a tiny blob of glinting white, painted on the iris, could do. Then she added a touch of yellow and pink to the white paint, and started adding touches on the bridge of the nose, the forehead, the chin, and along the cheekbone.

She stood back to see the effect. Mrs Henry Ermintrude II, Pearl to her friends, was going to be thrilled out of her tiny mind. The portrait was destined to hang in their Dakota apartment and Pearl had specially worn a pale green silk dress to be painted in, 'Because the colour will go so perfectly with our decor'.

Madeleine grimaced, and then signed the canvas with a flourish, in dark brown paint: Madeleine Delaney. She gave it one more appraising look, then started to clean her brushes. It was only lunchtime, but she wouldn't be able to paint any more today as she had something more pressing to do. She checked the address where she was going: Tenth Avenue and Twenty-sixth Street, not far from Penn Station. A block called Altman Buildings. She didn't have an appointment. She could only hope he'd be there and that she'd get to see him.

Altman Buildings turned out to be a tall building, housing over fifty companies, their names listed by the elevator in the lobby. Not a smart building, by any means, she observed, running her eye down the list of occupants who mostly seemed to be in the con-

314

struction or machine tool business. Taking the creaking elevator to the eleventh floor, she stepped straight into a small cluttered reception area, the walls lined with battleship grey metal filing cabinets, a couple of battered desks, and a film of grime clinging to everything like a patina of poverty. In one corner an ancient coffee machine gurgled lethargically, as if it, too, was depressed by the surroundings.

A blowsy looking girl with bleached hair, tortured into an artful concoction of curls piled high on top of her head, sat at one of the desks, a telephone receiver wedged between her shoulder and jaw. She was deep in conversation.

'Aw, gee, honey, I told him straight – I don't like it that way! I said I'm not going to date you again unless you treat me like a lady . . . and what d'you think that cunt said? He told me I was frigid! Me! Frigid! Well, then I tells him he can shove it up his own arse for all I care!'

Suddenly the girl looked up, a resentful expression on her face at having been disturbed. 'Yeah?' she asked Madeleine.

'I'd like to see Mr Hank Pugsley, please.'

Insolent brown eyes looked her up and down. 'Is he expecting you?'

'No, but please tell him it's very important,' said Madeleine firmly.

The girl gave a sigh of irritation and spoke into the phone again. 'Dorothy? . . . Yeah, sorry about this. Will ya hang on a minute . . . I'll be as quick as I can.' Flashing Madeleine another reproachful look, she pressed the button on the office intercom.

'Hank, there's someone here to see you,' she bellowed.

Madeleine winced, and the girl addressed her again. 'Name?'

'Delaney. Madeleine Delaney.'

Another pause after the girl had repeated her name and then another question, sharp and unfriendly. 'What's it about?'

By now Madeleine was trying to keep her temper in check. One thing was obvious: Hank Pugsley ran a shoddy cheapjack outfit and the girl probably got paid peanuts. But then of course he wasn't into reinvesting in Brandt's Motors; he was too busy feathering his own nest in Switzerland.

'Tell Mr Pugsley,' said Madeleine with a hint of aggression, 'that I have to talk to him on very important business, and I won't go away until he sees me.'

The girl looked taken aback, but not for long. Her voice twanged nasally. 'She says it's important, Hank.' There was a pause and then she looked up at Madeleine again. 'Last door on the right, along the corridor,' she said grudgingly.

'Thank you,' replied Madeleine with pointed politeness. As she strode away along the corridor she could hear the girl on the phone say: '. . . Dorothy, are you still there? . . . Sorry about that! As I was saying . . .'

The wording painted on the door was grandiose compared to the conditions of the office. 'President. Hank Pugsley. Brandt's Motors.' Knocking, Madeleine entered to find a large man in his shirt-sleeves, his red face bloated with fat, his bare forearms covered with black hairs. From between his teeth a cigar protruded, so much a part of him that she wondered if he slept with it clamped between his lips like a baby with a dummy. Small wary eyes regarded her sharply, as he remained seated.

'Well?' demanded Hank Pugsley.

Madeleine stepped forward, an incongruously elegant figure in her simple cream dress. She pointed to the chair facing his desk, and asked with exaggerated good manners: 'May I sit down?'

Hank watched her with widening eyes and a slackening of the lower lip. 'Sure. What can I do for you?' he asked with a touch more deference.

'My name's Madeleine Delaney,' she began, 'and I have something to tell you which I think you ought to know.' Her heart was fluttering wildly now, wondering how he was going to react. At all costs, she reminded herself, she must keep Carl's name out of this.

Hank looked alarmed and Madeleine could tell he was guilty of a dozen misdemeanours by the way his eyes were registering varying degrees of anxiety as thoughts passed through his mind. She could guess he was thinking: Has my wife found out I've been going with hookers? Has the Department of Trade discovered I'm producing inferior goods? Worst of all, are the IRS on to me?

Madeleine let him simmer for a moment, allowing his obvious panic to settle and subside.

'What sort of thing?' he asked in a hoarse voice.

Madeleine leaned forward confidentially and dropped her voice.

'Firstly, I must ask you to respect the fact that I am talking to you in complete and utter confidence, and that I will not answer any questions as to how I came about the information I am going to give you.'

Hank took several seconds to digest this.

'What's . . . er . . . what's it about?' he gulped.

'Do you undertake not to question me about my sources?' Madeleine insisted.

He shrugged his great shoulders and spread his spatulate fingered hands on his desk. He hesitated. 'It depends.'

'I'll tell you everything I know, and it is to your advantage, Mr Pugsley, I assure you, but that's all I can do.'

The desire to be put out of his suspense, coupled with acute curiosity, made him reply: 'Okay. Whatever you say.'

Madeleine took a deep breath. 'I believe you know a girl called Kimberley Cabot?'

A glint of fear appeared in his eyes. 'Are you a private dick? Has my wife sent you?'

'Nothing like that,' said Madeleine, 'this has nothing to do with your private life. But you were unwise enough to tell Kimberley that you were evading paying all your taxes by transferring dollars to a phony company in Zurich.'

That did it. Hank shot up two feet in the air, his face grey, his eyes terrified.

'I deny it!' he blustered breathlessly. 'Who the hell d'you think you are . . . barging in here . . .'

'Listen, Mr Pugsley. It's no concern of mine what you do with your money!' she spoke sharply. 'I'm not from the IRS, or any other official department for that matter. I'm here because Kimberley Cabot is ripping you off and I think you should know about it.'

Confusion, relief, suspicion and finally incredulity passed like changing masks across Hank's face. He sank back heavily into his chair. 'What the fuck are you talking about?' he asked weakly.

Madeleine explained swiftly and in a decisive voice. She told him exactly what Kimberley was doing, making it seem like a one-woman operation so as not to involve Carl. 'I can't tell you how I found out,' she concluded. 'All I know is that every time you arrange to transfer dollars to Switzerland, she diverts them to her own numbered account. I even have the number of that account.'

Convinced at last, Hank sat slumped and again she could see his brain trying to work out what he could do. Report Kimberley to the FBI? Complain to the Central Manhattan Bank? Have it out with Kimberley in person?

Madeleine saved him the trouble of trying to find a solution. She spoke earnestly. 'There's nothing you can do about it, because you'd be in big trouble with the IRS yourself, and Kimberley knows it. She's banking on your keeping silent if you find out. That's why she's sure she can get away with it.'

'The fucking little cunt!' Hank exploded. 'And I thought she was a model! Some model!' He spat in disgust. 'What am I gonna do? D'you know how much of my money she's stolen?'

'How often do you put through a transfer?'

'Every coupla weeks . . . around three hundred thousand dollars each time.' He groaned despairingly.

Madeleine raised her eyebrows and did a quick calculation. 'Then she's probably got over a million dollars, by now. Maybe a million and a half.'

'Holy shit!' Hank sat stunned, gazing blindly at the papers on the desk before him, not seeing them but only seeing his precious money being stolen from him. 'I could do with a drink,' he mumbled. Fumbling in a drawer of his desk, he produced a bottle half full of whisky, the glass blurred with imprints of sweaty fingers.

'Want one?'

'No, thanks.'

He poured the amber liquid into a paper cup and gulped noisily in the silence of the dreary little office, his eyes registering pain. For a moment Madeleine felt quite sorry for him.

'There is something we can do, if you'll co-operate,' she ventured.

'Tell me something first – no, two things.'

Madeleine shook her head. 'I told you at the beginning that I can't tell you how I found out.'

'But you can tell me what's in it for you,' he shot back.

'There's nothing in it for me, except to see justice done; maybe a very rough sort of justice, but nevertheless I'd like to see Kimberley Cabot put out of action . . . probably as much as you would,' Madeleine replied evenly.

'Has she been screwing your husband?' His little

eyes suddenly looked shrewd with understanding.

Madeleine averted her gaze, as if the subject was distasteful, but inside she felt a pang. His remark was unnervingly accurate, and she had to master her emotions for a few seconds before she could reply. Then she turned to him with a calm smile.

'My father happens to be the President of the Central Manhattan Bank. I want Kimberley stopped because sooner or later she'll bring disgrace on the bank, and that would hurt my father. Nothing like this has ever happened before and it would affect him deeply.' And Carl, and me, she thought to herself.

Hank sniffed loudly. 'So what are you proposing? We get a hit man to look after her? I don't like the idea. Once you get in with the Mob . . .'

Madeleine looked shocked. 'Nothing like that! My God, no! That really would be fatal!'

'So what are you suggesting? Oh, Jesus Christ, I've just remembered!' He slammed the palm of his hand to his brow, and there was a slapping sound as flesh hit flesh.

'What's the matter?'

Hank looked greyer than ever, his skin a dirty bleached colour now. 'I sent off another transfer first thing this morning, for three hundred and thirty thousand bucks! Fuck, how can I stop it? I'd better call up the bank and say . . .'

'It's all right,' said Madeleine urgently. 'Don't do anything! It will make her suspicious if you cancel it now, and anyway she won't be able to put it through.'

'How d'you mean?'

For the first time Madeleine gave a satisfied smile.

'Unless I'm very much mistaken, she won't be able to divert your money to her own account any more, not unless she can think up another way of doing it. This time your money will end up where it's supposed to: in your account instead of hers.'

'Yeah? How did ya fix that?' Hank asked sceptically.

'I can't tell you, but I do think your money's safe, now and in the future. In the meantime, Mr Pugsley, how would you like to get what was stolen back again?'

Hank drained his paper cup of whisky, filled it up again and took another swig. 'Lady, you make me nervous. I'd like you to stop talking in riddles. You look like a classy dame, but how do I know you're on the level? And why should you want me to get my money back? How do I know I can trust you?'

'You've nothing to lose by trusting me, have you, and you can easily check that I'm Jake Shearman's daughter. The way I see it, I'd like to put to rights the loss you have suffered at the hands of an employee of the Central Manhattan Bank. And I'll be frank – I'd like to see Kimberley deprived of that money.'

Suddenly Hank seemed to be on her side and his attitude towards her changed. They had a purpose in common now, a desire to get even with Kimberley Cabot, and Madeleine could sense a new respect in his attitude.

'So what do we do?' he asked.

Madeleine outlined her plan. Hank's expression changed to one of total agreement and approval. 'Jeeze!' He whistled through his teeth. 'You're quite a dame, aren't you!'

'So you'll help me?'

'Sure! It'll be my pleasure!' The hint of a smile filled his flushed face. 'This has given me the fright of my fucking life. I'll never risk doing this sort of scam again. Christ, you don't know who you can trust, do you?'

Madeleine's smile had a touch of irony in it. 'You're right,' she agreed.

A few minutes later she left Hank's office and went along the corridor to the elevator. The girl behind the reception desk was still chattering on the phone to her friend.

'Is that you, Jessica?' Andrew braced himself to hear her voice again, knowing its light dulcet tones would cause him pain.

'Andrew!' She sounded shocked, although she must have been expecting him to return her call. He could imagine her going pink in the face, hands gesticulating wildly. 'Oh, Andrew! Did Maddy explain that I left London in such a rush I barely had time to even say goodbye to my parents? Are you terribly angry with me? Was it a terrible thing to do? I'd no idea you'd be *upset*!' Breathlessly, in a way Andrew knew so well, Jessica rattled on, hardly letting him get a word in edgewise.

'. . . and then when I landed in Boston, and telephoned Maddy, she said you'd been in touch,' she concluded. 'Anyway, how *are* you?'

'I'm okay,' he replied, determined to resist that overwhelming charm of hers that was as natural and uncalculated as a child's, and yet could have such a devastating effect on other people. For a moment, actually, he had a strange sensation that they were still together, that the last few months had been nothing but a silly quarrel, which they were about to patch up. 'And you're well?' he asked.

'I'm fine.'

There was an embarrassed silence where once there would have been an easy intimacy, reminding Andrew that they were no longer together; that Jessica was now thousands of miles away and with someone else.

'Good,' he said. 'So . . .' The silence between them became an eternity of unspoken words and unformed thoughts, and Andrew realised how deep was his loss. He wanted to ask Jessica: 'Why? Why did you give up your entire career for this other man, when you couldn't even give up a little bit of it for me? Why were you able to turn your back on the three years we had together for someone you hardly knew?' But all he was able to say was: 'So, you'll be doing a lot of travelling now, I suppose?'

Jessica spoke hurriedly, as if glad the lull in the conversation was over. 'That's right. I'll be living out of suitcases from now on! It's lucky I like hotel life, I must say . . .'

I'm glad she's not talking about *him*, Andrew reflected, as she chattered on. Then he thought: This is hurting much more than I thought it would. I can't believe I was such a fool as to let her go. He closed his eyes and heard her talk about visiting Moscow and how she was looking forward to it. 'That'll be interesting,' he heard himself say, while the pain ripped through his heart with lacerating swiftness and his mind cried out in silent anguish.

Andrew didn't remember much about the rest of their conversation. When he hung up he felt sick with cold misery and a feeling of utter defeat, made all the worse because he was convinced it was all his own fault.

As soon as Madeleine left Hank Pugsley's office she went straight back to her studio, not to paint but to sit down and quietly assess the position. Luck had been on her side so far; incredibly, she'd managed to get into Kimberley's apartment to talk to her, and she'd also had good fortune on her side when the PA had been called out of her office and she'd been able to examine the Filofax. And now she'd had her meeting with Hank Pugsley. Everything was going her way so far, but she wondered how long it could last. The next thing she needed was an excuse to go to Europe without awakening either Carl's or Jake's suspicion and curiosity. That might prove difficult.

Madeleine stayed for several hours in her studio, gazing absently at the canvases hung round the walls or stacked on the floor below. Occasionally she glanced up at the skylights, where through the glass, white clouds could be seen scurrying across a blue backcloth like an ever moving picture. Then she would glance at the faces of all the men and women she'd painted; some famous, some not; some beautiful, others quite ordinary; all bearing testimony to the years of hard work she'd put into her career. But her eyes weren't focused and nothing around her seemed real because all she could really see was a pale feral face framed by a mass of red hair, the mouth lewd, the eyes coldly brutal. It was as clear to her as if she had painted it: the face of Kimberley Cabot.

With shock, Madeleine realised she was consumed by revenge. She would not rest until she had brought about this woman's downfall, and for a second she felt a pang of shame. Doesn't this lower me to her level? she asked herself. Then she remembered hearing somewhere that you had to fight like with like. This was not the time to turn the other cheek and be forgiving. Her whole future with Carl was in jeopardy while Kimberley was allowed to get away with what she was doing. All Madeleine had to do now was find a plausible reason for flying to Europe.

It was as if her wish had been granted. When she got back to the apartment, there was a letter from Mr Marks, the solicitor, saying she was needed urgently in Devon.

Chapter Twelve

'Dinner at the White House! But I've nothing to wear!' wailed Jessica.

They were sitting in their very English suite at the Ritz-Carlton in Boston, and Bernard was calmly reading aloud his itinerary for the coming few weeks. Jessica had arrived two days before, to a rapturous reunion with him, but now she was trying to get to grips with the day to day routine that would be her future life. Strangest of all was finding that although she was still living in a hotel, she'd joined the ranks of the rich and privileged and was no longer concerned with the running of the place.

Suddenly her mildest wishes had become someone else's most pressing duty, with Bernard ordering everyone around them with the same command that he used to conduct an orchestra. Miss McCann wishes to have her hair done; or her dress pressed; or her shoes shined. Certainly, Sir. Miss McCann would like an extra pillow; another drink, a little snack . . . Yes, Sir. Certainly, Sir. No sooner had Jessica muttered that it would be nice to have something, than the figurative baton was in action again, and Bernard had everyone running round in circles.

With the unerring instinct of someone who relishes life to the full, Jessica flung herself into her new life with the velocity of a bullet leaving a gun barrel, but she greatly missed not being in control any more. She'd been so used to giving orders at the Royal Westminster, and to being responsible for the smooth running of the place, that now she felt disconcertingly disorientated, and strangely lost.

'The President and his wife are having one of their big dinners,' Bernard was explaining, 'when anyone who is anyone gets to go. This time that includes me and my lovely lady friend!'

Jessica pulled a little frown. 'Bernard, I hate being referred to as your "lady friend". It's an awful expression! The next thing is, I'll be referred to as "your constant companion"!'

'You could do worse, my darling,' Bernard demurred.

'And I could do a lot better!' Jessica flashed back. 'What's wrong with "girlfriend"?' She almost added as a joke, 'or fiancée or wife', but Bernard seemed to have lost a little of his sense of humour since she'd arrived in Boston. Instead she said seriously: 'Darling, what shall I wear for this dinner? Will it be terribly formal?'

Bernard looked up at her as she paced their suite, her small feet in their spiky heels almost high stepping like a pony in her agitation. Suddenly she felt unsure of herself, and very nervous. Everything seemed to be beyond her control now.

'You must have something suitable,' he observed mildly.

Jessica spun round, looking unhappy. 'I haven't got anything that would be right! Oh, if only you'd told me before I left London I could have got something at cost. I know all the designers at home.'

'We are "at home" ', Bernard said pointedly, 'or as much at home as we'll ever be. You'd better get used to it, Jessica, because we'll never be more settled, except when we're at my house in Sardinia, than we are now.'

Jessica stood still for a moment as the words registered. What he said was, of course, true. She'd known when she left London that for the rest of her life 'home' would be wherever Bernard was. Mistaking her silence for sulking, he rose angrily to his feet.

'Good God, what a fuss over a dress!' he suddenly roared. 'Every city has dress shops. Go out and look now. There are plenty of dress shops in Boston, for Christ's sake!'

Jessica stared at him, taken aback by his manner. Of course she had to admit she was making a fuss over a dress, but it was because she wanted him to be proud of her, and it wasn't every day one got to go and have dinner with the President of the United States.

'Okay, I'll go!' she said brightly. 'I'll go right now and come back with something that will stun you!' She went to get her coat and purse from their bedroom. When she returned to the living- room Bernard was absorbed in the score of the symphony he was conducting that night with the Boston Philharmonic Orchestra. Jessica realised he'd completely forgotten she was there.

'Fine!' she said to herself, with a comical expression. 'And enjoy yourself, Jessica! Get yourself a nice dress, Jessica! Have a nice day, Jessica!'

Leaving the Ritz-Carlton, which she'd heard described as the grande dame of Boston hotels, she walked along Arlington Street, where on the opposite side of the road fine public gardens blazed with flowers and grass as green as emeralds. She had to find a store where she could buy a stunning dress, and maybe shoes and a purse to match, and she was just about to ask an incredibly handsome young policeman she'd spotted where the main shops were, when something suddenly struck her with unpleasant force.

In the past, she had lived on her earnings, sharing the cost of running the flat with Andrew and being able to be financially independent. From the age of nineteen, she'd paid her own way, proud of the fact she didn't have to ask anyone, not even her parents, for money. But what was going to happen now? She'd saved a few thousand pounds of her salary while she'd been living in at the Royal Westminster, but that wouldn't last her long, especially if she was supposed to buy expensive clothes to go with Bernard's lifestyle. There was no way she was going to be able to work again with the constant touring. A fragment of her newfound euphoria crumbled away as she walked slowly on, she knew not where. Why hadn't she thought of the money side of living with Bernard before? Would he give her an allowance, or would she have to ask every time she even wanted a pair of tights? The thought was galling. It would make her feel like a kept woman and she hated the idea.

When Jessica got back to the Ritz-Carlton, nearly two hours later, having spent much more than she wanted to on a simple white crêpe evening dress, she had worked herself into a state of great agitation. She must know where she stood, and the sooner she discussed it with Bernard the better. She found him where she had left him, sitting in the living-room of their suite. He was talking to someone on the phone.

'*Si*, Prague!' bellowed Bernard into the mouthpiece, 'and after Prague, I go to Madrid. *Si*!'

Jessica went through to their bedroom, hung up her new dress and waited until she heard him replace the receiver. Then she rushed back into the living-room, her expression a mixture of anxiety and anger.

'Bernard, I must talk to you,' she began.

'Hush!' Bernard lifted the receiver again and asked the hotel switchboard to get him a number in Paris.

Jessica hovered about impatiently, watching him as he talked, wishing she could get the matter settled quickly. This whole scene is too humiliating, she thought distractedly. I'm not used to being so dependent on anyone. I'm a working woman who has always got a kick from having my own money and . . .

Bernard came off the phone. Jessica flung herself on the sofa beside him. 'Bernard . . . I *have* to talk to you!'

Bernard looked slightly surprised at her vehemence, but she could tell his mind was still miles away.

'I've realised I can't go on working now, and so I wondered what I'm going to do about money!' she blurted out, realising it sounded crass but desperate to get his attention before he started to make any more calls.

'Money?' Bernard looked at her so blankly she

might have been talking about nuclear energy or splitting atoms. 'What d'you mean?'

'Money! For buying clothes . . . and things!' Jessica had flushed so deeply her blonde hair looked white by comparison. 'I shall need money, and I haven't much of my own, and I'm used to earning . . .' She broke off lamely, mortified at having to ask for an allowance. Bernard should have made this easy for me, she thought, with a sudden burst of anger. He should have said something, right at the beginning, when they were planning their lives together; something that would clarify the situation. Instead, here she was fumbling for words, trying to preserve some shreds of dignity.

Bernard waved his hand airily. 'Oh, just put everything on my credit cards. I'll get your signature authorised, so it'll be no problem.'

'Yes, but . . .' She still didn't feel entirely happy. Supposing she wanted actual cash? Supposing she wanted to buy him a present, and she didn't want him to know how much it had cost? She wriggled uncomfortably. 'I'd rather have money in my bank account,' she added plaintively.

Bernard rose and stretched. His voice sounded angry. 'What's the matter with you? Why all this fuss . . . first about a dress and now money? My financial advisers look after everything for me. They take care of my bills and my taxes, so that I don't have to be bothered with this sort of thing. I don't even want to have to think about money. It bores me. My life is music . . . not how do I pay for a pair of shoes or a new shirt or some such trivia.'

'That's all very well for you!' Jessica retorted, the bit between her teeth now, filled with an insane desire to pursue the subject to the limits, almost as if she'd been spoiling for a fight. '*You're* earning the money in the first place, and you can do as you like with it! For the first time in my life I'm not going to be earning anything and . . . well, it makes me feel insecure, and . . . and *beholden* to you! It makes me feel like a kept woman!'

For a moment Bernard stared at her and then he threw back his head and gave a bellow of laughter. A moment later he had his arms around her, hugging her close. 'You funny girl . . . you funny girl,' he repeated, rocking her gently, his face buried in her hair. 'Scratching like a little wild cat who does not want to be looked after!'

'But, Bernard . . .' Jessica said weakly, leaning against him.

'Is this what women's lib does for you? Makes you unable to accept a man's love?'

'No, of course it doesn't!' she retorted, pushing him away slightly. 'Love has nothing to do with this. Love is something you *give* . . . money shouldn't come into it at any point. I don't like the feeling you're letting me spend your money, just because you love me!'

'Is that what your mother said to your father? I don't suppose she complained about being looked after financially, any more than my mother did,' Bernard replied. 'You young girls have got it so screwed up . . . you feel it is a disgrace if you can't pay your way like a man, whilst I think it is a man's duty, not to mention his pleasure, to look after a woman in every way.'

Jessica broke away from his arms, her small face determined. 'I don't agree. I like to be able to spend my money as I like. How can I do that if it's your money?'

'Shouldn't you have considered this before you came away with me?' Bernard asked reasonably. 'You must have known you'd be giving up your career?'

Jessica hung her head, feeling childish and foolish. 'I never thought,' she said, almost sadly. 'It all happened so quickly.'

With a swift movement, Bernard took her in his arms again, kissing her face with light fluttery kisses, looking adoringly down into her eyes. 'I know, my love. I know,' he murmured softly. 'It must all be so strange for you, and you must still be jet-lagged and tired. I've been a fool to rush you like this, without stopping to consider how you must be feeling.'

Jessica returned his kisses, feeling her body responding to his, though doubts still hovered in her mind. She did belong to a generation of young women who guarded their financial independence fiercely. Most of her friends had continued to work, even after they'd married and had children, and she'd always supposed it would be the same for her. If she had married Andrew, she'd have had to continue working in any case for them to afford the style of living they had both wanted. Andrew. Her parents. England. How far away they all seemed.

Bernard was carrying her in his strong arms into the

bedroom now, and she could feel his mounting desire. Confusedly her body was filled with a longing for him too, although her mind had been shafted by tiny thrusts of misgiving. In time she would resolve her feelings, but for now here was Bernard, soothing and arousing her with magical hands, kissing away her fears and bringing to the surface a passion she never knew existed.

She didn't even remember taking off her clothes. The next thing she knew Bernard had placed her astride him as he lay on the bed under her, and he was thrusting upwards with such strength that he was lifting her, penetratingly and violently, with each push. With his sensitive hands holding her hips in position, he took first one small breast and then the other in his mouth as she leaned over him, sucking deeply on her until she felt as if her whole body was inflamed. With each thrust the intensity increased until she convulsed and begged him to stop. Only then did he allow himself to climax, giving himself to her with a rush of passion and a cry of joy.

Madeleine read the letter quickly, trying to understand the pedantic legal phraseology that all solicitors love to indulge in. By the time she'd got to the third 'whereunto' and 'wheretofor', she reached for the phone and dialled the Devonshire number of Spindle, Coutts and Marks. Mr Marks came quickly on the line, shouting slightly, as if to make sure his voice carried across the air-waves of the Atlantic.

'I've heard from your father, Mr Jake Shearman,' he said in a loud voice, 'but he hasn't given me any details that will help to verify the existence of your mother's death certificate.'

'I see.' Madeleine didn't know her father had been in touch with the solicitor at all. Why hadn't he mentioned it to her? 'What exactly did he say?' she inquired.

'Well, he asked me to fly over to visit him in America – quite out of the question, of course.' Mr Marks dismissed the idea as being as crazy as if he'd been invited on a spaceship to the moon.

'Why did my father invite you over here?' Madeleine asked, mystified.

'I'm afraid I don't really know. He said it was a confidential matter, so even if I was aware of the facts I would not be able to impart them to you,' he added primly, his voice still raised to a tremulous shout.

'So what happens now?' Madeleine felt deeply irritated. Why on earth couldn't Jake co-operate so that this whole business could be settled once and for all?

'I'm afraid we'll have to go ahead with bringing the case to court, to get an order of presumption of your mother's death, and you will have to appear. Even if I had the time to get away, which I haven't,' he added hastily, 'it's too late to cancel the hearing. That's why I wrote to you.'

Madeleine's mind worked quickly. The last thing she wanted was to have to attend this court case, which would be held in Okehampton Assizes, and would no doubt attract a lot of local gossip and speculation. On the other hand, she desperately needed a valid reason to go to Europe right now and this was a trip Carl wouldn't question. She'd tell him Mr Marks

336

demanded her presence, and that while she was in England she'd make arrangements to hold an exhibition of her work the following summer, in London. That should satisfy him; more importantly, it would be a perfect cover for what she really had to do.

Tonight, she and Carl were dining with her father. Aunt Patti would be there! Suddenly, Madeleine realised it would be the perfect opportunity to kill two birds with one stone. She'd tell them she had to go back to Milton Manor for the case, and she'd ask her father why he'd wanted Mr Marks to fly over to see him.

When Carl returned from the bank shortly before seven o'clock, Madeleine was in their bedroom, changing for dinner.

'Hi, darling,' she called out, when she heard his step in the hall. 'Like a drink while you're getting ready to go to Daddy's?'

Carl entered their bedroom and saw Madeleine sitting at her dressing-table, putting the finishing touches to her make-up. She was wearing a brilliant yellow silk jersey dress, her black hair a riot of curls around her exquisite heart-shaped face, and he thought he'd never seen her look more beautiful. He went over and kissed her tenderly on the side of her neck.

'I'd love a drink,' he said with feeling. 'It's been one helluva day and I'm whacked!'

'Why don't you get into the shower while I fix it,' said Madeleine, jumping to her feet. She gave him a brief loving look and then went into the living-room to fix his favourite dry martini with an olive. When she got back to the bedroom he was undressing slowly, as if every movement was an effort.

'So what have you been doing today,' he asked, taking the drink from her and sipping it appreciatively. The gin, sharply iced, hit his stomach explosively. Leaning back on the white sofa at the foot of their bed, he closed his eyes.

Madeleine went and stood over him, gently massaging his neck and temples in a way she knew he liked. 'Oh, nothing much,' she lied in a soft voice, 'but I did get a letter from Mr Marks telling me I'll have to go to England for the court case.'

'Yeah?' Carl wondered why he felt a momentary stab of relief. He'd miss her as he always did when she was away, but right now the strain of having to carry on normally was proving too much for him. He'd started to use sleeping pills lately and he'd lost so much weight his trousers were in permanent danger of falling down. Madeleine was bound to notice soon. It would give him some breathing space if she was away for a week or so.

'I shall miss you, honey,' Carl said truthfully. 'I wish I could go with you, but it's impossible right now.'

Her fingers, rotating gently round the nape of his neck, were easing the tension, but he still felt strung out.

'I'll be back as soon as I can,' she promised. 'You know I can't bear to be away from you for too long, either.'

'Good,' he said absently, the gin taking effect. Hank Pugsley was due to put through another transfer any day now, and Carl lived in sickening dread of those moments when he saw the signed authorisation placed on his desk by Kimberley. She had a way of laying it right on top of all his other papers so that he saw it first. Now he knew that behind her gesture of leaving it prominently displayed lay an element of psychological warfare. She despised him for his initial moment of weakness in allowing himself to be seduced by her, and it gave her a kick to torture him every time Hank's transfer came through; remind him that if he hadn't been such a fool, none of this would have happened; remind him also that he was in her power and he'd have to do as she wished.

Would Hank's transfer come tomorrow? Carl's stomach contracted painfully. Instead of feeling easier with each successful transfer, he was getting increasingly panic-stricken. Kimberley had been lucky so far, but suppose somebody came into the computer room, at the exact moment when she had the copy of the tape from Jake's office in operation? Supposing they came up to her and, seeing the layout on the green screen, asked: 'Hey, Kimberley, what are you doing?' Supposing someone met her on her way to the computer room, or on her way back, with the tape in her pocket and the details of Hank's latest transfer in her hands? Supposing . . . here Carl's heart gave such a bound that he was sure Madeleine, stroking his neck, would feel the hammering of his pulse through her fingers . . . supposing Jake were to ask one day why Brandt's Motors seemed to have stopped paying regular invoices to Michaux Internationale in Zurich? And supposing he then called up Hank Pugsley to ask if everything was all right? Carl squeezed his eyes shut in inner agony.

'I think we should go away for a long vacation when this is all over,' he heard Madeleine say.

He caught his breath sharply. 'When what's all over?'

'This business with the solicitors and my grand-father's Will, of course! We were just talking about it!'

'Yes. Oh, of course.' Christ, he'd been miles away, the worry eating into him, making him paranoid. In an hour they were due at Jake's house. Better get showered and changed.

'Could you fix me another drink, Maddy?' He held out his empty glass.

'Sure.' She sounded surprised. 'But you'd better not arrive at Daddy's in an alcoholic state. You know how he likes to indulge us with his special wines.' Jake considered himself to be something of a wine connoisseur.

Carl managed a laugh. 'I know.' He imitated Jake. 'At a hundred dollars a bottle we shouldn't spoil our palates by drinking spirits first.'

Madeleine giggled. 'If Daddy had his way, I shouldn't wear lipstick when drinking wine, either, because it spreads a layer of grease on the surface of the wine and affects the taste. And he says I shouldn't use perfume. "Destroys the delicate bouquet". Honestly, I think he goes over the top at times!'

Carl smiled, longing to feel as merry as Madeleine obviously did. And then it struck him . . . when had he last felt really happy?

* * *

Jake Shearman's house, set in a quiet cul-de-sac off Beekman Place, overlooked the East River, far below, and was one of the few that were still privately owned. Built with the formal symmetry of a dolls' house, it was stone-fronted up as far as the second floor windows, and above that, red-bricked. Somehow retaining the quiet elegance of a bygone era, and far enough away from the heavy traffic of First Avenue, the cul-de-sac was part of a quiet oasis of tree-lined streets in which purring limousines waited for their owners to appear. Madeleine had spent her childhood in this tranquil house, and when she'd left to marry Carl, Jake decided to stay, looked after by the servants who had been with him for over twenty years. After all, he said, where else could he house his possessions? The Shearmans had been one of New York's most revered and rich families for three generations and, having originally made their fortune in tin mining, they had invested that money in priceless paintings and antique furniture and objets d'art that would more normally be found in a museum.

Now, as President of the Central Manhattan Bank, Jake looked upon the Beekman Place mansion as a perfect setting for formal entertaining. The classy ambience was something you couldn't buy in a restaurant. The new money of yesterday had become the old money of today.

When Carl and Madeleine arrived for dinner the beauty of the house, which would one day be hers, struck her afresh, as it did every time she visited Jake. There was something so wonderfully warm and welcoming in the softly lit rooms, where French and

341

English antiques blended together under the fine oil paintings that hung on the walls, and where marble and gilt, natural polished floors strewn with silk oriental rugs, and raw silk draperies at the windows, gave the whole atmosphere a feeling of rare elegance.

Jake was waiting for them in the drawing-room where great Chinese vases, full of white lilies, added to the air of opulence.

'Hi, Daddy!' Madeleine swept forward, very much a figure of the eighties with her fashionable cloud of black curls, in this setting which was so eighteenth-century. Her yellow dress stood out dramatically against the pastel shades of the room.

'Hello, Maddy.' Jake leaned forward to kiss her, and then he shook hands with Carl although he'd only seen him at the bank a couple of hours before. 'Good to see you, Carl.'

As drinks were being poured Madeleine looked round the room, her eyes automatically straying to the wall above the mantelshelf. It was as if she always hoped for a miracle, hoped that one day the portrait of her mother would suddenly reappear so that she could study it, especially now she'd seen all those old photographs of Camilla at Milton Manor. Had the artist seen into Camilla's soul, the way she saw into the souls of her sitters? Had he, too, found those eyes mockingly evil?

'Daddy . . .' she began, curiosity suddenly consuming her. After all, why shouldn't she ask where the painting was?

'. . . and with interest rates being what they are I said to the President . . .' Jake had his back turned to her, deep in discussion with Carl.

Madeleine sat down on the sofa facing the fireplace, waiting for the men to stop talking. Suddenly she heard Jake say: 'I saw that glamour girl you've got working for you in the lobby yesterday!' He paused, his brows furrowed. 'What's her name? Something to do with a diamond.'

Carl shifted his feet avoiding Madeleine's eyes, and said abruptly, 'Kimberley. Kimberley Cabot.'

Jake beamed as if he'd remembered it himself. 'Of course! Kimberley, like the diamond mines! Well, she said . . .'

Madeleine realised both she and Carl were straining forward, eager to catch each word. She recovered herself first and sipping her drink with seeming nonchalance, heard Jake continue: 'She said you'd had a lot of meetings in connection with Third World debts.'

The atmosphere in the room instantly relaxed, grew warm, and Madeleine had a delicious floating sensation as if the champagne bubbles had lifted her bodily as well as mentally, and were making her drift upwards. She heard Carl reply: 'We've had a few problems, but there's nothing that won't right itself in time . . .' before she felt herself crashing downwards again at her father's next words.

'Carl, that was a large transfer of dollars you put through to Ireland at the beginning of the week. Loan for a new car plant, is it?'

Madeleine watched Carl closely; maybe there was more going on than she realised, and perhaps Jake had got wind of it. The muscles of her stomach tightened sickeningly and she held her breath, waiting for Carl's reply.

'Yes. The Morgan Company. They're opening a plant just outside Dublin. Oliver Morgan, from Wisconsin, is President and he's over there now setting everything up,' said Carl calmly.

'Of course.' Jake nodded. 'I remember now. It should bring a lot of employment to Ireland where it is most needed.' The two men smiled at each other and continued to discuss business.

For Madeleine it was enough. She didn't want to spend the whole evening on an emotional switchback with Jake giving her these frights every time he opened his mouth. She tried to keep her voice light and jokey.

'Now, that's enough, you two. No more business talk! You've got all day at the bank to talk shop so let's discuss something else.'

Jake grinned indulgently. 'My little girl getting bored?' But Carl looked surprised. Normally Madeleine showed an interest in what was happening and never cut short a business discussion.

At that moment Patti arrived, alone because Sam was attending an all male dinner at the New York Yacht Club.

'I hope you're not expecting any other guests,' she remarked tartly, after greetings had been exchanged.

Jake looked mystified. 'No, there's just us. But why?'

Patti settled herself on an upright chair, a cigarette in one hand and a drink in the other. She surveyed them sternly. 'Because I've had enough of making polite conversation to boring socialites to last me a lifetime! Today I had lunch with twelve other women.

This afternoon I was with the committee for the Arts Educational Trust to discuss their gala benefit night . . . and you can imagine the jealousy there is on the ladies' committee, not to mention the bitching. And this evening, I had to go to a drinks party on the way here!' She closed her eyes, as if the rigours of socialising were too much to bear. The gentle blue vapour of her cigarette rose round her perfectly coiffeured head and gaunt face, making even her diamonds look smoky. For a moment she seemed withdrawn from them in her suffering.

Jake's mouth twitched. 'Patti, you don't have to go to all these things! You know you only do it because you really enjoy it.'

Her eyes opened with a snap and regarded him fiercely. 'You talk a lot of rubbish, Jake . . . and where are the ashtrays?' Her head swung jerkily, stiff with age, from side to side. 'Why do you never have any ashtrays around, for goodness' sake?'

'One ashtray coming up!' said Carl, swiftly placing a tiny china dish by her side, a grin on his face. 'This will hold precisely one butt and a little ash, and then I'll find you another one.'

Patti laughed, and it was like the sound of rusty machinery that hadn't been used for years. 'Thanks,' she replied, 'and you look tired, Carl. Jake, are you working this boy too hard?'

'I'm a slave driver, Patti, you should know that by now,' Jake said, with a glimmer of humour.

'Yes,' quipped Carl. 'He chases after us with a whip! No slacking's allowed at the Central Manhattan!'

Patti looked from one to the other, and then turned

to Madeleine. 'And you look as if you need a break. I'm not sure that yellow dress doesn't make you look like a ripe banana! Never mind, your hair's very pretty tonight.'

Madeleine roared with laughter. 'That, I must tell Calvin Klein! I'm not sure he won't sue you. But we can't all look like Marlene Dietrich on a good day, Aunt Patti.'

'Cheeky girl,' chided her aunt. 'Marlene Dietrich has the most appalling taste in clothes.'

'Another drink, Patti?' Jake said.

'I thought you'd never ask! Of course I'd like another drink. And are we going to eat some time tonight? I can't live on canapés, you know.' The exhausted socialite of a few moments before had become the ebullient scene-stealer, as she held court in her brother's drawing-room as if he'd invited thirty guests instead of three.

Patti was in her element, teasing one moment, charming the next, playing her little audience along like a fisherman trying to land a salmon, but knowing when he did he would let it go free. The others enjoyed the little charade, pitting their wits against her razor sharp repartee and gimlet-like mind, trying to hold their own in the face of her volley of insults, none of which were meant to hurt or be taken seriously.

For Jake and Madeleine it was easy; both had known Patti all their lives and were used to her acerbic tongue. Jake gave as good as he got, while Madeleine trod more delicate ground, aware that she belonged to the younger generation and must temper her ripostes with good manners. Carl was in a more

346

difficult position. It had taken him nearly five years to get used to Patti Ziffren at all, much less engage in astringent badinage with her, but he had finally hit upon an act of cheerful guileless boyishness and she loved him for it; especially when he pretended to flirt with her. Then Jake was reminded of the Patti of his childhood, a high-spirited young woman, eleven years his senior, and the toast of New York with young men falling over themselves to take her out. But that, Jake reflected sadly, was before a loveless marriage to Samuel Ziffren, and being unable to have children, had made Patti take cover behind a façade of asperity, so that she might protect her real feelings.

'That's the third cigarette you've smoked since you arrived, Patti,' said Jake with some anxiety.

'So, who's counting?' Patti retorted, and promptly fell into a coughing fit. She was still wheezing when the butler came in to announce dinner.

Jake Shearman's dining-room was no less formal than the drawing-room, hung with Brussels tapestries and furnished with Hepplewhite chairs and table. A dazzling display of silver and crystal glittered in the glow of many pale blue candles, which Patti complained made it too dark to see what you were eating but was, on the other hand, a very flattering form of lighting. 'And God knows, Jake, you and I need all the flattering we can get!' she added, as she took her place opposite him.

Madeleine had decided to wait until dinner was over and the servants withdrawn before producing Mr Marks' letter. Her stomach tensed as the time drew nearer. Once Carl and her father had stopped talking business the evening had become pleasant and relaxed, but she knew that as soon as she spoke about her mother, there would be acrimonious repercussions. She was about to speak when Patti, whose eyes had been flickering round the table observing everyone with her usual acuity, turned first to Carl and then to Madeleine.

'What's the matter with you two?' she demanded. 'I've heard more conversation in a cemetery on a wet Sunday.'

Madeleine seized the opportunity, withdrawing the solicitor's letter from her purse. 'I've heard from Mr Marks, Daddy. Here is his letter. I'd like Aunt Patti to read it too.' She handed Jake the stiff white sheet of paper, which had the name of the company discreetly printed in small black lettering along the top. 'Why did you write to Mr Marks, Daddy, without tellling me? What could you tell him that you couldn't tell me? I have to go to England again in a week's time, and I've got to have some answers before I go.'

Jake's eyes were skimming the letter, his bonhomie vanished at the mention of the solicitor's name. In silence he handed it across to Patti. When she had read it, she looked up at him, her eyes unfathomable holes of darkness in her drawn face. The atmosphere in the room was suddenly charged with expectancy, an anticipation that was painfully palpable.

Carl was the first to speak, and his tone was quiet and reasonable. 'Look, I think it's time everything came out into the open, don't you? It's embarrassing for Madeleine not knowing what the hell's going on, and it's beginning to put her in an awkward position with Mr Marks. As it is, she's now got to appear in court to try and get an order of presumption of her mother's death. Wouldn't it be simpler to spare her all this and just tell her what happened?'

Madeleine's expression, as she looked across the flickering candlelit table to Carl, was one of gratitude. Carl's supportiveness meant the world to her, especially at this moment.

Patti spoke before her brother. 'I think Carl's right, Jake.'

He stared down at his tiny china coffee cup, stirring the black liquid absently with a small gold spoon. 'I had hoped this whole thing could be settled quietly and without fuss,' he said slowly. 'I was prepared to talk to Mr Marks, if he came over.'

'But why not to me, Daddy?' Madeleine pleaded. 'It's not much to ask. All I need to know is when and where my mother died, and then the matter can be settled.'

'Go on, Jake!' urged Patti, as if she could hardly wait for the tale at last to be told. 'It'll be worse for Madeleine if she hears it from someone else.'

Something cold and prickling and tingling swept across Madeleine with a suddenness that made her give a little gasp. Jake rested his elbows on the table and covered his face with his hands. The only sound was the occasional hiss of a guttering candle flame and far away the desolate wailing of a police siren, growing louder then fading away again.

Something was to be revealed at last, a curtain of silence and conspiracy to be lifted. Madeleine sat rigid, knowing that it was about to happen, while her mind silently shrieked: 'Tell me . . . tell me . . .'

The shock when it finally came burst upon her like an explosive shower of sparks; stinging, burning, scorching her brain.

Jake had taken his hands away from his face, and his eyes, as they looked into hers, were full of pain. But his voice was sharp and clear.

'The truth of the matter, Maddy . . . is that your mother is still alive.'

Chapter Thirteen

'My mother's still alive?' Madeleine repeated Jake's words in disbelief. 'How d'you mean . . . she's alive?'

Jake looked at his daughter as if the truth, wrenched at last from his soul, had left him raw and bleeding.

'Alive?' echoed Carl, incredulously.

'She's not dead as we led you to believe,' cut in Patti, in a clear concise voice. 'I'm sorry, Maddy, but under the circumstances both your father and I felt it was better to let you think she'd died when you were small.'

'But why?' Madeleine felt the room spinning round, as her mind tried to absorb this unbelievable thing; that the mother she'd always thought was dead; the mother whose love she'd craved when she'd been a child; the mother whose guidance she'd longed for as she grew up; the mother whose support and encouragement she'd so wanted in recent years . . . was alive and well and presumably living in England! The blood rushed to her head, as angry tears blinded her. She turned to Jake, who sat there in silence.

'How *could* you!' she lashed out in fury. 'How could you deprive me of my mother, all my life! I don't care what she did to you,' she continued wildly, 'I don't care how much she hurt you, you had no right

351

to keep me from her. Oh, God, I always wanted my mother so much!' Her voice ended on a sob and she seemed to crumple and grow smaller in her chair. Carl rushed round from his side of the table and put his arms around her, holding her close.

'You mustn't blame your father,' she heard Patti say. 'He did what he thought was best, and I backed him all the way.'

'Was it because she was involved in black magic?' demanded Madeleine. 'Why didn't you take her away from England then? Why didn't you bring her back to the States?' Her questions, tumbling out one after the other, caused Jake and Patti to look at each other, exchanging knowing glances. Madeleine intercepted their looks and a cold wave of fear swept over her.

'Is she . . . is she still involved . . . in witchcraft?' she blurted out wretchedly.

Patti shook her head violently, the ash from her cigarette falling into a little grey roll on the table's polished surface. 'No. No, she is not, Madeleine. She hasn't been involved in . . . that sort of thing since . . .' Her voice drifted away and again she caught Jake's eye. Something in his expression silenced her.

'Since you were little,' Jake finished the sentence for her. 'Please believe me when I say that what I did, I did for your own good, honey. You know me well enough to know that I would never do anything to hurt you.'

Madeleine knew her father was telling the truth. Ever since she could remember he'd put her first, caring for her in every way, even though the bank had always made great demands on his time. Somehow he'd managed to get home in time to read her a bed-time story at least twice a week, which was more than many of her friends' fathers did, and at weekends he'd always take her out and spend time with her.

As she sat at the dining-room table now, looking at him, she believed him when he said he'd never do anything to hurt her, and yet . . .

'So why did you never tell me my mother was alive, Daddy?' she cried out piteously. 'God knows, I've asked you often enough. It wasn't until I went to grandfather's house that I even found out what she looked like. All these years you've kept me in the dark, and so have you, Aunt Patti, and I want to know why?'

'Yes,' Carl broke in loyally, his arm still round Madeleine, stroking her shoulder comfortingly. 'There'd better be a damn good reason for you to have kept Maddy in the dark all these years, and I, for one, would like to know what it is!'

Madeleine turned her head to look at Carl, grateful for his support, and it flashed through her mind that once they were out of this nightmare of her problems with her family, and his problems with Kimberley, they'd be such a strong unit together nothing would ever be able to break them. She reached out and took his hand, and he returned her grip with a tender squeeze. A heavy silence fell on the room, and when Jake at last spoke his tones were measured.

'You have to realise, Maddy, that you were only three when your mother and I . . . er . . . parted, shall we say. Far too young to be told anything, and like all small children you accepted her absence at first

353

because you had me, and a very good Nanny, and of course Aunt Patti.'

'But I remember asking about my mother, all the time!' Madeleine protested. 'You wouldn't tell me anything at first, and then you said she was dead. Why did you tell me she'd died, Daddy, if she hadn't?'

'Perhaps because . . .' Jake paused, as if searching for the right words. 'Perhaps because she was and always would be, dead to you and me,' he finished quietly.

Madeleine's dark eyes grew round. 'I don't understand.'

Jake leaned forward and his eyes were filled with sympathy and compassion for a daughter he loved so much, and on whom he was having to inflict pain.

'I'm afraid, my darling, that your mother is in a mental asylum. She's been hopelessly insane for over twenty years.'

The mocking eyes, hundreds of them, closed in on Madeleine, threatening her with their malevolence, terrifying her with their feral venom. It was dark. She was in a padded cell, so soft-walled and sound-proofed that her cries could not be heard, and round her wrists tight bindings held her fast. There was no escape; she had been banished from the light a thousand years ago, and held in this place where the walls were made of glittering eyes and the silence was the silence of the tomb. Her throat ached with screams that could not be heard, and in a frenzy she struggled to free herself of the shackles . . .

'Madeleine! Darling! Wake up!' Slowly, through the dark mists that enveloped her, Madeleine struggled to the surface of consciousness, aware that her nightdress was soaked with sweat and that her hair clung about her face and neck.

'It's all right, sweetheart,' she heard Carl saying repeatedly, holding her flailing wrists with both hands. 'You've had a nightmare. Wake up! It's all over now. You're all right, darling.'

Madeleine opened her eyes, and looked around as if to reassure herself that she really had been dreaming. 'God . . . it was all so vivid,' she muttered, burying her face in Carl's shoulder. 'I dreamed I *was* my mother . . . and that I'd been held in a padded cell for years and years.'

Carl turned on the bedside light, bathing the silky room in a rosy glow. Then he took Madeleine in his arms, holding her close.

'I could kill your father for springing that information about your mother on you like that, tonight,' he said angrily. 'You've had the most tremendous shock, Maddy. I'm not surprised you had a bad dream.'

'Oh, Carl . . . it was awful!' Tears streamed down her cheeks as she pressed herself close to him. 'Daddy never said what made her go crazy . . . do you think it's hereditary? I felt I was mad in that dream just now! Is that why he hasn't told me about my mother before . . . because he knew it could happen to me too?'

'No, I don't think that was the reason. I think something happened . . . something traumatic, from which she never recovered,' Carl said gently. 'You found out she was involved in black magic. I suspect it had something to do with that.'

Madeleine raised a tear-stained face to look into his, seeking reassurance. Carl didn't know it, but she had so much on her mind at present she felt she *could* easily go crazy. Kimberley Cabot and the bank embezzlement, and the deal she'd made with Hank earlier in the day, were enough to send anyone off their trolley, even without being told their mother had been totally insane for years!

'You're probably right,' she said, trying to get a grip on herself, though small dry sobs still caught her breath, 'but I feel scared of going to sleep again.'

Carl kissed her cheek warmly and tenderly. 'You'll be safe with me,' he whispered, tightening his grip. 'I'll see that nothing happens to you.'

But as she drifted off to sleep at last, the irony of his words struck her. It was she who was really trying to see that nothing happened to him.

They met at Mortimer's for lunch, greeting each other joyously and a little curiously, having exchanged all their news on the phone the previous day. Madeleine wondered if Jessica would have changed in any way as a result of falling so dramatically in love with a stranger, even to the point of giving up her old life. Jessica was consumed with interest to find out Madeleine's reactions to finding her mother was alive after all.

'It's *so* good to see you!' Jessica crowed, doing a little jig. She looked vibrantly alive in a scarlet suit with lots of brass buttons, but for once her hair was in a firm tight chignon and her large gilt earrings made her face look more diminutive than ever. 'But, Maddy, you're looking pale,' she added accusingly.

Madeleine made an attempt at flippancy. 'Well, it's not every day you find out you've got a mother, when you've spent most of your life thinking you haven't!' she quipped. She looked thinner than usual, and there were dark shadows under her eyes. 'Anyway, let's have a drink. I'm longing to hear all your news, it sounds amazing!'

'It is! And I want to hear all yours! When did Jake spring all this on you, and *why*, my dear?' Talking non-stop, Jessica settled herself at the corner table they'd been shown to, ordered a spritzer, and then turned her full attention on Madeleine. 'Seriously, Maddy, are you all right? You look dreadful!'

Madeleine burst into laughter. 'Thanks, Jessie! That's just what I wanted to hear. Now I feel terrific.'

Jessica snatched her arm earnestly. 'You know I didn't mean it like that, sweetie. I'm worried about you. You said you were flying to England in a couple of days' time . . . is it to see your mother?' Jessica couldn't help shuddering inwardly; the story her journalist friend, Peter, had told her coming back to her. It had been so horrific she'd kept it to herself all this time. She wondered how much Madeleine knew, even now. At the time she'd pretended she hadn't been able to get hold of Peter again, so that her friend wouldn't probe further.

'I don't know whether I shall see my mother or not,' Madeleine replied honestly. The truth was she was still using the revelation about her mother, plus the fact she had to discuss Milton Manor with the solicitor, as an excuse to go to Europe. There would be no court case now to prove her mother dead; Jake had held the power of attorney of Camilla's estate for years so Madeleine would inherit automatically.

'I couldn't believe it when Jake told me she was still alive,' Madeleine continued, as she slowly sipped her drink. 'To think she's been in an institution all these years, with Daddy sending regular payments, and I never knew! He still won't tell me what happened . . . why she went mad . . . but I think it's got something to do with the black magic cult or whatever it was that she was involved with.'

Jessica's face was inscrutable, giving nothing away. 'Perhaps she just had a nervous breakdown,' she said carefully.

Madeleine shook her head. 'No, I'm sure it was to do with the witchcraft. In any case,' she straightened her shoulders, and looked more cheerful, 'I shall find out now. I shall ask the doctor who's looking after her at the institution. Even Jenkins, the gardener, might spill the beans when he realises I know she's really alive after all. Hell, I might even ask her herself!' Madeleine gave an edgy laugh, with a thin vein of hysteria running through it.

Jessica frowned. 'Maddy, you *are* uptight! Oh God, I wish I could be in England when you go over. Isn't it the most maddening thing,' she demanded, 'that just as I arrive in New York, you buzz off to London? And I suppose I'll have left for Milan by the time you return.'

'Oh, I should think so,' Madeleine replied carefully, not wanting Jessica to suspect that she intended to stay in England until a great deal more than the affair of her mother had been sorted out.

'Oh, damn! Then I won't see you again for ages. You must keep in touch and tell me *everything* that happens, and exactly what Camilla's like.'

'I will,' Madeleine promised. 'And so you'll be touring with Bernard Scheller most of the time, will you?' she added, with a sudden feeling of embarrassment. It had been Andrew for so long . . . Andrew whom she'd grown really fond of, and Andrew whom she'd always supposed would become Jessica's husband one day. It was strange and awkward to have to refer to a man she'd never met and who, from what she'd heard, wasn't exactly right for Jessica.

'My dear,' said Jessica excitedly, 'do you realise that I'll be living out of suitcases for the next five months? That's twenty-four weeks! Talk about a gypsy existence.'

'Some gypsy!' teased Madeleine. 'Staying in five star hotels around the world, being given the full VIP treatment wherever you go. Jessie, you're going to be living like a film star, so don't expect any sympathy from me. What's this Bernard like?' she added almost shyly.

Jessica wasn't in the least embarrassed or inhibited about her new found love.

'Maddy, wait till you meet him!' she breathed. 'He's the most electrifying man you've ever met. He oozes charisma. I bet he'll knock you sideways when we all meet for dinner tonight. He is, my dear, *totally* divine!'

Madeleine regarded her friend with undisguised

amusement. Jessica had always been given to exaggeration and dramatisation but she seemed to have gone completely over the top this time.

'And you're not going to miss the Royal Westminster?' she asked gently. 'You worked so hard to get on in the hotel business, Jessie, are you sure you're not going to have any regrets?'

'None,' replied Jessica, a shade too swiftly. 'I realised when I met Bernard, that never in my life again would I find a love like this. You've no idea what it's like, Maddy.' She turned her round blue eyes, sparkling with earnestness, on Madeleine. 'He's a *fantastic* man, there's no other word for it, and he really is as much in love with me as I am with him. Of course I felt a dreadful pang the day I left the hotel, but one can't have everything in life, and I reckoned that Bernard was worth a dozen hotels, or a hundred careers.'

Madeleine's smile was genuinely warm. 'Then I hope you'll be tremendously happy, Jessie, and I'm really glad for you.'

Jessica grinned back, moved almost to the edge of tears by her friend's sincerity. 'Thanks, Maddy. You'll see what I mean as soon as you meet Bernard.'

'Which reminds me . . .' Madeleine looked at her askance. 'Have you called up Andrew?'

Jessica's face fell, as if a puppeteer had let loose all the strings that controlled her smile. 'Yes, I called him as soon as you gave me his message,' she replied sadly. 'I really do feel dreadful about him, but what could I do? We'd finished anyway when I met Bernard, so I saw no point in telling him what had happened. I didn't think he cared any more about me. At least, that's how it seemed when he broke it off because I went to live in the hotel.'

'I think he hoped that one day you'd grow bored with hotel life and return to him,' said Madeleine quietly, 'and of course what really hurt him was that you weren't prepared to work less hard to please him, yet you were prepared to chuck in your whole career to go off with Bernard.'

Jessica hung her head, like a woebegone child. 'I *know* you're right, Maddy, and I know I behaved rather badly. But on the other hand,' her head shot up and for a moment she looked self-righteous, 'why should it always be the woman who gives up her job to please a man? Whoever heard of a man giving up his job to please a woman?' Then they both laughed, Madeleine thinking of Carl and his dedication to the bank, and Jessica thinking of Bernard, to whom music was life itself. No, men were not prepared to make sacrifices in the way women were. 'And it's jolly unfair!' Jessica declared, tackling her Salade Niçoise with gusto.

'So, we're all meeting for dinner tonight at Elaine's?' Madeleine asked.

'Yes. I've booked in Bernard's name, of course. Might as well ensure we get the best table!' joked Jessica.

'I can hardly wait,' replied Madeleine, with an unaccustomed touch of dryness.

'I've had enough of London,' Andrew remarked morosely, as he sat looking out at the wet Knightsbridge pavements. The large window of Jason

361

and Seymour Partnership held displays of photographs and details of des. res. properties, from ten-bedroomed mansions to bijou mews cottages and modern flats, representing an ever increasing turnover in a booming market.

'You've what?' Sandy demanded as if he hadn't heard right. 'Don't be such a bloody fool! This is where the money is. Properties are going up by fifteen percent a week! What the hell will you do if you leave London?'

'Properties are increasing in value in the country too. Old barns and cottages can be picked up for about forty thousand pounds, then you spend another fifty thousand on them, and they sell for two hundred and fifty! It's happening all over. Rich, affluent people in the south of England are looking for weekend places, more and more. I reckon we should cash in on the upsurge in country developments.'

Sandy regarded Andrew with interest. 'You could have a point,' he said slowly, 'and if we did branch into selling country property, you'd be prepared to run a country agency?'

Andrew nodded. 'I've always wanted to live in the country, you know that. Of course, I'd planned to marry Jessica and set up home . . .' His voice faltered, and painfully he averted his gaze.

'Oh, I realise that,' Sandy said swiftly. Then diplomatically he continued: 'This is something we must discuss seriously. We'd have to get bank loans for the expansion, you know; we'd have to take on more staff, and you'd have to find somewhere to live, as well as opening up a new office.'

362

'I'll get a small fortune for my flat in Chelsea,' observed Andrew. 'It cost me eighty thousand seven years ago, and now it's worth over a quarter of a million.'

Sandy grinned. 'And who said we're not in the right business? Jesus, I wish we could buy, do up and sell, instead of just negotiating other people's buying and selling. We could be millionaires by now.'

'But think of the hassle. I'd hate to spend my time improving a place, only to sell it to the highest bidder. When I buy a house, I want it to be my home.' The wistfulness in his voice portrayed the hurt he felt inside. Sandy looked away, embarrassed. He'd always managed to remain fairly fancy-free himself, with as rapid a turnover of girlfriends as he had of new cars. With Sandy it was easy come, easy go, and as long as he had lots of money in his pocket and some female's bed to sleep in, he was happy. The thought of settling down horrified him, even more than the thought of being away from the bright lights. He jumped to his feet restlessly, walked around their office for a minute or so, and then turned back to Andrew. The scheme wouldn't suit him, but it would be perfect for his partner.

'I think you're right, I think we should go ahead with a country agency,' he said. 'It's a good idea.'

'Great,' Andrew replied. 'I'll get the wheels in motion and go and talk to the bank tomorrow. I might as well get on with it as soon as possible, because there's no reason for me to stay in London any longer.'

Kimberley gave a little sigh of relieved satisfaction when she saw Hank Pugsley's transfer authorisation among Carl's papers on his desk. She'd been expecting it any day now; in fact it was overdue. She picked it up and looked at the amount. Three hundred and thirty thousand dollars! Dated three days ago, so it had got delayed in the mail.

When Carl walked into his office a few minutes later, she gave him a knowing look. 'Hank's putting through another one,' she remarked succinctly. 'It's late this time.'

Carl threw her a haunted look and said nothing. He too been expecting another transfer from Hank Pugsley any day now, but he'd been clutching at a faint straw of hope that perhaps Hank wasn't going to send any more money to Switzerland. Maybe he'd decided to change his bank, or move to the West Coast . . . or perhaps he'd been arrested for tax evasion! Carl shook his head despairingly. Hank was alive and kicking and still up to his old tricks, and to suppose anything else was wishful thinking.

'I'll put it through late this afternoon,' Kimberley said with quiet relish, as if it were something delicious she was going to eat or drink.

Still Carl said nothing, as he wondered how much more he could take. For the past few weeks he felt as if he'd been swimming against the tide, struggling against currents that were stronger than him, being bashed against the rocks every time he saw another transfer from Hank lying on his desk; and now he longed for the tide to turn and bring him back to a safe resting-place where he could stay still and get his breath back. His eyes sought Kimberley's for a moment, searching for a tiny gap of weakness in their translucent grey depths, wondering if the strain wasn't proving too much for her too; but he was met with a solid resistance to his unspoken plea to call it a day. Her eyes held the flat stony lifelessness of a carved figure and were totally devoid of feeling. Abruptly Carl turned away, sickened by the whole business.

At lunchtime, Kimberley went back to her apartment to collect the precious computer coded tape from where she kept it among the few books on her shelves, then she took a cab back to Wall Street. All afternoon she worked in a state of elated anticipation, seeing in her mind's eye the dollars flash up on to the green screen, seeing the number of Hank's current account, then the number of her own Swiss account: 23007 4810 66792. Kimberley knew it by heart now, had it engraved on her mind in numerals a foot high. No longer did she need to check in the index of her Filofax before putting through the transfers; it was right there in the forefront of her mind, like the amount that had shown on the last bank statement she'd received from Zurich . . . Over one-and-a-half million dollars. Today's transfer would bring it up to nearly two.

A smile hovered round Kimberley's mouth as she did her work and embellished her fantasy, one she'd begun as a twelve-year-old kid, standing on Times Square; a fantasy that took her to the shores of the Mediterranean where she imagined the sea would be as blue as sapphire and the sky an endless dome of sunshine.

At four-thirty Carl announced he had a meeting.

'Okay,' Kimberley replied. 'I'll see you after – later,' she corrected herself, in case anyone was within earshot. The minutes ticked slowly past, and her stomach knotted tighter with a mixture of nerves and excitement. At ten to five, she slipped the tape from her purse into her pocket, adding the pack of cigarettes again in case anyone noticed the bulge. At five to five she ran through the operation once more in her mind; any mistakes or delays could prove fatal. At two minutes to five, she went down into the deserted lobby, and passed unnoticed as she stepped into the elevator that would take her to the basement where the main computer room was situated, next to the vaults.

To her relief it was empty; the dreaded Liz had already departed along with all the other computer operators, and only one of the security guards, in his office along the corridor, glanced up casually as she passed. They smiled briefly, having known each other for nearly two years, and then Kimberley hurried into the computer room and took her seat at the keyboard.

First, remove the current account programmed disc from the computer. Kimberley did this, watching the screen go blank and dark like a television set that has been turned off. Then she whipped the foreign transactions disc out of her pocket and, loading it carefully, watched for the screen to glow brilliant green again, and for the flickering black lettering of the programme to reveal itself so she could type in Hank Pugsley's details and then the secret code for her own foreign account.

Suddenly she stiffened in her seat, and craned forward anxiously. Something had happened. Something was terribly wrong, and for a moment she felt a shaft of panic pass through her. Kimberley tried again, removing her tape and then reloading it with care, but still the screen remained dark. There was nothing. The screen looked back at her, just a piece of thick glass as grey and blank as the eye of a great dead fish.

Kimberley glanced swiftly round the room. She still had a few more minutes before the security guards did their rounds, so as an experiment she loaded the original disc in the computer again. Within seconds there was a happy sort of bleep and the screen sprang to life, green as freshly mown grass, alive with a mad flutter of names and figures, as the records of clients' current accounts appeared. Kimberley stared, appalled, the colour draining from her face so it picked up the green tinge of the screen. It could mean only one thing, she thought. Recklessly, in a desperate effort to prove herself wrong, she removed the disc once more and for the third time re-loaded her own. Again nothing. A dead screen with not a flicker of life, a hostile square of glass that mocked her in her anguish and offered her no comfort from its sterile depths.

Tight-lipped, Kimberley slipped the disc back into her pocket, replaced the original one and strode out of the computer room, too angry and upset even to notice the security guard beginning his round of inspection.

Back in her office she lay in wait for Carl to return from his meeting, disappointment and frustration jostling with fear and apprehension.

As soon as Carl appeared, she sprang from behind

her desk and rushed into his office, closing both her and his door to the corridor. 'Something's gone wrong with my computer disc,' she said in an urgent whisper, 'I couldn't put through the transfer.'

Carl's face grew haggard and pale as he sat slumped, looking up at her. His voice was dangerously quiet and calm. 'What happened?'

Kimberley shrugged in an exaggerated way. 'I don't know, I tell you. All I know is that my computer disc has been wiped clean. There's nothing on it! You'll have to get the original from Jake's office again so that I can make another copy.'

'You know perfectly well I can't!' snapped Carl. 'Jake has recently introduced tighter security methods. Those master discs are kept under lock and key twenty-four hours a day, and only Jake and his deputy have access to them. There's no way I can even get near them.'

Kimberley knew he was speaking the truth and the knowledge increased her rage. 'Fuck it!' she spat, keeping her voice low with an effort. 'How am I going to transfer Hank's money now? What can we do? Of all the goddamn things to happen!' She began to pace up and down his office, beside herself with a fury she was finding it harder by the minute to control. Suddenly she swung on Carl, her eyes blazing. 'I bet you've done something to sabotage my disc! I've had it in my office all afternoon –!'

Carl eyed her coldly, a tiny creeping sense of relief stealing over him. If her disc had been wiped out there was no other way he could think of that she could transfer Hank's money to her own account. Her scheme might be forced to grind to a halt here and now. The thought made him momentarily dizzy. Could the end really be in sight?

'I haven't even been in your office today,' he heard himself say. 'If you will recall, I've been in here with clients, or in the boardroom at a meeting.'

Kimberley turned sullenly away, unable to deny he was telling the truth. 'Then what the fuck's gone wrong?' she demanded hoarsely.

'I don't care what's gone wrong. All I do know is that tomorrow, first thing, Hank Pugsley's transfer of dollars has to go through in the normal way,' said Carl.

'Like hell it has!' stormed Kimberley.

'It must!' Carl insisted angrily. 'The date of transfer has got to show up on his current account bank statement. The dollars have got to be taken out of his current account and if they aren't, he'll wonder why. Every month his statement shows the debit side of his current account, don't you see? We've got to transfer the money by tomorrow. I just hope the manager of his bank in Zurich doesn't contact him and ask why this is the first time in weeks he's sent money over.'

Kimberley let out a low moan like an animal in pain as she sank on to one of Carl's office chairs. Her long fingers covered her eyes in a gesture of despair. 'What can have gone wrong?' she whispered. 'Everything was working so perfectly.'

'Too perfectly, perhaps,' said Carl crisply. He didn't like it himself. Why should Kimberley's disc have been wiped clean, and who could have done it? That was the thing that worried him most. Someone, apart from himself, was anxious to put an end to her activities, and that person had deliberately sabotaged the disc.

If one nightmare was over, another one might just be beginning.

Chapter Fourteen

'And this is Bernard!' exclaimed Jessica with a flourish, as she introduced him to Madeleine and Carl that evening while they had drinks in the bar of the Plaza, where they were staying, before going on to dine at Elaine's.

They all shook hands, grinning self-consciously, uttering the usual social banalities and eyeing each other with curiosity.

'I've heard so much about you from Jessica,' Bernard said suavely to Madeleine, 'and you're even more beautiful than she described.' He held both her hands in his, and stood looking at her as if he found her enchanting. Madeleine returned his gaze evenly, summing him up, slightly shocked that he was even older than she'd thought. There was a fine network of wrinkles spreading from around his hooded eyes and deep lines at the corners of his mouth.

'Thank you,' she said simply.

'Let's have some champagne,' Jessica was saying, as they seated themselves at a table in the corner, away from the mass of people drinking and talking. She signalled for a waiter, her gold bangles rattling on wrists that seemed slimmer than ever. 'Oh, isn't this divine! I've been *longing* for us all to get together, and here we are at last!'

The waiter placed little bowls of nuts and green and black olives on the table, and Jessica grabbed Bernard's hand in a rush of excitement.

Carl asked him, 'Do you travel a great deal?'

Bernard, having decided that Madeleine was not going to succumb to his charismatic charm, and was not even going to flirt with him, seemed to be losing interest in the proceedings.

'I'll have been touring eight months this year,' he replied casually, his eyes roving around the bar area to see if there was anyone he knew. 'I'm giving concerts in all the major cities, including Tokyo.'

'Then we have four months off!' interjected Jessica. 'Touring isn't all glamour, I've discovered. It's living out of suitcases, catching planes, checking in at different hotels every few days, and as for Bernard's fan mail . . . My dear, he gets *sacks* of letters! But,' she squeezed Bernard's hand, 'we're actually having four months' break in the spring. Did I tell you Bernard had a house in Sardinia? It's on the beach, I gather, and – oh! Oh, Bernard! I've had the most wonderful idea!' Jessica's small face suddenly blazed with delight. 'Maddy and Carl can come and stay with us, can't they? Wouldn't that be fantastic! The house is on the Costa Smeralda, and we could go snorkelling and sailing, and there's riding and tennis, isn't there, darling? And then there's the Pevero Golf Course! Oh, just think what fun we'll have, and how *brown* we'll get!'

Bernard looked taken aback and a glint of annoyance showed in his eyes. Not noticing, Jessica insisted: 'Wouldn't that be fabulous, Bernard?'

He hesitated, his smile contrasting chillingly with the warning look he seemed to be giving Jessica. 'Well . . .' his voice trailed away, his tone discouraging.

'I don't know when Carl and I will be able to get away,' Madeleine cut in hurriedly. It was obvious Bernard was not going to make them feel welcome, and for Jessica's sake she felt it was better to take avoiding action.

'Of course you can get away! Don't be silly!' declared Jessica impatiently. 'What's wrong, Bernard? Aren't there enough bedrooms?' She was sitting very upright now, in a way Madeleine knew so well, her cheeks flushed and her attitude that of a persistent child determined to embarrass a grownup. 'We'll never get to see our friends if we can't have them to stay with us.'

Madeleine, amused, took a swift gulp of her drink to hide her twitching mouth, not daring to look at Carl who was studying the ceiling of the bar. Out of the corner of her eye she saw Bernard run a caressing hand down Jessica's arm. Then he spoke in a polite but firm voice, but as if Madeleine and Carl had not been there.

'I bought the house as a private hideaway, not for entertaining,' he was explaining. 'It's where I write my music; it's where I go to get away from people, and have a bit of peace. I do not want guests.' Then he turned to them as if he'd just remembered their presence, giving them a patronising smile: his adoring fans, honoured to be in the presence of the great man himself.

Jessica's flush deepened and for a fleeting moment

she looked like a disappointed child who might burst into tears, but Madeleine's eyes narrowed as she looked at Bernard, and in that instant she realised she disliked him deeply. He was an arrogant, conceited bastard, and she wondered how Jessica could have fallen in love with someone so utterly wrapped up in himself. She also knew in that instant that the feeling was mutual. A flash of hostility had passed between them as they'd exchanged looks, and she knew it was partly because she hadn't pandered to Bernard's vanity when they'd been introduced and partly because he resented Jessica having close friends from her past.

'So you do all your composing when you're in Sardinia?' Carl asked conversationally. 'Does it take you long to write . . . say . . . the theme music for a film like *Silver Apples of the Moon*?'

Bernard cast world-weary eyes round the crowded bar area, making it clear that he was sick of always being asked the same sort of questions. 'It depends . . .' he shrugged nonchalantly. Then he looked at Jessica and gave her a conspiratorial wink, a look that said, Won't it be nice when these dreary people have gone and we'll be on our own again.

'Are you all right, darling?' he whispered intimately.

'I'm fine!' Jessica replied with a perky smile, though she still looked slightly deflated. Then she turned to Madeleine and Carl. 'Now, I want to hear all your news. Carl, you're looking divinely distinguished! Still taking Wall Street by storm? And I *adore* that dress you're wearing, Maddy. It's to *die* for! Who designed it . . . Bill Blass?' Her slim little hands fluttered over the silk of Madeleine's skirt, and her smile was one of undisguised admiration. 'You always look so good,' she added generously.

Madeleine laughed. 'Thanks, Jessie, but there's no need to overdo it!'

Undeterred, Jessica continued: 'God, how I wish we were going to be in London when you're there. We'll be in Milan, won't we, Bernard?'

His brows had gradually been drawing together in a deep frown while Jessica had been prattling happily on, but now he seemed to reach flash-point.

'I'm more concerned about where we're going to eat tonight,' he snapped, slamming his glass down on the little table. 'I've been rehearsing all day and I'm tired. I certainly don't want to hang around this place all evening, drinking. Let's go now.'

Jessica rested a placatory hand on his arm. 'All right, darling. There's no need to get in a state.' She turned to the others. 'Would you mind if we had dinner a little early? Bernard suffers from low blood sugar when he's been working very hard, and he feels awful if he doesn't get something to eat straight away.'

'That's fine,' Madeleine replied lightly, thinking it was less a case of low blood sugar and more a case of raised temper that was making Bernard behave in this way.

Then, as she watched Jessica take his arm, looking adoringly and with concern into his face, Madeleine realised just how much in love her friend was with this talented but irascible man. She seemed bewitched and bedazzled, a satellite encircling a star with selfless

375

devotion. And Bernard knew it, of that Madeleine was certain. With a triumphant look on his face at having got his own way, he was striding out of the Plaza bar with Jessica running after him in her spiky heels in order to keep up. His head held high, he pointedly ignored the stares and nudges and admiring whispers of the other people in the bar when they recognised him.

God help her, thought Madeleine, as she and Carl followed. He's already got her running round in circles, pandering to his every need. What about her own career? What about that lively independent spirit who knew exactly what she wanted and where she was going? Already Jessica seemed changed totally from the young woman who had told Andrew that she was a person in her own right. Already there was a submissiveness about her that had not been there before. By falling in love, Jessica seemed to have lost a little of herself in Bernard.

'I didn't like him, did you?' Madeleine said to Carl as they got ready for bed that night. It had been a difficult evening, with awkward silences and stilted conversation, so unlike the previous times she and Carl had spent with Jessica.

'He's okay,' said Carl, 'but I wouldn't have thought he was Jessica's type. Far too temperamental and volatile. Very different from Andrew.' Carefully he laid the gold cuff-links Madeleine had given him in his jewel case. 'What d'you suppose she sees in him?'

Madeleine thought for a moment, sitting at her dressing-table brushing her hair until it gleamed blue-black in the soft lighting of their bedroom. 'Excitement, I think . . . and maybe a challenge. Andrew was the only serious boyfriend she's ever had, so maybe one of Bernard's attractions is that he's completely different. And he *is* charismatic, I'll give him that!' She turned to look at Carl, a worried expression in her eyes. 'I hope she's going to be happy, but I'm afraid Bernard just wants a glorified PA and someone to go to bed with regularly, and that's not going to be enough for Jessica.'

Carl raised his eyebrows. 'Maddy, you really do amaze me sometimes.' He walked over to her and placed his hands on her shoulders. Then he lowered his head so they were cheek to cheek, looking into the mirror at their reflected images.

'Why do I amaze you?' she asked, rubbing her cheek softly against his.

'Because I always suppose you're in a dream . . . painting some great picture . . . imagining some scene . . . and then you suddenly come out with a remark that shows you're as on the ball as anyone!'

Her dark eyes widened, thinking of Kimberley, thinking of all the things she knew that were going on at the bank, thinking of her own well laid plans to get even with a woman who had tried to ruin her happiness. Then she looked down at her hands lest her expression should give anything away.

'Oh, I don't know,' she replied lightly, 'I'm in a dream most of the time really.'

Carl kissed her ear, then ran his tongue around the lobe, tugging it gently with his lips. 'Are you coming to bed?' he asked, his voice suddenly thick with longing.

Madeleine nodded, leaning back against him, feeling already the arousal of his body as he pressed himself against her.

'I agree with Bernard about one thing,' whispered Carl, as his hands slid to her breasts, which strained full and rounded against the satin of her nightgown.

'What's that?'

'I like having someone I can go to bed with regularly, too!'

'So I should hope,' she cried, in mock horror. 'How dreadful it would be if you didn't!'

'You were very rude tonight!' Jessica scolded Bernard, as soon as they'd climbed into bed, back at their suite at the Plaza. 'Madeleine and Carl are my oldest and greatest friends. Why did you behave so badly?'

Bernard rolled on to his back, his broad shoulders indenting the pillows, his head supported by his hands. 'I was bored, sweetheart,' he replied blandly. 'Carl is a typical banker, all he thinks about is money. Madeleine is your typical rich society girl, spoilt and empty-headed.'

Jessica shot into an upright position, her breasts bare above the fallen sheet, her face enraged. 'How can you talk such rubbish?' she stormed, her eyes round with indignation. 'Madeleine is *not* spoilt or empty-headed! On the contrary, she's a very talented artist who's had a lot of success so far. And she's amazingly shrewd. She was too polite to say anything tonight but I don't think she liked the way you patronised her, at *all*!'

378

Bernard turned to look at her, his hooded eyes unfathomable. 'Are we going to spend the night quarrelling about your little friend, or are we going to sleep?'

Jessica plumped her pillows angrily and glared at him. He seemed so changed since she'd joined him in Boston; grumpy, domineering and demanding. Where was the tender, passionate lover who'd confessed to being lonely?

'I don't want to quarrel with you,' Jessica said fretfully, 'but I don't understand why you didn't like Maddy and Carl! You could at least have been nice to them for my sake.'

Bernard snorted contemptuously. 'Life is too short to be nice to people one doesn't care for, and your friends committed the worst social sin of all.'

'What d'you mean?'

'They were boring! Utterly, desperately boring!'

'And I suppose the sycophants who surround you, aren't?' Jessica shot back. 'For God's sake, Bernard, that's the most intolerant and ridiculous remark I've ever heard. Some people can't help being boring!'

'Everyone can help being boring . . . it just requires a little effort. People who socialise have a duty to be interesting. They must be prepared to sing for their supper,' he added arrogantly.

Jessica jumped out of bed and flung on her blue satin robe. 'You're a conceited bastard, Bernard Scheller,' she yelled, making for the door, 'and if you think . . .'

Bernard was too quick for her. With a bound he was across the room, his naked body blocking her way, his strong arms encircling her. 'Hush, hush!' he admonished. 'You're getting too excited.'

'I will not listen to the rubbish you talk!' Her tiny fists flailed wildly in the air as he grappled with her, eventually catching her by the wrists. Then he pulled her close until she grew still and leaned against him.

'That's better,' he whispered soothingly, stroking her head as if she were a child. 'What a fuss about nothing. It was only a little dinner-party that turned out to be a bit dull, not the end of the world.'

Unexpectedly, Jessica found herself sobbing, as if she was indeed a child. 'I know,' she wept, surprised by her own display of emotion. The whole evening had somehow unnerved her and now she felt a painful reaction. It wasn't just that Bernard hadn't liked her friends. It was that her friendship with Madeleine represented security, something she'd known ever since she was a child but which suddenly seemed to be lost. Her parents had always been there in the background, loving and supporting, and now they were thousands of miles away. Her friends and all the people she'd worked with in the Golding Group were scattered far and wide too, and as for Andrew, alone in the little Chelsea flat they'd shared . . . She gave a loud sob. Up to now her life had progressed gradually from childhood to adulthood, each event and each person in it linked to the previous event or person, so that a continual chain had woven her destiny. That was, until she'd met Bernard.

Then her past had been severed with a suddenness that only now she realised had been traumatic. In a matter of weeks her job, her friends, her family and even the country of her birth, were a thing of the past, exchanged for a man she hardly knew, and for an existence which would be basically nomadic. There had been no talk of marriage or lasting commitment; nothing to replace the security she'd relinquished; nothing to give her a sense of having new roots to lay down. And suddenly, tonight, Bernard's rejection of Madeleine and Carl had made her realise how alone in the world she was with him. There were just the two of them, and she was utterly dependent on him for everything.

'I wanted you to like them,' she snuffled. 'They are my best friends.'

'Good. That's nice.' Bernard sounded as if he were humouring her. 'Friends are important, my darling, but don't forget that my life is very demanding and that I don't want to be surrounded by people any more than I have to be. I was trying to explain that earlier, about not wanting anyone to stay with us on Sardinia. It is bad enough having the servants, though at least they've learned to keep out of my way. But people staying – ? Impossible! Unbearable! I can't have any distractions when I'm composing!'

Jessica nodded, understanding, but the feelings of hurt and insecurity still lingered inside her. For a moment she felt a flash of panic, wondering what she was going to do with the rest of her life while Bernard worked, but she pushed the thought away.

'Come back to bed, sweetheart,' Bernard was saying coaxingly.

Back in bed he held her in his arms, rocking her gently, stroking her hair as it lay like a stream of gold silk on the pillow. Gradually she began to feel the knots of tension dissolve as his hands moved down her body, caressing her, arousing her, and all the while his voice, almost hypnotically was repeating: 'Little one . . . little one . . .'

As Jessica's senses began to be lulled, her fears abated, seeming now hysterical and irrational. After all, Bernard had been tired after rehearsing all afternoon and he'd probably have preferred a quiet dinner with her rather than having to meet people he didn't know. Little by little, her disappointment and chagrin faded as his hands and lips worked their magic, touching her just where she wanted to be touched, kissing her where she longed to be kissed. Then Bernard touched himself, his eyes closed, his expression absorbed. As his strong hand smoothed and stroked his erection, Jessica became consumed with passion. An instinctive urge – part love, part lust – filled her with desire to give this man his pleasure, to bring him to a peak of fulfilment, knowing in those moments she would have him utterly in her power.

With a swift movement she rolled over on to her knees, and taking him in her mouth sucked deeply. Groaning with an almost animal gratification Bernard rocked his pelvis with deep sensuality, thrusting himself until he touched the back of her throat, extracting every exquisite sensation he could from her tongue and luxuriating in the pleasure she was giving him.

'Yes . . . oh, yes,' he murmured. 'Stroke my balls, darling.'

Jessica glanced up for a second, and saw that he

was looking down at himself through half closed eyes, watching his own inflamed passion, admiring himself as she brought his precious body to a climax. He ran his tongue along his bottom lip and his hands pressed down on the flatness of his stomach. Then he relinquished himself to her ministrations, almost as if he were doing her a favour.

The doctor's face was grave. 'I'm sending you for X-rays, Mrs Ziffren. How long did you say you'd had that cough?'

Patti cleared her throat, and her voice was more gravelly than usual. 'Oh, pretty well as long as I can remember,' she said, with a touch of forced gaiety. 'It's only a smoker's cough, for goodness' sake! I came to see you because of my headaches. There's nothing wrong with my lungs.' She pulled the white cotton wrapper around her thin body and her eyes challenged the doctor to disagree with her.

'Well, we'll have to see about that,' he said slowly. He was a young doctor who had recently taken over the practice, and he refused to be intimidated by Mrs Ziffren. She might be one of New York's richest and most influential women, but to him she was just another patient, and a rather sick one at that.

'I'll tell you why you're getting headaches when you wake up every morning,' he continued. 'You tell me you smoke three packs of cigarettes a day?'

Patti shrugged bony shoulders. 'Yes, probably. Sometimes less. Sometimes more.'

'Then every morning, you're suffering from a nicotine hangover. That's worse than alcohol! You've got to give up smoking, you know. At this rate you'll be dead in a couple of years.' He spoke earnestly, his face full of concern.

Patti tossed her head. 'Never heard such rubbish in my life! I take a couple of aspirins and then the headache goes. I just wondered if there was anything better than aspirin?'

'Yes, there is. Quit smoking altogether, and then you won't get any more headaches. Meanwhile, we must have a look at that chest of yours. I'll arrange for the X-rays to be done first thing tomorrow morning.' The doctor didn't even ask her if it would be convenient. As far as he was concerned, Mrs Ziffren was underweight, with skin the colour of putty, and a cough that was tearing her apart.

As Patti got dressed again she knew, with a sickening feeling of dread, that the doctor was right. She *was* killing herself by smoking, but the hell of it was that she neither wanted to give up nor felt able to. The more Jake nagged her about it, the more contrary she felt. Sam had stopped trying to persuade her years ago, so she got neither support nor disapproval from him, but one by one all her friends had given up, and in the last year or so she had begun to feel she was being anti-social. Although she only lived two blocks from the doctor, she'd ordered her car to wait for her. It was absurd, she knew, but walking home those two blocks would have left her feeling tired and breathless. A jab of panic sent tingles of fear shooting through her; suppose what the doctor said was true? Suppose the X-rays revealed something? Supposing she only had a couple of years to live?

With unaccustomed weakness Patti's eyes filled with tears on the journey home. She didn't want to die yet. She wanted to live so that she could eventually see Madeleine's children, and watch them grow up as she'd watched her niece. Life is a precious thing, she thought, reaching automatically for a cigarette. It was lit, and she was dragging on it, before she realised what she was doing. This is crazy, she thought, and yet, as she inhaled, her worries seemed momentarily to fade. Doctors didn't always know what they were talking about, she reassured herself. She'd have got lung cancer by now if she was going to. After all, cancer didn't run in their family. Anyway, what was the point of being alive at all if you were miserable. And without cigarettes she was miserable. They made her calm and . . . she was seized by a fit of coughing that was so severe her chauffeur slowed down, glancing over his shoulder anxiously.

'Are you okay, ma'am?'

Patti could only nod. With streaming eyes, her body convulsed by spasms, she was unable to speak as cough after cough was wrenched from her throat. For a moment she thought she was going to choke, but with a final rattle she got her breath back. Exhausted, she leaned back in the car, her eyes closed. From between her manicured fingers her cigarette still smouldered. With a sudden movement she stubbed it out in the car ashtray, and taking a lace-edged handkerchief out of her handbag she wiped her eyes and dabbed the corners of her mouth. The doctor was right. This couldn't go on.

*　　*　　*

The Boeing 747 skimmed through the thick grey porridgey clouds that hung over southern England, dropping altitude as it approached Heathrow. In first class, Madeleine sat huddled under her blanket, feeling cold and shivery as if the clammy chilliness of the swirling cumulus had penetrated the aircraft cabin. It had been a long night and it seemed an age since she'd kissed Carl goodbye in New York.

The smiling steward brought steaming coffee and poured out a generous cup for her. Madeleine sipped it gratefully. The next few days were going to be the most nerve-wracking of her life. A lot would happen before she could go down to the comparative peace of Devon, and in the meantime Carl must be allowed to believe that she was in London, fixing up her next exhibition, prior to catching the train for Milton Manor.

'Please extinguish your cigarettes and fasten your safety belts,' a disembodied voice announced over the loudspeaker.

Madeleine's ears started to pop and she swallowed hard, partly to relieve the unpleasant sensation but partly with nerves. Everything depended on this trip being successful and she hoped and prayed that Hank had kept his side of the bargain. If he lost his nerve, Kimberley might still get away with everything and that was a thought Madeleine couldn't bear to contemplate.

The plane touched down, roared along the runway with its jets screaming, and eventually came to a halt near the terminus buildings. Half an hour later Madeleine was through Customs, and hurrying towards the taxi rank.

'The Royal Westminster, Hyde Park Corner,' she told the driver, remembering the last time she'd been to England when Jessica had been with her. They'd chatted all the way into the centre of London, discussing her grandfather and wondering what he wanted. Well, now she knew. Her mother was alive and in an institution, where Jake had been paying for her to be looked after for over twenty years now. But I mustn't think about my mother, she thought grimly. Not yet. There'll be plenty of time to think about her and decide whether I'm going to go and see her, when this business with Kimberley is over. Carl comes first, and getting him out of this mess without Jake discovering what has been going on, is the most important thing right now.

As the taxi rattled along the motorway, getting snarled up from time to time by the morning traffic, Madeleine ran through her carefully laid plans. Checking into the Royal Westminster first, although it meant she had to make the journey back to the airport a few hours later, was all part of the scheme. At lunchtime she'd call Carl and tell him she'd landed safely and would be out and about, meeting people, until she left for Devon. That way, if he should call her at any time, he wouldn't be surprised if the hotel switchboard couldn't locate her.

The Royal Westminster gave her the VIP treatment, including a glass of champagne while she checked in, but it seemed so strange without Jessica and her bright little face, alive with its welcoming smile, her hair glinting with gold under the formal chandeliers. To Madeleine it seemed as if a light had gone out in the hotel, and at that moment she would have given anything to have had her friend with her. No matter how serious the situation, Jessica always managed to inject a shaft of humour into it. Right now she would have been so supportive, such a help in the dreaded task that lay ahead.

Madeleine had been given a magnificent suite overlooking Hyde Park. As she stood staring out of the window, the soldiers of the Queen's Household Cavalry jingled past on their magnificent black horses, breastplates and plumed helmets glittering in the early morning sun, the clatter of the polished hooves reminding her that before the days of cars, horses had been the only means of transport in this great old city.

Unpacking her cases, she showered, changed and then repacked an overnight bag. She wasn't going to need much, just a nightdress, one complete change of clothes, her wash bag and make-up. Then, pulling the telephone towards her, she lay down on the bed to make the first of her phone calls.

It was to Mr Marks, the solicitor.

'I'm in London for a couple of days,' she told him, 'and I'll be coming down to Milton Manor, to see about my grandfather's property, on Wednesday.'

'That will be very convenient, Mrs Delaney,' she heard him say. She could just imagine him sitting in his office, surrounded by stacks of dusty legal papers, his moth-like eyelashes fluttering as he talked.

'As I told you when I called you from New York, my father has given me all the information I need, regarding my mother and the estate,' continued Madeleine. 'I will tell you all about it when I see you.'

'Indeed. Well, that is very good, isn't it? We shan't have to go to court now.'

'That is correct.'

'Well, I'm sure that's a relief for you, Mrs Delaney. I'll see you on Wednesday then,' said Mr Marks primly.

'Twelve noon, at the Manor. I'll be there.' Madeleine hung up and then she got the switchboard to get her a number in Zurich.

'Schweizerhof Hotel. Can I help you?' asked a German-accented voice, when she got through a few moments later.

'Could I speak to Mr Hank Pugsley,' said Madeleine. Oh, God, let him be there, she thought, digging her nails into the palm of her hand. Supposing he hasn't arrived yet? Supposing he's decided to chicken out, in spite of the plans we made?

'Hullo?' she heard a man's voice say, cautiously.

'Hank Pugsley?'

'Y-yes,' admitted the voice, still sounding doubtful.

'This is Madeleine Delaney. I've just landed in London and I'm catching the afternoon flight to Zurich.'

'Good,' said Hank. 'I was waiting for your call. Everything okay?'

'Everything's fine,' said Madeleine, 'and we're meeting as arranged in the Banque Internationale de Zurich on the Bahnhofstrasse tomorrow morning at nine-thirty?'

'I'll be there. It's a long street, by the way. The bank is near the centre, near Barengasse Strasse. It's a big building; you can't miss it.'

389

'Thanks.' Madeleine's mouth twitched. Hank was obviously enjoying himself. He was talking in a James Bond sort of voice, clipped and secretive, and she could just imagine him, sitting in his hotel bedroom, shirt sleeves rolled up ready for action. I hope to God he hasn't got a gun or anything like that with him, she thought, in sudden alarm. Hank's next remark caught her off-guard.

'Why don't we meet for dinner tonight?'

Madeleine, remembering his fat greasiness, thought quickly. Doing a deal with him to outwit Kimberley was one thing; having to spend an evening socialising with him, was another. She tried to let him down gently so as not to hurt his feelings.

'I don't think that would be wise,' she explained. 'My husband thinks I'm going to be staying in London, and if one of his business contacts spotted me in Zurich in the company of a man, well . . .' Her voice drifted off, leaving the sentence unfinished.

Hank was quick to cotton on. 'Oh, no, we don't want that,' he agreed. 'Right, well, I'll see you tomorrow morning, and we'll cook the little bitch's goose once and for all!'

'I'll see you then,' said Madeleine, hanging up. She had two hours to kill. She closed her eyes, trying to sleep, but tension held her in its grip. She found her mind going over and over the details for tomorrow. It was going to be a highly risky business, and if the bank in Zurich became suspicious . . . She shut her mind off to the dangers; she had set out to get the better of Kimberley and now she had to go through with it. At twelve-thirty she put through a call to Carl, who had just woken up.

'Yes, I'm fine, darling,' she assured him. 'I'm off to see a gallery in Bond Street,' she continued, hating having to lie to him, 'and there are one or two in Chelsea that sound interesting. Anyway, I'll call you when I've settled on something. Don't bother phoning me because I'm going to be out most of the time,' she added firmly.

'Okay, sweetheart,' she heard him say. 'Take care of yourself. I hope you'll find what you're looking for.'

Madeleine smiled to herself. 'Oh, I'm sure I will,' she said with a touch of irony, knowing Carl would think she was referring to a suitable gallery. Then she picked up her overnight bag, walked out of the hotel and caught a cab round the corner, out of sight of the main entrance. There was no point advertising the fact she was returning straight to Heathrow airport.

Four hours later, Madeleine landed at Kloten Airport. She was directed by a helpful official to an adjoining railway, where, within minutes, she was on a train to Zurich. Tired and feeling strained, she sank thankfully on to a seat as the train pulled swiftly out of the station. To her amazement and relief the journey only took ten minutes, and when she alighted she found herself at the Hauptbahnhof, in the centre of Zurich. She jumped into the first of a waiting line of cabs. 'The Baur au Lac Hotel, on the Telstrasse,' she told the driver.

Sitting gazing out of the windows as tempting shops and inviting cafés and restaurants flashed by, Madeleine realised that apart from being one of the world's leading financial centres, it was one of the most affluent cities in Europe. She could see

391

prosperous young bankers returning home from work, hopping on clean-looking blue trams that skimmed smoothly up and down the well-kept streets, for Madeleine remembered that only 'foreigners' drove their smart cars to work. Beautifully dressed women were shopping in the many boutiques that lined Zurich's principal boulevards. And then she saw it! The Banque de Zurich, just as Hank had said, half-way down the main street.

The Baur au Lac Hotel, which she'd chosen from a travel brochure as she didn't want to involve her usual travel agent, turned out to be sensationally beautiful and elegant, a favourite haunt of bankers and industrialists, with a pretty pavilion set in its extensive gardens and a view over the Limmat River from its windows.

Madeleine ordered supper in her room and went to bed early. Tomorrow was going to be a big day.

Jake came into Carl's office, shortly after he got in that morning.

'Heard from Madeleine?' he inquired. Jake was never happy unless he knew his only daughter was all right.

'She's arrived okay. I spoke to her before I left the apartment and she was in great shape.' Carl replied. 'She's going to be looking at London galleries today.'

'That's good.' Jake looked relieved. 'Now we've just got to make sure Patti's all right, and our problems will be over.'

'Patti?' Carl repeated. 'What's wrong with her?'

'She's got to have a chest X-ray,' he replied grimly.

'I told her she smoked too much; she's had this terrible cough for a long time now.'

'Oh, my God!' Carl looked anxious. 'I hope she's going to be all right. Does Maddy know?'

Jake shook his head. 'This only happened yesterday, but she doesn't want Madeleine to know anything unless . . . of course . . .' He sighed deeply, breaking off. Patti was the only family he had left, apart from Madeleine, and if anything should happen to her, he knew he'd be devastated.

'I'm sure she'll be okay,' Carl said comfortingly.

'I don't know . . .'

'When will she get the results of the X-ray?'

'I expect they'll be able to tell her right away. I asked her to call me as soon as she knew.'

'If there's anything I can do, Jake.'

He smiled absently, his eyes still troubled. 'Thanks. Right now, we can only hope . . .' He broke off as, with a flourish, Kimberley Cabot hurried into Carl's office, unaware that Jake was there.

'Oh!' She started, stopping in her tracks. She looked quickly from Carl to Jake, wondering what was going on.

'Good morning.' Jake greeted her politely.

'Good morning, Mr Shearman,' she said demurely. 'I'm sorry. I didn't realise you were in here.'

Carl sat, his face a dull red now, his expression uneasy.

'What did you want?' he asked her bluntly.

Her grey eyes widened innocently, and she looked almost hurt. 'There's so much work on, I thought I'd make an early start.'

Carl watched her performance of the poor-little-me-I-only-wanted-to-be-helpful look, with a sense of incredulity. She was so convincing it was incredible, and Jake was totally taken in.

'Mr Delaney sure is a lucky man to have you as an assistant,' he said, smiling down at her. 'You were working late last night too, weren't you?'

Kimberley's lips curved round her teeth when she smiled, in a way most men found deeply attractive. Carl watched as Jake fastened his eyes on her mouth, and knew exactly what he was thinking. She'd had the same effect on him once upon a time.

'I try to make it a rule to clear my desk before I go home at night,' she said earnestly. 'That way we don't get a backlog.'

Jake looked impressed. 'Very good! Quite right!'

'I don't need you for the minute, Kimberley,' Carl cut in smoothly, 'why don't you come back when I've gone through these transfers?'

She looked at him from veiled eyes. 'Certainly, Mr Delaney.' A moment later she had slipped back to her office, closing the communicating door behind her.

Jake dropped his voice to a barely audible whisper. 'Lucky you're a happily married man,' he joked.

Carl's smile was sickly. 'Quite. You'll let me know anything when you hear from Patti?'

'Yes, of course.'

Two hours later the phone in Jake's office rang and his secretary said it was Mrs Ziffren for him. Jake grabbed the phone with shaking hands.

'Yes?'

'Is that you, Jake?' It was Patti, and to Jake's

horror it sounded as though his sister, who was never known to shed a tear, was crying her eyes out.

Hank arrived first at the Banque Internationale, trying to look inconspicious in a raincoat over his suit, although it was a dry day. He hovered just inside the main door, highly visible, deeply unattractive and obviously a foreigner. When Madeleine walked quickly into the bank, his moon face was already gleaming with sweat. With lumbering gait, he went up to her.

'Good morning,' she said tensely.

Hank didn't reply. Regarding her with anxious eyes, he looked as if he wasn't sure it was really her as she looked so different.

'Okay?' she asked shortly.

'D'you think it's going to be all right? I mean . . .' He looked round the busy bank lobby as if it scared the hell out of him.

'Watch me,' replied Madeleine, with more confidence than she felt, 'and don't say a thing!'

She wasn't sure whether Kimberley had come to Zurich in person to open her bank account the previous year. If she had, there might be someone who would remember her, so before leaving the hotel she'd put on shades, a dark blue turban that completely covered her hair, and heavy make-up with thick dark red lipstick. It wasn't a likeness of Kimberley, but it gave an *impression* of her, and Madeleine hoped that would be sufficient. Of course it would be a disaster if the bank teller knew Kimberley well. Apart from being of medium height and slim, the women bore no resemblance to each other at all.

Her eyes moved swiftly along the row of bank tellers, deciding which one to choose. They were all busy with a line of people waiting to draw out, or pay in, and she decided on a pale thin young man who looked particularly harassed; if he was busy he might not have the time to look too closely at her. He had steel-rimmed spectacles, pale brown hair receding at the temples, and an instantly forgettable face. Madeleine joined the line of people waiting to be attended to by him. Hank remained at her side, tense and silent as if he were going to his own execution.

At last Madeleine reached the counter, and the teller looked at her questioningly, his grey eyes magnified by his glasses so they looked sharp and foxy.

'I'd like to transfer some dollars from my account and pay them in to another account,' she said, managing to keep her voice steady.

'Your account is in this bank?' he asked, in broken English.

Madeleine nodded. He passed her a slip of paper.

'Please to fill it in,' he said, in an expressionless voice.

Without faltering Madeleine filled in where it said Account Number. Holding the pen firmly she wrote 23007 4810 66792. Below it she signed Kimberley Cabot.

'Will you wait a minute,' said the teller, snatching up the slip of paper without looking at it. Madeleine watched him go to a colleague who sat at a computer. The two men exchanged a few terse words, and the second man seemed to be tapping something into the keyboard in front of him. Then they both watched as a rippling tide of clients' names and details shimmered from the bottom of the screen to the top. While Madeleine waited, watching out of the corner of her eye, she saw them peering intently and muttering something. She knew she had perfected forging Kimberley's signature from the memo she'd taken from her office, but had she got the account number wrong? After all, it had only been by means of deduction that she'd thought the orthodontist insurance number in Kimberley's Filofax had been her Swiss account number. Maybe it wasn't! She felt an icy clutching in her stomach now as she stood there, trying to look unconcerned. Perhaps Kimberley had got there first, and had already removed all the money . . .?

Something seemed to be wrong, for the teller and the clerk were still muttering to each other, and at one point the clerk looked back over his shoulder and pointed her out. Casually Madeleine opened her handbag, withdrew her gold compact and powdered her nose. It was the sort of thing Kimberley Cabot would have done. Then the teller nodded to the clerk and vanished through a door marked *Privé*. Madeleine replaced the compact in her bag, keeping her face expressionless, aware that Hank, by her side, was breathing heavily now. At any moment she expected some top bank official to appear, to accuse her of attempting to steal funds; of embezzlement; of forgery. She imagined Carl and Jake, in New York, being informed that she'd been arrested and charged in Zurich. Her heart started thumping thickly, and she could feel the blood drain away from her face. She glanced at the main doors that led to the street, wondering if she should make a run for it, but already she was too late. The teller was bounding out of the door marked *Privé* again and coming towards her. Madeleine braced herself for an interrogation.

'How much do you want to transfer?' he asked, with a friendly smile.

Relief swept over her, bathing her in sweat. She was sure her face had turned scarlet.

'I'd like to close my account,' she said, amazed at the coolness of her voice. And then, taking a gamble, added: 'I can't remember how much I have in this account, but if you would be good enough to transfer it all to the account of Mr Hank Pugsley . . .' She indicated Hank, still standing by her side as if his feet were glued to the floor.

The teller glanced quickly at the slip of paper he held, and then wrote something on another slip which he handed her, having discreetly folded it in half first.

Madeleine opened the piece of paper and stared, stunned for a second by the amount he'd scribbled down. Then she pulled herself together quickly and said: 'Yes, that's right. I'd like to transfer it all, please.'

'Sign here, please,' said the teller, and once more she scribbled Kimberley Cabot. Then Hank gave the number of his account and it was all over. Five minutes later they were out in the busy boulevard again, and Hank was gasping:

'I could sure do with a drink!'

Madeleine glanced at the fat man as he shambled

clumsily by her side, and for a moment she almost liked him. In the past fifteen minutes they'd shared a nerve-wracking experience, and it had made her feel quite close to him. They could have been arrested, and it would have been very difficult to have convinced anyone to believe their story. Now that it was over, and they'd outwitted Kimberley Cabot between them, she felt elated, but there was still a need for caution. She wouldn't feel really safe until she was back in England. She grabbed Hank's elbow and hurried them along the Bahnhofstrasse, past shops and inviting-looking bars and cafés.

'I could do with a drink, too, but let's get away from here first,' she said, glancing over her shoulder. 'If they suddenly discover what I've done, they might try and come after me!' As she spoke, she whipped off her turban and shook out her black curls, instantly transforming herself from an older, chic-looking woman into a wildly pretty young one. She reached in her pocket for a tissue with which to wipe off the scarlet lipstick, and then she put her shades in her pocket.

'You're right,' cried Hank. At that moment they saw a cab and he raised his great beefy hand to flag it down. 'Where are we going?' he turned to ask her.

'My hotel . . . the Baur au Lac, on the Telstrasse,' she told the driver as she jumped in. 'I have to pick up my bag to catch the next flight out of here, but we've time for a drink first,' she added, as Hank sank on to the seat beside her.

He looked at her dubiously. 'Do you think we're being followed?' he asked nervously. He craned his neck to look out of the back window.

Madeleine shot him a warning look, her fingers to her lips, indicating the driver. 'I don't think my husband actually saw us,' she said loudly and clearly.

For a split second Hank looked at her with totally blank eyes, before he cottoned on. 'Oh! That's good! Okay then! We don't want your husband to find out about us, do we?' he almost shouted.

They ordered two brandies in the bar of the hotel, and sat in an alcove where they could not be seen. Madeleine was the first to speak.

'You're flying back to the States today?'

'Yup! And you're going to England?' he inquired.

'Yes. I have some family business to attend to.'

'You don't want to be in New York when Kimberley finds out what's happened?' Hank asked curiously.

'No way. And I don't want my husband to be there either,' said Madeleine, sipping her brandy slowly, feeling her nerves gradually settling.

'Is he going to join you in England, then?'

Madeleine gave Hank a dry smile. 'He doesn't know it yet, but yes, he is.'

Hank nodded understandingly. 'You could be right,' he said. 'When the shit hits the fan, it's sure going to go flying around the place!'

Jessica glanced round the hotel bedroom, shrugged her shoulders and decided they must be in Milan. It was the old joke; this is Thursday so it must be . . .! Only the joke was wearing thin so far as she was concerned.

They'd been flying from country to country, staying in city after city, living in hotels, never having time to even unpack properly, and she had the terrible feeling that they were never going to *arrive*! But arrive where? she asked herself. There *was* no point of arrival, no moment when they could say: 'At last we're here'. They were on a journey that had no ending and all she could long for was next spring, when they finally got to Bernard's house in Sardinia. But next spring! That was still months away.

Jessica jumped up from the dressing table, where she'd been putting on her make-up, and went to look out of the window. Ahead lay Milan Cathedral, blackened with age, as awe-inspiring as a great peaked rock, dwarfing the tourists who milled around the large square in which it stood, imposing its majesty on the historic city. Could she wait until next spring? Then what? She and Bernard would have a few months at his home, and then they'd be off again, for another eight months, jetting around the world in a never ending spin. Depression ate a great hole in her heart as she leaned her forehead against the cool windowpane and thought about how lonely and bored she felt. For a moment she almost wished it hadn't been a false alarm and that she was pregnant, but the memory of Bernard's face when she told him she thought she was going to have a baby, still sent an icy chill through her when she thought of it. Bernard hadn't wanted a baby. He'd made it very clear.

Jessica had said nothing at the time, partly relieved herself because she'd been wondering how she'd manage on tour with a baby; but now, as she thought about what he'd said, it added to her depression. She'd always planned to have children one day, and if she wasn't going to have a career in the hotel business she might as well get on with it now, surely? What was she waiting for? When she and Andrew . . . Jessica caught herself up short, startled to find herself thinking of Andrew again.

'Are you ready?' bellowed Bernard at that moment, from the living-room of their suite, where he'd been on the phone for hours. They were due to have lunch with the publicist of his Milan concert, and after that he was being interviewed for *Gente Mese* magazine before going on to rehearsals. Apart from lunch, Jessica faced the rest of the day, and most of the evening, alone.

'Yes, I'm ready,' she replied, running a brush through her hair and picking up her purse. She joined him in the next room where he sat, surrounded by papers and notes, the phone still in his hand.

'You will have to replace the third violinist!' he was shouting at someone on the other end of the line. 'I cannot work with an . . . an *amateur!*'

Jessica sat down opposite him waiting for him to finish, and when he put down the receiver she jumped to her feet.

'Okay. Shall we go?' she said brightly.

'*Momento, momento* . . .!' Bernard said vaguely, as he started to dial another number.

Jessica planted herself before him, her slim straight figure and long legs in their high-heeled shoes set in an attitude of indignation.

'Don't "*momento*" me!' she stormed. 'You asked me to go to this lunch with you and I'm ready to go. It's you who made such a fuss about our being on time!'

Bernard continued to talk on the phone, barely acknowledging her presence in the room. Jessica watched him angrily, her pent-up frustration at having nothing to do increasing her irritation. Never in her life had she hung around for anyone. Her time had always been tightly scheduled, her hours filled with work and purpose. Sitting around now, waiting for something to happen, was driving her crazy, especially as Bernard barely noticed her presence. What had happened to the ardent lover who had declared he was so lonely as he travelled the world by himself? What had happened to the pleading man who had said he needed her with him, because life on his own was a desolate desert? What has happened, thought Jessica spiritedly, is that Bernard likes having someone in tow, just in case he has an idle minute, away from the sycophantic adulation of his fans! An idle moment during which he might be forced to entertain himself! He doesn't want *me*, Jessica thought furiously, he wants a bimbo with which to decorate his bedroom! Someone who is always there, looking pretty and sexy, ready to boost his ego and pander to his needs.

'If you're not ready to go to lunch – I am!' she exclaimed, flouncing towards the door.

'Wait!' Bernard commanded, raising his hand.

'What for?' she retorted. 'To starve to death?'

But that night as she sat in the concert hall, watching as Bernard conducted the great orchestra and his music filled the air with its unbearable sweetness, her irritation and growing resentment vanished. The magnificence of his melodies as they washed over her stirred her deeply, filling her with worship for this talented man whose music thrilled millions. And he's all mine, Jessica said to herself, overwhelmed by the thought. He is mine to care for and look after; mine to love and adore. I am the person with whom he spends his nights . . . And at that moment she realised how envied she must be by other women. Bernard was not only a rich and highly successful man, he was a star in his own right, and a musical genius. She was lucky to have him in her life, she told herself, as the violins sang out with pathos, and the muffled drums found an echo in the thudding of her heart. And she should appreciate him more, she reflected as full throated trumpets took up the melody and the cymbals exploded in a spine-chilling crash of excitement. Bernard is a great man, Jessica reminded herself as her eyes grew moist at the passion of the music, and I love him with all my heart and mind and soul.

At breakfast the next morning, which they had in their suite, an altogether more prosaic atmosphere prevailed as Bernard grumbled about one thing after another. The concert had been lousy. The first violinist ought to be shot. The party at the end of the concert had been a disaster, and why had the car been forty minutes late to collect them afterwards? He'd slept badly because the room was too hot, and he'd been woken at dawn by road works going on under their bedroom window! On and on he went, finding fault with everything and everyone, until Jessica finally lost her temper. This was not the god-like creature she had put on a pedestal the previous night, but a petulant, spoilt little boy who seemed to think the world should revolve around him.

'Oh, for God's sake, Bernard, do shut up!' she

exclaimed crossly. 'You're *never* satisfied! You always find something to complain about. Why can't you relax? You don't seem happy unless you've got something to be unhappy about!'

'Rubbish!' he raged. 'I just don't like inefficiency. Look what happened a minute ago! I tried to put through a call to Paris . . . and the stupid operator cut me off!' He looked as offended as if he'd been mortally insulted. 'Now it means I must try again, and I have better things to do with my time than waste it fighting with stupid little girls on a switchboard!'

'I'll try and get through for you,' said Jessica resignedly. 'Anything for the sake of peace,' she added sotto voce.

'What was that?' roared Bernard.

'I said anything for the sake of peace,' repeated Jessica sullenly. 'You get so worked up about everything, and frankly life's too short.'

'No, I don't!' he retaliated. 'I've a right to expect telephone operators to work efficiently, . . . and I don't see why I should put up with a hot noisy bedroom in a five star hotel, do you? Well, answer me, do you? Were any of the guests at the Royal Westminster subjected to massive road works going on right under their bedroom windows, and the central heating turned on during a heatwave?'

'Don't be ridiculous! The heating was *not* turned on last night . . .'

'Why do you always argue with me?' he cut in, his tone aggrieved. 'Why do you never take my side, when something goes wrong? I expect loyalty from you, Jessica . . .'

'Oh, this is bloody absurd,' she exclaimed, banging down her coffee cup and rising. 'I'm going to have a shower.' She hurried to the bathroom, closing and locking the door behind her. Bernard had made her so angry that she didn't trust herself not to *throw* something at him! How, she asked herself, could a mature man of such enormous talent, sink to the level of behaving like a super-brat?

When she went back to the bedroom to dress, she heard Bernard talking on the telephone in the next room, as blithe and cheerful as if nothing had happened. Which is all fine and dandy for him, she thought, but I'm getting a bit tired of living on an emotional switchback!

It wasn't until they arrived at their next destination, Paris, the following day, that Jessica realised the full extent of Bernard's moodiness.

They were booked in at the Hôtel George V, near the Étoile, in Paris, and two nights later Bernard was to give a concert at the Théâtre Musical de Paris. As usual, they were given the best suite in this hotel, which had once been a French palace, and the full VIP treatment.

When they'd arrived from Milan it had been so late they'd gone straight to bed and hadn't wakened until noon the next day. According to the itinerary Jessica saw this was a 'free day' for Bernard, but from experience she knew that didn't mean a thing. He wouldn't be happy unless he was talking on the phone all morning, contacting friends, acquaintances, and colleagues, no matter whether they were in Europe,

Australia or America. And then he'd set up meetings to check on every detail of the forthcoming concert, although there were plenty of people whose job it was to do that. Finally he'd arrange to meet a score of people from lunchtime onwards. It was always the same; a restless round of self-inflicted commitments that left Jessica either hanging around waiting for him, or trailing along after him. Today she decided to do her own thing. She hadn't been to Paris for ages, and she would combine looking round the city again with some shopping.

Bernard's reaction to this was to throw up his hands in a gesture of helplessness. 'Shopping again?' he almost moaned. 'Dear God, don't you do anything but buy clothes? You must be spending a fortune with my credit cards!'

'But it was you . . .!' gasped Jessica, stung to the core by the injustice of his words. '*You* who insisted I should use your credit cards! *You* who said I shouldn't make a fuss because I'm not able to earn my own living any more, and it was . . . *and I am not spending a fortune on clothes*!' Incensed, she had jumped to her feet and was hopping angrily in front of him, her eyes blazing.

Bernard's hooded eyes swept coldly over her. 'You're always buying clothes,' he retorted accusingly. 'Every time I see you you've got on something different; every concert I give it's another evening dress! Why do you bother anyway? You're not the one who's in the limelight, you know! Who's going to be looking at you, anyway?' He waved an imperious hand as if to dismiss her, and went back to reading his newspaper.

'That's the nastiest thing I've ever heard,' Jessica exploded, dumbfounded by his rudeness and arrogance. 'Don't you dare talk to me like that. I may not be a star, but I am a person. And don't you *dare* throw up in my face that you have to pay for my clothes. You know I'd much rather be earning my own living.'

Bernard shrugged as if he were already bored by the subject. 'Well, stop spending so much of the living *I* earn.'

Jessica grabbed her purse, whipped out her wallet and wrenched all his credit cards from one of its pockets.

'There!' she yelled. 'And there! And there!' Plastic cards rained down on Bernard, bouncing off the edge of his coffee cup and showering the breakfast table. 'Take back your cards. I'd rather *die* than use them now! You're the meanest, nastiest, most . . .' Her voice trailed away as tears of rage plopped out of her eyes, and splashed down on to her satin robe. She gave a loud sniff.

Bernard looked at her, his eyes crinkled, and then with a guffaw he doubled up, rocking with laughter. His shoulders shook and his face had turned scarlet with mirth.

Jessica mopped the tears from her cheeks with the back of her hand and looked at him suspiciously.

'What's so funny?' she croaked.

'You . . . you . . . Ah-h-h . . .!' He went off into another paroxysm of laughter, rolling his head from side to side as, helpless, he flopped back on to the sofa.

Jessica gathered her robe closer in an effort to look

dignified, but it wasn't easy, with her hair dishevelled and her eyes red-rimmed. Her chest heaved in an involuntary sob.

'I don't see what's so f-funny.'

'You are!' gasped Bernard, wiping his own eyes. 'You're hysterically funny! I've never before seen an adult woman turn into a four-year-old child in ten seconds flat!' He gave another gurgle of mirth. 'You should see yourself! Why are you so upset?'

'Because you're being unfair, unjust and I won't be talked to like that!'

'Come here, little pet.' Bernard held out his arms to her, his eyes gentle through their deep amusement, his voice soothing. 'Come to me, my little pet . . .'

Jessica allowed herself to be cosseted, although she was aware that he was manipulating her. He was kissing her face softly now, holding her close, in a way that was partly fatherly and partly like a lover, and all the time he was whispering endearments. But these swings in mood were treacherous and Jessica knew it. Sometimes she wondered if he wasn't nasty to her on purpose, either to prove to himself his power over her, or because to see her upset amused him. Either way, she was beginning to feel like a dice, shaken and thrown down at regular intervals, never knowing which way she'd land.

Chapter Fifteen

Milton Manor was as Madeleine remembered it, except that the seasons had changed and the soft Devonshire landscape had hardened and grown bleak with winter, its soil frozen and its trees now almost stripped of leaves. Once again Jenkins met her at the station, silent and morose, and drove her along the ice-bound roads and under overhanging branches lacy with frost.

And I have changed since I was last here, she thought, as she sat in the back of the old car gazing out of the window. I, too, have hardened like the chilled earth, by being exposed to the biting wind of reality. There have been moments when I thought I would perish. She thought of Carl, in bed with Kimberley while she visited her grandfather in this very house last summer, and she thought of the scheme Kimberley had put to Carl, blackmailing him into going along with it. Then she thought of the months of self-control she had been forced to exercise, hiding from Carl the fact that she knew what was going on, while all the time laying a trap for Kimberley to fall into. What amazed her most, looking back, was her own strength. If someone had told her five months ago that she'd have to endure this living hell, while pretending to be bright and happy, she'd have said it was impossible. Yet she'd done it, because she loved Carl and wanted to save their marriage; most important of all, because she knew Carl loved her.

But it wasn't over yet. Kimberley could still bring about his downfall.

Hunter greeted her with his usual formality but she could tell he was pleased to see her again, and glancing round the house it was obvious that he and the other servants had been keeping it in pristine condition. Jenkins had also been at work in the garden, for there was not a dead leaf or twig lying on the ground and the paths and lawns looked orderly and neat.

'Is there anything I can get you, Madam?' Hunter asked, taking her case.

Madeleine had flown from Zurich that morning. On landing at Heathrow she had taken a taxi into the centre of London, collected her things and checked out of the Royal Westminster, then caught a train for Okehampton. She'd been away exactly twenty-four hours and there was just one message for her: would she please call her husband in New York? He'd called at six o'clock the previous evening, English time.

'I'll take a shower,' Madeleine told Hunter, 'and then I'd like some coffee in the library. I've got some phone calls to make.'

'Certainly, Madam.'

The pretty chintzy bedroom had been prepared for her again and it was warm and cosy as she entered. A log fire crackled in the pink marble fireplace, and a bowl of Christmas roses, white and delicate-looking as porcelain, stood in a vase by the bed. The curtains had already been drawn.

Twenty minutes later, bathed and changed into a long green woollen housecoat, her hair still damp and held off her face by a scarf, she sat at her grandfather's desk in the study and dialled the number of the Central Manhattan Bank.

'Can I speak to Mr Carl Delaney,' she said, as soon as she got through.

When Carl came on the line he sounded anxious. 'Maddy? I've been trying to get hold of you! Where on earth have you been?'

'I'm sorry, darling. I had to look at so many . . .'

'There's been a panic here, and I desperately needed to get hold of you.' Carl's tone was slightly reproachful.

Madeleine's heart skipped a beat. 'What d'you mean? What sort of panic?'

'It's Patti. She's not been well, and the doctors insisted she have some chest X-rays done . . .'

'Oh, my God. Is she all right, Carl?' This was something she hadn't expected; she'd been so sure something had gone seriously wrong at the bank. 'What did the doctors say?'

Carl let out a long breath. 'She's been lucky, Maddy. She's got a chronic chest infection, but it's not lung cancer. We've all had a bad fright, though. Patti didn't want you to know when we were afraid it was something serious, but I knew you'd want to and that was why I was trying to get hold of you.'

'Oh . . . Carl!' Madeleine felt quite drained with shock. If anything had happened to her beloved aunt,

413

she'd have been distraught. As it was, relief made her feel choked so that what she had to say next sounded more plausible.

'Carl . . . please come to England to be with me. I feel absolutely strung out . . . it's scary enough, having to go and see my mother in the institution, but thinking what might have happened to Patti . . .' Her voice broke off in a little sob. 'Please, darling,' she begged, 'please come to England to be with me?'

'Sweetheart, you know I can't get away,' said Carl reasonably. 'We're up to our eyes in work at the moment. It's quite impossible.'

'Listen, Carl.' Madeleine wasn't having to act now. Real desperation to get him to leave New York gave her voice a genuine ring of fear and her hands were shaking. 'You've no idea how badly I need you here. I can't cope with having to see my mother on my own . . . and there's this house . . . Oh, Carl, I don't often ask you a favour, but please, just this once . . . even if it's only for a few days, please fly to England?'

'I don't think I can, much as I'd like to, Maddy.'

'Carl, you *must* come,' she broke in. If what Hank Pugsley said was true, Carl must be a million miles away from the bank when the balloon went up. 'Please, sweetheart, I'll talk to Daddy. He'll arrange for you to get away!'

'All right, all right,' Carl said soothingly. 'I'll come, darling. Don't get in such a state. I'll fix it with Jake, myself. What's gone wrong, Maddy? You weren't worried about meeting your mother before you left here. What's suddenly scared you?'

She let out a little sigh. 'I don't know. This place

maybe. All I know is that I want you here. Can you fly over tomorrow?'

'Tomorrow!' Carl sounded startled. 'For God's sake, I can't just walk out of the bank like that.'

'Please, Carl.' Never in her life had she used her powers of persuasion with more force. If only she could tell him the truth! If only she could tell him the months of fear and misery were almost over! But right now she had to use her own fear of facing her mother as an excuse to get him to fly over, and she prayed to God it was a strong enough reason.

'Okay,' she heard him say at last, and her heart swelled with relief.

'Let me know when you're arriving, Carl, and I'll meet you,' she said. 'And thank you, honey. You've no idea how good I feel now that I know you're coming over.'

When she'd finished talking to Carl she put a call through to Jake. She wanted to get her side of the story in first, and she wanted her father to realise how much she needed Carl at this time.

'That's fine,' said Jake, when she told him. 'He could do with a break anyway, he's looking very tired these days. How long d'you think you'll both be away?'

That was something Madeleine couldn't answer. To see her mother and wind up the estate with Mr Marks would probably only take a few days; to put paid to Kimberley's activities might take longer, and that was now up to Hank Pugsley anyway.

'I'm sure we won't be away long, Daddy,' she said, 'and you'll encourage Carl to come over here, won't you? I really need him.'

'Of course, honey. Don't worry about a thing.'

Madeleine let out a long sigh of relief. So far, everything was working out just as she'd planned. In the morning she'd call up Mr Marks to confirm their appointment, and she might even call Hank, just to ask how things were going.

Mr Marks arrived promptly at noon the next day, delighted to accept Madeleine's invitation to stay on for luncheon, after they'd discussed business.

'So kind . . . quite delightful . . .' he muttered, eyes blinking rapidly when he saw her.

Madeleine had asked Hunter to light a fire in the drawing-room and they now sat in front of it, Mr Marks with his glass of sherry, Madeleine with a gin and tonic. She looked rested and refreshed after a good night's sleep, and knowing that Carl was on his way had taken a great load off her mind.

'You said you had some information about your late mother,' he began pedantically, 'has your father been able to give you the details . . .?'

'Yes.' Madeleine smiled gently, knowing what she was going to say would be a great shock to him.

'Ah . . .' he paused delicately. 'You have traced the death certificate?'

'There is no death certificate. My mother is apparently alive.' Briefly, Madeleine told Mr Marks what Jake had told her. 'I have these documents for you,' she continued, handing him a large brown envelope. 'When she became ill my father was given power of attorney, with the permission of my grandfather, so there should be no problem about my inheriting this

416

house now. I'm afraid she'll never come back here.'

'So . . . so she's at the Meredith House Institute, is she? My goodness me. My word.' Mr Marks was deeply baffled. 'And you never knew? All these years she's been alive . . . and you thought she'd died? That must be why your grandfather never made a new Will; your mother was alive, and perhaps he thought she'd get better?'

'That may be the answer,' Madeleine replied. 'That was certainly what he wanted to tell me, so that I'd go and see her sometimes; so there'd be someone to care.'

'What an extraordinary story!' exclaimed Mr Marks. 'I've never heard anything like it! All these years . . . and your father knew, but he never told you!' He continued to shake his head in wonderment.

'It's been rather a shock,' Madeleine remarked, looking at him candidly. 'My husband is flying over tomorrow and as soon as he arrives we'll go and visit her.' As she spoke, she felt her stomach muscles tighten. She was actually going to be seeing her mother within the next couple of days; the mother she'd wondered about ever since she could remember; the mother she'd so wanted when she'd been a child; the mother she'd so feared on her last visit here. In the past week or so, the existence of Camilla had been overshadowed by her other worries, but now she was about to come face to face with the woman of a thousand eyes, who kept a journal about her black magic experiences, and whom no one had talked about for over twenty years. Madeleine shuddered violently, as if a cold wind had touched her, and Mr Marks looked up anxiously.

417

'Are you all right, Mrs Delaney?' he asked.

'I'm fine,' she said quietly. Mr Marks wasn't exactly the type of man she felt she could confide in. After he had left, Madeleine tried to settle in front of the fire with a newspaper and a novel she'd bought at the airport, but she felt restless and on edge, as if she were waiting for something to happen. She looked round the drawing-room – pretty and innocuous as any room in a typical English country house, now that all the pictures of Camilla had been removed – and wondered why she still felt uneasy. The fact that she now knew her mother was alive should have lightened the atmosphere because the living do not haunt, but still she seemed to feel a ghostly presence in the room. After a few more minutes, she left it and went into the hall. Jenkins was walking towards her with a basket of logs, and as their eyes met Madeleine knew the moment had come when she must get him to tell her everything. She followed him back into the drawing-room and stood watching, as he transferred the logs from his basket to the side of the fireplace. The only sound in the room was the crackling and sizzling of the fire, and in Madeleine's head, the thudding of her heart.

'Jenkins,' she began . . . then waited for him to turn and look at her. His back view was stern and unbending, and for a moment she wondered if he was going to ignore her. 'I'd like to have a few words with you, Jenkins,' she said more authoritatively. 'You see, I know my mother's still alive . . . and I know she's in a mental home . . . and I also know it's got something to do with the black magic and witchcraft

418

she was involved in . . .' Madeleine broke off, as Jenkins spun round to look at her. She couldn't tell from his eyes what he was thinking, but there was something fearful in his look.

'Who told 'e that?' he croaked, his Devonshire accent rich and strong.

'My father told me,' replied Madeleine, watching him closely, 'but he wouldn't discuss what had caused it. You know, don't you, Jenkins? It was you who took from the library the diary she'd kept, relating her Satanic experiences, wasn't it? All along you've known what happened, what made her go crazy . . . I'm asking you to tell me now, Jenkins. Please. I am an adult and I shall be going to visit her as soon as my husband arrives from the States. It would help me a great deal if I knew what had happened; it would help me to cope with her . . . and the situation.'

While she'd been talking Jenkins had remained on his knees in front of the fire, his gnarled work-worn hands nervously rubbing the brass fender, his eyes fixed on her face.

'Dear Lord . . .' he seemed to be offering up a prayer, as if asking for guidance, and for a moment he closed his eyes.

Madeleine dropped on to her haunches beside him, her full-skirted grey dress falling into heavy folds around her feet, her black hair tinged with blue by the light of the fire. Tentatively, desperate now to get him to respond, she stretched out a hand towards him.

'Please, Jenkins? You've no idea how much it means to me to find out the truth.'

She watched his face and the deep lines seemed to

deepen, and there was wetness round his eyes. His mouth quivered.

'Lord bless you, Miss, and you were such a bonny little girl,' he said gruffly. 'It would have been murder if anything had happened to you that night!'

Jostled by crowds scurrying home from work at the end of the day, Kimberley walked the last two blocks to her apartment that evening. She wanted to buy some groceries, but more importantly, some liquor. Her men friends had a habit of calling up unexpectedly and inviting themselves round and she liked to keep a well stocked bar. Not that she was expecting anyone tonight, thank God, she thought, as her high-heeled boots crunched on the icy sidewalks and the piercingly cold wind bit through her clothes. She had planned a quiet evening on her own: wash her hair, have supper and watch a movie on TV. The sort of evening she liked to have occasionally, when she could relax and do her own thing. She bought herself a steak, some salad and some fruit, and then as an afterthought a section of rich dark brown chocolate cake from the delicatessen across the street. Hell, she reflected, as she entered the lobby of her apartment block, who cares about a few extra calories! Her figure was superb, without a trace of fat anywhere. No need to worry about dieting yet.

There was a letter for her in her mail box; the moment she saw the Swiss postage stamp and the familiar white envelope, her heart gave a little bound of joy. Taking the elevator up to her apartment, she let herself in and hurriedly dumped her shopping on the floor, lit one of her lamps and ripped open the envelope with fingers that shook with excitement.

Kimberley knew it was risky, having the Banque Internationale de Zurich send her monthly statements, but she couldn't resist seeing, in black and white, exactly how much money she had deposited in Switzerland. To see it made it seem more real, to count it was as comforting as counting the cookies in a jar for a small child. The words 'Credited' and 'Balance' were like music in her ears. Each month showed under 'Credited' how much she'd transferred into her account, and each month the figures under 'balance' rose steadily, the number of fat noughts increasing all the time. It reassured her to know every month that she was now a very rich woman. Soon she'd be able to vanish from New York, pick up the cash in Zurich and then disappear into Italy. Kimberley Cabot would no longer exist.

She pulled out the folded statement, thinking, If Hank can resist seeing how much he had stashed away, I can't! She liked to check that every transfer had gone through and then double check the final total. Even the best banks made mistakes; no one was going to make a mistake with *her* account. Today, she reckoned her balance must stand at one million, seven hundred and eighty-two thousand dollars. Exactly. Of course if only she'd been able to put through the last transfer, that would have been a further three hundred and thirty thousand dollars! She bit her lip, still deeply vexed that her computer disc seemed to have been wiped clean. It was something she couldn't understand. The tape was permanently in her possession. How could it have been erased? And she still had to think of a way of getting round Jake's new security methods, so that she could make another copy.

Feeling an almost physical thrill, she unfolded the statement, and smoothed it flat on her knee, her eyes sweeping down the 'Balance' column. Then she started, eyes popping out of her head. That *couldn't* be right! Something had gone terribly wrong with the Banque Internationale's computer! It had made a mistake and she must call up Zurich right away . . . Her heart was hammering now as her panic-stricken eyes swept down the columns. Just under four weeks ago she'd transferred three hundred and twenty-one thousand dollars . . . yes, there it was in the 'Credit' column. Relief swept over her momentarily until she caught sight of a row of figures in the 'Debit' column. DEBIT, her mind shrieked, but she hadn't withdrawn any money! And then she saw it . . . the amount she had expected to see at the bottom of the 'Balance' column. One million, seven hundred and eighty-two thousand dollars. But it had all been withdrawn the previous week! The only thing at the bottom of the balance column were the words, 'Amount: Nil. Account closed'.

Kimberley slid off the chair to her knees, sobs of rage tearing at her throat. Someone had taken her money – ALL OF IT! She pounded the floor with her fists as tears of fury poured down her cheeks. Spitting obscenities and cursing with rage, she clawed the air and rolled on the floor, beside herself with wrath.

'My money! My money!' she moaned as a mother

will cry out in anguish at the loss of her child. 'My money!' Convulsed, tearing at her hair, her face twisted in a paroxysm of bitter passion, she writhed about as if demented. It was HER money! HER savings! She was the one who had taken the risks, and she was the one who deserved to be rich! It was her future too . . . all that she had ever dreamed or planned for. Gone! As if it had never been. The deep pain of her loss coursed like a virulent poison through her veins and for a moment she felt capable of killing.

'I'll get him for this!' she screamed, picking up an ashtray and hurling it across the room. Then, with a violent move, she kicked over a lamp and it went crashing to the ground. 'That fucking bastard! He'll not get away with this. I'll see him dead first,' she screamed. Inflamed into a passion in which reason played no part, Kimberley thrashed around her living-room, smashing what she could pick up and throw, kicking or pushing over what she couldn't. And everything she threw and kicked and punched was Carl; she'd get him for this! She'd go to Jake Shearman and all the other directors of the Central Manhattan Bank, and then she'd go to the FBI and she'd bring about Carl's ruin if it was the last thing she did. Thoughts of revenge, like a towering black wave, swamped her and drenched her, carrying her along a treacherous path where she saw herself bringing about the final downfall of Carl . . . and his damned wife too. Flinging herself on to the sofa, which stood amidst the destruction she had wrought, she stared into space, her grey eyes wild, her hair a tangled mess. Her mind was already formulating a plan. She had been cheated, but she'd get even! The bastard was not going to get away with it, sitting in his fucking Fifth Avenue apartment, with everything he could ever want, while she slogged it out for the rest of her life behind a desk.

Kimberley closed her eyes for the moment, gathering her thoughts. She'd say that Carl had forced her to make a copy of the computer disc he'd stolen from Jake's office, because he wanted to embezzle Hank Pugsley's money. She'd say he blackmailed her into doing it – threatening to expose the fact she'd once been a prostitute unless she did as he said. And as she'd wanted to keep her job at the bank . . . Kimberley nodded to herself, pleased with that line. Yes, it would work very well. Then she'd say Madeleine barged into her apartment one day – which was true – and threatened her.

That was it! Kimberley's inflamed mind worked frenziedly, making sure her story was watertight, and making sure that what she had to say would ruin them both forever!

She went over her story again and again, until finally her rage exhausted itself and gave way to tears of sheer misery. Kimberley sobbed for her lost fortune as if her heart would break, knowing that her dreams would never come true now. The little girl who had stood on Times Square, dazzled by the lights that blazed their tempting message of prosperity, was still inside the woman who crouched huddled on the sofa, so that now, together, they mourned their loss; the dream was but a dream. The string of lights would never become a string of diamonds now, and her tears were as much for sorrow at the little girl's disappointment as for her own.

The room was in semi-darkness now, lit only by the one lamp she'd switched on when she'd got back, and through the uncurtained windows the blackness of an icy night, friendless and stark, lay like an uncharted sea. Of course she didn't have to tell the FBI anything, she thought, as she wiped her face with the palms of her hands, smudging the eye make-up. She wanted revenge, more than anything, but wouldn't she be cutting off her nose to spite her face? Common sense began to prevail, as she got a grip on herself and tried to control the occasional childlike sob that shook her frame. Crushed by her loss, and filled with exhausted despair, she nevertheless began to realise that in making Carl and his wife suffer, she'd only be adding to her own suffering too.

If she did nothing, no one would ever know what had happened. Certainly Carl and Madeleine weren't going to talk, so . . . Supposing she left her job at the bank, got another job, maybe in modelling? Her fertile mind began to write a whole new scenario with herself, as always, the central figure, the heroine.

When her doorbell shrilled in the darkness of her apartment lobby, she paid little attention at first. She was still too couched in misery, too much in a state of shock, to want to see anyone. But it rang again, strong and persistent, demanding attention.

Slowly, stumbling over the wreckage she had created, Kimberley went to the door, accidentally tripping over the bags of groceries and liquor she'd placed there earlier. Swearing, she fumbled for the lock just as the bell rang out again. It scared her this time, ringing out with piercing loudness just by her ear, and inflamed with irritation she grabbed the handle and jerked the door open. Too late, she realised she'd forgotten to put on the safety chain, because she'd been in such a hurry to open her mail . . .

A second later, Kimberley's terrified screams echoed and re- echoed along the deserted corridors of her apartment block, heard only by those who chose to mind their own business. In the dim light she could make out the great bulky figure and sweating, moon-shaped face of Hank Pugsley.

'Murder?' Madeleine repeated, shocked. 'My grand-father said something . . . what was it? Oh, yes, he said something had nearly led to my death, but I don't understand, Jenkins. What happened?'

The old gardener remained on his knees in front of the fire, dabbing his watery eyes with a red and white spotted handkerchief.

'You really wants to know, Miss?' he asked, almost in a whisper, his rich Devonshire accent thick and pronounced. 'Sir George, he hushed up the whole thing at the time, though everyone in the village knew what had happened. And your father, Miss, Mr Jake Shearman, he threatened to sue anyone and take them to court if they so much as breathed a word of what happened that night. That's why I durstn't tell you nothing when you asked before, not even when all the village people at Sir George's funeral looked at you, curious like. But they remembered 'cos it would be hard to forget, it would.'

Madeleine leaned forward, straining to hear and understand every word he said. 'But I do want to know, Jenkins. I must know if I'm to meet my mother. What happened? Was there an accident?'

Jenkins shook his head morosely. 'It were no accident, Miss. It were the doing of the Devil.'

Something in the way he said it made Madeleine catch her breath. 'So my mother *was* involved in witchcraft?'

'Oh, aye.' The old man nodded vigorously. 'Your mother, she got involved in a witches' coven. They were led by a man who called himself the "Master". They used to meet on Friday nights, up in Warreners Copse, where there used to be an old barn. Strange things did happen on them nights. Bad things. Put the fear of God in me, all right, did those bad things.' His accent and way of speaking made Madeleine lean closer, listening intently.

'How did my mother get involved?'

Jenkins shrugged and looked down at his strong old hands as if seeking some answer to her question. 'I don't rightly know,' he said at last. 'Maybe it was because she got low after Her Ladyship died. Proper hold they had on her, though. All the time your father was working in London, she was gettin' deeper and deeper in, and I warned Sir George, but he wouldn't listen.'

'My grandfather knew what was happening, but he did nothing to stop her?'

'As far as Sir George was concerned, Miss Camilla could do no wrong,' Jenkins replied.

Madeleine smiled at the respectful way the old

gardener still referred to her grandparents and her mother. 'Did my father know?' she asked.

'I didn't think it was my business to go telling your father. After all, I was just the gardener here. Then, one night I went up to the barn on Warreners Copse, over Pendlebury way, where I knew the coven used to meet, because I heard strange noises.' His voice dropped to barely a whisper and his eyes took on a fearful expression, as if the memory of that night still haunted him.

'They'd just sacrificed an animal . . .' he continued. 'I could hear them chanting and I looks through a crack in the window, and I think they were smearing someone with blood. It was terrible to see the strange things that were going on! Then, all at once . . . I heard them say your name.'

Madeleine stiffened, knowing before he said it what was coming. She could just imagine the old barn with a make-shift altar set up in the middle, surrounded by the men and women wielding phallic symbols and dancing and chanting, naked in the candlelight around the sacrificed animal.

'It was to be you next time . . .' Jenkins breathed almost inaudibly.

'No!' Madeleine sprang to her feet, horror making an icy shiver crawl down her spine, and her face blanch to whiteness. 'No!' It was a protest, a wild cry to blot out the terrifying images that sprang before her eyes. Her own mother had been prepared to have her sacrificed!

'That can't be true,' she whispered brokenly. 'You must have heard wrong! That's too horrible an idea.

My mother would never have . . .'

Jenkins continued as if she hadn't spoken, gazing down at the burning logs in the fireplace. 'Then I runs back to me cottage, not knowing what to do, like. It's no good going to Sir George again, because he won't listen. And there wasn't much time. I'd heard them talk about Midsummer Eve, and that was just two days away.'

The silence was so heavy in the drawing-room that it seemed to close in on Madeleine like a tangible force, blocking out all outside sounds, as if she were at the bottom of a deep pool. Only the roaring in her ears of her hammering heart made her believe this moment was real. What Jenkins was saying had the quality of a nightmare, with her and her mother as central figures, moving like ghosts in another time and age. She looked down at her hands, slim artistic hands, with only Carl's gold wedding ring for ornamentation, and she wondered if these very hands had held on trustingly to her mother . . . a mother who had led her as a child, from her cot, and taken her to a place of unspeakable evil . . . a mother who had been ready to sacrifice her to some Satanic god, for reasons best known to herself. Had she cried out? Clung to her mother's skirts? Begged to be protected?

Madeleine closed her eyes, feeling sick. 'What happened?' She spoke so low Jenkins could barely hear her.

He turned his weatherbeaten face towards her, and in its deeply carved lines there was a certain nobility, an honesty and integrity that made her realise at that instant there was something very special about him.

The faded blue eyes, still moist with emotion, looked at her with something like compassion.

'I gets in touch with your father, in London,' he said slowly, as if measuring each word, trying to spare her the worst of the shock and agony that already she knew was to come, 'and your father, he came down as quick as he could, because he didn't believe what I had to say. But he believed me, all right, when he arrived late at night, all the way from London, and neither you nor your mother could be found in the house. Sir George, he said he didn't know where you'd gone, and then your father got real worried. Rushed round the house, shouting and hollering your names: "Camilla," he yelled. "Where are you? Where's Madeleine?" And then Sir George got anxious too, and they both looked at me.'

There was a long pause as Jenkins seemed to re-live that moment, probably the most important in his life, when a child's fate hung in the balance, a child he had the power to save. Madeleine held her breath, spell-bound, hanging on to his words.

'I said to 'em, "Follow me", and I led them to the barn up on Warreners Copse,' Jenkins continued.

Madeleine could hardly bear to hear any more, feeling the cold wind sweeping across the lonely copse, seeing the barn, the candles, the altar standing ready . . . She closed her eyes and buried her face in her hands and suddenly she was trembling with a remembered terror that flashed through her mind. A knife, chanting voices, naked flesh and eyes, dozens of eyes, that burned like lasers into her body as she lay there . . . and a man's voice.

'Oh, Christ!' she cried out. 'Oh, dear God!'

'Aye,' Jenkins said ponderously. 'We got there in time, your Dad and me. He ran forward and grabbed you off the make-shift altar they'd built, and I caught hold of Miss Camilla . . .' The tears started to roll down his cheeks again and he dabbed them ineffectually with his spotted handkerchief. 'I'd known her since she was a little girl too. Wild she was, that night. Screaming and raving! It took me all me time to get her out of the barn and drag her back to the house here. You weren't harmed, though you were bawling your head off, and Sir George rang for the doctor. Your dad rang for the police.'

Madeleine was crying too now, crying for the lost mother and the lost child and the terrible night which might, but for Jenkins, have ended in a heinous crime. It was as if something that had been locked inside her all her life had been revealed, exorcising dark memories that had always been just beyond her reach before. Now she had something positive to come to terms with, it would be easier to rid herself of her childhood fears.

Jenkins continued: 'They couldn't do nothing with your mother. Gone clean off her head, she had. Doctor said something about her being in a trance when your father and I broke into the barn, and the shock turning her mind, or sommat. But we'd got you out all right, and that was the main thing.' There was quiet pride in his voice now, as if he'd grown a beautiful rose or planted a bed of fine lilies.

'You saved my life,' said Madeleine looking at him, as he knelt with dignity, the only sign of emotion the

clutching and reclutching of the red spotted handkerchief, 'I shall always be grateful to you for that,' she
added with sincerity. 'I had no idea . . . What happened when the police arrived?'

'Well, of course they'd all run off, and left the barn
empty, hadn't they? Scarpered all over the country,
leaving the place in a mess. There was one old woman in
the village who was charged with being an accessory to
attempted murder, but it came to nothing. Got into a
lot of newspapers, though. Made a real stink. That was
why Sir George was so angry with your dad. Had a real
fight, they did. Sir George said the whole thing should
have been hushed up to protect the Dalrymple family,
and that the police should never have been called. I
think your dad was right, myself. Those wicked people
should have been caught and punished!'

'And my mother?' Madeleine asked painfully. 'Did
she go into . . .?' She couldn't finish the sentence. The
whole thing was a tragedy; a beautiful young woman,
married to a wonderful and successful man; a lifetime
before them of golden happiness with their little girl;
and then a dark nightmare casting its shadow over
them all, ruining Camilla's life and causing Jake deep
suffering.

'Miss Camilla was sent to hospital for treatment, but
it didn't do no good,' said Jenkins, answering her
unspoken question. 'She must have been at Meredith
House going on twenty-two years now. She don't
know anyone, of course. Don't even know who she is
herself,' he added sadly.

Madeleine looked up, surprised. 'You've been to see
her?'

432

'I go from time to time,' he replied shyly. 'I takes her a few flowers from the garden.'

'Thank you, Jenkins. Thank you for everything,' said Madeleine, rising. 'I shall always be grateful to you for caring about my mother. And me, when I was small. Also for all the years you gave to my grandfather. I think the Dalrymple family owe you a big debt of gratitude.'

He looked embarrassed, bundling his handkerchief into his pocket, then rubbing his hands before the blazing fire as if to warm them.

'I want you to know,' Madeleine continued, 'that I shall see you are always looked after. Do you own the cottage you live in?'

'Why no, it's part of the estate, Ma'am,' he mumbled, looking startled. 'Sir George just let me and me wife live in it while I works here.'

'Then I shall get the solicitor to draw up the necessary papers, making you the owner,' said Madeleine, 'and apart from the bequest my grandfather left you, I shall give you sufficient income to live comfortably on, when you retire.'

Scarlet in the face, hands shaking, Jenkins thanked her and she could see he was overwhelmed.

'I just hope I can go on working the garden when you sells the house,' he added. Then he turned and looked out of the drawing-room window at the stretch of lawn with its outer edges fringed by great elms and oaks and beech trees. 'I loves that old garden, I do,' he said simply.

Madeleine nodded, understanding. 'You can rely on me to do all I can to persuade the new owners to keep you on. I'm sure it won't be a problem. And at least you can be sure of a roof over your head, and your own bit of garden, for the rest of your life.'

'Yes, Ma'am. Thank you very much, Ma'am. The wife will be right pleased.' At last he turned to her with a beaming smile before walking slowly to the door. Then he stopped, and gave Madeleine a final grin.

'I'm right pleased to have got that lot off my chest at last, too,' he said with relief.

Madeleine held Carl in her arms as if she could never bear to let him go. 'God, I've missed you,' she whispered, pressing her cheek to his. 'Thank you for coming over. You've no idea how badly I need you.'

'Well, I'm here now, sweetheart!' He hugged her back and she thought how tired and strained he looked. Jake was right. Carl badly needed a break, although only she knew why.

'Did you have to abandon everything to fly here?' she asked as they clambered into the back of her grandfather's old Riley, which Jenkins insisted on driving at thirty miles an hour.

'More or less. I was able to delegate a lot and Jake was very good about the whole thing. It's a particularly busy time of year though; I'd never have got away if I hadn't been married to the boss's daughter!' Carl joked.

'But of course you've got Kimberley; she can look after things in your absence, can't she?' Madeleine asked smoothly, keeping her eyes fixed firmly on the passing wintry countryside.

Carl sounded equally non-committal. 'Yes, she can look after things.'

Madeleine felt inward relief. It looked as if she'd managed to get Carl out of New York in time. If Kimberley was still working in the bank, then the balloon obviously couldn't have gone up yet. All she had to do now was to keep Carl in England with her for perhaps another week, and with any luck it would be safe for them to return home.

'How's Aunt Patti?' she asked cheerfully.

Carl grinned. 'You'll never believe this . . . she's given up smoking!'

Madeleine's face lit up. 'No! Really? Thank God for that! How on earth did she manage it?'

'She was recommended to a hypnotherapist. Apparently he has a high rate of success, and after five hours with him she threw away her Marlboro's, and walked out, saying she'd never smoke again.'

'That's fantastic! D'you really think she'll stick to it? It would be wonderful if she did.'

Carl sounded positive. 'She got one hell of a fright, you know. Really thought her number was up. I don't think she'll touch another cigarette as long as she lives. Already she's started to complain about other people smoking.'

Madeleine laughed. 'Now that does sound like Aunt Patti!'

Soon the car was turning up the drive that was so familiar to Madeleine now.

'So this is Milton Manor,' exclaimed Carl. 'I must say it's impressive-looking. Are you sure you want to sell it, darling?'

'Yes, and I've already spoken to Andrew about it. He thinks he's found a buyer though he wouldn't say much at this stage. But, as I told him, the best gardener in the world goes with the property so whoever buys it is very lucky.' Madeleine smiled at Jenkins as she got out of the car, and he beamed in response. It was as if a great weight had been lifted off his shoulders in the past twenty-four hours.

'Who is he?' Carl whispered, when they were alone. 'He's like a little garden gnome!'

Madeleine burst out laughing, amused by the accuracy of Carl's description. Then she told him all about Jenkins and what he'd told her the previous day. Carl listened with growing horror, hardly able to believe his ears.

'You mean in this day and age –!' he said incredulously. 'My God, the whole thing sounds mediaeval! I can hardly believe it. You mean you were going to be killed as part of some Satanic ritual? And that your mother was a part of it?' He shook his head, bemused. 'Thank God for Jenkins then, and thank God for your father. I'm not surprised he refused to tell you all this. It's a terrible story.'

'I know,' agreed Madeleine. 'It explains so much, and I can understand why Daddy wouldn't have it mentioned. And I'm scared, Carl. What's she going to be like? Apparently she won't have any idea who I am. Jenkins said she doesn't know anyone, but I'm still nervous of having to meet her. That's why I wanted you here.' It was true. She'd used her fear of meeting her mother as an excuse to get Carl away from New York, but now it had become a reality.

Without Carl by her side, she didn't think she could get through it.

'Whatever happens, I'll be with you, Maddy,' he assured her tenderly. 'It's probably just as well she doesn't know anything. Imagine how she'd feel if she did!'

They went up to bed early that night, in the pretty chintzy bedroom where one of the maids had lit a fire and turned on the softly shaded lamps. The flower-patterned counterpane had been folded back to reveal an inviting downy nest of pure white linen and lace, and when Madeleine saw it she felt a sudden stab of desire. How long was it since she and Carl had made love – really made love, away from the pressures of the bank which had hung over them both like a towering shadow? She sat down on the chaise longue before the fire, gazing into its glowing depths, wondering if Carl felt the same. Or did he still think of Kimberley and remember what she'd been like in bed? Madeleine forced the thought out of her mind, and concentrated instead on the logs that flamed and flickered before her.

Carl undressed, and putting on his blue silk pyjamas, came and sat down beside her.

'Are you all right?' he asked, looking at her profile, wondering what she was thinking.

Madeleine stretched out to caress his thigh. The silk felt sensuous beneath her fingers and her hand slithered higher.

'I'm fine,' she said softly, 'but I've missed you.' As she spoke she could see the stirring of his passions, and looking deeply into his eyes her hand slid higher

437

still. Carl took her hand and held it tightly.

'God, I've missed you too,' he replied, and Madeleine could detect that same quality of desperation she'd noticed before, during that weekend at Oyster Bay. It was not the desperation of frustrated passion but of a deep sadness and regret, as if he could never undo what he had done, and as if he'd lost something precious he'd never find again.

'I love you, Carl,' she said softly, as she looked at his beloved face in the flickering flames of the fire. 'You know that, don't you?'

Carl put his arms around her, his eyes shut. 'And I love you, too, Maddy,' he said simply.

They kissed with tenderness, her hands cupping his face as his tongue gently explored the softness of her mouth. Then he removed the long velvet dress she'd worn for dinner, slipping it off her shoulders and revealing her perfect breasts, pulling it down over her slim hips, his hands caressing her skin as he did so, his mouth leaving a fiery trail of kisses.

Madeleine whispered with longing: 'Oh, Carl, I want to feel you inside me.'

'Maddy, my darling Maddy . . .' Carl kissed her deeply as if he could never bear to let her go, reassuring her that he loved her. She let herself relax, melting in his arms, blocking her mind to everything except the strength of his arms, the heat of his body and the sound of his voice. Together they lay in front of the fire, their bodies glowing pink in the firelight, their breathing the only sound in the room.

'My love . . . oh, God, my love,' Carl cried out as he entered her. She was clinging to him with a fever of passion now, wanting him to fill not only her body but her mind; to wash away the pain and anxiety that had blighted her for so long; to restore the trust and belief that it was only her he loved, and to give back to her the peace of mind that once she'd taken for granted.

'Love me . . . love me forever,' she begged, between her kisses.

'I'll love you as long as I live,' he vowed, thrusting deeply inside her. 'Take me, Maddy. Take me. I'm all yours.'

In the dim red light she could see the outline of his golden body as part of hers now, as they moved in unison, transported to a level of such intoxication that they were unaware of their surroundings, heedless of the ringing of the bedside phone. As wild tumultuous waves of piercing pleasure drove Madeleine demented with the desire for fulfilment, Carl climaxed with a wrenching rush that left him shuddering and calling out her name.

Beached, as if giant waves had thrown her high and cast her down again upon some distant shore, Madeleine lay dizzy and drained by the violence of her emotions. Then, as if from a long way away, she heard Carl say something.

'Is anyone going to answer that damned phone?'

She became aware of the incessant shrilling of a bell, but then it stopped and she snuggled closer to him, feeling the pounding of his heart as he lay struggling to get his breath back. A few minutes later there was a tap on their bedroom door.

Carl raised his head and looked unbelievingly towards it.

'Yes, what is it?' he shouted, pulling Madeleine's velvet dress over them both.

They could hear Hunter's voice, clear and concise. 'I'm sorry to disturb you, Sir, but there is an urgent call for you. It's from a Mr Shearman at the Central Manhattan Bank in New York, and he says he must speak to you immediately as something has happened at the bank.'

Chapter Sixteen

It was in Sardinia, where the turquoise sea lapped along the sun-drenched platinum beaches, and the perfume of wild thyme and rosemary and rock myrtle lingered in the air, that Jessica realised with a shattering suddenness that she was no longer in love with Bernard.

The previous week, after the concert in Tokyo, he had decided in a temperamental flurry of anger that he wished to return to his home, bringing to an end his tour, there and then.

'I am tired!' he declared petulantly. 'I cannot be expected to continue week after week like this. I am not a machine! I am exhausted!'

Jessica felt torn between longing for a break herself, and thinking Bernard was behaving unprofessionally.

'But you'll throw the whole tour!' she told him. 'What about all the people who have bought tickets? What about the organisers? The advertising? It's going to be a major disappointment for a lot of music lovers.'

'Why should I care about other people?' he shot back. 'My health is more important, and my creative ability. To hell with other people. I couldn't care less.'

Jessica remained silent, seeing what a bad mood he

was in and knowing it would do no good to argue; this was a very different Bernard from the man she had fallen in love with. Gradually, over the weeks, she had come to notice his moodiness and irascibility and it was dawning on her that maybe this was what he was really like. Had she only imagined him to be good-tempered and considerate, blinded as she'd been by love? Or had he put on an act at the beginning, in order to seduce and ensnare her?

Now, a week after they'd arrived at the Villa Roccia di Volpe, she was sure that was what had happened. Accustomed to switching on the charm when he met his friends or fans, none of whom he ever had to spend a long time with, he was unable to maintain those more pleasant facets of his character for any length of time. Yes, thought Jessica, stripped of his veneer of charm, Bernard was a very different person.

Unable to sleep, she rose at dawn and wandered through the cool white marble rooms to the verandah. Wrapped in a misty dawn, the Cala Di Volpe bay lay beneath, its turquoise waters as smooth as silk. She curled up on one of the large bamboo seats and watched, with unseeing eyes, the first grey veil of dawn spreading itself over the landscape.

How could she have fallen out of love? Her head spun at the impossibility of the thought, and yet increasingly she'd grown tired of having her independence taken away from her, grown bored with not having a life of her own, and most of all, perhaps, become fed up with always having to dance to Bernard's tune. A smile flickered across her face at the unintended pun . . . Bernard's tune indeed!

In the garden of the villa where tall cypress trees and exotic shrubs and flowers grew lush and ripe in the rich soil, Jessica could hear the gardener, who came every day, setting up hoses to water the rough grass. Soon the steady and soothing phut phut of sprinklers filled the morning air, and going into the kitchen, Jessica decided to make herself some coffee.

When she got back to the terrace it had grown lighter, and already the heat of the coming day was rising in warm bands, carried inshore by the trade winds. The scent of marjoram, sweet and pungent, mingled with the perfume of wild rosemary and myrtle, and from the shrubs came the soft shrilling of awakening cicadas. This is idyllic, she thought, propping her bare feet up on the low stone wall that edged the terrace, drinking in the beauty of the island's dawn.

And then, as if she had foreknowledge, she knew that it was going to be very difficult to leave this place. Already she loved the villa, the gardens, and beyond them the beach with its strange-looking rocks, sculpted by thousands of years of wind and water. A part of her would remain here forever, she thought emotionally, rooted deep into the soil like the olive trees. On this island her soul had been touched by the beauty of nature, and she dreaded saying goodbye to it all. And yet a part of her knew that that was what was going to happen, sooner or later.

At noon, Bernard appeared, tousled-haired and naked under his towelling robe. Jessica, who was sunbathing after a swim, opened her eyes and smiled, longing for him to smile back so that she could reassure herself that her love for him was as great as ever; but he scowled instead, seating himself in the shade of a striped umbrella, cursing someone who had just phoned him from Rome, wakening him.

'But it is nearly lunchtime,' Jessica pointed out reasonably. 'You're missing the best part of the day by sleeping all morning.'

'Rubbish! Anyway, I was working until late last night on the score of the new concerto I'm writing.' Bernard glanced round angrily, as if displeased with everything he saw.

'What's the matter, Bernard?' Jessica suddenly demanded. She knew she was treading on delicate ground because when he was in this sort of mood, to question him only made it worse, but something inside her couldn't resist needling him, almost as if she wanted to bring this whole discordance between them out into the open.

'Nothing,' he replied sullenly.

'There must be something wrong. You're like a bear with a sore head!' With slim brown hands, she pushed her blonde hair back, peering at him through the loose curls that floated round her face. 'People don't get bad-tempered for no reason! Are you feeling ill?'

He gave a snort of annoyance, then raising his voice, bellowed to the servant who was laying the table for lunch: 'Bring me some coffee, and make sure it's strong!'

Jessica ignored the fact he was ignoring her, and reaching for the bottle of sun oil, remarked drily: 'Perhaps you're drinking too much coffee! It's supposed to make people feel stressed.'

'Don't talk to me about feeling stressed,' Bernard snapped. 'You're the one who's stressed.'

'I'm not!' She sat bolt upright with indignation. 'Why should I be stressed?'

'That's what I want to know.' His eyes narrowed as he regarded her, making her feel vulnerable and exposed, though she wasn't sure why. It was true she was edgy. She felt she was nearing some crisis in her life, and half of her felt as if she was running away from whatever it was while the other half seemed determined to bring it to a head.

'It's just that . . .' she began, but then paused. How do you tell someone, after you have given up everything to be with them, that you think you are no longer in love? It sounded crazy. It *was* crazy! There was no way it made sense, but right now, neither did she, she reckoned. Something was falling apart inside her and she no longer knew how to hold it together. Why had she fallen out of love with Bernard when she'd been so besotted with him such a short time ago?

Later, as she lay on the terrace reading, she could hear him in the living-room, playing his latest composition on the piano. The music came floating on the still air, stirring her emotions, sending little thrills up her spine. She closed her eyes, letting the sweet cadences wash over her, and gradually she began to feel all her senses melt like ice in the sun. Her body felt languorous and her blood seemed to flow thickly through veins suffused by desire. Her hand touched her breast accidentally as she put down her book, and a thrill, strong and vibrant, shot through her, making her realise how much she still desired Bernard. The music continued, seductive and rapturous, winding its way like tendrils round the strings of her heart, invading her mind with images that cast her loose on an endless sea.

Oh, I do love him . . . thought Jessica, as she lay in a state of hot desire. Of course I love him. He's the most wonderful man I've ever known . . . passionate, with such tender feelings . . . brilliantly talented, a genius. I love him with all my heart. Deep happiness flooded through her, as she realised how lucky she was to have a man like this in her life; a man who could transport her, and millions of other people, with his music to heights of feeling they had not thought possible. So what if he was a bit temperamental. He was a creative artist and one had to make allowances. No doubt Beethoven and Chopin and Rachmaninov had their bad-tempered moments too. Jessica smiled, making allowances for Bernard as she always did. One couldn't expect someone as talented as him, she told herself, to be like other people.

The music continued, the top notes fluttering teasingly and then the melody flowing in the minor key, almost moving her to tears. A moment later the major chords, strong and powerful, made her smile again and so she lay on the terrace, letting the strains manipulate her as the clouds above were being manipulated by the winds; swept forward then held back, tossed about and then scattered until they disappeared altogether.

Then came a crashing grating discordance, a shouted oath, and the falling of something heavy.

Startled, Jessica opened her eyes and sat up. She could see through the windows into the music room, and to her horror she could see Bernard throwing something at a frightened servant, who stood too petrified to move. He was yelling abuse at her, and the sight sickened Jessica. Then Bernard pushed over a chair in rage and went storming out of the front of the villa.

It was as if an icy bucket of water had been thrown over Jessica, awakening her from her beautiful reverie. Shocked, she crossed the terrace where the stones were so hot they burned her feet, and entering the music room, looked round dismayed. So much damage had been done in those few seconds. Sheets of music lay scattered, a table as well as a chair had been overturned, spilling books on to the floor, and a vase of flowers lay smashed, the water a pool of spreading liquid on the red terracotta floor.

'What happened?' Jessica exclaimed, aghast.

The servant, a young local girl, was clutching her cotton skirts, a terrified expression on her face. Then she dropped to her knees and with trembling hands started to pick up the pieces of the broken vase.

'Are you all right?'

The girl whimpered and touched her head, where a bruise was starting to swell up on her forehead.

'You're hurt!' Jessica hurried forward, helping the girl to her feet. 'Leave this mess, I'll see to it. You go to the kitchen and put some ice on your head.'

The servant looked at her doubtfully, then shook her head in protest. 'I'm okay,' she whispered, in a heavy Italian accent.

'You leave this to me,' said Jessica firmly. She'd been used to dealing with staff of all nationalities at the Royal Westminster and this girl reminded her of many of their chambermaids. Jessica guided her in the direction of the kitchen. 'Lie down for a while, and put ice on your head. Now, don't worry about a thing, everything will be all right.'

'It often happens . . . for no reason,' whispered the servant.

'Then I think you should find yourself work in another villa, where the people are kinder, don't you?' Jessica suggested briskly. Inside she was seething with rage. How dare Bernard treat a servant like that? After she had cleared up the mess, she walked slowly back to the terrace, and it was at that precise moment that she knew exactly what was wrong with their relationship.

He reappeared an hour later and blandly took a seat under the awning on the terrace, as if nothing had happened. Jessica had no idea where he'd been for the past hour and she didn't really care. He was sipping his glass of iced Frascati, apparently unaware of her presence, as she set about planning in her mind what she would say to him.

Now that she knew the truth about her feelings, her instincts were to flee; to get away from Sardinia and Bernard and the whole terrible mess she'd made of her life, and to go and hide somewhere quiet where nobody knew her. She'd been such a fool, she thought. How could she, an intelligent, successful woman of twenty-six who'd been holding down a highly responsible, highly paid job with a great future, make such an utter fool of herself? At the time it had all seemed so right! But after falling madly in love with Bernard, which had blinded her to everything else, she now had to face the fact that the mists of infatuation had cleared and the stark truth had presented itself.

Bernard suddenly spoke. 'Shall we have a swim before dinner?'

'I'd rather talk,' she replied. He looked over to where she sat, cross-legged, on a lounging seat, a vividly coloured sarong showing off the glorious tan of her shoulders and arms, her blonde hair swept up on to the top of her head in a tumble of unruly waves and curls. Her candid blue eyes were looking intently at him and her small mouth was, for once, serious.

'I might as well have another drink then.' He poured himself another glass of Frascati, and then, as an afterthought, offered some to her. Jessica shook her head.

'What do you want to talk about?' he asked.

Her voice quavered slightly. 'You and me.'

'I thought so.' Thoughtfully, he sipped his wine and then he said in a quiet voice: 'I think I know what's coming.'

'You do?' The faint jangle of her gold bangles tinkled in the warm still air. 'You mean you've realised . . .?'

'That you are no longer in love with me? Yes. Yes. I've realised, Jessica.' He sounded weary, tired, as if he knew the score. 'I was afraid of this happening,' he added, almost sadly.

'But . . .! I don't understand. Why do you think

. . .?' She became lost for words, confused, barren of thought. How could he know? She was sure she'd given no hint of her feelings during those moments when she felt she had nothing in common with him.

'Tell me what you feel,' he urged, leaning towards her, his eyes penetrating, the whole strength of his great personality focused on her at that moment, so that she felt like a tiny insect being looked at through a giant microscope.

Jessica looked back at him, faltering, wavering under the power of his gaze. 'I think . . .' she began, then cleared her throat. 'I think it's your music I'm in love with . . . not you.' The last words were a whisper, barely audible.

Bernard nodded, seeming to understand her completely. 'Like some people fall in love with the character an actor plays, and not the actor himself,' he suggested.

Jessica pounced on the explanation. It so perfectly described how she felt. 'That's right! That's exactly how I feel. When I hear your music, I'm totally carried away . . . I'm transported . . .!'

'It's not unusual,' Bernard cut in. 'That's why my wife left me. She adored my music but she couldn't stand me, or living my kind of life. Music can be a very dangerous and potent thing, Jessica, as you have found out. It can have more effect on human emotions than anything else on earth, because it is the language of the soul. Through music any mood can be conjured up, haven't you noticed? Play a certain type of music and everyone jumps to their feet and wants to dance! Play another kind and everyone weeps! And play the type of music I compose, and you affect the heart and soul of the listener! That is what has happened to you, Jessica, the music has carried you away, but the reality of life, when the music stops, is something different.'

Large tears trickled down her cheeks at the wisdom of his words. They were so true. Always an emotional person, she had let herself get carried away by the music, crediting its originator with all the beauty and the passion that he'd created without stopping to examine the man himself. She hung her head, feeling so childish, so utterly stupid, like an adult who'd only just realised Father Christmas didn't exist.

'That's why I didn't ask you to marry me,' she heard Bernard say. 'I realised when my wife left me that marriage was not for me. Sooner or later, women always get fed up with me and my lifestyle. Music may be the food of love, as Shakespeare said, but unfortunately one needs something a little less romantic to keep one going on a day-to-day basis!' He smiled wryly and reached out to stroke her shoulder. 'Little Jessica, a born romantic,' he murmured. 'It is for women like you that I write my music. Anyone more prosaic wouldn't be so affected by it.'

She stared at him, the tears drying on her brown cheeks, leaving little streaks of salt. 'You thought this might happen?'

'I hoped it wouldn't.' Bernard sounded sincere and he continued to gaze at her thoughtfully. 'But I could see all the signs coming on as soon as we started travelling. Living in and out of suitcases isn't anyone's idea of romance. I know that only too well.'

'It isn't the travelling,' Jessica protested, 'it's just that you've become . . . well, a different person to the one I knew in London! I don't seem to know you any more.'

'You never did know me, Jessica. That's the whole point. There wasn't time. You came away with the person you thought I was, because of my music. When you got to know the real me, it was a different story. No man can match up to the dream lover a woman creates in her mind.'

Jessica shook her head, still bewildered. Bernard seemed to understand what she felt and was expressing it better than she could ever have done. 'I don't know what to do,' she said dejectedly.

'You can stay, or you can go home,' he said gently. 'It is up to you. But, remember, if you stay you will have to put up with the real me, and the way I live. I can't pretend to be the romantic hero of your imagination in order to keep you happy. My job is to write music, make records, go on tours; it is as exacting a life as a lawyer's or a financier's. There is very little time for romance.'

'But in bed . . .' Jessica faltered, painfully averting her eyes. 'You were passionate in bed, when we first met; you said you loved me. Were you acting then?'

He took her hand, holding it between his own two strong ones, smoothing her slender fingers. 'I am a man like all men, Jessica. Of course I fell in love with you, and I did everything I could to get you to go to bed with me. It was wonderful and, believe me, I enjoyed every moment of it as much as I hope you did, but . . . men are different, darling. Once the chase is

452

over, and the conquest has been made . . . what is left but to repeat the act again and again, until both the man and the woman are bored by it!'

Jessica looked up swiftly, angrily, wanting to deny his words, but he silenced her with a look before she could say anything.

'Relationships have to be based on reality,' he continued. 'They are not symphonies or grand operas, they are a part of real *life*.' He stressed the word as if to reach through the tangled dreams that filled her head, confusing her about her real feelings.

'I understand,' she said slowly.

'Think about it. There is no need to rush into making any decision. You may find you can carry on, or you may find that reality is too painful, too unpalatable. And if that is the case, you must go.' He spoke without self-pity, as if he'd set the rules of the game and was perfectly happy to abide by them.

Jessica had guessed it would be difficult to leave the island and now, as she packed her cases, a sense of finality lay over her like a black shadow, cold and bleak. It was the closing chapter of something that had started with a star-burst of love and laughter and wonderful prospects. It was mid-afternoon and her flight was taking off at five-thirty. Dry-eyed and numb, she methodically folded her clothes and stuffed paper into the toes of her shoes, going through the motions like a sleep-walker, while the villa lay wrapped in the sultry silence of the afternoon, and Bernard remained in his music room.

Resigned to the fact it was all over, Jessica calmly

fastened her cases and went out on to the terrace for the last time. It was the magnificence of the bay she wanted to look at once more, so the memory of its aquamarine waters and surrounding lush greenery should remain with her always.

The only sound to break the silence was the mad shrilling of the cicadas in the long grass. Feeling a sense of relief that it was all nearly over, Jessica leaned on the parapet, looking down on the water gently lapping the shore. And then she heard it – Bernard's music – evocative, haunting, stirring, creeping into her being like a vapour, weakening her senses as she leaned against the warm stones, filling her with feelings that clamoured to be assuaged. Raising her head, she looked up at the blue density of sky, and then, dizzily, she closed her eyes as the music seared her senses and ripped into her heart. With a quick bound she was across the terrace and through the glass doors into the music room. Bernard was sitting at the piano playing his latest concerto, a far away look on his face as his hands moved over the keys.

'Don't you dare try that trick on me now!' Jessica shrieked, waving her small fists above her head. 'That's the lousiest thing I've ever heard of. You *know* the effect your music has on me! It simply isn't fair!' Large tears splashed down her cheeks as she fought for control.

Bernard looked up at her, a knowing smile spreading slowly across his face. His hooded eyes bored into hers as he continued to play.

'You like this piece, do you?' he asked quietly.

'You know I do, damn you!' she yelled, quivering with rage. 'You . . . you deliberately set out to upset me . . . and I think it's really nasty of you!' Angrily she wiped away the tears and tried to pin up her topknot, which had come undone and was cascading down round her shoulders. 'Don't you dare do this to me!'

Bernard's mouth twitched. 'My darling, I'm not doing anything to you, you are doing it to yourself! I came in here to work on my music, and you get all excited and say I am playing dirty tricks on you.' As he spoke, he continued to play, filling the room with rising cadences and swelling chords that thrilled with a promise of ecstasy.

Jessica clamped her hands over her ears. 'Stop it! Stop it at once! I hate you, Bernard Scheller! You're a very dangerous man, d'you know that? You *know* what your music does to people . . .!' She turned and ran out of the music room, still blocking her ears. Bernard threw back his head, laughing richly.

Jessica's high heels could be heard clattering on the marble floors, and then there was silence. The smile faded from Bernard's face and he sat staring through the glass doors to the terrace and bay beyond. He should have known Jessica better than to imagine she could be seduced into staying. Even by his music.

The plane rose from the runway like a powerful bird heading out to sea, breasting the stiff breeze, setting course for the north-west. Below, Sardinia lay like a topaz in an aquamarine setting, growing smaller all the time. From her cabin window, Jessica looked at it for the last time, hardly able to bear the thought of the broken dreams she was leaving behind. She'd never be able to return; there was too much that reminded her of her own weaknesses and failure and the fact that she'd allowed herself to be overpowered by emotion. That was all over now. She'd said goodbye to Bernard for the last time, and now she had to look ahead. The dreams had gone, vanishing like the stars behind a cloud. Only one thing remained and that was something she would be sharing with the rest of the world: Bernard's music. It would live on after all the hopes and desires it evoked had faded away.

Carl's legs felt like lead as he crossed the bedroom to pick up the phone. A call from Jake, at this hour of night, saying there was something wrong at the bank, could mean only one thing. Cold sweat ran down his back, and in spite of trying to control himself his hand shook as he reached for the receiver.

'Jake?' Somehow he managed to sound casual. Madeleine had come to lie on the bed to be near him, but he turned away so that she wouldn't see his face.

'I'm sorry to disturb you . . . it must be quite late in England, isn't it?' Jake enquired genially.

'Er . . .' Carl was thrown. 'Well, it's fairly late, but not to worry. How's everything?' He had the receiver pressed to his ear, hoping Madeleine wouldn't be able to hear what her father was saying. Stupid really, he reflected. This was something he wouldn't be able to keep from her, not once it blew up in his face.

'It's about your secretary . . .' he heard Jake say.

'There's been a bit of trouble, and I thought you ought to know.'

This was it. The moment he had been dreading, the final terrible exposure of what he and Kimberley had been doing. It was obvious she'd been caught, and within no time now the net would close in on him. He knew what Jake was going to say even before he said it.

'I'm afraid Kimberley Cabot's been arrested, Carl . . . this afternoon. It's been a terrible shock, but I'm hoping we can keep it out of the newspapers, for the sake of the bank.'

Carl sank weakly on to the edge of the bed, feeling as if someone had punched him in the stomach. 'Arrested?' he echoed faintly.

'That's right.' There was a long pause on the line as Carl sat there, seeing the ruins of his life spread before him like a sea of wreckage. He'd really done it now. His marriage, his career, his whole future lay demolished . . . and he had only himself to blame. That one unguarded moment, when he'd felt lonely, had paved the path to his own destruction and now he must face those fatal consequences.

Jake's voice broke into Carl's thoughts. 'She's been charged with larceny . . .'

I know, I know, Carl's mind screamed in silent despair. You don't have to tell me. Nearly two million dollars worth of theft. Aloud, he said: 'What happened, exactly?'

'What is it?' Madeleine was asking. She was sitting on the bed beside him, trying to attract his attention. 'What's going on?'

Carl spoke into the phone. 'Hang on a minute, Jake. Madeleine wants to know what's happening.' Carl cupped his hand over the mouthpiece and, managing to avoid catching Madeleine's eye, outlined briefly what her father had said. Then he turned his attention back to the phone. 'You were saying, Jake?'

'Give my love to Madeleine! Now, about this girl, Kimberley. It seems she had a boyfriend called Hank Pugsley . . .'

I know, thought Carl.

'. . . and he had a grudge against her . . .'

He would have, Carl reflected.

'. . . so he called in the police and had her arrested for stealing . . .'

Like one and three-quarter million dollars, Carl said to himself.

'. . . some jewellery from his apartment . . .'

'*What*!' Carl clutched the phone, frowning deeply.

'Stealing some jewellery from his apartment,' Jake repeated. 'He was particularly upset about a pair of diamond earrings that had belonged to his mother.'

'But . . .' Carl paused, stunned. How could Kimberley have been such a fool? She'd been clever enough to think up a scheme which would rob Hank of millions, and then she'd got caught for petty larceny by pinching some earrings from his apartment. I didn't even know she'd been to his apartment recently, thought Carl suddenly. Since when had she been seeing Hank again?

'So, she's been arrested?' Carl asked lamely. Madeleine, he'd noticed, had wandered away from the bed, and was brushing her hair at the dressing-table as if she'd lost interest. Maybe I'll get away with it, thought Carl for one wild elated moment, but then he knew he was kidding himself. Kimberley was probably laying the blame for everything on him, right at this moment, and it was only a matter of time before the world knew of his involvement. Maybe it would be better if he told Jake everything now! Get it over with. Carl's mind worked quickly, wondering if confession might not be better than waiting to be found out.

Jake continued: 'Yes, she's being held at the local precinct now. They searched her apartment earlier, I gather, and found the stuff hidden under her mattress. They'll probably keep her in custody overnight and charge her in the morning.'

'Jake . . .' Carl began slowly. 'There's something . . .' How was he going to tell his father-in-law what he'd done? How on earth could he begin to explain what had happened? And yet the temptation to unburden himself, at last, of the secret that had tormented him for months now, was so great he gripped the phone and started to speak again. At that moment, as if she'd been listening after all, Madeleine came hurrying across the room, and took the phone from Carl.

'Hi, Daddy! Don't you want to say hello to your only daughter?' she demanded gaily. 'You interrupt my first evening with Carl to talk business, without a thought for me! Don't you want to know how I am?'

Jake laughed, always amused by her banter. 'I wouldn't dare talk to Carl and *not* ask how you are!' he responded.

Madeleine kept him talking for a few more minutes

459

and then she said: 'Is that all? Is there anything else you have to tell Carl?'

'No. That's it. I just didn't want him to call up his office, to find his secretary had gone missing because she was in gaol! Sorry I disturbed you, darling.'

'That's all right, Daddy. Just don't do it again!' she joked. When she hung up she turned to Carl and looked at him with an expression he didn't understand.

'You had nothing further to say to my father, Carl,' she said pointedly. 'Kimberley has been arrested, and I have a feeling that's the last you'll hear from her.'

'I didn't take his stuff. I haven't even been to his apartment for about a year,' Kimberley insisted.

She was being questioned and as she sat at the table in the interrogation room of the police department, she felt a mounting sense of fury. Hank Pugsley had set her up, and she'd walked right into his fucking trap! The bastard was too clever to get her for robbing him of his dollars because he'd incriminate himself, so he'd thought up this scam instead, leaving the evidence himself under her mattress.

I wish to God I hadn't lost my head when he came to see me the other night, thought Kimberley. If I'd kept my cool . . . but I was so sure he'd come to kill me and so thankful when he'd appeared friendly, that I was completely caught off guard. She remembered the terror she'd felt when she'd seen him, looming large and threateningly in the corridor outside her apartment door. She'd screamed, certain now he'd found out what she'd done, sure it was he who had taken back all his money and somehow managed to close her Swiss bank account. The sound of her cries, high-pitched and loud, echoed in her own head as they reverberated down the passage.

'Hello, Kimberley,' Hank had said gently, as if she hadn't made a sound, as if he'd only seen her a few days before. She'd stopped yelling when she saw he wasn't going to hurt her.

'Can I come in for a little drink? Long time no see.' Hank inched his bulky form through the door and automatically Kimberley stood to one side, wondering how she could ever have slept with this great slob of a man. Without replying, she led him into the wreckage of her living-room, picking up her shopping bag of liquor as she did so. Hank ignored the mess and dropped heavily into one of her suede armchairs.

'So, how have you been?' he asked conversationally.

Striving to keep calm, wondering now if he *did* know she'd been systematically stealing from him for months, she replied: 'Okay. And you?'

'Oh, I'm just fine!' He sounded quite perky. 'Have you got any Scotch? I've had a long day and I could do with a drink.'

'Yes. Okay.' Kimberley went into the kitchen to get some ice, her mind in a turmoil. Perhaps it *was* Carl who'd taken everything out of her account, after all? Maybe Hank had just dropped in for a drink, for old times' sake, and had no idea what had been happening? He was certainly being very friendly, she thought rapidly, the ice cubes burning the tips of her fingers as she put them into a bowl, and he wouldn't have come

461

round to be friendly if he'd suspected anything. Kimberley decided to be nice to him.

'Here's your drink,' she said, smiling, as she handed him his Scotch on the rocks. 'Will you excuse me for a moment? I just want to freshen up.'

Hank nodded benignly, like a sweating mandarin. Even the glass was sweating in his chubby hand. A few minutes later, Kimberley reappeared, her red hair brushed so that it fell in curls round her shoulders, and she'd slipped into a cream silk robe that fell open at the front, revealing her snowy cleavage.

'I'm sorry about the mess,' she said lightly. 'I was just about to clean up when you arrived.'

Hank spoke softly, almost in a whisper. 'That's all right. Don't worry about it. It's you I came to see. I've been thinking a lot about you recently.'

Kimberley's heart skipped a beat, and trying to keep her hand steady she poured out a drink for herself. 'You have?' she asked, trying to sound coy.

'Sure I have. Why shouldn't I? We had some good times together, babe.'

'We sure did.'

'In fact, you've been on my mind a lot recently.' Hank gulped noisily at his drink and handed her the empty glass to refill. 'Last time I saw you, you were planning to be a model. How did that work out?'

Kimberley poured more whisky into his glass and added some ice. 'I've done a little work, mostly fashion for the trades, but I'm hoping to get a new agent soon. I've met one and she thinks I could make the cover of *Vogue*.'

'Is that so?' Hank sounded genuinely interested.

'Well, you know, babe, you can count on me if you need anything. I'm not in the fashion world, as you know, but I do have my contacts.'

'That's very kind of you, Hank.' She curled up on the sofa, covering her bare feet with the skirt of her robe.

'You'd like to be rich one day, and successful, wouldn't you?' Hank asked reflectively, never taking his eyes off her face.

Kimberley shrugged and gave a little brittle laugh. 'Who wouldn't?' Then she thought about the two million dollars that had been hers, *hers*, and a shadow passed over her face. She'd never, as long as she lived, get over the loss of that money.

'Anything wrong, babe? Anything troubling you?'

She glanced nervously at Hank, forcing her stiff face into a smile, willing her mouth to turn up at the corners. 'No. Why should there be? Tell me your news, Hank?'

'Ain't much to tell. Business is as good as ever. Get a bit lonely at times, of course.' In the semi-darkness, his eyes seemed to glint lasciviously.

'Perhaps we can do something about that.'

'Perhaps we can,' Hank replied. 'Are you sure I'm not disturbing your evening? Perhaps you're expecting someone?'

Kimberley felt surprised at his consideration. She didn't remember him being that thoughtful in the past.

'No. I'm not expecting anyone.' Suddenly she rose, longing for it to be over, longing to be alone with her misery and her heartbreak at her loss. 'Shall we go then?' With a nod of her head she indicated the bedroom.

'I'll finish my drink first, babe. You go right ahead,' Hank replied.

Kimberley was lying on the apricot sheets, naked and with her hair spread out, when Hank entered the bedroom. He sat down on the side of the bed and undressed slowly. His weight made the mattress sag and as Kimberley lay there, looking at his back, she gave a little shudder of revulsion. But at least he was being nice to her, so he couldn't suspect a thing. She closed her eyes with a sense of relief that was even greater that her sense of disgust.

Two days later she had been arrested as she was leaving for the bank. Under her mattress the police had found a gold watch, two pairs of gold cuff-links, an antique silver cigarette case and a pair of diamond drop earrings. She was charged with stealing them from Hank Pugsley's apartment.

'Hank Pugsley came to *my* apartment!' Kimberley told the policeman who was questioning her, with increasing desperation. 'He must have planted the jewellery then. He was angry with me because I wouldn't let him stay all night. This is his means of revenge.'

But she knew it wasn't. It was Hank's revenge for something much greater and she knew he wouldn't rest until he had exacted his pound of flesh from her. She also knew there wasn't a damned thing she could do about it.

Carl eyed Madeleine nervously. 'Why do you say that?' he asked. 'Why do you say I won't be bothered with Kimberley any more?'

'Daddy called to say she'd been arrested, didn't he?' said Madeleine, feeling nervous now that the moment had come to tell him everything.

'Yes, how did you know that?' Carl looked at her, startled.

Madeleine levelled her gaze at him and said with a flicker of a smile, 'Because I helped set her up.'

'You *what*? How d'you mean? What do you know about Kimberley Cabot?'

'Everything, Carl. Everything.' Her voice dropped to a whisper and for a moment she averted her gaze, unwilling to let him see the pain in her eyes. 'I've known what's been going on between you two for a long time now.'

Carl's face flushed dark red, his skin suffused so that the veins stood out at his temples. 'How?' The single word, dragged from his dry throat, asked a million questions.

'I happened to be in the washroom in your office one day, when I heard you and Kimberley quarrelling . . . and I heard what she was doing, and how she was blackmailing you . . .' The pain in Madeleine's voice was raw now, and she was finding it difficult to find the right words.

'Oh, my God,' breathed Carl, looking at her with anguish.

'And I heard her tell you that what you were doing was safe . . . that you'd never get caught . . . that

Hank would never find out.' Tears filled Madeleine's eyes now as she remembered the shock and agony of that day. Then she told Carl all that she'd overheard.

'At first I didn't know what to do,' she concluded, 'then I remembered hearing you say to Kimberley that you loved me.' She turned to look at him then, her eyes suddenly blazing with passion. 'If I hadn't believed that was true, Carl, I'd have left you immediately.'

'Oh, Maddy.' Wretchedly, he held out his hand to her. 'It's such a mess . . . such a goddamn awful stupid mess! I never stopped loving you; not for a moment. I hope you'll always believe that. If it hadn't been for you, I don't know what I'd have done. I never loved Kimberley. It was one of those crazy things . . . no more than a one-night stand, that went hopelessly out of control. Then when she sprang this ultimatum on me . . . well, I sort of panicked. I should have told her to go to hell.'

Madeleine took his hand and squeezed it tightly. 'I know, Carl. I can understand how you felt. The most important thing is that my father should never find out any of this. Things would never be the same again if he were to know what Kimberley did, with your help.'

'But what about Hank? Will he be content to have Kimberley charged with petty theft, when she's got two million dollars of his?' Carl protested desperately.

'She *had* two million dollars of his,' Madeleine corrected him. 'Hank and I took the money out of her account in the Banque Internationale de Zurich last

week, and transferred it to Hank Pugsley's account.'
Carl's mouth fell open in utter astonishment as
Madeleine told him about getting Kimberley's bank
account number out of her Filofax, and then learning
to forge her signature.

'This is unbelievable,' he said at last, shaking his
head. 'You, Maddy, who have always been such a
dreamer . . . I always believed you were so impracti-
cal, so in need of protection . . . and now you tell me
you and Hank actually met in Zurich when I thought
you were looking at London art galleries, and you
took the money out of Kimberley's account and gave
it back to Hank?'

Madeleine nodded, the colour slowly coming back
to her cheeks. Relief that the long drawn out ordeal
was nearly over, and that Carl was no longer in danger, was making her feel quite light-headed. If
Kimberley, out of spite, were to accuse Carl of
embezzling funds, she'd no longer be able to make it
stick. Hank had his money back and he'd say it had
been in his account all the time.

Suddenly, Madeleine thought of something. 'Carl,'
she asked, 'did Kimberley try and put through a transfer a couple of weeks ago, only to find her computer
disc was blank?'

Carl's eyes widened and he looked at Madeleine
incredulously, as if he couldn't take much more.

'Yes,' he croaked. 'Why?'

Madeleine gave a smile of deep satisfaction. 'Brilliant! I'm so glad it worked!'

'What did you do? I remember she was wild,
because Hank was transferring a lot of money to

467

Switzerland that day, and she couldn't get her hands on it. She'd no idea what had gone wrong, though.'

'I don't suppose she had,' Madeleine replied drily. How well she remembered the visit she'd paid to Kimberley Cabot's apartment, that Saturday afternoon. She'd asked for some coffee and, sullenly, Kimberley had gone into the little kitchenette to make it, leaving Madeleine alone in the living-room. She'd overheard Kimberley say to Carl that she kept the copy of the computer tape she'd made in her apartment for safety's sake, and Madeleine's eyes had flickered round the room hopefully. It was probably locked away . . . but as she glanced at the books on the shelves, she suddenly saw it, recognising it because she had seen many tapes like it in her father's office. She could hardly believe her luck. Moving swiftly, she'd slipped the disc inside her jacket, and holding it there, wandered into the kitchen on the pretext of chatting to Kimberley.

As soon as the girl's back had been turned, she'd slipped the tape on to the counter beside the microwave oven, casually drawn a tea cloth that was lying there over it, and then switched on the microwave. Distracting Kimberley by remarking on everything in the kitchen, she was able to switch off the microwave again, retrieve the disc, and then wander back to the living-room where she replaced the disc among the books without Kimberley's ever having been aware of what had happened.

Carl looked blank. 'I don't get it!'

'I read somewhere that a famous TV comedian kept all his jokes on a disc,' said Madeleine. 'Everything

468

was fine until he left it in the kitchen and his wife switched on their new microwave.'

'You mean . . .?'

'Exactly. The tape was erased.'

Carl drew in a deep breath. 'So you made Kimberley's disc blank? You wiped out the computer code . . . everything?'

'Everything! I must say, I'd have loved to see her face when she got a blank screen!'

'My God . . .' Carl, shocked and amazed, sat gazing at Madeleine, as if he couldn't believe all he'd heard. That his gentle and artistic wife had been strong enough to outwit Kimberley Cabot was a stunning revelation. 'And I never knew you had any idea what was going on. All this time my main worry was that you would find out!'

'That was one of my worries, too,' admitted Madeleine. 'I was afraid you'd find out I *did* know everything! I knew you'd never have been able to carry on without Kimberley suspecting somehing. I wish I could have let on sooner, Carl, for both our sakes, but this was the only way.'

He could only hold her hand in both of his, so deeply had he been affected by finding out what Madeleine had done. Later, there would be a time for laughter and tears and explanations, but right now he just felt the need to be close to her.

The cold blue light of a wintry dawn was stealing through the chinks in the bedroom curtains when at last they lay down together, the terrible misery and anxiety of the past few months washed away by their talking. When at last the sun rose, weak and milky over the Devonshire countryside, Madeleine lay with her eyes closed and her hand still in Carl's. She was exhausted, but she had never felt so happy or so close to him. His words of love and appreciation for what she'd done still echoed in her mind, and she thanked God that the long ordeal was over.

Chapter Seventeen

The familiar sight of the lofty flower-filled lobby of the Royal Westminster Hotel made Jessica's heart give a great lurch. It seemed to her as if she'd been away a lifetime, and yet nothing had changed. The same hotel staff in the same dark green uniforms were going quietly and efficiently about their work, and there was the usual hustle and bustle of comings and goings, the same stacks of luggage, the same expensive smell of polish and perfume, and leather and lilies, and the same muted murmuring of voices in a dozen different languages.

With a sense of déjà vu, Jessica paused and looked around, hoping against hope that she might be able to return to work here, feeling in many ways as if she'd never left, as if the whole episode with Bernard had been some extraordinary dream. She glanced at the revolving glass doors, almost expecting to see him stride through, his hooded eyes taking in everything. Then she looked over to the cluster of seats arranged under the oasis of plants and remembered sitting there talking to him. Had it all really happened? It seemed that another person in another time had clicked her way in high heels across the gleaming marble floor, brimming over with enthusiastic love for a man she hardly knew. And now that same person, feeling considerably older and wiser, stood here wondering what she could recapture from the past.

On the phone yesterday, the General Manager, who had always liked her, said he could see her at eleven-fifteen. Jessica's hopes had soared, seeing herself back in her old position, back in harness, her mistakes forgotten as quickly as possible. She had only one idea in mind: to get back to work and resume her old life. Only by doing that could she hope to obliterate her sense of failure and foolishness. That morning, as she'd driven up from her parents' house in Surrey, she'd sworn to herself that never again would she be so impetuous or crazy. Letting her heart rule her head had proved fatal, and she might even have lost her career because of it.

Jessica glanced at her watch. It was ten-past eleven. By the time she got up to the executive offices on the second floor, it would be time for her appointment. With a mounting sense of excitement, she got into the elevator. Already she was feeling a part of the place again. As she passed a console table outside Kenneth Wolfson's office, she gave the arrangement of flowers a proprietorial look and paused to straighten a bloom. How did I ever imagine I could exist without this life? she thought.

Kenneth Wolfson greeted her cordially, looking just the same with his shining clean pink face and sharply pressed Savile Row suit. A pleasant aura of Paco Rabanne aftershave moved with him like a perfumed shadow.

'Well, this is a nice surprise, Jessica,' he said, shaking hands with her. 'I didn't think we'd see you again for a long time!'

In spite of her resolve to keep cool, she found herself blushing to the roots of her blonde hair as she took a seat opposite him. Suddenly, she felt more nervous than she had during her first job interview when she'd been eighteen.

'I didn't think I'd be back either!' she replied, trying to sound jokey. 'I'm afraid it was all a great mistake.'

Kenneth Wolfson smiled kindly. 'I'm not going to say I told you so. Let's just be thankful things are not worse. For example, you could have married Bernard Scheller, or had a child.'

'I know,' Jessica nodded fervently. 'It's been awful, but it could have been much worse, I suppose. I just wish I hadn't got so carried away in the first place.'

'It's all part of the learning experience, Jessica. My generation had to live by our mistakes. We didn't have the chance to discover things were wrong before we got married, and afterwards it was too late! We were lumbered.' He sighed again, as if he spoke from personal experience.

'So I was wondering . . .?' Jessica began hopefully, her eyes wide and candid, her mouth curving in an eager smile.

'Yes. I asked you to come and see me this morning because I wanted to explain the position to you.'

Something in his tone sent a chill through her, a premonition that it was not going to be as easy as she'd thought to persuade him that she really intended to get back to work again.

'I promise you I won't go off like that again,' she

said earnestly. 'I know it was a kind of madness, but I've got it out of my system now and I really want to resume work in the hotel business again, more than anything.'

Kenneth Wolfson leaned back in his opulent leather chair and his hands fiddled with a letter opener shaped like a dagger. Without looking at her he said slowly: 'It's not your reliability I'm referring to. I know you're a professional to your fingertips and I appreciated the way you were prepared to continue last time until we found a replacement for you. Why I wanted to see you myself is because I wanted to tell you that I'm afraid we don't have any vacancies in the hotel at the moment.'

Jessica's face fell, distress showing in every feature. 'There's *nothing*?' she gasped.

'Not a thing, I'm afraid. Every position is filled and I honestly can't say when a vacancy is likely to occur again. I'm really sorry, Jessica. There's nothing we'd have liked more than to have had you on board again.' His smile was genuinely sympathetic as he noticed how upset she looked.

'Do you think there'll be anything going in any of the other Golding Group hotels? Oh, I can't *bear* this!' she wailed.

'I made a few inquiries on your behalf yesterday,' he told her, 'but head office said there was nothing available at present, except for the job of Deputy Banqueting Manager at their Dubai hotel. But you haven't got the qualifications for that, anyway. You're purely on the sales side, and right now all those posts are taken.'

Disappointment hit Jessica like a body blow. Never for a moment had she imagined she'd be unable to get another job in the Golding Group; even if it wasn't in the Royal Westminster, she'd been certain there'd be something in one of their other hotels.

'Oh, God . . . I wish I'd never left now!' she exclaimed. 'How could I have been such a fool?' She wrung her hands despairingly. 'How could I have been so crazy? I've thrown away my career! – my whole future! – everything I worked for!' Her little red-pointed nails stabbed the air dramatically and she looked ready to burst into tears.

'I'm awfully sorry, Jessica,' said Kenneth Wolfson, in an effort to sound soothing. 'I really am. If anything comes up I'll let you know immediately. In the meantime, why don't you take a break? Have a little time to yourself?'

'I've just had a break!' Jessica responded spiritedly. 'Such a long break that I'm bored to tears. I want to get some work or *I'll die*!'

Kenneth's mouth twitched. One of the things he'd always liked about Jessica was the way she dramatised everything, making it sound sensationally interesting even when it wasn't.

'It might be worth your while applying to one of the other hotel groups,' he suggested. 'They might have some vacancies.'

'I'll try, but it won't be the same. Oh, are you *sure* you couldn't squeeze me in somewhere?' Jessica's blue eyes were beseeching.

'I wish I could, my dear.' He shook his head sadly.

'Well, that's that, then.' Regretfully she rose. 'If

you hear a loud bang in the corridor, you'll know I've shot myself!'

He laughed outright. 'Don't make too much mess on the carpet then. We're short staffed when it comes to cleaners, if not sales people. Goodbye, Jessica, take care of yourself,' he shook her hand warmly, 'and the best of luck.'

'Thanks. I need it!' Pretending to be light-hearted in order to disguise how deeply depressed she felt, Jessica pranced down the corridor, out of the hotel and into the street, where the Hyde Park Corner traffic swept relentlessly past, numbing her senses with its roar.

Damn, damn, damn! she thought, as she hurried down Knightsbridge in the direction of Harrods. She didn't know where she was going or what she was doing, so flattened did she feel, so utterly deflated. She had no job, and nowhere to live. The fact that she had no boyfriend either was a minor consideration by comparison. Men she could live without, especially right now. Work she could not; and she couldn't bear the idea of burying herself in the country. Her parents were very sweet but life didn't exactly buzz in Surrey.

Then she had a brilliant idea. She'd fly over to New York to see Madeleine. That would cheer her up! She'd spend a couple of weeks catching up on everything with her best friend, and then she'd think about getting another job.

In the sleepy village of Sherston, the people awoke to a morning of sparkling frost and chill mists that swirled round the old thatched roof cottages and plucked at the icy ground. Up at Milton Manor, servants were lighting fires, drawing back the thick curtains at the windows, preparing breakfast in the large country-style kitchen. Jenkins, in his best serge suit, shiny at the seat and elbows, hovered expectantly in his cottage nearby, having given the Riley a good polish. Today, he was driving Madeleine and Carl over to the Meredith House Mental Institute to see Camilla, and he felt quite nervous. 'Dodgy like,' he'd informed his wife.

'Then why take them?' she demanded. 'They can drive themselves, can't they?'

'It wouldn't be right,' Jenkins insisted. 'Miss Madeleine is goin' to need someone who knows what's what! Mr Delaney, he won't be much good. When I sees him last night he was more worked up than her!'

Mrs Jenkins protested. 'But 'e is her husband!'

'Aye, but I knew Miss Camilla, and 'e didn't. If anything goes wrong, I wants to be there, to protect Miss Madeleine like!'

'What could go wrong? I thought you said her mother was like a cabbage . . . didn't know no one?'

Jenkins nodded in agreement. 'That's right, but you never know. At the sight of her daughter, something might come back to her,' he added darkly.

Madeleine and Carl were waiting in the hall when Jenkins brought the car round to the front door. Wrapped warmly in a thick red coat and black leather boots, Madeleine got into the back, holding Carl's hand all the time.

In the last couple of days they'd grown closer together than ever, their relationship strengthened by Madeleine's ingenious scheme which had removed

Kimberley from their lives, and proved to them both the solidarity of their marriage. Nevertheless, she felt very emotional at this moment. The time for wondering about Camilla was almost over; the mystery almost unveiled. In an hour she'd come face to face with her mother and she couldn't help wondering what she'd find. What sort of woman could have been prepared to offer up her child as a sacrifice to some Satanic god? Involuntarily, Madeleine shuddered, and Carl slipped his arm round her shoulders.

'You don't have to go ahead with this,' he said gently.

'I know,' she agreed, 'but it's something I feel I must do. Lay the ghost once and for all; put an end to over twenty years' speculation and doubt. I want to satisfy my curiosity too, you know. If I don't see my mother now, I'm going to be wondering for the rest of my life: what was she really like.'

'You will remember, won't you, darling, that she was a very sick woman and that these evil people only got a hold of her because she was in a very vulnerable state at the time? She couldn't have been herself on the night she took you up to the barn; she couldn't have known what she was doing,' Carl assured her.

Jenkins cleared his throat from the front of the car, with a scraping sound. 'Mr Delaney is right,' he interjected. 'Miss Camilla was a lovely young woman before they cast their spell on her and led her astray.'

'Those are the words my grandfather used,' said Madeleine. ' "Led astray". Even so, I find it impossible to understand. How any woman could do such a thing!'

Carl hugged her tenderly. 'Try not to think about

478

that side of it. Try to remember that you are going to visit a woman who had a total breakdown a very long time ago, and who has been virtually catatonic ever since.'

'I'll try,' Madeleine said doubtfully.

Meredith House looked surprisingly ordinary; a large redbrick building set in spacious grounds, hidden from the main road by a high wall. Security gates, manned by a uniformed guard, were the only hint it was not the estate of some rich landowner. The long curved drive, bordered on each side by high rhododendron bushes, was well kept and the lawns in the hazy winter morning were smoothly mown and looked well cared for. A few people, huddled in thick coats against the sharp edge of the wind, walked briskly in pairs and a nurse in a dark cloak pushed an elderly woman in a wheelchair.

Madeleine's heart plunged with a swift surge of pain before resuming its thick beating. Then she got out of the car and walked with a firm and determined tread towards the entrance. Carl followed, and Jenkins came slowly after them, a few creamy Christmas roses from the garden of Camilla's old home clutched in his hand.

The institutional smell of disinfectant and floor polish assailed Madeleine's nostrils as she entered a large square hall, sparsely furnished but with a pleasant and warm atmosphere. A wide staircase led up to the floor above, and on either side of the hall passageways led to a series of private rooms, all with numbered doors. Madeleine hesitated, wondering where to go. There was no reception desk or obvious inquiries office, and she was just about to turn to Jenkins for help, when her elbow was suddenly gripped from behind and squeezed almost fiercely. She let out a small cry as panic engulfed her. Whoever had come up behind must have recognised her, and she spun round fearfully, half expecting to see the deranged face of her mother. Then she let out a gasp of relief.

'Daddy!' she cried. 'Oh, Daddy, what are you doing here?'

Jake, smiling and distinguished-looking, put his arms around her and hugged her close.

'You didn't think I'd let you go through an ordeal like this without me, did you, Maddy?' he asked.

Madeleine leaned against him, relief weakening her limbs and almost reducing her to tears. 'Daddy, I'm so glad to see you! But how did you know . . .?' Then she looked questioningly at Carl, who grinned back at her. It was he who had told Jake she was going to visit Camilla today! Carl who had asked Jake to fly over so that she could have him by her side now.

'Thank you,' she whispered gratefully. She knew he would have preferred to have avoided seeing Jake so soon, in case he got drawn into discussions about his ex-secretary's activities, but for her sake he'd asked her father to come.

'I thought you needed Jake at a time like this,' Carl whispered.

'I've already seen the matron,' said Jake. 'Camilla's in her room now. Shall we go and see her?'

Madeleine looked up into her father's eyes, feeling again like the little girl who'd once depended on him for everything.

'Daddy?' Then she hesitated.

'What is it, Maddy?'

'I know everything now, you know. About her belonging to a Satanic organisation, about her being a witch, and offering me as a sacrifice; and I know if it hadn't been for you and Jenkins, I might not even be alive today.' Her voice had sunk to a whisper.

Jake looked down at her, a sad troubled expression in his dark eyes. 'Now you know why I wouldn't have her name mentioned; why I never wanted you to know. I was scared of the psychological effect it might have on you. Imagine! A child, finding out its mother was prepared to watch it being killed as part of some ghastly religious ritual! The truth was so terrible, Aunt Patti and I decided to say your mother had died . . . it wasn't such an awful lie, was it? After all, from the moment Jenkins and I rescued you and broke up the ceremony, she's been dead to the world anyway. She doesn't know what's happening and they tell me she never will again.'

'How did you bear it, Daddy?' Madeleine asked.

Jake didn't answer at first, and the lines on his face looked more deeply scored, but then he smiled again and bent forward, kissing her cheek. 'Because I had you, sweetheart,' he replied simply. Then he added quietly: 'Shall we go?'

Madeleine nodded, and while Carl and Jenkins waited in the hall, she and Jake mounted the stairs to the first floor room where Camilla awaited her husband and her daughter, although she was not even aware of it.

*   *   *

The peal of the front doorbell echoing round Milton Manor brought Hunter, who had been down in the cellar selecting bottles of wine for the weekend, panting to open it. On the worn stone steps stood a petite blonde in a fluffy cream wool coat, black woollen stockings and high-heeled black boots. She was stamping her feet to get warm, her head cocked to one side.

'Is Mrs Delaney at home, please?'

Hunter raised his eyebrows, noticing a local taxi behind her, with the driver unloading a lot of luggage. He remembered the young lady now. She and a gentleman friend had stayed earlier in the year.

'I'm sorry, but Madam is out,' he said, then he added carefully, so as not to give offence: 'Is she expecting you, Madam?'

'No, that's the whole idea! I'm surprising her. I called her up in New York and they told me she was here. Will she be out for long?'

'Several hours, I should think. She and Mr Delaney have gone visiting,' he added diplomatically.

The little figure clapped black woollen-covered hands in delight. 'Perfect! I can get installed before she comes back, and she'll get the shock of her life when she finds me here!'

She certainly will, thought Hunter, but he said nothing. Years of training as a butler had long since taught him when to speak and when to keep his mouth shut.

Blue doll-like eyes smiled into his, sparkling with fun. 'Do you remember me? I've stayed here before. My name's Jessica McCann, and I'm Mrs Delaney's oldest and best friend, and I *promise* you, she'll be delighted when she sees me. I'd hoped to spring a bit of a surprise on her anyway, but as she's out it's even better. Wait until she walks in!' Jessica hopped from foot to foot with anticipation while the driver carried her cases into the hall. Then she handed him the fare plus a generous tip. Hunter was still hovering in deep consternation, not knowing what to make of this extraordinary young lady, when she turned to him, her face serious and concerned.

'Look, I know you think I'm mad but I really do want to surprise Mrs Delaney. She thinks I'm on the other side of the world. I haven't come to steal the silver or anything, and I promise you she really will be glad to see me when she gets back.'

Hunter's resistance crumbled. With a weak smile, he ushered her into the hall. 'Would you mind waiting in the library, Madam?' he suggested. 'There's a nice fire in there, and perhaps you'd like a cup of tea while a bedroom is being prepared for you?'

Jessica's eyes widened with appreciation. 'Hunter, you should work in a five star hotel! You're *wasted* in a private house. You'd make the most fabulous major domo.'

Looking startled, Hunter led the way to the library, lost for words.

'Thank you,' Jessica said, removing her large woolly coat, which he took from her with as much reverence as if it had been made of priceless sables.

'Hunter, could you do me a big favour?' she begged, clasping her slim hands together. 'Could you *hide* my luggage?'

'Hide it, Madam?' His resonant tones filled the library.

'Yes, you know! Put it out of sight somewhere,

then if Mrs Delaney returns before my bedroom is ready, it won't give the game away.'

Hunter's mouth twitched against his will. 'Very well, Madam.'

As Jessica sat by the blazing log fire in the library, she looked round with interest. The carved ceiling and old stone mantelshelf and walls lined with books from floor to ceiling, gave the room an atmosphere of quiet tranquillity that made her feel instantly at home. Milton Manor was just the type of house, she thought, that she'd like to have if she ever went to live in the country. There was something solid and gracious about it that appealed to her, and when she went to look out of the window the charming gardens looked inviting in spite of the frost. On the lawns, large black rooks flapped about like clerics in a hurry and Jessica smiled to herself, somehow reminded of her own secure childhood in the countryside. It was all very reassuring.

Hunter brought her tea, impeccably set out on a silver tray with Rockingham china.

'Your room will be ready in a few minutes, Madam. I am most sorry for the delay. Is there anything else I can get you in the meantime?'

'No, thank you,' Jessica replied, more impressed than ever by his manner. He was exactly the type of person they were always looking for at the Royal Westminster: polite without being servile; anticipating guests' requirements without bullying them into having something they didn't want; friendly but never, ever familiar.

'Have you ever thought of working in a hotel?'

Jessica asked suddenly, as Hunter added another log to the fire.

'I've always been in private service, Madam. I wouldn't mind working in a small, shall we say, exclusive hotel, but I don't think I'd like to work in a big place. They're so impersonal, I always think.' He stood, waiting for her to give that almost imperceptible indication, known to all well-trained servants, that the conversation was about to be politely terminated. Jessica, who had spent the past seven years learning the finer points of dismissing staff from one's presence without appearing to do so, smiled knowingly. The man was a treasure. If Madeleine had any sense she'd take him back to America with her.

When Jessica had drunk her tea, fragrant Lapsang Souchong with a thin slice of lemon, she decided to freshen up before Madeleine returned. Hunter had told her where her bedroom was so, slipping out of the library, she crossed the hall, making for the staircase. The drawing-room and dining-room doors were open, revealing tantalising glimpses of the rooms beyond. She hadn't noticed the extent of the beauty of the house on her last visit, because she'd been too fraught at having to tell Andrew about her promotion; but now, as she wandered into the rooms, she realised just how exquisite they were, with their big bay windows overlooking the gardens, and their handsome marble mantelshelves and ornate plaster ceilings. Just the sort of place that would . . .

Suddenly she clapped her hand over her mouth, stifling a gasp. She'd just had the most wonderful idea! A staggeringly fantastic amazing idea! Oh, why hadn't she thought of it before? She clasped her hands in an ecstasy of excitement; her idea was so perfect it *must* be made to work! Leaping up the stairs two at a time, she paused at the top, making a quick calculation. Counting the top floor as well, there were probably eighteen or nineteen bedrooms; of course, there wouldn't be enough bathrooms, but they could easily be put in . . .

With excitement rising in her like a fever, she rushed into the bedroom she'd been given, and opening the little secretaire in the window, grabbed some sheets of thick cream writing-paper embossed with the address of Milton Manor in dark blue. Sitting on the chintz-covered bed, she started doing some calculations. On her last visit, she remembered Andrew telling Madeleine she'd probably get over half a million pounds for the sale of the place. Add to that various conversions and redecorating, installing a commercial kitchen with the best stainless steel equipment from Germany, plus crockery, cutlery, beds, three sets of bed linen and blankets . . . on and on the list grew until at last she drew a thick line along the bottom of the figures and started to add them up.

Taking a deep breath, she finally added in the total. It would cost around seven million pounds to turn Milton Manor into the five star exclusive country hotel of her dreams! Her calculations continued as her ambitions soared. The running costs would be heavy too; heating, lighting, first-class staff, a Rolls-Royce to collect guests from the station, flowers in every room, superb food and wines . . . Hugging herself with delighted anticipation, Jessica continued to sit on the bed, day-dreaming. She might be able to persuade her parents to provide some capital, and surely she'd be able to raise the rest, she thought. After all, her experience in the Golding Group would show that she knew what she was doing. But firstly, she had to tell Madeleine she wanted to buy the manor, though that wouldn't be a problem; she knew Madeleine had been wanting to sell it from the moment she inherited it.

Cream paint and green linoleum, discreet grilles on the windows and locks on the doors, distinguished Meredith House as a mental institution. Not that there was anything prison-like about it, Madeleine reflected, as she followed her father along a corridor. The atmosphere was more that of a private nursing home, with strong security.

Room 18 was not locked, except at night. Jake opened the door and entered quietly, followed by Madeleine. Seated in an armchair by the window, her hands folded on her lap, sat a middle-aged woman, plain and dumpy, her grey hair cut short, her blue eyes lifeless. Like an empty husk with all life gone from it, Camilla gazed vacantly before her, unaware even of their presence.

'Hullo, Camilla,' Madeleine heard Jake say.

The woman's face, as devoid of make-up as it was of expression, showed no signs of having heard him.

'I've brought Madeleine to see you,' Jake continued, and there was pain in his voice. The lovely young woman he had married, and the mother of his child, had borne no resemblance to this zombie-like creature whose eyes never flickered. 'Do you remember Madeleine?' he asked her, peering into her face though he knew it was useless. Camilla was not capable of understanding anything, and perhaps, he reflected, for her sake it was a good thing. But the waste of it all, his heart cried out wildly. He had lost a wife and Madeleine had lost a mother, and all because of some evil people who had sought to take command of a young woman's mind and spirit. Whatever demon had insinuated itself into her being, brainwashing her into believing in Satanism, had long since lost its power. The empty shell that had survived couldn't help but fill him with pity. Jake reached out and took her hand. All that remained was an ineffectual, ordinary-looking woman who no longer even knew who she was.

Tears suddenly sprang to Madeleine's eyes, childish tears that had not been shed since she'd been a lonely little girl wanting her mother. Then in her imagination Camilla had been like a fairy queen, warm and loving, and she'd made up wonderful stories about her. In recent months the pictures had changed and grown dark and sinister and fearful; now, it was something of an anti-climax to be faced with this broken woman who was lost to the world, and was neither threat nor comfort.

Jake broke the silence. 'I'm afraid she's always like this, darling.'

'You've been here before?' Madeleine looked up at him in surprise. 'I never knew that.'

'I come every few years, and of course I keep in touch with the doctors, in case there's any change.'

Madeleine glanced at the blank face, embarrassed

to be talking in front of Camilla like this, as if she wasn't there at all. 'And she'll always be like this?' she whispered.

'I'm afraid so.' Jake sounded full of compassion. His rage had faded and died over the years as he'd come to realise it was useless to blame Camilla for what had happened. Her mind, already vulnerable after the death of her mother, had been corrupted and finally destroyed, and she had ended up being as much the victim as the perpetrator of evil.

Madeleine rested her slim hand on Camilla's shoulder, longing to bridge the emptiness between them, wishing fervently she could make contact.

'Hullo . . . hullo, Mummy,' she breathed softly, the tears spilling down her cheeks, but Camilla moved her head away to look out of the window and did not appear to have heard.

'Don't be upset, sweetheart,' said Jake, putting his arm round her, 'I think she's quite happy . . . where she is.'

They stayed a few more moments and then slipped out of the room again, still unnoticed by Camilla.

Madeleine took Jake's arm as they walked slowly back along the corridor. 'Daddy, can I ask you something?'

Jake smiled and there was a touch of weariness in his expression. 'Anything you like, Maddy. I've no more secrets from you now.'

'Why did you never marry again?'

'Because your mother and I are still married.'

Madeleine turned to him, horrified. 'What? You never got divorced?'

'How could I divorce her, Maddy? Think about it. It was the trauma of Jenkins and me breaking up the ritu-alistic ceremony, when she'd been put into a trance, that sent her over the edge. I've always felt a sense of guilt about that. We had to do it to save you, but it undoubtedly wrecked your mother's already delicate mental state.' Jake sighed, as if the burden of knowing this had lain heavily on his shoulders for a very long time.

Madeleine paused halfway down the corridor, and looked up at him, her face full of sympathy.

'Oh, Daddy, that must have been dreadful for you. I'm sure you're not to blame. If my mother was that near the edge of insanity, anything could have tipped the balance.'

'You may be right, Maddy. Anyway, I couldn't divorce her then; she was no longer with us in the true sense of the word, and to have divorced her would have been like betraying her when her back was turned.'

Madeleine squeezed Jake's hand. 'Did I ever tell you, you were a very special person?' she whispered, 'and that I'm the luckiest girl in the world to have you as a father?'

'You haven't told me lately,' Jake replied with a teasing smile.

Carl was waiting for them down in the lobby. With-out letting go of Jake's arm, Madeleine reached for-ward and took his hand.

'Everything all right, Maddy?' he asked anxiously.

She nodded. 'Yes, and I'm glad I came.'

Jenkins, who had left his roses with a nurse to give to Camilla, was standing in the drive, chatting to the chauffeur who had driven Jake from the airport.

'Carl, why don't you go with Jenkins, and I'll go in Daddy's car,' said Madeleine pointedly. She wanted to find out from Jake if there were any more developments about Kimberley, and it would be better if Carl was not involved in the conversation. Understanding, he winked imperceptibly at her.

'Fine,' he agreed. 'See you back at the house.'

Madeleine settled herself comfortably beside Jake in the back of the hired limousine. 'So, how's everything at the bank?' she asked conversationally.

'We're busy as usual,' replied Jake. 'I'll be glad to have Carl back in New York, of course, although I think he needed this break. He's looking much better.'

'Yes, I think he is. What's happened over that girl who was arrested? He told me she'd been charged with stealing.' Madeleine spoke evenly, her eyes fixed on the tangled hedgerows as the car sped along the country lanes.

There was a moment's pause, then Jake spoke. 'Kimberley Cabot, you mean? Oh, she's being held on a charge of robbery and I think she'll be sentenced. What a fool! She had such a good job at the bank, and she risked everything for a thousand dollars worth of trinkets! After this, she'll never get a decent job again. Anyway, Carl will be pleased to hear that his old assistant, Averil Fielden, is coming back to work for him. She missed New York, apparently, and can't wait to get back.'

Madeleine let out a little secret sigh of relief. Jake spoke of Kimberley as if he had already half forgotten her.

'That will please Carl,' she said lightly, 'he was sorry when Averil left.'

Jessica heard the scrunch of the cars coming up the gravel drive, just as she finished her calculations. Peering out of the bedroom window she saw Madeleine with Carl and Jake come into the house and a minute later their voices, laughing and chatting, could be heard coming from the drawing-room below. Brimming with excitement, she slipped out of her room and down the stairs. She could just imagine their surprised faces when they saw her.

Pushing open the drawing-room door, she struck a pose, arms outstretched.

'Hi there, everyone!' she called out gaily.

There was a stunned silence as the others turned to look at her. Madeleine was the first to recover.

'*Jessica*! What on earth are you doing here?'

'That's not much of a welcome!' chided Jessica, running over to hug her.

Carl and Jake greeted her with amazed affection, exclaiming as Madeleine had done: 'What are you doing here?'

Jessica stood in the middle of the large room, her hands on her hips, making an effort to pretend to look insulted.

'You'd think you weren't pleased to see me! I come from England, remember? I *live* here! . . . Well – er – I do now!' she added lamely.

Madeleine looked at her anxiously. 'You mean . . .? What's happened to Bernard?'

'Bernard, for all I know, is still throwing the china at his servants on Sardinia!'

'You've left him?' asked Carl, wonderingly.

'I've left him, my dear,' Jessica repeated flatly. 'The whole thing was a ghastly mistake, right from the beginning. I must have been mad, quite mad! Anyway, I'll tell you all about it later. All I'm longing to hear right now is your news, Maddy.' She glanced at the others. 'And why are you all here?'

Madeleine slipped her arm through Jessica's. 'We've been visiting my mother,' she said quietly. 'I'll tell you all about it later.' She'd already made up her mind that not even her best friend would know everything that had been happening in the past few months. That was something that only she and Carl would share.

At that moment Hunter brought in afternoon tea, setting the silver tray on a round table in front of the fire. He was followed by one of the maids with plates of sandwiches, scones and a homemade walnut cake. Jessica clapped her hands in delight at the sight.

'Perfect! Every detail is perfect!'

Madeleine looked at her questioningly. 'How d'you mean?'

Jessica laughed and shook her head mysteriously. 'Oh, it's nothing really. I was just thinking how pretty the tea things looked.'

After tea Carl and Jake wanted to walk round the gardens, in spite of the cold, so Madeleine and Jessica sat by the fire, catching up on all their news.

When Madeleine had described Camilla and repeated the dreadful story Jenkins had told her, Jessica looked at her thoughtfully for a moment. Then she spoke.

'I've known all that for some time you know,

Maddy. My friend, Peter Thorn, who works on the *Evening Standard*, told me all about the ceremony in the old barn because he reported the incident. Of course I couldn't tell you; it was all too horrible, and I knew you'd be terribly upset.'

'My God, I'd no idea you knew!'

'Oh, I can be discreet sometimes!' Jessica grinned.

'Now, are you going to tell me what happened between you and Bernard?' asked Madeleine, intrigued.

Jessica's face grew pensive and there was suddenly a sheen of unshed tears in her eyes.

'I've made the most awful mess of my life, Maddy,' she confided in a low voice, as she curled up on the chintz sofa. 'I must have been mad to have given up everything and rush off with Bernard. He wasn't at all like I'd expected – he was grumpy and demanding. I lost my feeling of independence and I had nothing to *do*! Oh, God, it was awful. I suddenly realised I'd fallen out of love with him as fast as I'd fallen *in* love; it was all a disaster.'

'Jessica!' Madeleine remonstrated gently. 'How could you make a terrible mistake like that? What did Bernard say? Wasn't he upset . . . or angry?'

'Oh, he understood. His wife left him for the same reason, I found out. You see, I fell in love with his music, and I thought he *was* his music, and then when I found out he was quite different, not a bit like I'd imagined . . .' Jessica's voice trailed off as she looked at Madeleine, her expression beseeching. She was longing for her friend to understand and sympathise. To her relief, Madeleine smiled warmly.

'It must have been awful for you,' she said. 'Thank God, at least, you didn't marry him. This way, hopefully, you can get back to your career and, as Dad always says, "put it down to experience".'

'That's just it,' Jessica wailed, dashing a tear away from her cheek, 'I've *blown* it, Maddy! I can't get my job back and there aren't any vacancies at all in the Golding Group. I've been such a *fool*, right from the beginning. Why didn't I stay with Andrew? Why wasn't I content just to work in the Royal Westminster without having to claw my way up the ladder! Now I've got nothing, nothing at all. No job and no Andrew.' She was silent for a moment, gazing disconsolately into space. 'I really regret losing him now,' she added softly.

Madeleine looked at her with astonishment. 'You do? Are you sure that isn't because everything else has gone sour? You'd no hesitation in hurting him, right in this room, the last time you were here, because you wanted to give your all to the hotel. Jessie, are you sure you do know what you want, honey?' She hated talking harshly to her friend, but she was worried. Jessica, who had always seemed so together in the past, now looked as if she were about to crack up.

Jessica's reply surprised her. 'Yes, I know what I want now, Maddy. As far as Andrew is concerned it's probably too late, I'm afraid, and I do have some pride. I'm not going running to him. But as far as work is concerned, I've had the most brilliant idea!' She dabbed her eyes with a small lace handkerchief and sat bolt upright.

'You're planning to sell this place, aren't you? Well, I'd like to buy it!'

495

Madeleine looked at her blankly. 'What on earth do you mean?'

'I want to raise the finance to buy this house, and turn it into an exclusive, deluxe, five star hotel! Oh, Maddy, I've been making the most wonderful plans while I was waiting for you to get back, and you know how I've always dreamed of having my own hotel!' Jessica spoke earnestly and excitedly. 'The potential is fantastic. All the staff could stay on . . . and we could build tennis-courts, a swimming-pool . . .'

Madeleine broke in with a touch of anxiety, 'Jessica, do stop and listen to me for a moment.'

'What's the matter? You *are* planning to sell the house, aren't you?' She looked crestfallen, seeing her wonderful new dreams smashed before her eyes. 'Don't tell me you've changed your mind?'

'It's not that.' Madeleine looked distressed. 'What I'm trying to tell you is that Milton Manor has already been sold.'

'Sold!' Jessica looked ready to weep again. 'You can't mean it, Maddy. Oh, that's dreadful. How can you have sold it so quickly?' She sounded almost reproachful.

'I'm really sorry. Once the solicitor knew I had the legal right to sell, I put it on the market.' Madeleine opened her mouth as if to say something else, then changed her mind.

'What were you going to say?' asked Jessica, noticing how abruptly her friend had stopped talking.

Madeleine flushed uneasily. 'Nothing. Just that the house has been sold. I think the contracts were exchanged yesterday.'

'Oh, hell.' Jessica sat disconsolately, her brow furrowed with annoyance and misery. Nothing was going right for her these days. She'd been a headstrong fool, and now she was having to pay the price. She'd let Andrew slip through her fingers and she'd walked out on the best job she'd ever get. How could she have done it? she asked herself, as she curled up more tightly on the sofa in her anguish. How could she have walked away from everyone and everything she knew and cared about, including her parents as well as her friends, for a perfect stranger? What lunacy had swept all else away so that she could pursue the dangerous madness Bernard's music had evoked? Like someone drugged on melody, bewitched by cadences, besotted by the strains of a sensual rhythm, she had let his music dull all her other senses; she'd become deaf to all other warning sounds and blind to what was obvious, and when the harmony had disintegrated and the music had stopped, nothing was left but the discordance of her own feelings and the frustration of knowing that she had no one but herself to blame.

Madeleine was looking at her watch. 'Will you excuse me, Jessie? I've got a few important phone calls to make. Carl and I are flying back to the States in a few days and there are some loose ends I want to tie up first.'

'Of course. Go ahead.' Jessica forced herself to sound cheerful.

As Madeleine hurried out of the room, Carl and Jake returned from their walk, stamping their feet and clapping their hands with cold. Madeleine drew them in to the library for a few minutes, speaking rapidly and quietly.

'The Central Manhattan could finance the project,' Jake whispered, when she'd finished talking.

'Are you going to call him now?' asked Carl.

Madeleine nodded. 'Go and chat to Jessica, will you? She's rather low and needs cheering up.'

At dinner that night, Madeleine announced she and Carl were holding a luncheon party the following day, before Jake flew home.

'Who's coming?' asked Jessica. 'Do you know any of your neighbours?'

'I've invited someone called Alice Stewart; she was a life-long friend of my mother's and she's awfully sweet.'

'It'll be nice to see her again,' observed Jake.

'And you say her son, Philip, is coming too?' said Carl.

'Yes. Apparently we met as small children, although neither of us remember,' said Madeleine with a smile.

Jessica let out a groan. 'Oh, I get it! You're setting me up with a blind date, aren't you, Maddy? Oh, God, you're hoping I'm going to like him, and forget all about Andrew and Bernard.'

Madeleine's mouth twitched. 'No, I'm not. Philip isn't your type at all. I was actually hoping you'd hit it off with the new owner of Milton Manor. He's coming too.'

Jessica cast her eyes to heaven. 'This is going to be more than I can bear!' she declared dramatically. 'How could I possibly even *like* him? He's bought the one house in England I wanted, and now you're expecting me to be friendly with him. Honestly, Maddy!'

The next morning it was colder than ever. The winding lanes that led to Milton Manor stretched like glittering trenches through the frozen countryside, and icicles hung like crystal stalactites from the eaves of thatched cottages. At ten o'clock a large van trundled up the drive to the front door. Painted on its side was: 'Sewell. Removals and Storage. Okehampton.'

'They haven't come to take the furniture away already, have they?' Jessica demanded, looking through the window.

Madeleine looked puzzled. 'No. I haven't arranged for anything to be moved until next week. I wonder what they want!'

A minute later, Hunter came into the library where they were sitting. 'There's a delivery for you, Madam,' he said. 'An item that Sewell's have been storing for many years, I believe.'

'What is it, Hunter? And who asked them to bring it here?'

'I did, darling,' said Jake, coming into the room at that moment. 'Get them to bring it in here, Hunter.'

'Very well, Sir,'

'What is it, Daddy?' Madeleine repeated. 'I didn't know we had stuff in storage here.'

'This is something I had shipped over from the States, a very long time ago. I had it put in storage as I didn't want to upset your grandfather by letting him know I didn't want it,' Jake explained.

Two men in overalls came staggering through the

doorway, and she could see they were carrying a canvas, wrapped in sheeting. She looked questioningly at Jake, and slowly he smiled and nodded.

'Is it really . . .?' she breathed.

'Yes, my darling. I thought you'd like to have it now.'

The delivery men propped the canvas against the wall and Madeleine stepped forward and lifted away the covering. There, in colours as fresh and vibrant as if it had been painted yesterday, was the portrait of her mother that she remembered from her early childhood.

'Oh, Daddy,' she breathed, gazing at it. It was a masterpiece; a perfect example of the work of Philip de Laszlo, showing the sweetness and innocence of the young Camilla, in a creamy lace dress, with a cascade of pearls falling from her neck. This was the Camilla that Madeleine had based all her imaginative ideals on; this was the vision that had inspired a thousand childish fantasies, and now Jake had given her back the mother of her dreams.

'Thank you, Daddy,' she said, a catch in her voice. 'I always wondered what had happened to it.'

'I'm glad you're pleased,' he said, also moved by emotion. 'This is the way we should both remember her; this is what she is really like inside, I believe. The other Camilla was possessed by some terrible evil force; this is the woman who was my wife and your mother.'

'I agree,' said Madeleine softly. 'I shall hang it in the living-room at home in New York.' And she turned to kiss him impulsively.

*　　*　　*

Alice Stewart and her son arrived at half-past twelve, and within minutes she and Jake were chatting away as if they'd only seen each other a few weeks before.

'My dear man,' Alice flattered him, 'you look more distinguished than ever, and of course Madeleine is the image of you!'

Jake roared with laughter. 'Well, I can tell that *you* haven't changed, Alice!' He turned to Philip. 'Did you know that in her day your mother was the most outrageous flirt?'

Philip grinned. 'She still is!'

Everyone was talking and laughing, while Hunter took round glasses of champagne on a silver tray, when Jessica, who was being rather quiet, suddenly looked at Madeleine.

'I can hear another car arriving,' she observed. 'Is it . . .?'

'Yes, it's probably the new owner.' Madeleine went over to the window and looked out. 'Yes, it is.' There was a certain satisfaction in her voice.

'Oh, I'm going to hate him!' exclaimed Jessica. 'This is dreadful!'

'Oh, it could be a lot worse,' said Madeleine casually.

'I don't see how . . .' began Jessica, peering over Madeleine's shoulder. Then she let out a shriek and turned scarlet. 'But it's Andrew!'

Madeleine nodded knowingly, smiling with deep amusement.

'But I don't understand . . . Why didn't you tell me? What does he want this big house for?' Jessica was babbling, her eyes round with wonder.

'Why don't you ask him yourself?' said Madeleine, laughing.

'But Maddy!' Jessica clutched her arm in an agony of bewilderment. 'Does he know I'm here?'

'Yes, of course he does. Stop panicking! When you told me you wanted this house for a hotel, I called him up, and he was just in time to stop the sale by telling the other buyers I'd changed my mind and wanted to keep it! Then, with backing from the Central Manhattan Bank, which Daddy and Carl arranged, Andrew bought it himself . . . for you! You can have your hotel, Jessie, and Andrew as well. But I think you'd better let him tell you that bit himself,' said Madeleine, pushing Jessica gently but firmly into the hall.

Jessica clasped her hands together, looking scared. Then she watched as Andrew came up the front door steps. 'Oh, my God, Maddy! I don't believe this! You mean . . . Andrew wants me back?'

'Go and greet him. Go on, Jessie, you're being hopeless,' teased Madeleine, giving her friend a final push. Then she went back into the drawing-room and closed the door quietly behind her.

'Everything all right?' murmured Carl, smiling at her conspiratorial expression.

Madeleine crossed her fingers. 'I think everything's going to be just fine,' she replied. 'And I've got a feeling that we'd better ask Hunter to put some more champagne on ice!'